THE
ENCHANTED
CROWN

THE ENCHANTED CROWN

Copyright © 2019 by Bethany Atazadeh

Contact Info: www.bethanyatazadeh.com

Cover design : Stone Ridge Books
Editor: Enchanted Ink
Formatting Template : Derek Murphy

ISBN: 978-1-7332888-1-1 (paperback) 978-1-7332888-7-3 (hardcover)

First Edition: March 2021

10 9 8 7 6 5 4 3 2 1

THE

BOOK FOUR IN THE
STOLEN KINGDOM SERIES

ENCHANTED
CROWN

GRACE HOUSE PRESS

ALSO BY

BETHANY ATAZADEH

THE STOLEN KINGDOM SERIES :
THE STOLEN KINGDOM
THE JINNI KEY
THE CURSED HUNTER
THE ENCHANTED CROWN

THE NUMBER SERIES :
EVALENE'S NUMBER
PEARL'S NUMBER

MARKETING FOR AUTHORS SERIES :
HOW YOUR BOOK SELLS ITSELF
GROW YOUR AUTHOR PLATFORM
BOOK SALES THAT MULTIPLY

OTHER :
THE CONFIDENT CORGI

SIGN UP FOR MY AUTHOR NEWSLETTER

Be the first to learn about Bethany Atazadeh's new releases and receive exclusive content for both readers and writers!

WWW.BETHANYATAZADEH.COM/CONTACT

RUSALKA

DRAGON CLIFFS

KESHDI

AZIZ

PIRUZ

BARADAAN

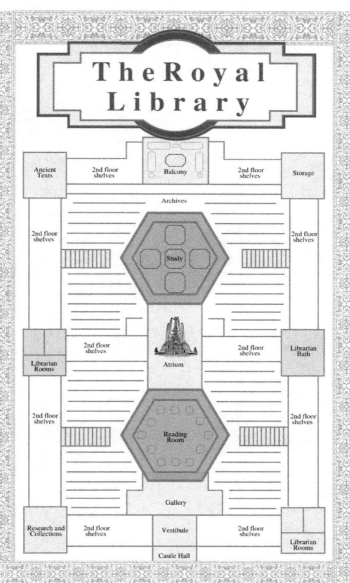

The Royal Library

Ancient Texts

2nd floor shelves

Balcony

2nd floor shelves

Storage

Archives

2nd floor shelves

Study

2nd floor shelves

Librarian Rooms

2nd floor shelves

Atrium

2nd floor shelves

Librarian Bath

2nd floor shelves

Reading Room

2nd floor shelves

Gallery

Research and Collections

2nd floor shelves

Vestibule

2nd floor shelves

Librarian Rooms

Castle Hall

Chapter 1

Arie

"HAS ANYONE SEEN THE queen?" Kadin's warm, deep voice floated through the library door from out in the hall, tense and clipped.

The servant's response was inaudible.

I strained to hear their thoughts but was met with silence—a painful reminder of what I'd lost when my Gift was Severed a couple months ago.

Muffled footsteps grew louder, heading my way.

I'd found a dark pocket of space beneath the library stairs, which the sunlight didn't know existed, and neither did anyone else.

There was an old rolled-up rug, left forgotten in the tiny space, which I used as a cushion to sit on. I leaned back and stared out at the small triangle of light in front of me. It revealed the last few shelves of a dusty bookcase in the corner, as well as the legs of a single chair and table. The main library door and the rest of the room were out of sight, which meant I was too.

Still, I pressed farther back into the darkness, tucking my slippered feet beneath the heavy skirts of my black mourning dress. Mourning the loss of my father. Of my Gift. Of my entire life as it had once been.

Leaning my head against the wall, my fingers idly traced the patterns of the cracks. There was a chip in the paint. I picked at it.

"Arie?" Kadin called, inside the large room now, breaking library etiquette to raise his voice. "Are you here?"

Reluctantly, I pulled my gaze from the wall.

His boots strode past my hiding place as he took the stairs to the second level.

"If you're here, you're needed in the dungeons." He raised his voice to reach the entire library, which I assumed was empty, though I hadn't checked thoroughly before crawling under the stairs.

His steps overhead grew louder, then quieter, then louder again as he paced down one row of books after another, likely hoping I'd materialize behind one of them.

It should've bothered me that he assumed I was ignoring him.

Instead, tears welled up as I noticed the empty space where his thoughts should've been.

I heard nothing.

Only a chair squeaking across the floor as he moved it in his search.

I sank back against the wall and closed my eyes.

My Severance had been incredibly effective. It'd cut me off from my abilities and myself in ways I'd never imagined.

Gideon had told me once that a Severance was like losing a limb or a lung, that a Gift was a part of you.

I'd scoffed at the idea then.

But the loss was *more* than both of those things combined. My whole body tingled, and my hands twitched restlessly, as if searching for something that wasn't there. The absence of my ability carved out something inside of me, leaving me hollow and too light, floating along through each day without an anchor to hold me to reality.

Kadin was still calling out, although softly, as if worried the wrong ears might overhear. His voice grew closer as he came back down to the main level. "The people need their queen, Arie. Please. We need you." His voice hitched just a bit but came back clear and strong. Maybe I'd imagined it. "There's... someone you need to see."

Someone.

In the dungeons.

Kadin's effort to be discreet was a waste of time. The servants already knew the guards had caught a spy this morning. I'd overheard them whispering about it earlier when I'd hidden behind a tapestry. *Is he from King Amir's kingdom or another's?* they'd asked each other. *Is there a war brewing while the kingdom of Hodafez is left defenseless?*

I played with a little purple thread I'd pulled from the carpet, wrapping it around my finger, then unwrapping, then wrapping again.

I should care.

It should've bothered me that I didn't.

Kadin's sigh pulled me out of my dark thoughts. Leaning forward on my hands and knees, I snuck a glance at him from the depths of my hidden alcove.

There were dark circles smudged blue and purple under his golden-brown eyes. His dark hair had grown past his ears, and his beard had begun to fill in. A muscle in his jaw twitched as he gazed around the room one last time, frowning.

"Have you found her?" It was Gideon's voice, somewhere just out of sight.

How long has he been there? Normally I'd have sensed him immediately—that tingle of another Gifting present. Not anymore. Whenever I poked at the place my Gift had been, it was like poking at a hole in the gums where a tooth had been:

surprise and confusion followed swiftly by loss, and sensitive to the touch.

Kadin only shook his head, lips pursed.

I crawled backward to the rug again. Carefully, to avoid being heard, I unrolled it to lie down, lifting my heavy crown from my head and placing it at my feet so I wouldn't have to look at it.

"I could move forward without her, but I would prefer her permission." Gideon's soft voice washed over me like a distant wave.

I tried to tune him out.

"The queen of Jinn uses human spies as well," he added. "We may need to consider that possibility." They moved toward the door and back into my line of vision. "Enoch hasn't returned since he left to spy on the queen, so I can only assume they've found him and that he's been imprisoned... or worse."

"Do you trust him now?" Kadin asked. His back was to me. From the stiff way he stood, I guessed he didn't.

"I do," Gideon replied, eyes dropping to the floor. "He was controlled by the queen's amulet, just as I was."

"I notice you give him grace but blame yourself." Leave it to Kadin to say what Gideon and I had danced around for months. We'd avoided each other's presence. I knew my Severance wasn't his fault.

It wasn't.

Repeating it had yet to change the memory of a bitter iron taste on my tongue from biting it, or the twisting fear that spiraled up inside me in his presence.

"You speak the truth," Gideon whispered in his way of an answer without answering anything. His usually sharp blue eyes still gazed aimlessly at the floor.

"If King Amir had forced Enoch to do the Severance instead of you, as he'd originally intended, would you have held him accountable?"

"No." Gideon's voice was flat.

"It was the king's vendetta," Kadin insisted. "You were only a tool."

"A tool would not feel responsible." Gideon's expression flickered, and he straightened. "It's neither here nor there. My focus now must be on not making the difficulties worse. To ease her burden however I can. Which means this situation must be taken care of."

Kadin nodded, rubbing a hand across his face. Turning away from Gideon, he stared toward my section of the library.

I held my breath and didn't move.

When he didn't think anyone was looking, his expression grew hopeless. Where his lips normally quirked upward with a spark of mischief and adventure, they now flattened in a grim line.

Gideon continued. "While Queen Jezebel won't declare outright war on the human world until after the Crowning Ceremony, I can only guess at what she's doing behind the scenes."

Kadin's shoulders rose and fell in a heavy breath, and his eyes roamed the shelves in front of him aimlessly, crossing over my hiding spot once more. His expression didn't change. He turned to face Gideon. "It's been this way for three months now. If you want to act in Arie's best interest, I'd recommend not waiting for her when you know what you need to do."

I frowned at his back. Had it really been three months since the Severance? It felt as if it'd just happened yesterday, and at the same time as if it'd taken place years ago.

Rolling over to face the wall, I curled my legs inward and wrapped my arms around myself, closing my eyes. Two sets of footsteps made their way out of the library, and the door shut behind them.

The silence wrapped around me like a thick shell that kept everything else out. Some small part of me, as insubstantial as a shadow, whispered that I should follow, while another larger part wished they would leave me alone permanently. I wasn't who they thought I was. I couldn't be what they needed. It was better for everyone this way. The shadow side agreed. But another small voice wished someone would find me…

A soft scuff of a footstep sounded.

My eyes flew open, and I spun around to find the object of my thoughts crouching in the little triangular opening. He'd seen me after all.

"Is there room on this rug for two?" Kadin asked softly.

I dipped my chin in a nod, averting my eyes.

He tucked himself inside the small space beside me, our knees knocking together.

I rolled onto my back to make room.

I didn't want his pity.

What I hadn't expected was his arm gently wrapping around my waist and arm. Holding me. His warmth seeped into me, making me aware of my icy skin. My arms drew up to cover his instinctually.

The minutes passed as we lay there without speaking, and his breathing evened out until he began to snore softly. This gave me the courage to glance over at his face, so close to mine. The worry lines relaxed in sleep, and his lips parted slightly.

I stared at the low ceiling above us as tears threatened to escape. One trickled down my cheek into my ear.

The shell was still there, but this time I wasn't alone inside it.

Chapter 2

Rena

MUNCHING ON AN APPLE, I peered out from the kitchen at the argument breaking out in the great room. One of the noble Shahs sat on a bench, gesturing wildly as he hissed to the others at the breakfast table, "Princess Arie isn't capable of leading this kingdom. She hasn't even left her chambers!" His face was the color of a ripe tomato, and his fervor only increased as he continued.

I tilted my head at the way these humans carried on. Back home such talk would've ended with a trident through the heart from my father. But I supposed Arie's father was dead. She had no other family to speak of, and the man was right about one thing: Arie had barely left her bed in weeks. The kingdom was light on trident-throwers at the moment.

"Watch your tongue!" An equally sweaty man slammed his drink down for emphasis. "The *queen* of Hodafez deserves our support. We're not all fools like you who can't put their pants on without someone telling them what to wear. Would you prefer King Amir return?"

"Of course not," Tomato Face grumbled, voice nearly lost in the protests of the other Shahs. "I just think someone else should take charge of Hodafez. One of us, perhaps. The queen clearly isn't capable of ruling."

"She just needs time to heal from the Severance," another Shah protested. "And between this council and Captain Navabi, Hodafez has more than enough leadership for a temporary absence."

More arguments broke out. The way they repeated what they'd said just moments ago made me shake my head. Such strange creatures, these humans.

"Where's Captain Navabi?" I asked one of the guards at the great hall entrance.

"The dungeon," he replied.

Tossing my apple to one of the castle dogs, I headed for the stone staircase that led to the dungeon.

Sure enough, the captain stood with Gideon discussing something in hushed tones. Though I slowed down, careful not to kick any loose rocks in the dimly lit stone hallway, they both fell silent and turned to face me.

"What is it?" the captain asked in his gruff voice. He reminded me of my father.

"Your Shahs think they should run the kingdom," I said bluntly.

The captain was moving past me before I'd even finished speaking, headed for the stairs.

"Great hall," I called after him, though no doubt he'd hear the fuss.

When I turned back, Gideon shifted in front of the open cell door, blocking whatever was within.

Frowning up at him, I dodged to the side to peer through the cell bars before he could stop me. Inside, a prisoner stood chained to the wall. A stout human with more hair on his chin than on his head glared at Gideon's back while pressing himself against the stone. So a Jinni scared him. That wasn't really that unusual. Was this the spy the servants had been whispering about?

The human's narrowed gaze turned on me as Gideon sighed. "You shouldn't be here."

Jinn had such trust issues. "If you can't confide in me by now, you should have kept a lot more secrets than this," I joked.

He didn't even crack a smile. He just stared into the cell, where the stubby human squinted at me rudely.

"So, who's this fellow?"

"I'm afraid I can't say." Gideon's tone was polite. He crossed his arms casually, not moving out of the doorway. "Did you need something?"

"No." I fought the urge to cross my arms as well. Just because I was sixteen and at least a century younger than him didn't mean I liked being treated like a child. Or maybe he was distant because he still thought I had a crush on him. If so, he was being ridiculous. That was long over.

Since Gideon was blocking the door with his tall frame, I stepped up to the bars, wrapping my fingers around them, trying to figure out what was going on. Conversations that included chains and cells hinted strongly at an interrogation. "He's the spy they're talking about, isn't he?"

"I don't know what you mean."

That was a yes. If it wasn't true, he would've just said no. Why wouldn't he let me in on the fun?

"I'd like to stay." My voice came out more girlish than I'd intended, like a little-Mere instead of my fully grown and mature sixteen—almost seventeen—years. I cleared my throat and added, "I know how to use a trident, if you'd like help." I definitely did not. But we would cross that ocean when we came to it.

"No need," Gideon replied, brushing his vest off as if wiping away the very mention of a spy. "I am finished for the moment."

I slipped around his arms through the gap he'd left and entered the cell, peering at the strange bald man. "You found out who hired him, then? Is it the queen of Jinn, like you feared?"

A hiss came from Gideon as the spy began to shimmer in the air, growing translucent. There was a small smirk on the man's grimy face as he winked out of existence just like Gideon did when he traveled. The manacles that had been around his wrists clanked heavily against the stone wall, empty.

"What happened?" I jumped back, eyes wide. "Where'd he go?"

Lips pressed together, Gideon leapt into the cell where the man had stood and flashed out of sight. He came back a moment later, then flashed away again.

Finally, he came back, shoulders hunched. "There's no trail."

"Is he…" I blinked, unsure what to ask. "How did he get away? Is he dead?"

Gideon shook his head, touching the manacles, then the wall, searching for something I couldn't see. "Not dead. Escaped. I was trying not to activate the magic I sensed over him, but it seems your question was the trigger."

"That's not my fault," I muttered under my breath. "You could've warned me."

"Even a warning would've likely had the same result if he'd overheard," he reassured me as he gave up and left the cell. "Unfortunately, we now have no way of knowing why he was here."

"You're not serious?" Now I was the one who smirked. "It's more than obvious. You don't send a spy to another kingdom unless you hope to see where it's vulnerable." Even I, the youngest daughter of the Sea King, knew that.

"There could be other reasons."

Gideon didn't want to see it. It was his home, after all. "Don't be delusional. If there was magic, I didn't see it, which means it was Jinni magic. And if the queen of Jinn's name is forbidden, then you can bet this spell came from her. The only real question is *why* does the queen of Jinn want to know the weaknesses of a human kingdom?"

Gideon said nothing. The silence stretched while we stared at the empty cell as if the spy might somehow reappear.

Finally, he turned to face me. "Jinni magic may rule out the Mere and the humans, but that doesn't immediately incriminate the queen."

"Who else would it be?"

"Perhaps one of the Jinn she banished?" He studied the floor in thought.

"To what end?" I kept my face smooth and blank, hiding my giddy excitement. Unraveling this scheme was almost as thrilling as a shark hunt.

Gideon was clearly at a loss.

"Wouldn't sending someone like this and using a spell to steal him away with whatever secrets he has"—I gestured to where the spy had been—"be against your Jinni code?"

"The Three Unbreakable Laws," he murmured, shaking his head. "It's a gray area. That doesn't mean anything."

"It does," I insisted. "It's too big a risk for a banished Jinni. If the queen found out, there'd be consequences." I didn't wait for him to confirm the obvious. "But who holds the queen accountable? Who can stop *her* from breaking the Indestructible Laws?"

"Unbreakable," Gideon corrected. He blinked and shook his head a little, as if trying to clear it, rubbing a hand over his face once more.

"Sometimes the truth tastes like a Bitterfish." I repeated the Mere saying into the lengthy silence. "But better a Bitterfish to survive than a Nightfin's sweet poison."

"You're right." Gideon winced. "I know you're right."

It was a struggle not to grin and rub it in, and I might've faltered for a moment, but fortunately he wasn't looking at me.

He rubbed his face with both hands and then crossed his arms. "If it's truly Queen Jezebel spying on the human world—on Hodafez and possibly other kingdoms—I can only see one reason: she plans to attack, most likely immediately following the Crowning Ceremony when her Gifts are strongest."

My shoulders hunched toward my ears. Now I was the one recognizing the taste of a Bitterfish. "She's coming here? The humans are all but defenseless against the Jinn..."

"I know."

The urge to nervously flap my tail came over me, but of course, I couldn't. My toes twitched under my gown. "The Mere could help if they wanted to... but I don't think they will."

"I know," he said again, eyes closed, one hand pinching the bridge of his nose.

"We have to warn the humans." I bounced on my toes as the nervous energy tried to find a place to go. "They need to prepare, to find some sort of protection..." I trailed off, not knowing what that would look like.

On a long sigh, Gideon said once more, "I know." He dropped his hands to his sides and fully met my gaze for the first time since I'd arrived. "Would you gather everyone in the queen's reception chamber?"

I nodded, turning to go, but stopped. "Where are you going?"

"I'm going to help the captain maintain order," Gideon replied, vanishing. He didn't believe in interfering with the kingdom's politics or using his many Gifts to influence human behavior—something about those debatable laws of Jinn—yet he was happy enough to flash upstairs to the great hall where just his simple presence would cause the discussion to break up and end. At least for the day.

I shook my head in frustration.

In Mere, we did what we wanted when we wanted. All this tiptoeing around felt as idiotic as taking a swim during a hurricane.

* * *

I STARED AT THE dark mahogany door that led to Arie's room. I was overdue for a visit. At first I'd come every day, but now I tended to only come by when the others visited.

I sucked in a deep breath and held it, as if that would keep the misery from infecting me. But Arie's pain always became my own. Avoiding heartbreak was impossible when it stared you in the face.

Entering the dark room, I could make out her form lying in the bed. Mirrors and dressing tables and another set of couches decorated the room. They sat collecting dust.

"That's it," I muttered. "This isn't helping." Going to the window, I flung back the floor-to-ceiling drapes, coughing at the dust that floated through the air.

The gloom immediately lifted. Sunlight spilled in and touched the bed, making Arie stir.

"Stop," she mumbled, shielding her eyes as if I'd forced her to stare directly at the sun. "Close them…"

I ignored her. This was for her own good, even if she didn't agree.

Coming around to the bed, I pulled back the curtains that surrounded it, tying them up as well. "Did you know it's just past noon?" I asked in a cheerful tone as I worked. "You would never have guessed it walking in here, but it's actually a beautiful sunny day. I've grown quite used to the sun now. I prefer to be in it whenever possible."

She glowered at me but didn't say a word. I was one of the only people in her entire kingdom she couldn't chastise. At least, not effectively.

"So…" I dropped onto the bed and let the word drag out to emphasize how one-sided this conversation was. The others could coddle her; I didn't believe in it. In Mere, we addressed a problem directly.

When she didn't reply, I gave up on conversation, just for the moment. "Gideon asked me to gather everyone for a meeting in the sitting room, if you're up for attending."

She only shrugged.

This wasn't the Arie I knew. I needed to do something. "When are you going to stop feeling sorry for yourself?" I winced as I heard myself. It sounded like something my sister would say.

Oddly enough, it seemed to light a tiny fire in her dead eyes. "Excuse me?"

"You know." I waved at the dirty room the servants were afraid to enter, searching for nicer words. "When are you going to stop all this and start ruling your kingdom? They're not going to wait forever." That wasn't much of an improvement. Still, picturing Tomato Face downstairs, I figured if I didn't find a way to say it now, someone else might later, and it wouldn't end with time to think about it.

She frowned at me, which made me smile back. I was finally getting somewhere.

Arie's gaze shifted past me to stare at the wall. The fire in her slowly died, and she curled in on herself. "They didn't want me as queen when I was Gifted, and they certainly don't want me to be queen now."

"That might be true." I shrugged. "But it doesn't really matter. The fact is, you *are* the queen and you *are* without a Gift, whether any of you want it this way or not. Maybe it's time you take a good look at who you actually are and try accepting it for once."

Though I'd tried to keep my voice matter-of-fact, I threw my hands up at the glare she gave me. "I'm just speaking the truth. Someone should. You've spent enough time in this bed to recover at least three times. It's time to get up and see if your legs still work."

When she lifted a brow, I smiled as if I was joking. *Who knows how legs work?* I'd only had mine for a few months. They seemed sturdy enough, but not nearly as strong as a tail. "You're my friend. If no one else is brave enough to say these things to you, I will."

When we'd first met, Arie might have sarcastically thanked me, though I wouldn't have known it was false at the time. Today she just rolled over and put her back to me, pulling the covers over her head to block out the sunlight.

"Well." I stood to leave, adding lightly, "I'll be waiting in the sitting room for someone to talk to who can hold up their end of the conversation."

Even that didn't bring the fire back. I held in a sigh, trying not to be disappointed, and left without waiting for her reply since it often didn't come.

In the connecting room, Bosh stood by the large window, idly playing with the gold tassels of a pillow on the window seat.

I wove through the tables and chairs, treading softly until I was directly behind him. Then I cleared my throat.

He jumped and let go of the pillow as if he'd been caught red-handed. "Oh, Rena, I was just... I mean..." He gulped. "Hi. How are you?"

"I'm well." His reaction made me smirk.

It wasn't just the fact that I'd learned to sneak up on a thief; it was also adorable how he seemed determined to give that life up. For me, I hoped.

After my last attempt at forcing love with Gideon, this time I planned to hold back and see what floated to the surface on its own.

That said, I still *had* to tell him everything I'd found out since I'd seen him that morning. "Did you hear about the spy?"

Chapter 3

Kadin

WE WAITED FOR GIDEON and Arie in the queen's sitting room. Bosh murmured something in Rena's ear. She giggled.

I'd sent a message to Daichi and Ryo to come if they were free. They preferred to stay at the tavern in town; the castle made them uncomfortable. According to Ryo, "We're supposed to steal from queens, not serve them." With Naveed scouting for the next possible job and Illium having left our crew altogether, that left just me and Bosh.

Which might as well have meant I was alone since he spent his days with Rena.

The shift in dynamics from leading my crew to being someone in the background threw me more than I wanted to admit.

While the Shah's Council met daily with the captain of the guard, Navabi, the eight of us had formed a second "unofficial" council on Arie's behalf.

When the door opened, Ryo and Daichi entered, surprising me by attending after all. Their eyes darted around the room, cataloguing items. The gold inlaid over the backs of chairs. The ivory statues. Even the pillows and rugs were exquisite. I recognized the habit as easily as I did my own. They were restless.

My men stayed in Hodafez for me, but for how long, I couldn't say. Our crew was breaking apart. The toothpick I chewed on snapped between my teeth. I threw it away and pulled out a new one. The future was about as clear as the path to Jinn.

When Arie slipped into the room from the opposite door, hope inflated my lungs. For her sake I pretended not to see her and nodded along with Ryo's story.

"She asked about my tattoos," he was saying as he held up his arms. They were covered in ink from the wrist to the shoulder, disappearing under the sleeves of his tunic and crawling out from beneath it onto his neck. Raising a brow for emphasis, he added, "All of them. You try to tell me she's not interested when she wants to sit and listen to an hour's worth of stories. About skin." He smirked.

Arie settled into the window seat across the room from us, pulling her faded red robes around herself. Her dark hair lay flat and lifeless, and her eyes gazed dully at us, but at least she was here. It was something.

Before Ryo could go on, Gideon flashed into the room. His eyes landed on Arie, and she stiffened. His wince was almost imperceptible. Turning to the rest of us, he moved toward the side of the room farthest from her. "Good, you're all here."

Ryo and Daichi sat up straighter in Gideon's presence, while Rena glanced over at me, practically bouncing in her seat.

She looked away when I held her gaze. It was an effort not to frown at her.

Gideon moved into the circle of chairs, kindly not pressing Arie to join us, and began without preamble. "I owe all of you an explanation. When we first met, as you know, I was pursuing a lamp that could help me return to Jinn." He perched on the edge of the sofa, perfectly still besides fidgeting with his cane, which for him might as well have been wild pacing. "What I've never shared is that just prior to my leaving Jinn, I had learned that the prince of Jinn was missing."

"You told me," Rena said, grinning at the rest of us, proud she'd known a secret. I could remind her that she'd told me too, but I let it go.

"He disappeared over a year ago," Gideon continued. "What you may not know"—his voice grew sharp, and each word snapped—"is that when I pierced through the enchantment and began to discover hidden truths beneath the surface, the queen banished me from Jinn."

Rena coughed.

"Some of you knew that as well," Gideon amended.

"Is that normal?" I spoke for the first time, keeping my voice mild, though this new information shocked me.

"It shouldn't be," Gideon said darkly. "But this last century, it's happened more and more frequently. This last year of my banishment, I've spent every spare moment searching for a way back into Jinn to find the lost prince."

"That's why you wanted that lamp," Bosh interrupted, nudging Daichi beside him, who nudged Ryo. "We knew it had to be important."

"I thought so." Gideon pulled that same oil lamp from his pocket, holding it by the golden stem and staring at the green glass orb on top. "But since Arie's Sever—since three months ago, that is…" We all kept still and silent, careful not to glance in Arie's direction as Gideon faltered and continued on. "When Enoch revealed that the prince is not even in Jinn, I began to wonder if the queen banished her own son. I've spent these last few months searching the human kingdoms instead for any trace of him."

"The queen?" I sat forward. I couldn't help myself. Growing up on tales of Jinn, it was difficult to separate facts from fairy tales, but one of them stuck out in my mind, about a compassionate queen who took over the throne and ruled fairly after her husband passed away. Those bedtime stories had painted her out to be a saint, which I'd always found a little hard to believe. Still, I'd never expected a truth like this. "She'd banish her own son?" *Just when I start to trust the Jinn, I'm reminded what they're truly like.*

"Queen Jezebel's involvement in the prince's disappearance is too strong to ignore." A muscle twitched in Gideon's jaw, and his blue eyes were like ice when he turned to me. "For the past year, my entire focus has been finding the prince before the Crowning Ceremony of Jinn. Crowning him instead is the only way to prevent the queen from ruling for another fifty years. The crown enhances her Gifts, making her stronger than any other Jinni. Crowning her would renew her strength and tie my people to her for another half century. But—" he glanced at Rena, and they exchanged a weighted look—"I've reason to believe there's a new concern that affects the human world as well."

He turned in his seat to address Arie directly for the first time. "It's no longer just the prince of Jinn who needs saving, but the human kingdoms as well. Without a plan of action, it may be mere days after the ceremony before the queen of Jinn attempts to take over."

Take over. "What exactly would that look like? Turning the humans into slaves? Killing them?" I forgot to watch Arie. This was exactly what I'd always been afraid of. Memories of growing up powerless with Jinni Gifts hurting my family flooded back. My little brother lying dead in the road. I clenched my fists. The Jinn had always exploited their power. Why should I be surprised?

"Both. Worse. The queen sees humans as lesser beings."

I clasped my hands and rested my chin on them, trying to maintain a calm demeanor that I didn't feel as my men glanced between us. "I thought we at least had the Jinni laws protecting us."

"We do. Or we did. The queen has worked hard to revoke them. When she goes through the Crowning Ceremony and regains her full ruling strength from the spells, I have no doubt she'll overrule anyone who disagrees with her."

"She has to be stopped," I said, mostly to myself.

Gideon nodded. "I've called you here because it's no longer just a matter for the Jinn alone. Our problems will very shortly spill over into the human world as well, which brings me to my main request."

Rena scooted to the edge of her seat, and the room seemed to hold its breath.

We waited.

"The queen of Jinn is trying to start a war." Gideon tapped his cane on the floor, as if to knock out the words that wouldn't quite come, and said softly, "And I think it's time we give it to her."

I was shaking my head before he'd even finished speaking. "Absolutely not. Humans can't win a war against the Jinn."

"It's not an easy request." Gideon's fingers curled around the elegant cane. His voice wavered almost imperceptibly as he continued. "When the queen's daughter disappeared years ago, I could have come to the humans for help. We could've worked together. But pride kept me from it. Perhaps if I'd been willing to bend, she could've been found." He stared at Arie as he said this, though her gaze was on the floor.

"The humans need a plan," Rena declared in the silence that followed. "We've seen firsthand what happens when the queen of Jinn involves herself in the human world." She gestured to Arie, adding, "No offense intended."

Arie straightened a bit, lifting her chin to nod in agreement. "No, you're right. I don't want what's happened to me to happen to my people."

"And that brings us back to the main topic at hand," Gideon said gently but firmly. "We need to discuss ways the humans can store up defenses against the coming invasion. More importantly, we need to discuss offensive tactics and, if possible, find a way to challenge the queen's rule and fight back."

I knew he was right, but we'd seen what the Jinn could do. My gaze slid across all the fine castle furniture, which I'd seen during daylight hours far more than I'd ever expected, to land on Arie. She'd slumped back against the side of the elaborately carved window seat, eyes closed.

Our constantly present proof of Jinni strength.

Impossible to ignore.

Her Severance was like her own private torture chamber I couldn't rescue her from, no matter how hard I tried. If that was the result of just one Jinni... well, it was difficult to imagine what would happen if the queen sent an army.

I sank back into my chair. Creating the perfect plan was usually a pleasure. This was the first time in years that I felt utterly defeated as I came up blank.

I couldn't save Arie any more than I'd been able to save my little brother all those years ago, or my family from their fate. How, then, was I supposed to rescue the entire human race?

Chapter 4

Arie

"WHAT IF…" MY VOICE was rusty, and I had to clear my throat. "What if we could get more Jinn to join the humans?" It felt good to focus on something outside of myself for a change. It helped lessen the pain. "Not just you and Enoch, but dozens of other Jinn? If the queen has banished so many, could there be more Jinn out there who might want to take our side? To end her reign?"

There was a long pause. Not even the sound of breathing. Was it really *that* shocking for me to speak?

Rena grinned at me, hands raised to her mouth as if she might even clap. Bosh, Daichi, and Ryo glanced between me and Kadin, whose expression was carefully neutral.

Gideon was the first to answer, hesitating before he slowly said, "I'm afraid that could take weeks, perhaps months." His voice was soft, the way you'd speak to an injured animal, as he finished, "We don't have time for that, unfortunately. The Crowning Ceremony is barely more than a month from now."

This was my home. I wouldn't let myself give up, no matter how desperately I wanted to. "Remember how you told us you sensed the Jinni Key when it was unveiled? That it called to you and all other Jinn?"

His brows rose. "You're saying we could use the Jinni Key as a beacon."

"To call any Jinn nearby," I agreed. A brief smile touched my face. The feeling faded too quickly to hold on to.

"Not just Jinn nearby," Gideon whispered, leaning forward in his chair and growing completely still. "It could be sensed by Jinn across entire kingdoms. We could build an *army*." He stood in excitement. "If we return to Jinn with such a large crowd of witnesses, we might be able to take a stand at the Crowning Ceremony and challenge the queen's reign peacefully."

"Just one thing," Rena said, glancing worriedly at me.

I recalled the problem even before she spoke.

"I don't have the Key anymore." She pursed her lips and shook her head. "When Gideon said he didn't need it, I gave it to my sister. She always wanted it, and I thought... I thought I was doing something nice..." She trailed off, muttering to herself, "How could I give something so important to Yuliya, of all Mere..."

I sank back in my chair. "You're right. It was a stupid idea."

"Not stupid," Kadin murmured, leaning toward me. "Just... not feasible."

The others nodded, trying to be encouraging.

Tears pricked my eyes. When would a day come that I didn't cry for no reason? I blinked carefully, trying to hide them, and stayed silent.

"What's the worst that could happen if we did nothing?" Bosh asked, and they slowly returned to debating our options.

The sunlight slowly crossed the window seat, crawling up my arm and neck until it warmed my face. I leaned against the soft pillows in the corner of the window seat and closed my eyes as I listened.

Without meaning to, I fell asleep.

A soft shuffling of a chair moving closer roused me. Blinking sleepily, I found Kadin seated across from me, elbows on his knees.

"Any progress?" Guilt at falling asleep made that small spark of concern for my kingdom rise in my chest again. It flickered weakly and went out. They were doing a far better job than I would. Who was I to save my kingdom when I couldn't even save myself?

"Nothing worth trying yet," he said softly. In a louder voice, he called across the room to the others where they sat in their circle, "I think we should come back to the Jinni Key."

A voice called back, "We don't have it, boss." Bosh. Shoes knocked on the hardwood floors as he and the others came to join us.

I sighed and uncurled a bit to sit up. No matter how much I wished I could shut my eyes and go back to sleep, a queen should keep her feet on the floor in public.

Kadin shook his head at Bosh, half smiling. "There's no reason we can't get it back."

Rena stopped behind a chair, resting her hands on the top, shaking her head. "Yuliya would never part with it. Even if she hates it as much as I did, she still wouldn't give it back to me."

Everyone was silent. It took an enormous amount of energy for me to form my thoughts into words. "Would she consider a loan?"

Rena frowned, lowering her gaze to the floor as she contemplated the idea. "A bargain for temporary ownership?" On a deep breath, she said in a rush, "I suppose if the offer was enticing enough. Yuliya loves a good trade as much as the next Mere. Maybe more." Her eyes brightened. "We'd only need the Key until the end of the month"—she glanced at Gideon—"right?"

Arms crossed, forehead wrinkled, he nodded. "But how would you convince her?"

"I have an idea of what she might want." Rena headed toward the door, almost tripping over her skirts in her excitement. "If this is our only option, then there's only one way to find out if it'll work. I have to face my sister."

Chapter 5

Rena

"HOW WILL YOU REACH her?" Bosh asked from a few feet behind me on the beach. He'd stopped when he reached the water, but I'd stepped into it and let the waves of home wash over my feet.

"The Mere put migration communication rules in place for travelers," I said absently, eyes glued to the horizon where the late afternoon sun was setting over the ocean.

This time of year, it would be the orcas. Fortunately, my underwater home in Rusalka was only a short distance from Hodafez, otherwise this type of communication often took days. "We're not as barbaric as the humans, incapable of going anywhere without being out of contact for months."

"It's really that common to travel as a Mere?"

"Of course." I left the water to wander the beach, searching for a conch shell that would project the farthest. "I'm the youngest."

For some reason, that didn't clear things up for him. His bare feet appeared in my line of vision. "What does that have to do with anything?"

This shell should work. Holding the conch, I dropped onto the sand with a sigh, making a little hill to prop my feet up so I could stare at my toes as they wiggled. "Eldests stay home and prepare to rule. Middles learn politics and war. Youngests have the most freedom and usually travel as ambassadors to other Mere kingdoms, maybe even to human kingdoms in the past. Why? What did your parents teach you?"

"I never met my parents." His voice was soft. *Fish eggs.* As their human saying went, I'd put my leg in my mouth again. Or was it toes? I'd never quite figured out how that worked.

"Well, don't worry." I fumbled past the awkward silence, avoiding his words. "It's not that common for Mere to visit the human world. Yuliya would never bother coming here if I didn't ask her. Let's just hope asking is enough."

I played with my shell necklace, subtly pulling out an especially pretty shell that released the fragrance of a flower from the depths of the ocean. It wasn't as potent here on the surface as underwater, but I stood and stepped closer to him to make up for that. If only I had my glorious tail now instead of these two scrawny legs hidden beneath a dress. No Mereboy had ever resisted the shine of my red scales.

Bosh didn't seem to notice any of my attempts at flirting. Shading his eyes, he studied the water.

I sighed. Back home, he'd be expected to ask my father if we could swim for an hour a day to get to know each other. It was a very intentional type of courtship—not this unplanned, unspoken thing between us where we ran into each other and stayed until we didn't. *Wait to see what floats to the surface on its own,* I reminded myself.

Not that I minded spending most of my days with him. Not at all.

Sure, Bosh didn't do anything the normal way, but to be fair, it was difficult for him to ask my father's permission; I could forgive him for that.

I shrugged, letting go of the shell and the flirting to focus on the task at hand.

If any orcas grazed in these waters, it was almost time. The sun had dipped below the horizon, but that soft golden light lingered. Close enough.

I stepped into the tiny waves that lapped at the shore.

"Wait, what're you doing?" Bosh panicked, following me into the water. "Are you leaving?"

"Of course not!" I laughed. "I'm just going to call an orca in. At night they rest nearer to the surface, so it's our best chance to reach one."

"Call an... orca." His face paled.

Did I forget to share that bit? I shrugged, wading farther into the water, up to my waist. "I'll be right back," I called over my shoulder before I dove into the deeper waves and fully submerged.

After so long on land, my gills strained to adjust to being underwater. I put the conch to my lips and blew three short blasts, paused, then three more, and so on. It didn't take long for a dark shape to form in the distance. I swam farther out to meet it.

The orca stretched the length of three horses, and his powerful teeth could have easily eaten all three as well, but his beady black eye was friendly as he circled me.

Using the conch, I blew another series of blasts: short, short, long, a trill, and a drop. It was a complex language, but like every royal Mere, I'd learned to speak orca at a young age.

When I stopped, he trilled in response that he understood. With a flap of his tail, he rose to the surface to blow out the water and take in new air—Bosh would see a sudden fountain—and then he flipped to face Rusalka and swam off.

When I returned, Bosh stood in water up to his chest, eyes wide. "That was—it was huge! What if... how did you...?"

I grinned. "I gave him the message." My smile faded, and I gazed out past the crashing waves to the stillness beyond. "Now all we can do is wait."

* * *

WE CAME BACK TO the sandy shore frequently, sometimes with Kadin, Daichi, or Ryo. Sometimes even with Gideon, though he rarely stayed long. Arie never came.

There was no word the first day, nor the first part of the second, but in the evening on the second day, I jumped to my feet at the sight of pale blond hair rising from the depths. Glancing up at the castle on the cliffside above, small and pale in the distance, I wished I hadn't told Bosh to stay behind to help Kadin. The empty beach that had seemed so large and inviting now felt narrow and threatening. Too close to water. I should have told her to meet me at the castle.

Yuliya used the shell that gave her legs, a duplicate of the one she'd given me, before approaching. Once on solid ground, she strode out as gracefully as any Mere who'd had a tail the previous minute could, only tripping once or twice. She stopped where the waves still lapped at her bare ankles. "You dare summon me, Sister?" She sneered, but there was curiosity underneath the usual layer of contempt.

She wore a short dress of seaweed, another reminder that she knew more of the human world than she'd ever deigned to share with me.

I answered with the same degree of bluntness. "I'd like to offer you a bargain."

Yuliya's cool blue eyes lit up with interest, taking in the kingdom above and behind me, though her voice remained distant. "I'm listening."

"I'm sure you've noticed that the Key doesn't grant you your own desires, only the desires of others," I began.

"What of it?" she snapped, no longer indifferent. Behind her, the setting sun lit the sky, outlining her with vibrant gold and pink.

"Perhaps I'd be willing to turn the Key for you, as I'm sure you do for others, to grant your greatest desire." I'd done so many times before, and I would happily do so again if it meant saving the human world. I was completely confident Yuliya had never used the Key for someone else since she'd won it from me. She wouldn't risk the pain that came with granting someone's greatest desire, especially if it was a larger desire—which most were.

"Out of the kindness of your heart, I suppose?" Every word dripped with sarcasm. "Are the humans rubbing off on you so much already?"

Every word mattered in a bargain. I chose mine carefully. "This offer would come with an agreement to lend me the Jinni Key"—it was important to always name things with incredible detail in a bargain to avoid ending up with something unexpected, like a regular old key—"for the span of a month and a day. At the end of that time, I'd turn the Key to grant your desire and then give it back."

"Ha, at the end," she scoffed. "So you think I'd give you a whole month to find your way out of the deal? Or perhaps run away with the Key into the mountains"—she pronounced it mon-tayns—"and disappear forever? Absolutely not."

I kept my own façade of indifference intact and shrugged. "Well, I'm not going through the pain of granting a desire for nothing. Knowing you, it's likely a large desire and difficult to accomplish any other way." I hoped to twist the knife in how badly she wanted it.

Her eyes narrowed.

I crossed my arms, adding, "I can tell from your silence that the desire is substantial, so asking for a full month is hardly too large a bargain. If anything, it's too small. It's either this or there's no deal."

We stared across the water at each other, not speaking. Now that she was considering the deal, I hoped Bosh would take his time. This was the crucial moment.

After a long minute passed, I accepted her refusal with a nod and turned toward the path to leave.

"You'll grant the desire *first*," she declared, making me pause and turn back. "And only once the desire is granted will I allow you to have the Jinni Key for the span of a month and a day."

I checked every word of the deal carefully. It seemed reasonable. Better than I'd hoped, really. I hadn't been sure until this very moment that she'd even consider parting with the Key.

Between the crashing of the waves and the tall grass along the path to the castle, I wouldn't see or hear Bosh or any other humans coming, which worried me. Yuliya didn't like others to see her spells. She might withdraw out of spite. Thankfully, though, he didn't show.

As before, our contract was sealed with a spell; the imprint of the shell she used would remain on my skin like a brand until the contract was complete.

When Yuliya placed the cold metal of the Jinni Key in my palm, the crescent moon at the top dug into my skin, creating the feeling of a tiny school of fish in my stomach all swimming at once.

Now that I'd agreed, all that was left was to grant her desire. One more glance over my shoulder at the path through the tall grass. Still alone.

My sister looked as hungry as a shark with blood in the water.

When I turned the Key in the air, an inky cloud grew above her head, showing me a vision of her deepest desire. I could still back out if it turned out to be too much.

I expected to see one of the Meremen who frequently chased her tail. Instead, the vision revealed our father on his throne, naming her as his successor.

As the sky deepened in color and the sun drew closer to the water, making the vision even darker by contrast, I scrunched up my nose, trying to judge the cost that the Key would extract from me physically for granting this particular desire. On the one hand, Father *would* eventually name Yuliya his heir. However, he was still in his prime, with at least a century ahead of him, if not two. It was rare for a ruler to name a successor before the end of their reign. Unheard of, truthfully.

The edges of Yuliya's pale hair shimmered with gold as the sun dipped slowly below the water. She didn't say a word as I considered. We both knew I couldn't steal the Key, as much as I wanted to.

It was time for my decision.

A desire could only be granted if it didn't force someone else's will—the fact that the Key gave me the option to grant this desire meant it would be within my father's will to name her. I clenched and unclenched my hand; this debate could go on all night, but, ultimately, I knew what I would do. Better to just get it over with.

Holding the Key, I slipped it into the keyhole at the bottom of the inky cloud and unlocked the vision.

My ankle rolled to the side with an audible snap. I fell to the ground, gasping.

It was agony.

Through the fog of pain, Yuliya waded into deeper waters to bring her tail back. Another blink, still trying to clear the tears, and she'd dove beneath the surface, leaving me alone.

The bargain was struck.

Breathing hard, I tried to stand but fell back, clutching my throbbing ankle, unable to do anything but lie there with tears streaming down my face. My entire ankle had swollen to twice its normal size. Tentatively, I touched my fingers to the bone. Agony made my vision go black for a moment.

The gray sky grew darker. Stars would come out soon. Bosh had to have realized something was wrong by now.

I closed my eyes, focusing on my breathing.

This was what happened to fools who wanted legs instead of a tail. Stupid, breakable human bodies. *The Key always has a cost,* I reminded myself. *It would've been something else.* Right now, that wasn't comforting in the slightest. *Maybe this time the price was too high.*

"Rena, what's wrong? What happened?" Bosh's frantic voice cut through the throbbing. He'd finally come.

When I opened my eyes, it was pitch-black and I could barely make out his silhouette.

His hands were on my arms now, then my face, checking for the cause of my pain.

Catching his arm, I stopped his frenzied searching and said on a heavy breath, "It's my ankle."

"What happened? Did you sister do this to you? Can you stand?" he asked as he offered his hands to help me up.

I hissed through my teeth as I stood on one foot and attempted to put weight on the injured leg. Shooting pain radiated up my leg, pulsing, making my stomach churn and my head spin. I couldn't think straight. "I can't put weight on it," I said, shaking my head, trying to sit back down. "I think I'll just stay here tonight."

"You're *not* staying here." He stopped me, putting my arm over his shoulder. "Lean on me, and I'll help you. We need to get you to a healer."

I had to stop and rest a dozen times along the path before we drew close enough to the castle for Bosh to run and get help.

It was only as Bosh and the healer settled me on a low cot in the sickroom that I finally remembered the Key. My fingers curled around the now-warm metal still in my hand.

I slumped back with a sigh of relief that accidentally turned into a yelp when the healer prodded the bones of my ankle. "Hold still, child."

She pressed a few places, asking if it hurt.

I nodded with new tears streaming down my cheeks.

Finally, she wrapped it and stepped back to speak with Bosh in the doorway for a few long minutes.

When he approached my cot, he took a deep breath before blowing it out. "She said the swelling means there's been some pretty bad tearing, but she doesn't think it's actually broken."

I snorted. "Are you sure she's a healer?"

Bosh's face and shoulders relaxed a bit, and he smiled. "You're sounding more like yourself," he teased. "She said you'll need a few days to heal, maybe a week or two, but you'll be walking again soon enough."

I hoped she was right.

That night as I lay with my hands clenched through the pain, unable to sleep from the throbbing ache in my foot, I comforted myself by wrapping my hands around the Jinni Key and remembering the look on everyone's faces when I'd held it up.

Now that we held the Key, we held hope.

Chapter 6

Nesrin

WE SAT AT THE four-course dinner with my entire family. My three siblings, mother, and even my father all took turns staring at Malakai, the Jinni in their midst.

This dinner—and our dinners for the next decade, really—was all thanks to him. When Malakai had given me a dragon's egg and allowed me to bring it home, he'd saved every single one of them from a life of slavery to pay back the mountain of debt my father had accrued.

His nearly translucent skin with the tiniest hint of blue set him apart, as did his sharp jaw, pitch-black hair, and clear blue eyes that had an otherworldly silver in them.

That alone was enough to awe them into an awkward silence, even if they hadn't also known he was the prince of Jinn. Shadi and my mother thought we should tell everyone in town, but my father had fortunately backed me up when I told them it needed to be a secret. My mother had shrugged and muttered, "Maybe that's for the best. After all, even though he's a prince, he's still a *Jinni*." Scrunching up her nose at the thought, she'd let it go. For now. We'd see if it lasted into next week.

"Doost—ah, Malakai—would you like another serving?" I asked. My voice, which normally would've been drowned out by my siblings, sounded overly loud. I blushed at the slip in front of my family, but I'd grown used to calling him by the name I'd given him in his dragon form.

"I can get it for you," Shadi said, ladling a generous scoop onto his plate before he had a chance to answer.

My eldest sister twirled her dyed-red hair to draw attention to it, smiling when Malakai thanked her, and quirked her brow at me when he returned his attention to the plate.

None of them knew the full reason Malakai was staying here. I'd brought him to my father and begged him to let him stay. All he knew was what I'd told him: that I'd met Malakai during my travels to find the egg. "I owe him, Baba," I'd tried to explain while keeping the details vague. "I hoped I could repay the favor by offering him a place to stay while he's in town."

My father had agreed to keep our secret, however hesitant. After all, no one would turn away a Jinni outright anyway. But no one in my family, not even him, realized just how much they owed to Malakai.

Silverware—recently bought back, also thanks to Malakai—clinked against plates, and the only other sounds were chewing and swallowing.

As dessert arrived, I glanced up to find him studying the shivering confection where they set it down. It shook and bobbed like a liquid contained.

When he met my gaze, his lip quirked.

I grinned, lifting one brow as if to say, *You've never seen gelatin before?*

Our silent communication reminded me of how it'd been when I'd first met him as a dragon. I'd learned to read him better than anyone and knew without him saying a word that lifting his chin and shaking his head meant, *I prefer solid foods.*

Someone kicked me under the table.

I startled.

Zareen glared at me from across the table. She'd expressed her interest in Malakai the moment she'd seen him, declaring she'd make him fall in love with her within the day. It'd been a week.

Fury at my innocent interaction with Malakai rolled off her.

I shook my head at my plate. I'd be hearing about this tonight. Not for the first time, I considered telling her how I felt about Malakai... but I didn't really have a clue. He was a friend. That was all the claim on him I really had. My spoon dangled over the plate, forgotten. Did I want more? I'd never been in this position before.

Malakai's spine stiffened as if someone had poked him.

I leaned forward to glance at Shadi to see if she had.

"Is everything all right?" my father asked before I could.

"Yes," Malakai replied in a clipped tone.

Roohstam picked up the dessert plate and held it toward Malakai. It danced with the motion. "Would you like some more—"

"No," Malakai interrupted, palms slamming the table as he shoved his chair back and stood. The wooden legs wobbled, and the chair nearly tipped and fell before it settled back down.

I half stood as well. So did Shadi, and our wide eyes met where Malakai had been.

"I'm terribly sorry." He backed up as we all stared. "I must go. Thank you for the meal. And the place to stay. I—"

My father's chair scraped the floor as he stood to shake Malakai's hand, only to receive Malakai's back instead. Our guest rushed out of the room as if a dragon had set him on fire.

Pushing my own chair out of the way, I avoided my family's gaze and hurried after him. Stepping into the hall, I rounded the corner and a hand caught my arm.

"I'm sorry, I have to go," Malakai whispered in my ear. I swung around to find his eyes wild, frantic. "There's no time to explain. I-I can't. I'm sorry!"

The warmth of his hand vanished as he disappeared completely.

I shivered.

Just like that, he was gone.

My hands, still stretched out toward him, fell back to my sides, clenching and unclenching.

After everything we'd been through. After I'd invited him into my home. Confusion and hurt warred inside me. *What in the name of Jinn? Did I do something wrong? Is he coming back?* My mind searched for an answer without success.

I couldn't go back to dinner. They'd want an explanation.

"Nesrin," my mother called, voice growing louder as she followed me.

Too late.

"What got into your friend? We were just about to ask him—" She rounded the corner to find me standing there alone.

Her mouth opened, but I cut her off before she could ask. "I don't know. I don't know where he went, I don't know why he left, and I don't want to talk about it. I'm going to bed."

I ran up the stairs before she could respond. Crawling into my four-poster bed, I lay awake in the dying light. The sun hadn't even set yet. It was too early to sleep.

My room felt more empty than usual—lonely—even though I'd never shared it with anyone.

I'd only known Malakai for the span of a few short months. I barely knew him. This rejection shouldn't have hurt. At least, not this much.

I rolled on my side and pulled the blankets over myself. Nothing seemed to help.

After a few more minutes, I flung the covers off. I wasn't a damsel in distress who would sit around waiting for him to come back. Grabbing my bag, I pulled on my favorite black boots and a warm jacket. Time for some late-night hunting.

It was safer with the dragons in their nests, I reasoned. So what if the lack of light made it more difficult? I needed a good challenge right now to keep my mind occupied.

Chapter 7

Arie

A GOLDEN RAY OF afternoon sunlight danced over the thick book in my hands. It touched my skin. Made it a few shades lighter. Reminded me of my Jinni heritage that I didn't feel like I belonged to anymore. I pulled the hand back into the shadows.

I leaned back in the tall chair, giving up on even pretending to read. Dust motes danced in the light above the page.

Rena burst through the library door, hobbling toward us with Bosh trying to offer her his arm. Gideon followed a few paces behind. They made their way across the library toward me.

Kadin stepped out from between the shelves where he'd been searching for books on Jinni history.

"Our plan seems complicated at first glance," Rena declared in lieu of an opening. She was relentless. "But when the tide goes out, what's left behind is simple: we unveil the

Key and draw Jinn in, one at a time. Convince them to join our war against the queen of Jinn. Repeat."

Bosh nodded and shrugged. "Simple."

Without a word, Gideon moved past all of us to stand by the window, facing away.

Dropping into a chair across from me, Kadin slouched back, swinging one leg over the arm. "Will they really be so easy to sway?" He hid his anxiety well, except for the muscle in his jaw that ticked uneasily.

Rena grinned, licking her lips and clasping her hands like a child about to tell a secret. She was as easy to read as before my Severance, in part because the Mere were immune to Giftings, so I'd never heard her thoughts in the first place, but also because she wore her feelings in her every expression. Right now she was the exact image of a Shah who knew they'd won an argument. "I don't think it matters."

Gideon finally spoke without turning around. "May I remind you, not everyone has your immunity to Jinni Gifts."

Her musical laugh only made my headache worse and my melancholy deeper.

"Don't worry," she said as she and Bosh moved to sit. "They won't hurt any of you."

Gideon shook his head. "The Key will lure them in. Any chance for a Jinni to go home, even if they have to slip back in secretly, will be impossible to ignore. Since we can't give it to them, they'll be furious. Probably violent."

"No, no." Rena shook her head, auburn hair flying. "I mean they won't be *able* to do anything. I'll put spells in place."

Kadin stroked the scruff on his chin. "I might need a few more specifics."

"It'll be simple." She grinned. "The first spell, of course, will be a boundary spell so they can't leave after they learn our secrets."

"So we'll trap the angry Jinn in a confined space… with us." Kadin closed his eyes and tilted his head back. "Remind me again how this will be safe?"

"Easy!" Rena waved a hand in the air. "They're all the standard spells back home. This is the kind of stuff you learn as a little-Mere. I'll spell the Jinn who arrive so they can't use their Gifts once they're here. Or I suppose I could spell any humans within the boundary so that Jinni Gifts don't affect them instead." She chewed on her lip. "Maybe both?"

I tried to clear the dust motes from my throat. "Will it really be that easy?" Rena was well-known for exaggeration.

"Easy might not be the best word," she admitted. "It might take a day or two to accomplish on my own, but as long as we keep our efforts small, it should be doable."

"I believe she can do it," Gideon said softly. "The Mere are known for their boundary spells; it's one of the reasons there's peace between the Jinn and the Mere. We try to replicate it, but they have centuries of practice and a refinement beyond our own."

We absorbed the surprising information: something the Jinn weren't skilled at.

Kadin nodded to himself, twisting to face Gideon. "Do Jinn need to practice their Gifts like humans?"

Gideon nodded at the window, still not facing us, hands behind his back. His knuckles grew white.

"Then I vote for the second option: protect the humans." Kadin shifted in his seat. "And also that we keep this between us and begin as soon as possible to avoid spoiling the one thing we have going for us."

"What's that, boss?" Bosh asked.

"Surprise," Kadin and I said at the same time.

I glanced at him, then lowered my gaze to my book and picked at a loose thread poking out of my chair. I shouldn't have been surprised. He had a natural talent for leadership. What I'd been taught growing up came to him instinctively.

"It's settled then!" Rena clapped, practically bouncing in her seat at the idea of pouncing on unsuspecting Jinn.

My stomach twisted. Just like that, without a glance in my direction, they'd decided. To be fair, it was a good decision. Better than doing nothing. I had no reason to be upset.

Taking a deep breath, I searched for the energy to speak. "It's far from settled. We'll need to pick a place for this 'boundary' spell where humans won't enter unnecessarily." I had to drag each word out of the mud before I could share it. "Then we'll designate which of us *can* go in and how, exactly, we'll be protected." Rena would need to prove she could keep my people safe before I'd allow this. "Most importantly, we'll need to work out how to convince them to fight against their own queen. If it comes to that."

I could sense Kadin's approval without even looking. I avoided his gaze. This wasn't noteworthy; this was the bare minimum I could do for my people. I would do my duty like I should have from the start, even if it tore me apart.

"Agreed." Gideon tapped his cane on the floor for emphasis. "But there is some hope. After all, any Jinni who senses the Key will be somewhere in the human realm, which means there are very good odds that they were also banished."

"They'll hate the queen as much as we do!" Bosh crowed. "They'll join us for sure! This plan is perfect."

But Kadin shook his head. "Not necessarily."

"Why not?" Rena asked the question I'd been too tired to voice.

"It's not that they won't join us, but more that we may not necessarily *want* their help." Kadin avoided Gideon's gaze, catching mine instead. "After all, if someone's been banished, it's usually for good reason."

Chapter 8

Rena

"WHAT IF THE AIR turns to fire?" Bosh challenged. "And then they attack us!"

I giggled and shook my head at his latest suggestion. "They can't do that." I paused, turning to frown at Gideon. "Can they?" They certainly couldn't back home in the middle of the ocean. It hadn't occurred to me that my spells might not be quite as perfected here...

Gideon didn't chew his lip or pace, but his finger tapped the top of his cane relentlessly. "I'd say the likelihood is slim, but there's always a small chance of a Gift I don't suspect."

Squinting at him, I threw my hands up and hobbled to a chair to sit. "I don't understand. How do you not *know* what all the Gifts are?"

We'd tested my boundary spell with Gideon, and everything had gone smoothly. Why did we have to go over *everything?* At this rate, we'd be ready to call the first Jinni to us about a week *after* the Crowning Ceremony.

Bosh answered the door at the servant's knock, ushering them in with the dinner trays.

Gideon sighed, rubbing the spot between his brows, but refused to answer until they finished setting the table and left the room, shutting the door behind them. "Gifts are considered private. Like many other things in Jinn, Gifts are kept secret whenever possible." He held up a finger. "Unless they're fairly common or you require the use of them frequently."

I shook my head at their cryptic world, following Bosh to the table to eat. The others would join us when they were ready.

"A Gift like that could easily go unused and unrevealed for quite some time," Gideon continued. I paused midchew. I'd forgotten what Gift we were even talking about. Oh, yes. Air turning to fire. I rolled my eyes.

"On the other hand, if someone discovered they had that particular Gift when anyone else was nearby, it'd be impossible to keep it a secret…"

I tuned him out and focused on the meal.

The boundary was ready. Gideon had tested it, and he couldn't leave, just as I'd promised. Yet here we were.

Bosh finished making his plate and sat next to me, brushing my arm with his as he did. It caused a whole school of fish to start swimming in my stomach. My face felt hot. I shifted slightly closer to him so that he could bump me again if he wanted to.

"We're almost ready. We've got the location," he reminded us, oblivious. By location, he meant we'd chosen the library. It was the largest room in the castle, besides the great hall—both of which could hold a couple hundred—and more importantly, it was the most readily available. We couldn't exactly keep our plan secret if we had to explain to all the Shahs why the great hall was off-limits.

Bosh continued. "The spells Rena put on us will protect us from anything thrown at us: mind spells, any weapons made of liquid or air." He ticked each item off on his fingers.

I sighed. They'd wrung every inch of excitement out of this adventure.

Arie and Kadin joined us on the opposite bench, but I ignored them, scanning the table for those red pastries with the glaze on top. They reminded me of a kelpie treat back home except with buckets of sugar heaped on top.

Home.

What would Mother and Father think of this—a daughter of the sea scheming in a war between the humans and the Jinn? They hadn't even *spoken* to a human in over a century, and the Jinn had been their mortal enemies for three times as long. They'd never get involved in this fight, which meant they'd be terribly disappointed in me.

I shrugged to myself. That wasn't anything new.

"We should prepare the room beforehand," Kadin was saying. "Have beds brought in. Maybe practice weapons?"

"Do Jinn even need weapons?" I blurted.

Only the slight scrunch of Gideon's nose showed his distress.

I could almost hear his thoughts: *a Mere shouldn't know about Jinni warfare capabilities.*

I sipped my drink and waited, brows raised.

"Yes." He said the word as if it were being pulled from him. "Most do. Many Jinn only have one Gift—contrary to popular belief—and often that Gift doesn't lend itself to combat."

"Really?" My curiosity was piqued now. "Like what kind of Gifts?"

"I don't feel it appropriate to share such… intimate details." Gideon stood to leave the table, as stiff and unyielding as a deep-seated rock at high tide. "They're not relevant to our situation."

Arie's quiet voice stopped him. "If we're going to face them, we need to know what we're dealing with."

"Agreed," Kadin's deep voice added, backing her up.

I hid my smile behind my cup as Gideon sat back down. But the rest of the meeting was as boring as watching fish eggs hatch one at a time.

It turned out there were far more Jinni Gifts than I'd ever imagined. Hundreds even.

Gifts of healing I'd heard of before. Weather workers, craftwork abilities, a strange communion with plants and animals, sure. But time-telling? What use was that? Could it even be categorized as a real Gift? And what about this "salter"? So what if he could create salt—the ocean was full of it. Give me a strainer, and I could do that!

"What does 'flamethrower' mean?" I asked, and Kadin groaned.

Bosh had more patience with me. "I think it means when they can take fire and make it go where they want, like tossing a rock or a stick... kind of..."

I frowned. "That's strange."

"Strange, but deadly," Gideon replied.

He was testy today. Everyone was. But I could forgive them. "When do we start?"

Kadin and Gideon exchanged glances. Why didn't they trust me? "My boundary spell is unbreakable—you tested it yourself." Boundaries were the first spells a Mere ever learned, not to mention the most important. They came easier to me than breathing. It was the protection spells that concerned me, though I didn't tell them that. My gills fluttered at the thought. Since I'd put them all in place, the only way to know now would be to test them.

After a long stretch of silence, Gideon gripped that cane of his and said in a low voice, "The Crowning Ceremony is less than a month away. If we mean to have *any* chance of disrupting it, we need to begin immediately."

Finally.

As I pulled the Jinni Key from the twine around my neck, the servants entered to pick up the meal. I whispered the spell to unveil the Key out of habit. Just because I trusted Gideon didn't mean a Jinni should know Mere spells. None of them even noticed until I finished.

Gideon's back stiffened, and he leapt to his feet, yelling, "Why in the name of Jinn did you unveil the Key?"

My chest tightened. I'd never heard him yell before. "You said we should begin immediately."

Kadin stood, pulling a small knife from his boot and gesturing to Bosh to do the same. A lot of good that would do them against a Jinni's Gift. Only Arie stayed seated. She spoke quietly with the servants who had unfortunately just overheard, asking them to keep what they'd learned to themselves for the sake of the crown. Maybe they'd listen, but I doubted it.

Meanwhile, Gideon stood frozen, distracted by the Key.

"We'll be fine," I reassured them. "Last time it took almost an hour for any Jinn to find me, remember?"

Kadin stepped into the furious stare between Gideon and me, holding up his hands. "It's done now. Let's make the most of it and finish planning before our guests arrive."

* * *

JUST UNDER AN HOUR later, Gideon stopped pacing and rejoined us in the center of the room. "Hide it. Someone's here."

I spoke the spell under my breath, then tucked the Key beneath my dress again. "Where are they? I don't see anyone."

"You're sure the protection spells you put on us are ready, right?" Bosh asked as he swiveled, trying to watch all corners of the library at once.

I nodded, hoping I was right.

"They'll likely try to steal the Key," Gideon began, but he was cut off as another male voice yelled, "Now!"

Jinn flashed in from all sides of the room—appearing and disappearing, more difficult to catch than floating plankton.

"Take them down! Find the Key!" shouted the Jinni who had to be the leader. At least four or five Jinn attacked at once—flames, knives, axes, water, all aimed at anyone standing on two feet.

A ball of fire flew in my direction. Only Bosh diving in front of me warded it off, flinging it into the nearby shelves as his spells kicked in.

My nose scrunched up. I'd forgotten to put a protection spell on myself.

Flames licked across one bookshelf and onto the next.

I wished we'd spent more time planning for fire now that I saw it in action, but the damage was already done. The books curled up and turned black as they burned.

At least now I knew what a flamethrower was.

This was a disaster.

"Rena!" Gideon yelled, cracking one of the Jinn across the back and then the legs with his cane, dropping him in a handful of seconds. "Do something!"

Five at once? I didn't know where to start. Offensive spells were far more difficult than defensive.

I stuck my tongue between my teeth as I focused on the green-eyed Jinni before me, shackling him with the very water he spewed, causing him to crumple to the floor.

That only antagonized them.

All remaining upright and offended Jinn turned on me. Bosh yanked me into his arms just in time for a knife to glance off the air at my back. Flames shot past next. The barrier held, but Bosh held on to me almost as tight as I held on to him.

Overwhelmed, I squeezed my eyes shut and froze.

Only Gideon's shout over the madness stopped them. "In the name of the Unbreakable Laws, cease this instant!"

"Is that...?" Their leader held up a hand, and the chaos ceased, though the Jinn surrounded us, circling like the sharks they were.

I stepped out of Bosh's arms reluctantly but remained close. There were more of them than I'd first thought.

"Impossible," the leader said as he straightened, smiling unexpectedly. "Is this *High Commander* Gideon, son of Levi, son of Elijah, standing before me?"

He was the tallest Jinni I'd ever seen, towering two heads above me. He looked barely older than Gideon, although I'd learned that didn't mean much. He was handsome, even with a hooked nose that looked to have been broken at least once, if not a dozen times, and there was a distinctly dangerous air about him. "Tell me, *Commander*" —the title didn't sound terribly respectful on his lips—"why should I listen to *you*?"

I'd take care of this. I'd just begun whispering spells to myself when an invisible hand gripped my throat, cutting the words off with a gurgle. My feet lifted off the ground, and I clawed at my throat, feeling the sting of my nails without relief.

Bosh struggled against the female Jinni who'd grabbed him, but was no more effective than me. My spells had failed. They stopped Jinni Gifts from hurting Bosh and the others but didn't stop the Jinn themselves.

"Are you truly allied with a *Mere*?" the leader snarled at Gideon. He said the word the way the humans swore at their refuse.

My clawing pulled my hair back from my gills, further exposing my secrets for any Jinn who hadn't seen.

The room started to spin.

Spots danced in front of my eyes.

"Put her down!" Bosh yelled, struggling to wrench free from the Jinni who held him.

"You heard him, Jedekiah!" Gideon yelled. "Release her at once!" Metal on metal sounded as he pulled a thin sword from his cane, brandishing the weapon at any Jinn who dared to approach him.

I stopped kicking.

"Please," I mouthed, unable to speak. My vision grew black along the edges.

"I'm the queen of Hodafez." Arie's voice rang out. "And you will unhand my subject immediately."

That was the last thing I heard.

My eyes slid shut.

Chapter 9

Arie

"I LIKE YOUR SPUNK," Jedekiah said with a wink in my direction, ignoring Rena as she fell to the floor.

I swallowed but held his gaze. In the corner of my eye, Bosh dropped to his knees to check on Rena. "She's still breathing," he said, working to pick her up with Kadin's help. They escaped through the atrium in the center of the library where its greenery hid them from sight.

I let out the breath I'd been holding once they were out of sight, hoping the Jinn didn't notice.

Their leader stood with shoulders back and head high. He had a strong jaw and an easy smile, though there was a bump in his nose as if it'd been broken at least once, if not many times.

Clearly, he expected more of a reaction to his flirtation.

As it was, I only stared back at him. "I don't appreciate what you've done to my library." A few stray flames still licked at the archives behind me. I hated the way the burning books made me want to cry.

I stood tall. *Never show weakness.* These Jinn reminded me of the local Shahs on a council day—except more violent.

"Apologies, Your Majesty," Jedekiah said, bowing low. He waved to one of the Jinn behind him, who extinguished the flames consuming the books with a snap of their fingers. Wisps of smoke curled up from the frames of the shelves and the burnt black remnants of the books. "You've invited us into your home as guests. We do hope you'll forgive us the damages. They weren't intentional."

He left a pause for me to agree, but I only crossed my arms and frowned at him. If they weren't intentional, it was only because they'd been aimed at my face.

"Perhaps you might show us your beautiful home," he continued, approaching me with a confident smile. "I'm particularly interested in your treasury. Would you mind giving me a tour?"

I snorted, half laugh, half indignation.

Jedekiah stopped his advance, glancing at Gideon with an unspoken question.

"They've all been spelled to resist your particular 'charms,'" Gideon told him.

My brows rose at this before I smoothed my face over, but they were too busy glaring at each other to notice. "*Charm* is an actual Gift?" I whispered to Gideon, heart starting to pound. "Is it anything like King Amir's persuasion?"

He shook his head, and I let out a soft breath of relief. "Amir persuaded others, forcing his will onto theirs," he replied softly. "Jedekiah's charisma can only influence your opinion of him. Similar to someone with a powerful personality, but amplified."

If Jedekiah had been using a Gift on me, I hadn't known it. Rena had warned us that we'd feel a tingle—a prick of magic tickling our skin. I'd felt nothing.

Thinking of Rena made me take a casual sweep of the room, pretending to scan the Jinn there. Rena, Bosh, and Kadin were all gone, hopefully to see the castle healer.

The other Jinn loomed over us. One sat on top of a shelf, feet dangling in the air. Her short hair was shaved close to the head, and her deep purple eyes were hooded in black liner. She played with a small dagger and smirked down at me. Beside her on the ground was a muscular Jinni male with tattoos. Up on the balcony on the far side of the room stood two dark-haired, green-eyed Jinn, identical enough to be twins, each holding his weapon at ready—matching blades. How many others hid throughout the library, I didn't know. Gideon's hold over the room seemed tenuous at best.

"Jedekiah-Shah," I began, taking a deep breath to maintain my mask of self-control. "I propose that you and your fellow Jinn join us at the table for refreshments and hear us out. We have an opportunity for you that I think you may be interested in."

One thick brow rose, and he blinked lazily at me before asking Gideon over his shoulder, "Jedekiah-Shah?"

"It's a human term of respect," Gideon snapped with a heavy dose of disrespect toward the Jinni.

"If a discussion does not interest you"—I raised my voice so they couldn't ignore me further—"feel free to *try* to leave. And if you can get to the treasury, you're welcome to help yourself." I winked at their leader—his charm must have rubbed off on me. Was that a small smile in response before he caught himself? "When you're ready for a rational discussion, I'll be waiting."

Waving for Gideon to follow, I turned my back on the Jinn.

Confidence is a magic all its own, my father had always said. I felt a sharp stab of sadness at the memory. *What would he think of all this?*

Sitting down at a small table across the room, I chose to stay within eyesight but far enough that the singed smell didn't burn my nose. I picked up the cucumber yogurt and spread it across flatbread, stuffing it with savory meat, tomatoes, and lettuce before taking a bite. The servants had set out a small meal, just enough for our group plus one arriving Jinni. We hadn't expected so many to arrive all at once; that was a problem to consider later.

Jedekiah's hesitation was almost imperceptible. A chair scraped across the floor, and he dropped into it, facing me with a dark glare that made my heart skip a beat.

I took a sip of my drink to cover my reaction.

Silence stretched between us.

The others followed, filling the two remaining chairs and standing when all seats were taken. There were at least two more Jinn than the original five I'd seen, although I only caught them out of the corner of my eyes, refusing to glance away from Jedekiah as I set my glass down. "You decided to talk."

"I'm considering topics," he replied, leaning back to match my calm but with fire in his eyes. "Such as how it might be fun to spit you over an open fire and see how long you last before revealing your secrets."

"Don't waste your time." I waved a hand at that, taking another piece of bread. "I'm happy to answer your questions. This conversation won't require any prediscussion torture, I assure you."

Brows raised, he glanced past me at Gideon, who'd come around the table to guard my back. "She's a tough one, this queen of yours."

"She is indeed," Gideon murmured behind me.

I would've scoffed at that if it wouldn't have undermined my plan. "We hoped you might be the beginning of a growing force against the queen," I said stiffly. "At the very least, that you might stand with us against invasion attempts. But more importantly, we'd hoped you might join us in our attempts to stop the Crowning Ceremony itself." My whole body begged for me to give up; the long speech had exhausted me. "Gideon can explain the rest of why we summoned you here."

That made Jedekiah laugh and shake his head in disbelief. "Summoned, you say?"

His laughter didn't last long though. He was smart enough to think a few steps ahead.

With a flash, he left the table, reappearing above the second floor as the barrier stopped him from leaving. He crashed back onto the balcony as if an invisible hand had punched him, hissing in pain. In the next heartbeat, he traveled across the room to the atrium where he tried to escape through the glass ceiling, landing even harder on the decorative tile below. The crunch as his legs landed on one of the many potted plants made me wince. Shattered clay pieces and dirt clung to his clothing.

The boundary spell was as strong as Rena and Gideon had declared they would be—I hadn't fully believed it until now.

The other Jinn burst into action. Disappearing from the table in quick bursts, they reappeared all around us. The floor, walls, and ceiling all pitched them back.

Curses flew.

One of the Jinni twins barely avoided landing on top of us, disappearing just above my head as he traveled again. "I can't leave!" they called to each other. "What's happening?"

Something crashed against the shelves.

I winced.

Hopefully at least a few of our books would survive this encounter. I regretted choosing the library, but it was too late now. We couldn't lift the boundary spell without risking a Jinni running to tell the queen of Jinn our plans in exchange for permission to come home. I didn't know this group well yet, but it wouldn't surprise me if all seven of them took the opportunity to do just that.

Flashing back to his seat, Jedekiah loomed over the table to glare at me, all hard lines now, humor gone. "What have you done?"

He smelled faintly of smoke.

As other Jinn returned to our corner of the library, the odor grew stronger. What exactly did Rena's border do to them?

None of them sat now, except Jedekiah, whose charming façade was slipping.

"Like I said, Gideon can explain." I waved a tired hand, wanting my bed.

"I'd prefer to hear it from you."

I sighed. "It's a long story."

"Then you'd better begin. That spit is looking better and better by the second."

"Do what you will," I replied, glaring back at him as I stood. I'd had enough of his attitude.

Gideon stepped forward to hold up a hand.

Nothing happened.

I waited for him to speak, only to glance around and find their sharp gazes narrowing in on me. Jinni eyes in a rainbow of vivid colors studied my face as if seeing me for the first time.

Was Gideon speaking into their minds? How cruel to do so in front of me.

Jedekiah's fierce countenance shifted, brows drawing together as he turned to look at me more closely. "I do apologize, my queen. I wasn't aware."

I was not *his* queen.

The last word he'd said repeated in my mind, distracting me.

Aware.

Of what? My jaw clenched, and it was an effort to keep my hands open and relaxed at my sides. Did he mean my Severance?

How *dare* Gideon share that information with them. The worst part was this Jedekiah actually seemed sincere for the first time since I'd met him.

"I've had enough." I pushed my chair out of the way, its wooden legs screeching against the marble floor in protest and turned to leave.

This time, the other Jinn backed away respectfully. Even Jedekiah seemed more deferential, if a lack of argument could be counted as courtesy, staying where he was, hands in his pockets, studying me.

As I passed Gideon I hissed, "How could you mention the Severance?" Tears rose in my eyes, unbidden, and I furiously blinked them away.

"I did not," he replied, catching my arm. "I swear on all of Jinn. It was not that. On my honor."

Not my Severance. Another secret.

Jedekiah let out a low whistle from the table where he still sat. "First I've heard of a Severance," he said, unapologetically eavesdropping. "Would love to hear more, however. It's not every day you meet someone in your position."

My face burned. I refused to turn around, focusing on Gideon. "What *did* you tell them?"

"I can't say."

My lips parted. "Why?"

"It... has to do with the crown of Jinn. It's not something I'm at liberty to share, but it's nothing for you to be concerned about. You'll have to believe me."

For a beat, I took in his familiar face. He'd always been truthful with me. I didn't trust my voice to speak, so I nodded and turned to leave. Some distance would help me think. As I swept through the sunny atrium with its glass roof, I stepped over the cracked tiles and shattered pottery where Jedekiah had landed.

He followed me through the atrium and into the gallery, footsteps sounding on the marble behind me as he called, "Stay. Tell us about your summons. And this whole Severance debacle."

I ignored him.

Only once I stood in the vestibule, hand on the doorknob to the castle hall, did I turn, feeling a need for vindication and the last word. Jedekiah had stopped a few steps back. Though the others were out of sight, I raised my voice so they would hear me. "Don't feel sorry for me." I gestured toward the bookshelves all around us and the tall windows where the sun shone in. "*I'm* not the one who can't leave this place."

As I swung the door open, I winced. It was a terrible way to begin a truce, much less to ask for their help. I just couldn't stand another second of someone's pity.

I stepped up to the invisible line of the boundary, calling over my shoulder, "Thank you for your time. Gideon will explain the rest."

When I stepped forward, the barrier made the same loud popping sound. An invisible punch to my chest knocked me back.

I hit the marble floor hard, gasping for air, feeling almost like I'd been toasted on that spit that Jedekiah had kept referring to.

How is this possible?

I was still inside the library.

Chapter 10

Kadin

"GIDEON CAN'T LEAVE EITHER," I reminded
Arie, gesturing to where he still stood in the small doorway,
guilt-ridden as usual despite half carrying her into one of the
small librarian bedrooms in the corner of the library.

I couldn't meet his eyes. As casual as I tried to sound, I
was furious with this whole situation. Throughout the entire
planning process, I'd made it clear to Gideon that she
shouldn't be a part of it unless absolutely necessary. We'd
originally agreed that we'd stay away from the library and
leave Gideon to handle everything, but now she was trapped
here as much as he was.

Gideon stepped back. "I'll guard the door."

None of us answered.

The door shut softly, blocking the natural light from the
library's tall windows, leaving us with only the flickering
flame in the lamp on the small table by the bed. The librarians
who normally lived here had all been temporarily displaced
per Queen Arie's request. This one had left behind a small

collection of their own books on a shelf, a tiny chest for belongings, and a painting of a couple in which the woman pushed the man away. The art was uncomfortably familiar.

When I'd first met Arie in the bazaar all those months ago, she'd been just a beautiful girl. Mysterious, yes, but I'd had a chance. As queen, she controlled lives, holding the power I'd always hated, and yet she was still that same girl. Scared. Human. Trying to hide her pain.

Even though she was trembling, when I stepped closer and reached out, she brushed me off, moving toward the small trundle bed where Rena lay unconscious. The healer had just left.

Bosh perched on the edge of the bed, leaning forward and checking Rena's pulse again. Her eyes fluttered, but she didn't wake. "How long has she been unconscious, boss?"

"Not long," I reassured him. "She'll come to."

The shadows under Arie's eyes seemed deeper as she joined him and sat on the foot of the bed, leaning against the dark wall as if she might pass out too. Maybe we'd pushed her too hard. I didn't understand how the Severance worked, but I was determined to get her through it whether she wanted me to or not.

Somewhere in the shell before me was the girl I'd fallen in love with. I caught my restless hands before they could reach toward her, shoving them in my pockets instead.

Since there was nowhere to sit in the cramped room besides the bed that held all three of them, I leaned on the dresser, watching the small flame dance.

Both this bed and the room had originally been intended for Gideon to takeover, since we'd known the boundary spell would force him to stay here. That was the only part of our plot that had gone according to plan.

Rena shifted, blinking sleepily. Before she was even fully awake, she croaked, "That went poorly."

I snorted.

"Where are we?" she asked next, touching her throat as she sat up. Her voice was raspy.

Arie scowled. "Where do you think?"

"Why are we still in the library?" Rena's eyes widened in horror. "What went wrong? I didn't expect so many at once—" She cut off, wincing and touching her neck as she struggled to sit up. "Did my spells not work?"

I crossed my arms. *Now* she wasn't sure about those so-called "perfect" spells? Where was all that confidence from the last few days? I took a deep breath and stayed silent.

"Your spells worked fine," Bosh reassured her when I didn't, helping her swing her legs over the side of the bed and sit upright. "You just didn't put protection spells on *yourself.*"

In the lamplight, dark bruises showed themselves already forming around her gills and collarbone.

"How bad is it?" She tentatively brushed her fingers across her neck again and flinched.

"It's not that bad," Bosh said.

Arie and I glanced at each other, though she quickly averted her gaze.

I murmured, "Unfortunately, it *is* bad." I waited until they turned to face me and I had their full attention. "Arie *can't leave.*"

For the first time since it'd happened, she said in a tired voice, "It's not so terrible. I can stay here with Gideon."

"No," I snapped. "You *can't.*" It was unthinkable. I couldn't protect her from the Jinn. Memories of my little brother's death came rushing back unbidden, making my tone sharper than I'd intended. "I won't allow it." To Rena, I added, "You'll need to remove the boundary spell immediately."

"But I can't." Her voice cracked, protesting so much use. "We all agreed: once the Jinn are here, we can't let them leave under any circumstances. If they do, they'll warn the queen and we'll lose our chance."

The muscles in my jaw ached from clenching. I rubbed it, searching for a solution. I could always find a way around a problem.

When I didn't answer, Bosh cleared his throat and said to Arie, "If you're going to stay here, you're going to need a bed too. Right, boss?"

"Sure," I said, not looking away from Arie's dark eyes.

"We'll go let the servants know," he said awkwardly, glancing between Arie and me, before helping Rena stand. For once, the Mere girl seemed to read the room and didn't say anything else.

The door closed behind them.

Arie and I were left to a rare moment alone.

I stayed on my side of the small room across from the bed where she still sat.

"You can't stay here," I repeated, trying to soften my tone, not sure it was really working.

"You know I have to," she replied as she closed her eyes and laid her head back against the wall with a sigh.

"I'll stay with you then." I turned to the door, planning to call after Bosh and Rena and tell them to ask for a third bed. We'd make it work. My chest was tight, and my lungs couldn't seem to get enough air.

"No," she said as I turned the handle.

I stopped but didn't turn around.

"I need you to go." She said it so softly it was almost a whisper.

"Arie, don't give up," I began, turning to face her. "You can still try—"

"No," she interrupted, but had to stop and collect herself. She met my eyes, then dropped her gaze to the floor. This time she did whisper. "I can't... I can't lose you too."

My throat tightened, and the right words escaped me. Platitudes wouldn't help. She didn't need empty phrases, meaningless promises that I'd be fine. These were Jinn after all. What did she need? I opened my mouth, hoping the right thing would come out.

"I'm tired." Her voice was flat. Empty. "We're going to call more Jinn in tomorrow, and the next day, and the next. We should get some rest while we can."

I closed my mouth. "Sure."

As she crawled underneath the thin blankets and turned her back to me, facing the wall, I stepped up to the lamp and blew out the flame. The room went dark. The tiniest sliver of daylight crept through the crack under the door. Opening it, I waited a beat, then closed it again, letting her think I'd left. On silent feet, I moved to the open corner in the room, lowering myself to the cool stone floor and settling in.

I wouldn't give up on her.

When the Arie I knew came back, I'd be here.

∗ ∗ ∗

MANY HOURS LATER, SERVANTS had come and gone, bringing beds, dinner, and anything else Arie might need. She'd asked to be alone and had spent a large portion of the day sleeping or reading. When the captain of the guard and the Shahs asked for meetings, I met with them and made excuses. *She's indisposed. Perhaps you can speak with her tomorrow. Yes, I'll give her the message.* Fortunately, at this point they were used to neglect and accepted the apologies without question.

Gideon spent the afternoon and evening in the back portion of the library with the Jinn, whom I hadn't seen—or wanted to see—since their arrival. Just an hour ago, long after the sun had set, he'd returned, taking one of the empty librarian rooms right next to Arie's. He'd vowed yet again to protect her with his life.

It wasn't enough. He couldn't protect her from them. A nagging voice reminded me that I couldn't either. I ignored it.

I'd set up post outside her door, dragging a comfortable chair into a dark corner that gave me an advantage if someone came spying on her.

Which was how I spotted Naveed sneaking down the dark hall that led to Arie's room on silent feet despite his stealth. His dark skin hid him well in the moonlight.

Though he couldn't speak after the injury when we were young, he quickly signed that he had news. In silent agreement, we moved down the hall and left the library. There were too many prying eyes and ears in there. I fought the urge to look back and promised myself I'd check on Arie as soon as I returned.

Naveed respected me enough not to ask why I was here instead of sleeping. Instead, he signed that he'd found a job in Hoishi, where Daichi and Ryo were from.

They want to take it, he continued, hands moving slower than usual, as if he already knew my answer. *We'd leave tomorrow.*

I crossed my arms and leaned against the double doors, suddenly exhausted. I couldn't leave Arie, and I couldn't hold my childhood friend back. I'd never thought we'd take separate paths, but here we were. "You should take it."

But what will you do?

"I'll be here when you get back. It's only a couple months, right? A lot can happen in a few months." Arie could recover by then. The future might be clearer. Maybe we'd even find a solution to the impending Jinni invasion.

He waited patiently for me to look up before he signed in reply. *The Jinn aren't to be trusted.*

I sighed, rubbing the back of my neck. A few months ago, I would've agreed with him. After what we'd been through growing up, it was hard not to. "They're not *all* corrupt. Maybe we judged them too harshly." I was thinking of Arie, though technically she was no longer Gifted.

But Naveed thought I meant Gideon and grudgingly agreed. *He's kept his word so far. It's the others I'm not sure about.*

"I agree." I crossed my arms again. "But if there's a war coming, better to have some on our side than none."

We could avoid the war, he argued, but his heart wasn't in it. He knew what Arie meant to me even if I hadn't said it out loud.

My brows drew together, and a sudden chill made goose bumps pebble on my bare arms. "No," I said, more to myself than to him. "If the Jinn truly decide to attack the human world, I don't think anyone will be able to avoid this war."

Chapter 11

Nesrin

THREE DAYS, THEN FOUR passed without word from Malakai.

"Is this a Jinni custom?" my mother asked for the thousandth time since he'd left. She fluffed the pillows on my bed, then moved to stare out the window, checking the sky for dragons out of habit. Shuffling over to my jewelry box, she sorted it, though there was little out of order since I rarely wore any of it. "Do they always thank their hosts by flinging their plate and deserting their benefactors midmeal?"

Each day he was gone, the story grew, and they liked him less.

My jaw clenched at her harsh words.

"To think I'd even considered him for a moment," Zareen declared as she waltzed into my room and began sorting through my dresses.

"I don't know, Maadar." I repeated my standard answer, ignoring my sister altogether. My mother's energy only made me more aware of my stillness. After years of searching for a dragon's egg and devoting all my energy to that goal, my days seemed aimless now. I needed a new purpose.

They'd heard me say it a dozen times, but it hadn't stopped them from asking. And asking again.

"You would think he'd at least tell the girl he's interested in where he was going," Zareen said, tossing a dress on the floor, followed by another.

"He's *not* interested in me." I lifted my gaze to the ceiling so I couldn't see the mess I'd have to clean up later.

"Is that why he stared at you like you were his favorite dessert?" Zareen popped into my line of vision, leaning over me. She smirked at the blush in my cheeks, taking it as a win even though I refused to answer.

"The least he could do," my mother chimed in, "is grace you with an explanation since you so obviously like him."

"I *don't* like him, Maadar." The corner of my mouth twitched at the thought. I schooled my face into stillness once more.

Silence.

I risked tilting my head to the side to meet my mother's gaze.

She'd stopped flitting about the room and stood there, hands on her hips, brows raised. "You expect me to believe my cliff-jumping, dragon-taming—"

"That's a bit of an exaggeration," I mumbled.

"—huntress of a daughter is bedridden at the departure of a male suitor—"

"He's just a friend," I tried to interject, but she wasn't finished.

"This same daughter, who has no illness to speak of, can't find the strength to leave her bed, and yet she *doesn't* have feelings for this supposed 'friend'?"

"I *don't*!" I yelled back, sitting up and throwing my legs over the side of the bed to stand. "I'm just tired." And a little lost. After all, I'd gotten the dragon's egg and freed my family from our debts. What was I supposed to focus on now? *Not thinking about Malakai, for a start.* "If I never hear from him again, that's fine with me. In fact, I want nothing to do with him."

Leaving my bedroom, I slammed the door and stopped midstep in the hallway. Malakai's clear silver-blue gaze met mine.

He didn't say a word.

My mouth opened, but I snapped it shut and lifted my chin. *Why should I apologize? He's the one who left.* I swallowed my questions. I didn't need to know why he'd left or where he'd gone—he'd done it before as a dragon, and he'd do so again. Better that I get used to disappointment and not expect too much from him or anyone else.

He was the first to break my gaze, but only because my mother poked her head out to holler after me and gasped.

"Oh, what a blessing it is to have you back!" Her voice was breathy.

Zareen's footsteps came crashing toward us from my closet at the sound.

"Thank you," Malakai replied, returning his gaze to me. "I regret leaving so suddenly. Something—" His brows pulled together, and he glanced at my mother and sister, pointedly unwilling to share details in their presence. "Something called for my immediate attention. But it didn't yield any results."

"That's unfortunate," I finally said. My feet came unglued with my force of will, taking me past him down the hall. *Keep a distance. It will hurt less when he leaves again.* I made my voice light and indifferent. "Will you be staying for dinner?"

"Oh, please do stay," Zareen begged.

My lips twitched slightly. At least I didn't sound that eager.

"It'd be my honor," Malakai said.

I felt his eyes on my back.

Sneaking a glance over my shoulder, however, I found I was wrong. My mother and sisters fawned over him as Roohstam strode over from the other end of the hall to join them.

Again, I swallowed the hurt and disappointment, continuing down the stairs. I'd never felt this way before, had never cared much for anyone outside my family, much less someone who clearly didn't care for me. It was awful. There were hours until dinner, and all this energy needed somewhere to go. Pulling my dusty ropes off the hook on the wall, I gathered my gear and escaped from the house as if a dragon were chasing me.

* * *

BY THE TIME I reached the cliffs near the village, I'd calmed down somewhat. Enough to wish I knew why he'd left.

My muscles ached in protest shortly after I threw myself into the climb. I was out of practice. Where my callouses had grown soft, I'd have new blisters tonight. Still, the familiarity of climbing was a comfort, like coming home. I didn't slow down until my lungs were on fire.

"I should've known I'd find you here," Malakai said from somewhere above me.

I shrieked, losing my grip, and slid down the rock wall at an alarming speed. The sharp debris scraped my legs, arms, and face, but instead of feeling the sharp snap of the rope around my waist catching me, someone scooped me into their arms.

Very muscular arms.

I blinked rapidly, trying to clear the delusion. Had I fallen and hit my head?

No. That was *my* hand on Malakai's chest.

I didn't feel the calm of a dream or the panic of a nightmare; this reality made my heart race in a different way. Everywhere his hands touched felt hot.

"I didn't mean to upset you. You had more composure when we met on the cliffs before."

I couldn't meet his eyes, but that left me looking at his lips. I caught myself and glanced down at his feet instead.

They floated in midair.

Adrenaline rushed through my veins, drowning out his voice as my heartbeat pounded in my ears.

"I expect dragons when climbing near the Dragon Cliffs." My voice was breathy. "Not floating Jinn. Put me back."

He began to ascend toward the ledge I'd fallen from. "I wanted to speak to you—"

"Stop! Don't do that!" I hit him in the chest, then immediately froze, worried the movement might throw him off-balance.

When he obeyed, I tried to loosen my grip around his neck and speak without my voice shaking, keeping my eyes on his chin. "You know I hate flying. I just need you to set me down."

I didn't need to see his frown to know it was there. "I do apologize, but you asked—"

"I know what I asked." Lifting my chin to hide how foolish I felt, I squeezed the Jinni-spelled rope, making sure to keep my hand within the circle of his arms just to be safe. It tightened to the point it tugged us toward the cliffs, where it was attached to the hook I'd hammered in just minutes prior. "I'm attached. You just need to let go."

"Certainly not. I would never drop you." He proved it by floating toward a small rock shelf where he lowered me gently. Was there a Jinni word for this Gift of his? If there was, I didn't know it, but that was exactly what it looked like: floating.

When he set me on my feet, I embarrassed myself further by seizing the closest rocks and clutching them tightly.

"What're you doing here?" I demanded between gasps, trying to collect myself. It was difficult to run away from him while trapped on this little ledge, with clouds all around and one floating Jinni who wouldn't take his silver-blue eyes off me.

"I wanted to offer an explanation," he began.

I interrupted for the thousandth time. "I can't talk to you when you're hovering like that. It's unnerving."

"You've seen me fly before."

"*Fly*, with *wings*. I don't see any wings!" My voice rose to a new level of shrill, and I pressed my lips tightly together.

"The only place to land is beside you."

"Yes. Fine. Do it." I pressed my face against the rough rock, squeezing my eyes shut so I didn't have to watch this "landing," only to open them and find him close enough for his breath to warm my face. I bit my lip.

My only comfort in the whole situation was that for the first time since he'd arrived, he appeared distracted as well. He leaned a bit closer, eyes drifting to my lips.

"Go on then," I said, wishing my voice would lower to its normal pitch. I hardly recognized myself.

"It's actually a rather long story." He cleared his throat. "I sensed an object. It's known as the Key to Jinn, and it's incredibly valuable. If I had it, I could go home." He held my gaze, still close enough that he could close the slight distance between our faces in a heartbeat if he wanted to. Instead, he turned outward to the horizon and the forest below. "It's strange," he murmured, almost to himself. "It felt distant, too far to pinpoint right away. Then it just... disappeared." Frowning, he turned back to me, struggling to find words. "It did that again the next day, and the next. Each day I tracked it a little farther, but the sensation never lasts long enough to isolate where it comes from. All I can determine is it comes from somewhere in the west."

I let the information wash over me and latched on to one of the many questions whirling through my mind. "Does the fact that you're here mean you've found it?"

"What?"

"This so-called Key."

"Unfortunately, no."

"I see."

"But I'm sure you can see how it would change everything. I should have explained—I wanted to—but I feared that if I paused for even a moment it might wink out of existence and I would lose the opportunity."

He leaned closer, trying to catch my gaze, but that only reminded me how close we were. I'd never noticed that the small handkerchief he wore tucked into his vest was folded like a rose. How did he do that? I would have to ask him— after discussing his other surprise talents, of course.

"Nesrin, look at me." His voice grew deeper.

I shook my head stubbornly, then bit my lip. *Why am I being so childish around him?* On a sigh, I raised my gaze and forced myself to meet his eyes.

"I truly am sorry. I didn't mean for you to feel abandoned—"

"I didn't." I shrugged. "No need to worry."

We stood there on the ledge in the sky, staring at each other.

"All right then," he said. "Shall I go?"

I ignored him. "What else can you do? You vanished in front of me, you can float, or fly, or whatever it is that you were doing." I tapped a finger for each of his strange Jinni feats, forgetting to hold on to the rocks in my concentration. "And I'm almost certain that when you first spoke to me you were *invisible*. How is this possible?"

"Those are some of my Gifts."

"What do you mean *some*?"

"The word 'some' infers that there are others."

I could've slapped him. My eyes narrowed slightly. "Such as?"

"A Jinni's Gifts are personal," he replied, stiff and formal.

Right. Keep your distance, remember? I reached for the white powder in my bag, rubbing it on my hands as an excuse to look away from him, attempting to sound casual as I asked, "Could you do all these things as a dragon?"

He hesitated. "No."

"Ah." My mind spun with possibilities. "So that's why your mother cursed you, so that you couldn't do those things? Did you hurt someone? Are you dangerous?" I edged back, but only a fraction before my heel left the ledge and I stopped.

"Of course not!" He scowled.

"Well, you won't tell me why your mother did it." I shrugged again, growing to hate the gesture. "I can only assume the worst." I winced slightly. That was too harsh. His next words made me wish I could take it back.

"I don't truly know why she did it." His pale blue eyes squinted at the cliff wall beneath his hand. The more I stared at them, the more I noticed those bits of otherworldly silver. "I always knew she had ambitions but never expected she had the ability to betray family."

Swallowing, I worked up the nerve to apologize— something rarely done in my family, or in all of Heechi. My lips felt sewn shut.

"Come with me next time," he said. "If there is a next time, that is."

I frowned. "Next time?"

He gestured out to the expansive skyline, giving me a chance to admire his profile, clean-shaven with sharp cheekbones and a strong jawline. "I could sense the Key again at any moment. At least, that's my hope. There seems to be a pattern beginning to emerge where it's revealed in the mornings. I just need to sense it long enough to narrow down the city it's in, and then from there—"

"No," I said. "I-I'm needed here."

"But you told me that the egg was your entire purpose." He quoted my words back to me from our first days getting to know each other once he could finally speak. "You had said you didn't know what to do now."

"I'm joining the Dragon Watch," I said impulsively. What a stupid whim. The Watch had rejected me last year; there was no guarantee they'd consider me now.

I could almost hear my mother over my shoulder, *Nesrin, why do you insist on contradicting everyone? Would it kill you to let someone else lead for once?*

"The Dragon Watch," Malakai repeated, frowning. "I didn't realize you'd made plans so quickly."

"Well, you've been gone." I almost shrugged again but caught myself. "And it's something I've always wanted to do." That was only partially true. I'd wanted the prestige and honor, but the actual trials required to join the Watch had always seemed daunting.

I could've sworn his lip twitched as if ready to growl. Oddly enough, it was comforting, reminding me of when I'd known him as a dragon. I'd made him growl frequently then.

"What's so entertaining?" he snapped, drawing me back to reality.

"Nothing." When he glowered, I raised a brow. "It's hypocritical to keep secrets but think others can't do the same."

With a huff, he turned and stepped off the ledge.

"No!" I cried out, grabbing for his sleeve, only to remember his Gift belatedly. He wasn't falling, only putting space between us. I swallowed and pulled back, mustering the little dignity I had left. "Will you… be at the house for dinner tonight?"

He stood on thin air, hands behind his back, expression unreadable. "I will."

I searched for words, but all I could think to say was, "I'll see you then."

"You will." His reply faded as he disappeared. Once again, he'd vanished before my eyes.

"What's wrong with me?" I muttered, then flinched as I remembered his invisibility earlier. *Is he still here?* Such an unfair advantage.

I spent the next half hour as I climbed down imagining him in every rustle of trees and every breeze that blew past.

By the time I reached the ground, I was determined to ask him more at dinner. *Would it be madness to go with him like he asked?* I'd trusted him as a dragon; why was it so much harder to be vulnerable now?

Dragon Watch?

Or Malakai's quest?

Which one of these wild schemes would be less insane?

* * *

WHEN I ARRIVED HOME for dinner, however, Malakai was gone. Again.

This made up my mind.

"Shadi," I said over the barbari bread and honey. "I was thinking of going to the Blood Moon festival with you and Zareen. And Roohstam, if he's attending. Do you think there's time for me to get a dress?"

She dropped the cheese in her hand and screamed. She actually screamed.

Zareen came running in heels down the hall to the kitchen. "What happened? What's Nesrin done now?"

Shadi beamed, taking my hands and squeezing with a little shake. "I'm so proud of you."

"What did she do?" Zareen dropped into an empty chair at the table with a frown. "What's going on?"

Finally, Shadi turned away from me to face her. "Nesrin's going with us to the festival." She grinned.

Zareen leapt up, skirts tangling as she lunged for us. Both of them jumped up and down, giggling like five-year-olds.

I rolled my eyes, standing in place as they flung my arms up and down. Just because I was stooping to attend a festival didn't mean I'd lost my mind.

My mother poked her head into the kitchen. "Did I hear something about the festival?"

"Nesrin's going with us!" Zareen shrieked, and the jumping began all over again.

"Oh, Jinni save us, we only have two days to find something for you to wear," Shadi said breathlessly, abandoning the circle midjump to tug on my hand, dragging me upstairs to my closet. My mother and Zareen followed on our heels.

"No, no. Oh, that won't do at all. Nesrin, where are your actual dresses?"

"I don't know," I mumbled. "I think I have a few from last year in the back—"

"Last year?" Shadi squealed. "Don't even think about it! We are not going to be caught dead with you if you don't go in the latest fashions. Come." She took my hand, pulling me down the hall toward her rooms.

I sighed and let her.

I'd let them think I was going for the same frivolous reasons they were. But I had an underlying purpose, and I crafted my own plans as they worked. This was the perfect opportunity to gain information about the Dragon Watch without approaching them directly. I could make a few allies, inquire about vacancies, and decide if it was the right fit before I submitted a formal appeal. And equally important, I could distract myself from thoughts of Malakai and where he'd gone now.

Chapter 12

Rena

I BURST INTO THE library to find Gideon seated in the sunlit atrium next to the fountain in the center. Normally, this cheerful room with plants of all shapes and sizes throughout reminded me of home, like a comfortable patch of seaweed. The edge of the soothing fountain was my favorite place to sit. But today Gideon's companion—the tall leader of the Jinni crew lounging casually in the chair beside him—ruined it for me. Out of breath, I stopped to hold the hitch in my side.

Bosh nearly ran into me. His scowl challenged the Jinn, daring them to mess with us at their peril. The few within eyesight didn't notice.

Scanning the rows between the shelves as I approached the atrium, I kept an eye out for Arie, but she was nowhere to be seen. "Can you go find Arie and Kadin and make sure they're okay?" I whispered to Bosh.

He nodded and slipped away, disappearing under one of the balconies and reminding me how stealthy he could be.

Stepping into the tiled room and a ray of sunlight, I brushed past the tall ferns and stopped with a good distance between me and the one who'd choked me, the one Bosh had told me was called Jedekiah.

He flashed over to me, fingers slipping around the Key and pulling it up to dangle on its cord between us. "This little thing is the cause of all the fuss, hmm?" he murmured, turning it over to study it.

My spells didn't throw him across the room. I supposed he hadn't actually touched me. The moment I left this room, I'd fix that. Drawing on all my years of feigning indifference with Yuliya, I simply crossed my arms and stared up at him. The way he loomed over me made it more difficult to intimidate him, but I did my best.

"What happens if I were to, say, take this from you?" Jedekiah asked, meeting my gaze with an impish smile.

I did not smile back. "It returns to me. Not to mention you couldn't use it anyway since you can't leave." Under my breath, I added, "Fool."

"I heard that." Jedekiah dropped the Key, and it fell back against my collarbone.

My fingers closed around it greedily, tucking it underneath the fabric of my dress. I didn't like seeing it in a Jinni hand.

That same hand lifted toward my neck, lightly touching the bruises there. "I wonder if there's another way to break the barrier," he murmured as his fingers wrapped around the bruises, growing firmer.

I leapt back, clutching my shell necklace and muttering the spell I'd memorized and prepared for this moment.

"Don't take offens—"Jedekiah stopped midword to clutch his ugly pale throat.

"Touch me again and you'll regret it," I hissed at him.

Gideon jumped to his feet at Jedekiah's strange gurgling, frowning at me.

"Nothing can break the barrier except a counter spell. Killing me—or anyone else—will mean you *never* leave here. Is that clear?" I released him, and we shared a glare before he jerked his ridiculous vest back into place and returned to his seat, crossing one leg casually over the other.

"Quite the little army you've created," Jedekiah said to Gideon, as if he'd already forgotten my presence. "Certainly a downgrade from the last time we met."

I huffed, turning to grab a nearby chair and dragging it unceremoniously up to join their little circle.

"Not at all," Gideon replied, slowly lowering himself back into his chair as well. "These humans—and Rena—have been instrumental in my plans."

His plans? Didn't he mean Arie's plan? *Where is Arie?* I wanted to interrupt and ask him, but it was important to present a unified front, so I stayed silent, glowering at Jedekiah instead.

"I hope she tires of that soon," Jedekiah said, waving a hand at me, brows coming together skeptically. "Darling, you can relax," he enunciated dramatically, which only made my eyes narrow. "I've decided not to kill you. At least, not today."

"That makes one of us," I snapped.

He chuckled, shaking his head. "Suit yourself."

"I've explained our plans to gather a crowd of witnesses," Gideon told me. "And storm the gates at the main entrance to Jinn, using our numbers to challenge the queen's right to rule."

Before this whole debacle, he'd explained to all of us that traveling the distance to Jinn only required the combined efforts of three or four Jinn with a Traveling Gift. *The ability to arrive at the gates isn't the issue,* he'd clarified. *The problem is that unless we have a large enough company to overpower the Jinni Guard or a persuasive enough argument for our admission, we'll be turned away at the gates.*

To Jedekiah, he murmured, "As you know and have agreed to keep secret, I've had little luck in my search for the lost prince, so my only hope is that another suitable candidate for the crown will step forward."

"What if I would like to be a candidate?" Jedekiah asked smoothly, leaning into his hand with two fingers across his face, hiding his expression.

A slight shift on the balcony to one side made me glance up to find that more than one of Jedekiah's followers approached from the second floor shelves, listening in.

"You tried that once already," Gideon said in a clipped voice. "It ended with you here, in the human world, if I recall correctly."

"We don't need you," I said, filling in the strangely heated silence that followed. "We'll find others to help. We just need a month of silence until the coronation, and since you *obviously* can't be trusted, you'll be staying here."

This time I knew why the silence was heated.

"I'll consider it." Jedekiah studied his fingernails before looking up with a sigh. "Someone needs to stop that—"

Someone coughed in the rafters.

"Even so," Jedekiah said as if he'd never stopped. "She could have spies. I'm not sure I want to be seen on your side, especially if it's the losing side. We all have aspirations to return home someday, after all."

Gideon slid to the edge of his chair. "We can help you with that—sooner, rather than later." He ignored those watching, clasping his hands together. "You know me well enough to know I can be trusted. We were friends once, after all."

The other Jinni snorted at that but didn't interrupt.

"It was Queen Jezebel who banished you," Gideon snapped. "Not me."

"Yes, but you were the one who caught me."

"I didn't think the queen would banish one of the nobility. She'd never done so before."

"Would it have mattered?"

Gideon sat back, pursing his lips, and admitted, "No. The law is the law."

"You two were friends?" I broke in to ask Gideon.

Jedekiah answered instead. "He means that only in the loosest way, darling."

"What I *mean*," Gideon said, taking a deep breath as if losing patience with us both, "is that this is your opportunity to get justice. The queen removed you from Jinn, but now you have the chance to help remove her from the throne. Even you have to admit the queen shouldn't be allowed another fifty years."

"That, at least, we can agree on," Jedekiah conceded. "And if by justice you mean revenge, then I admit I'm intrigued. All right, my friend, I can't speak for the others, but I'm in."

Chapter 13

Nesrin

"YOU HAVE THE MOST lovely earlobes," said the dark-haired boy right before he danced on my foot. We spun around the town square, which was lit by lamps and starlight. The usual booths from the market had been torn down or moved to the edges of the square to make room, and half the town was dancing while the other half ate and drank at tables along the outskirts.

"Sorry," the boy said for the thousandth time, nearly stomping on my toes again as he tried to finish his thought. "I bet that you like—that you'd enjoy, um, jewels to, um, match... them?" He was a Dragon Watch candidate, and rumor said they were considering initiating him soon, which was why I was suffering through this unbearable conversation.

"Are you asking if I like earrings?" This wasn't the best song for talking in the first place; the steps were complicated. Though my sisters had forced me to learn so they could practice, it was difficult not to lead. He missed the switch of hands, catching it a beat too late. There was no way to look graceful with a partner like him. Even so, my mother looked on from one of the tables across the square, beaming, pointing us out to anyone within earshot.

I should have started with an initiate. At least they would have some idea of the true requirements to join. I endured the last few circles with a forced smile and stared up at the twinkling stars that danced along with us above the festive square; it was almost over.

When it finally ended, we bowed, and I made my excuses. It wasn't hard to escape. It was forcing myself to stay that was proving difficult. *Maybe I should just present myself to Avizun directly and save myself this torture.*

Despite those dark thoughts, I forced myself to continue, standing awkwardly alone at the edge of the dancing. Information was power. Knowing the secrets of initiation into the Dragon Watch before I began could help me successfully pass the tests. *Or possibly change my mind about joining altogether.*

Unfortunately, finding a reliable source proved harder than I'd expected.

Pressing my lips together, I accepted the hand of a freckled boy with a small gap between his front teeth. *Is he another hopeful or an initiate?* Most boys in town my age were one or the other. He bounced on his toes nervously, but he had a genuine smile that made his eyes crinkle at the corners. "How are you this evening?" he asked.

Oh, small talk. It would be the death of me.

"Very well, thank you," I murmured.

"That's good. I was worried for your toes when I saw you dancing with Hashem. If you'd prefer to rest, I would understand."

I chuckled before I could help myself, hiding my face in his shoulder, but the dance called for spinning, so I couldn't hide for long.

His responding wink made me laugh harder.

"Stop," I gasped, trying to maintain my poise. "Everyone is looking."

"Let them look." He grinned. "You're beautiful when you smile."

"So, ugly when I'm serious, then?" I teased, raising a brow, but I immediately regretted it. What was I doing offending the one sane person at this entire event before I had even asked a single question about the Watch? "I'm so sorry, I didn't mean—"

"Oh no, it's a fair question." He nodded dramatically as he swung me out. "The truth is, your somber face is terrifying."

Now I laughed outright, letting him pull me back in to swing to the side, step here, step there.

"It's the only reason I was even able to ask you to dance," he said, "If you hadn't scared everyone else away with that forbidding look, I dare say you'd be surrounded by admirers."

"Is that so?" I arched a brow, aiming for this supposed stare, but I smirked and ruined it. This was more fun than I'd ever had at a festival—maybe at any social event—which either said something about me or the town events. I didn't want to think on that too hard just now. "Well, that's unfortunate. I've always wanted admirers."

"We'll have to see what we can do about that." He swung me in for the final dip and lifted me back up.

It was over already. I hadn't had a chance to ask him a thing.

He bowed over my hand, brushing his lips over my bare knuckles.

Bowing back, I murmured my thanks, and he held my hand a bit longer than was polite as he replied, "I very much enjoyed it."

Making my way to the tables set up along the sides of the square under the guise of looking for a drink, I willed my cheeks to cool down.

I asked around until someone recognized the boy I'd danced with when I pointed: Adel Heydari, Dragon Watch initiate.

Strange fellow. But I liked him better than most.

More importantly, he'd already begun the two years of training and initiation required to become a full-fledged member of the Watch.

Standing there at the drink table, I took a deep breath before turning back to the dancing, hoping I'd have another chance to speak with him.

After the last few weeks of feeling adrift and aimless, it was good to have a goal again.

Chapter 14

Arie

"I TRUST YOU CAN handle the day-to-day affairs of the kingdom?" I asked Captain Navabi and three of the Shahs on my council. They'd come on short notice, yet I'd still expected more than three council members to show.

We stood in the privacy of the library vestibule where I'd asked them to meet me. The thick plaster walls and decorative carpets muffled our voices, and I made sure to speak softly in case there were any Jinn eavesdropping behind the door to the library—or servants lingering outside the door to the hall.

"Our Jinni guests would like to negotiate a treaty with the human kingdoms," I continued. Technically, this was true. "As you know, I've asked the librarians to take a sabbatical for the next month, as I understand negotiations can take quite some time." They nodded along as if they had any real precedence to go on. A truce with the Jinn was unheard of. Their wide eyes said they knew this, even if they refused to express the feeling in words.

"If any of you strongly desire to be a part of the negotiations, let me know." I paused.

They shook their heads vigorously. "No, Your Majesty, I wouldn't want to interfere," Captain Navabi was quick to say.

"We feel confident in Your Majesty's abilities and will do our part to keep the kingdom running smoothly," Shirvan-Shah said on the heels of Navabi's words, and the others agreed.

I knew I'd been right to keep them in the dark for our plans. The very presence of a Jinni was all they needed to know. That would keep all prying eyes far from here. "Have the servants bring meals into this room and ring a bell to let us know," I said as they turned to go before I'd dismissed them. Clearing my throat, I added, "No sense in scaring them unnecessarily."

The Shahs nodded in agreement, shuffling out of the vestibule. Maybe they assumed I would follow; I hadn't given them a reason to think otherwise. Captain Navabi paused in the doorway, noticing I hadn't moved. "Is there anything else, Your Majesty?"

"No," I reassured him. "I'll be here if anyone needs me."

He nodded, scurrying out of the library as quickly as possible. No one needed me, or perhaps the more accurate way to say it would be no one *wanted* me.

Kadin worried over my thinking this way. Like I might break. Didn't he know I was already broken?

Why am *I bothering then?* I didn't want to face the question. I didn't want to face anything, really. The Jinn were a welcome distraction. They gave me something to focus on besides myself. And despite everyone else's opinion that I should rest and try to heal, that was the exact opposite of what I wanted to do. This diversion was exactly what I needed.

I wandered back into the library through the shelves toward the study, expecting a similar scene to the day before, but at first glance it appeared empty.

"Hello?" I half expected to be shushed by a librarian, even knowing they'd all been removed days ago, complaining of their life's work being corrupted—and that was without even knowing we'd planned to invite the Jinn.

Meandering down the aisle in front of me, I inspected a section of books that had each been burned to different extents.

"You called?" Jedekiah's low voice rumbled mere inches from my ear.

I flinched, dropping the book in my hand.

He caught it. "Allow me." Placing it back on the shelf, he held out a hand. "We got off to a dreadful start yesterday. If you will, I'd like to make amends, starting by asking for your forgiveness for my rude behavior."

He had quite the silver tongue. Was he using one of his Giftings? A Gift of Charm, perhaps? It created a small chink in my armor, cracking open old wounds deep in my chest at the thought of a Gift being used so freely. With Rena's spell over me, I had no way to know for sure. In this instance, at least, he seemed genuine.

I warily accepted his hand.

He bowed low over it, clasping it between his own, not letting go as he straightened. Now we were just holding hands. "Please, my queen, your forgiveness. I'll beg if I have to." His eyes slanted as he smiled, and I had a feeling it wouldn't be the traditional style of begging on one knee.

"That's quite all right." I waved my free hand, mostly to get my other hand back. "I just came to…" I paused. Why had I come? I didn't fully know since Gideon had promised to handle everything. I spoke the first thing that came to mind. "Meet everyone."

"Of course," Jedekiah agreed smoothly. His smile never wavered as he let go of my hand and held out his elbow instead, leading me toward a circle of comfortable seats. "To me," he called out the command, doing something with his voice to make it carry across the enormous room, bouncing off the vaulted ceilings and falling back on us. "Our queen would like a word."

There he went again, calling me *their* queen. I could only guess he meant to charm me into giving him what he wanted. Instead, I focused on this newest Gift revealed, tilting my head. "Can I ask a completely inappropriate question?"

This made Jedekiah's lips twist in a grin. "I love the way your mind works. Ask away."

"What are your Gifts? I mean, what exactly can you do?"

He chuckled. "Oh my, that *is* an inappropriate question."

One of his crew flashed into the circle with us, and then another, and another. There were seven total—*if* they were all there. One of the female Jinn, a bit shorter than the others— well, short for their kind anyway—brought a large jug and drank straight from it before passing it around the circle.

I declined with a short nod and let it pass me.

"Kinsmen, you all remember our new queen," Jedekiah murmured once they were all there, and they nodded.

I nodded in return, gazing around the circle at each of them. Familiar icy-blue eyes stared back, along with shades of otherworldly silver, green, purple, yellow. A vivid shade of red on a thin white-haired Jinni made goose bumps rise on my arms. I blinked and moved on.

All seven of them had deep black hair and that pale skin that showed the blue veins beneath. Jedekiah wasn't the only one to sport old injuries; besides his broken nose, there was also a male missing a finger and a female with a long scar across her face.

All lounged with the false calm of those ready to fight at a moment's notice. It brought a crackle of energy to the air, and I found myself standing taller, enjoying it.

Finally, a different reaction to me besides pity.

Jedekiah introduced me, but not a single name stuck. I was more interested in what they could do.

"I'll make you a deal," Jedekiah said, finally answering my earlier question about their Gifts. "We'll trade a secret for a secret. Seems fair, don't you think?"

"You don't have to share anything you don't want to," Gideon said.

I flinched.

He stood at the top of the stairs. I'd completely forgotten he was here, but of course he was; he couldn't leave either.

"It's all right." I shrugged. "After all, I pick the secret, right?" It was meant to be a joke, but my lips forgot to smile, and it fell flat.

"Sure, sure," Jedekiah agreed, dropping into one of the nearby chairs and gesturing for me to join him. When Kadin said that word, it was reassuring. From Jedekiah, it felt out of place, false somehow. "Ladies first."

I took a deep breath and let it out, mulling over options. As I tapped my chin, I glanced up and caught the red-eyed Jinni frowning at me. His eyes darted away, but I knew that focus. Used to have it myself.

"First secret," I began with a short laugh, pointing lightly to myself. "I'm off-limits. As are my people. A friend of mine made sure a spell would guarantee it. You won't be getting any of my secrets without my choosing."

Jedekiah spread a dramatic hand over his heart. "Why, I'm offended, my queen. Whatever you think we might've done, I assure you—"

"Just Arie," I said flatly. I wasn't their queen; time to set that record straight. I stood. "And if you take me for a fool, I might as well leave."

Jedekiah flashed to my side in an instant. Gideon tensed but kept his distance, even when Jedekiah took my hand and bowed over it once more. "Please, my queen—Arie—it's the trickster in me. I've been roaming the human world for a long time. Old habits die hard."

"How long?"

"Excuse me?" Jedekiah's hand slipped out of mine.

"How long have you been in the human world?"

"He was banished over five decades ago," Gideon answered for him, finally leaving the second floor and approaching the circle to sit.

"It's hardly fair to share someone else's secrets," Jedekiah protested.

"I agree, it shouldn't count." I crossed my arms. "Why were you banished?"

"Ah, ha..." Jedekiah wagged a finger at me, moving back toward his seat.

I stared at his back, trying not to sigh again; he was buying time. "Gideon?"

"No, no, I'll share." Jedekiah held a hand up to Gideon, who closed his mouth. "It's a long story. But suffice it to say, I broke all three of the unbreakable rules of Jinn at once."

"That's one way to put it," Gideon muttered, seemingly to himself.

"All three?" I tried to remember what the rules even were. Something about stealing... or was it lying?

"Never use a Gift to deceive. Never use a Gift to steal. Never use a Gift to harm another," Gideon chanted, and the others nodded along.

Jedekiah just shrugged. "It is what it is."

He'd deceived someone. Stolen something. Harmed someone—maybe many someones.

I'd process that later.

"All right, we're dealing in partial secrets, I see." I returned to the circle with slow measured steps. "My next secret is that I'm not certain I can trust you." And I didn't know what to do about it.

"Ah, that one hits right where it hurts," Jedekiah said with a grin. "But I'd dare say it's not much of a secret."

"Considering Gideon is answering for you, neither are yours," I countered.

"Fair point." Jedekiah stepped into the circle where the drink was still being passed around and took a sip before giving it back. "All right. Let's give you a real secret then." He spun to face me, eyes narrowing on my face.

I blinked.

The Jinn held their breath.

Nothing happened.

"You're trying to use another Gift on me, aren't you?" I let out a laugh at his daring, surprised enough to smile. "You're optimistic, I'll give you that."

He growled and spun to face the smallest Jinni, unremarkable enough that I'd barely glanced at his face, who went flying from his chair, end over end, rising toward the ceiling like he'd been filled with air.

"Hey!" The Jinni floated above us. "Put me down or suffer the consequences!"

"Careful, Uziah," Jedekiah slurred, "If you make me too tired, I might drop you." Even as he said it, he began lowering Uziah back toward the ground. Or maybe that wasn't intentional.

"Don't you dare!" Uziah's fists were clenched, and his blue eyes bulged. "I'm going to—"

"Calm down." Jedekiah dropped him into a chair, turning his back on him. "It's good practice."

"Ha!" The shorter Jinni snapped, "I noticed you didn't try it on Samson."

"That's because my retaliation would be much more painful," one of the green-eyed twins said with a grin, holding up his palm, where sparks sizzled.

A bell rang at the other end of the library. The vestibule. The servants were signaling that the noon meal had arrived.

"He has a point," Jedekiah conceded, then snapped his fingers over the large table in the center of the study. The food that the servants had brought flashed onto the table. Another one of his Gifts. Was that a peace offering? I didn't have a chance to ask, as he waved to the other Jinn and said, "I'm starving. We can bicker later. Let's eat."

Hands reached in along with his, and the Jinn relaxed into the noon meal, almost as if they'd forgotten I was there.

Jedekiah closed his eyes, savoring a bite, humming in appreciation. It was all so… normal. My lips pulled up into a small smile.

No sympathetic glances. No overly helpful plate of food handed to me. No constant reminders of my shame. They just… let me be. It made me feel lighter, like the eyes on me had been a physical weight pulling me down.

Standing up, I began putting my own plate together, and decided to stay a while.

Chapter 15

Nesrin

THE MORNING AFTER THE festival, I came home flushed from a climb at dawn to find my mother waiting for me by the door.

"You'll never guess what happened," she called, running to meet me at the gate before I could even come down the path. She paused to catch her breath.

"Is Malakai back? Is he inside?" I hated the hopeful tone in my voice. My feet picked up the pace on their own.

"No," my mother said, wheezing, and I slowed. "Your sister ripped her dress on the stairs! We were terrified it might not be fixable, but fortunately the tear was clean."

Thankfully her back was turned as she opened the door, so she didn't see the face I made.

"Don't worry though," she added as an afterthought, heading toward the inner courtyard. "I'm sure Malakai will be back soon."

"Yes. I'm sure he will," I murmured, but my resolve to move on only strengthened. It didn't matter what Malakai was doing; his life was separate from mine. He was the *prince of Jinn,* after all. I needed to focus on the Dragon Watch.

Everyone except Adel had been a dead end last night. I could either try to find him and gather more information, or track Avizun down and demand to join the Dragon Watch.

Since Avizun still held a grudge from our last encounter in the forest just a few short weeks ago—where I'd kept him from killing Malakai in dragon form—I doubted he'd even let me speak. Worse, he was known to hold grudges for years.

"Do you know where the Heydari family lives?" I asked, following my mother into the courtyard.

Zareen gasped from the opposite doorway, Shadi right behind her. "You were dancing with Adel Heydari last night. Do you like him?"

I waved a hand. "I barely know him."

"You should invite him to dinner!" Shadi grinned at Zareen as if she'd invented the evening meal.

"Oh yes, *please.* He's dreamy."

Dreamy? I hadn't noticed. A potential ally against Avizun, on the other hand? Absolutely.

SHADI, ZAREEN, AND MY mother badgered me relentlessly until I agreed to ask Adel to dinner. Though it meant nothing to me, I still fought tingling nerves as I knocked on the carved double doors of his family home.

After staring at the fancy mosaic decorating the doorframe and knocking a second time, the door finally cracked open. A servant ushered me inside and left me in the entryway while she went to fetch Adel. I admired the lush carpet, vaulted ceiling, and potted plants. The Heydari family was well-off.

He grinned when he saw me. "Nesrin Ahmadi, good to see you."

I blushed and smiled at the potted plants behind him. I hadn't told him my name, which meant he'd asked about me too. After saying hello, I got straight to the point. "My family wants to know if you'd like to come over for dinner."

"I'd be honored to meet your family," Adel said, eyes crinkling again in that friendly way of his. "And I like a girl who knows what she wants."

I tensed. "Oh… no, ah…" Climbing the Dragon Cliffs was easier than talking to a boy, especially one with kind eyes and freckles. If I rejected him now, it'd also make asking questions much more uncomfortable. I gestured to the small bench built into the wall. "Can we sit?"

"Of course." He led the way.

I sat at the far edge of the unfortunately small bench, trying to put space between us, as slight as it was, and cleared my throat. "I've been wanting to ask you about the Dragon Watch," I began carefully. "What made you decide to join?"

"To protect my family, of course." He smiled. "And yours, and others in Heechi."

"Of course," I agreed. "And what made them agree to take you?"

"What do you mean?"

"You know." I lowered my voice. "The initiation. What did you have to do to prove yourself before they allowed you to join?"

He patted my arm. "Don't worry about that. It's not something you'll ever have to go through."

"Your mother is calling for you," the family servant said from the doorway.

"I'll be right there," Adel replied, smiling down at me and offering me a hand as he stood. When I took it, my hand tingled again. If nothing else, Adel was a good distraction from Malakai. I'd hardly thought about him in the last hour—well, until just now.

"I'll see you at dinner tonight," Adel said, lifting my hand and kissing my knuckles like an actual suitor. A small part of me regretted misleading him, but the other part nodded and smiled, scheming as I left their home. I'd gain his trust at dinner and let him think we were getting close. He wouldn't even realize when he began to spill his secrets.

* * *

BY DINNERTIME, MY MOTHER was in an absolute panic. Fussing with the silverware, she straightened the place settings for the thousandth time, coming over to pinch my cheeks. She tucked a loose strand of my dark hair back in with the rest where Shadi had swept it up onto my head, then stepped back to admire me in one of Zareen's nicest dresses—a heavier gold fabric with pretty crystal beading all along the hem and bare shoulders.

"Maadar, stop." I brushed her hands away. "You're going to put holes in them if you do that one more time."

"We want the young man to like you."

I nodded. What annoyed me was that I actually did want that.

All through Adel's arrival, introductions, and the first course, I considered him. He was funny, although in a more obvious way than Malakai. Darker skinned, of course, and muscular. Not nearly as secretive. Rounder in the face and just barely taller than me, while Malakai's features were chiseled and I had to tilt my chin up to look at him.

Why am I comparing them? Unlike Malakai, Adel was *here*. That was, in truth, all that mattered. I pushed my cucumber-and-tomato salad around on my plate, cutting the chicken kabobs into pieces to keep up appearances, too tense to eat.

"My mother cracks eggs over me for luck," Adel was telling my mother, who nodded in approval. She'd already whispered in the entryway that he dressed well and had good manners. I couldn't argue with that. He mimed the egg juice running down his cheeks and made a face. "She hopes it will help me meet a nice girl—like Nesrin," he added with a wink in my direction. I couldn't help laughing along with my family.

Next he mimicked how his mother threw salt on him each day as he left the house—also for luck. At some point, I needed to draw him away and ask more about the Dragon Watch, but this was entertaining. Almost captivating enough to ignore the empty chair at the other end of the table where Malakai usually sat.

"Excuse me," one of the servants said from the entry to the dining room. "Our guest has returned."

"I do apologize for the timing." I recognized the voice even before I turned to look. "I didn't mean to interrupt your dinner."

It was Malakai.

* * *

"PASS THE SUGAR?" MALAKAI asked me from the far end of the table beside my father. He'd sat in the open seat there, at my mother's urging, but he kept finding reasons to talk to me.

"I'll get it," Shadi said, grabbing the glass bowl of sugar cubes and leaning across the heavy oak table to give it to him directly. Her hair nearly dragged through the sauce on her plate. I caught it just in time, but she ignored me.

"How long will you be staying with us this time?" Zareen asked with a close-lipped smile.

"Zareen!" my mother chirped, dropping her silverware with a clatter. "He'll stay with us as long as he likes!"

My sister toyed with the green frond on one of the potted plants around us, pretending indifference.

"I'm sure business will call him away soon," I interrupted as I picked up my tea, added sugar, and took a sip. I kept my voice casual as I added, "He's very busy, after all. Isn't that right, Malakai?"

Adel's gaze shifted between the two of us. He didn't miss much. I bit my cheek to hold back anything else that might slip out. If Malakai kept interfering, I wouldn't even get a chance to discuss the Dragon Watch with Adel later. This dinner was a disaster.

Before Malakai could answer, I set my spoon down, ignoring the last few bites of my dessert. "I'm full. What do you say to a walk, Adel? I could use some fresh air."

My mother's hand fluttered to her chest in the corner of my vision. I ignored her too.

"I'd love to," Adel said smoothly, ever the gentleman. He came around the table to offer me his arm. "Everyone," he said with a bow, and to Malakai, another tilt of the head. "Good to meet you."

"You as well," Malakai replied, unreadable.

The inner courtyard with the small pool and handful of trees was just large enough to count as a walk if we kept to the edges next to the house and under the second floor balcony.

Away from the candlelight inside, the night was pitch-black. The moon hid behind the clouds. I blinked a few times, letting my eyes adjust to the darkness.

As soon as the door closed behind us, I cleared my throat. "I'm going to be straightforward with you, Adel. I want to join the Dragon Watch, and I was hoping you'd help me."

"The Dragon Watch," he repeated stiffly. It was too dark to read his face, but his voice was incredulous. "That's impossible."

"Why?" My urgent tone didn't match our casual stroll around the pool, which rippled a deep black in the moonlight. The banyan trees swayed lightly in the cool breeze.

Adel pulled us to a stop under the tree, letting my arm drop from his and stepping back, putting his hands in his pockets. His face was all shadows, angled toward the pool instead of me. "You're the girl who brought back an egg."

"You say that like it's related somehow."

"It is." He hesitated, then took a deep breath. "They're not going to let the girl who made a fool of them—us—join the Watch. Avizun hates you. He still talks about that day. It's just not going to happen."

"Avizun isn't the only one in the Watch," I argued, crossing my arms. "Maybe if you spoke up for me—"

"Was that Jinni the one Avizun and his men ran into a couple weeks ago?" Adel interrupted, focused on the door across the courtyard.

"Who? Malakai?" My heartbeat sped up, and I was glad for the darkness so he couldn't see my reaction. "It couldn't be. He was with my family when that happened."

"Ah, of course." His tone was neutral. I couldn't tell if he believed me or not. "It couldn't be him then."

"Couldn't be who?" Malakai's voice drifted toward us from the house.

I stiffened. He had the worst timing.

Malakai headed directly for us, a shadowy shape in the night. At least he wasn't invisible this time.

"Ah, hello." Adel crossed his arms, scratched his head, and then shoved his hands back into his pockets. Ever polite, he added, "Would you like to join us?"

"Absolutely." Malakai agreed immediately, not following the rules of etiquette at all. He was supposed to say, *Thank you, no. I wouldn't want to interrupt.* And then Adel would say, *You're not interrupting.* But Malakai would brush this off and repeat, *No, I couldn't.* And so on until we went our separate ways.

Instead, Malakai strode the remaining steps to the tree and offered me his arm at the same time Adel offered his.

I pointedly tucked my hand under Adel's elbow. "I'm not sure if you're aware, but this is a private walk." While Adel was too kind to be rude, I had no such fear.

"I thought you two might need a chaperone," Malakai said, winking at Adel, who gave him a forced smile in return. "So, what are we talking about?"

"How about a new topic of discussion?" Adel suggested. Heechi citizens distrusted the Jinn, and he was no exception. If he refused to share more details, and if he was right about Avizun and my odds, then my hopes of joining the Dragon Watch had just been shot down faster than a circling dragon. That would mean going back to having no purpose.

It was an effort to unclench my jaw and act relaxed as we began to walk once more, returning to the path along the edge of the house. I would salvage this somehow. "When Malakai and I met, I actually rescued him from a dragon," I blurted. It was technically true, even if he'd been the dragon and it had taken a month. "Avizun would be a fool not to consider me."

The muscles in Adel's arm tensed under my hand. "Is that so?"

From the other side closest to the house, Malakai's fingers brushed mine. I swallowed and pulled back, leaning closer to Adel to give Malakai more room.

"I suppose it is," Malakai replied. That wasn't the glowing praise I'd hoped for. Though I refused to look at him and wouldn't have seen his expression in the dark even if I had, I felt his eyes on me in question.

Adel patted my hand, offering the briefest answer possible in Malakai's presence. "As I said, Avizun might be a fool, but he's made his feelings about you clear." Changing the subject, he leaned around me to ask Malakai, "Where did you say you were traveling from?"

"Oh, you know." A bit of moonlight revealed his curved smile as he flashed to the path a few feet ahead of us. "Here." He flashed out of sight. From behind us, his deep voice added,

"There." Then from just on the other side of Adel, he whispered, "All over, really." He flashed to stand directly in front of us in a spot of bright moonlight.

Adel yelped, cutting off as he caught himself.

"Stop it!" I yelled at Malakai. "You're purposely trying to scare him!"

"Oh no." Malakai's voice was completely lacking dismay. "Is it true, Adel? Am I scaring you?"

Adel shook his head, choking out his answer. "Absolutely not. Not at all."

"See?" Malakai spread his arms wide and smiled innocently at me. "Besides, that's hardly frightening. Scaring someone would look more like this."

He vanished but didn't reappear this time. Smoke rose from the ground, drifting toward us, covering the flowers and rock paths unnaturally fast.

In front of us, Malakai's deep voice came from empty space. "Now this would inspire terror."

Despite knowing it was only Malakai, my heart picked up speed.

Adel jerked back. Stumbling over the flower bed, he continued backing up toward the house. "I'm so sorry, Nesrin. I think it's time I head home."

I stood there in the over-the-top gold dress I didn't even like, watching his long dinner tunic flap as he ran inside the main house without looking back.

I sighed, rubbing my forehead with my gloved hand. The fabric annoyed me, and I pulled them off.

"He frightens easily." Malakai's face reappeared in front of me, followed by his body, until he was fully visible. Hands in his pockets, he didn't close the space between us, but neither did he appear remotely guilty.

"I think he frightens the normal amount," I snapped. "Is what you just did even allowed in Jinn?"

"I didn't break the code," Malakai protested. "No one was harmed or deceived, and I didn't steal a thing."

"You just ruined my plans." I crossed my arms. I wanted to go inside and be alone, but my mother would no doubt pounce on me the moment I walked through the door. As far as she was concerned, if a suitor ran scared, it was my fault. She'd never believe Malakai was involved.

Malakai misunderstood. "You and I both know you need someone who can match your fearlessness, or you'll leave him behind. It was bound to happen eventually. You should thank me."

"Who says I need anyone at all?" My voice cracked on the last word. I swallowed and took a steadying breath; he was closer now. "But if I *did* choose someone, it'd be someone like him. He's kind, he has everything my family is looking for, and most importantly," I added with a sharp tone, "he doesn't just disappear." My point held less weight than I'd have liked after Adel's quick exit.

"I'm here," Malakai argued, taking a step toward me.

We both fell silent at that.

Did he just admit feelings for me? I was reading into it. Neither of us had really said anything important at all. *Or did we?* Was it even possible to reveal feelings if I didn't know what I felt?

"Your mother says you're considering marrying him," Malakai said softly into the heavy silence between us. "Is that true?"

"No," I replied quickly, shaking my head. Of course she'd told him that. "Not at all."

"Did *he* know that?" Malakai teased gently, but I couldn't smile back. This evening I'd been chasing a fantasy—I knew that now. But still, a fantasy was better than reality where I had no future at all.

He grew serious.

When he studied me like that, I couldn't meet his eyes. I turned to walk since I couldn't go inside.

Malakai joined me without invitation, and we finished the lap around the courtyard, then began another.

The silence was different than with Adel.

Not comfortable, exactly, because it was chock-full of unsaid words, but it was like... I pursed my lips, annoyed. *It feels like home.* What was wrong with me?

"Maybe... if you're looking for someone to marry, you should marry me," Malakai said out of nowhere.

"What?" I tripped as I swung around to face him. He caught me. I leaned into him for the tiniest moment before stepping back, putting a few paces between us. "You're joking."

"I'm quite sincere." He closed some of the space between us but stopped partway. "I don't know how the humans do this. In Jinn we would bring three presents—one a week—then speak with the family, then ask the lady after appropriate wooing."

It was hard to find words. I barely knew him. Then there was the fact that he was a Jinni, and marrying a Jinni was utterly unheard of in Heechi. And on top of that, he was a *prince*, although one without a country.

"I don't know if it's an exact science necessarily"—my voice came out a bit breathless—"but the wooing sounds accurate. You know, for women in general."

His eyes searched mine. "Is that a yes?"

Exhaling a shaky breath, I murmured, "Malakai, I'm not going to marry you."

"Why not? Is it because of the feud between our people? Or because of my throne?" He shook his head, and a mix of emotions crossed his face too quickly to read. "It's irrelevant, I promise you. I can't find the Key because each time I sense it and begin to track it down, it disappears. And without it, I can't go home."

I barely heard him past the burning question I'd wanted to ask for days. "How can I trust you when you just disappear without a word?" I didn't mean for the tears to fill my eyes. Blinking hastily, I tried to clear them away before they fell.

"Nesrin." Malakai's voice softened, and he closed the space between us, brushing his fingers against my cheek to wipe away the wetness. He cradled my face in his hand, and I couldn't help myself—I let him. Leaning into it, I closed my eyes, questioning my sanity. "You must know I care about you—I thought it was obvious."

Was it? I couldn't process his words with him watching me. My mind narrowed in on a less confusing question. "What did you mean when you mentioned a feud?" I opened my eyes and stepped back slightly. "You said 'between our people.' Is there a feud between the Jinn and the humans?"

"No," he said with a laugh, as if I'd said the most ridiculous thing. "Between the Jinn"—he pointed at himself, then gestured to me—"and the *Khaanevaade*."

The word was familiar, one of those terms Maadar Bozorgi had thrown around and I'd immediately shrugged off. I suddenly wished I hadn't. "Explain."

"You don't know? I just assumed with everything that you were aware. And what with the suppression—"

When he cut off abruptly, eyes glazing over, I reached out on impulse and caught his hand. "Don't go. Please." I had to know more. *Suppression?* That could mean a thousand things!

"I have to." His words spilled out rapidly as he lowered his head to touch his brow to mine. "I can only ever sense it for a few short minutes. Every second counts."

"Go then," I said, a bit more forlorn than I meant to, stepping back. But he was already gone.

Chapter 16

Kadin

I SLIPPED INTO THE library after a meeting with Captain Navabi on Arie's behalf. Voices drifted from deeper within, growing louder as I opened the door from the vestibule and stepped into the main room. At the other end of the long hall, past the shelves, Arie sat in the sunny atrium with a group of Jinn. Laughing.

One of the Jinn was showing off, creating a design of sparkling artwork out of the fountain water, letting it sprinkle down to water all the plants, narrowly avoiding the onlookers who laughed.

Ducking behind a row of bookshelves, I took advantage of the distraction and tried to get closer without them noticing. Arie might be fitting in surprisingly well, but I knew for a fact that I'd be like a humble trade coin next to rubies and emeralds, a simple human among magical creatures.

"You're as intelligent as you are lovely." Jedekiah's voice drifted through the shelves, and Arie laughed again.

My blood boiled. As I slipped closer, staying carefully out of sight between the books, I tried to get a good view of her face. Was she flirting back? I couldn't tell. A twinge of hurt twisted in my chest at the simple fact that he'd made her laugh at all.

"I'm told that two of your crew members declined joining us, but they understand they'll still have to wait out the month here until the Crowning Ceremony?" Arie was asking Jedekiah now. When he dipped his chin in a nod, she said, "I think it's time we call in more Jinn for this fight."

I reached the edge of the atrium, standing behind the closest bookshelf. Tall green fronds blocked my view of Arie's face. A few other Jinn lounged in the sunlight with her and Jedekiah, all relaxed and content.

"We don't really get along well with other Jinn, to be honest, my queen."

The Jinn rumbled their agreement.

Arie wasn't having it. "I'd like you to learn to get along. At least temporarily."

"We need to continue gathering forces. There isn't time to waste," Gideon said. He stood in the entrance of the atrium, just a few steps from me, though the foliage and shelves had kept me from noticing him until he spoke.

"I understand," Jedekiah assured them. "Perhaps you could spell another room in your lovely castle. Surely you have more than one available. I wouldn't want to interfere with your plans."

I recognized a smooth-talking criminal when I heard one. If only I could walk over there and punch him.

Straightening, I gathered myself, preparing to walk out and face them. There was no way I'd let these Jinn take advantage of her.

But she didn't need me. "Nice try." Her voice held a hint of amusement. "You'll be fine. You're all well-mannered guests, after all. Are you not?"

Of course, they couldn't answer without offense.

"I'll have Rena come by in an hour or two, and we'll begin," Arie said. "I would very much appreciate your help in calming the Jinn who appear."

"Mmm, yes," Jedekiah murmured, sounding less than pleased. "We wouldn't want to repeat the scenario from last time."

"I'm glad you agree," Arie replied.

I wanted to catch a glimpse of her. She sounded so much more herself: confident, fiery, and alive. I hadn't noticed before this moment of comparison just how lifeless she'd become.

"What are you doing here?" a low voice said behind me. I whirled, knife out and ready.

It was Gideon.

"You shouldn't sneak up like that," I whispered back, tucking the knife away before he could ask what I'd intended to do with it. I knew very well that bringing a knife to a Jinni fight was like bringing a toy sword to a battlefield.

I waved him toward the other side of the room, where we wouldn't be overheard, and he followed.

"My apologies," Gideon said, and he was kind enough to ignore the knife as well. "Is there a reason you were skulking in the book stacks?"

"I was checking on Arie." I crossed my arms. Not much use hiding it. "I'm worried about her."

"She seems to be doing better."

I nodded. That was what worried me. *But why? Jealousy?* She deserved to be happy, even if it was someone else making her smile. I ran a hand through my hair, struggling to focus. "What about you? What're you doing here?"

Now it was Gideon's turn to look glum. "I can't leave either, remember?"

"Ah, yes." It was a foolish question; I wasn't myself. If Arie didn't need me here, I'd find another way to help. "I overheard we're going for round two. I'll fetch Rena."

"Very good."

I pursed my lips as I turned toward the door. "I'll be back soon."

Slipping out of the room, I picked up my pace until I was practically jogging down the hall toward the kitchen, usually the first place to look for Rena—and Bosh too, for that matter.

The sooner we called in more Jinn, the sooner this battle of Gideon's could be put into motion, and the sooner Jedekiah and his friends would leave.

The next three weeks couldn't go by fast enough.

Chapter 17

Rena

"ARE YOU FULLY INSANE or only half?" I grumbled, taking a little cake from a plate as Kadin dragged me out of the kitchen. "You want to add more Jinn to that disaster in the library?" I limped down the hall, still favoring my ankle, though the swelling had gone down quite a bit in the last few days.

"This whole plan was insane to begin with," Bosh muttered as he tagged along.

I couldn't argue with that.

Entering the library first, Bosh held the door for us, offering a teasing bow as I passed. I giggled.

Once inside, I sobered quickly. There were already *seven* Jinn here. How many more did they plan to invite? My nose scrunched up. I knew the answer: as many as possible. It all depended on how many Jinn were in the human world in the first place. As far as that number went, I had no idea.

Dusting cake crumbs from my fingers as we made our way to the study where they seemed to congregate, I glanced up to find all Jinni eyes on us. It was exactly like swimming into a frenzy of circling sharks—and my presence was the drop of blood in the water.

"Let's get this over with," I said, coming to an abrupt halt as I pulled the Key from around my neck.

Spines stiffened in response.

"Wait, Rena," Kadin said, holding out a hand, but I'd already begun whispering the spell to unveil the Key.

"It's done."

"Everyone, get ready," Kadin called at the same time Gideon shouted, "Prepare yourselves!"

Each of the Jinn moved to the edge of their seat or stood, even Gideon. One even went so far as to take a step toward me, drawn by the pull of the Key, before catching himself.

"Last time it took an hour for anyone to find us," I reminded everyone. If my tone was a little snide, it was only because I was trying to hide my nerves. As I started to pace, I supposed that gave me away.

The silence was tense.

This is for Arie. For Gideon. For Bosh.

Repeating the reminder didn't help. I felt an outburst coming, mouth opening to tell this Jedekiah exactly what I thought of him.

Bosh spoke first. "Rena, have you met everyone?" he asked despite knowing for a fact that I hadn't. He went around the small circle, naming everyone, only needing a couple corrections. "And this is Uziah." He landed on the last Jinni, who stood a bit shorter than the others, closer to Bosh's height, though still a good head taller than me. "Check out what he can do!" Dropping into a chair, he grinned at Uziah. "Do your worst!"

Tensing, I scowled back and forth between Bosh and the new Jinni.

When Bosh slumped in the chair, eyes rolling back into his head and closing, I panicked. "What're you doing? Stop!"

I raced to his chair. Was he breathing? "Stop right now!" I shrieked, shaking him by the shoulders, harder when he didn't respond. Nothing. I swung around, clutching the shells around my neck, seeing red. "If you've hurt him, I swear I'll—"

Uziah threw his hands up. "He's perfectly safe. Jinni's honor." He waved to Bosh's still form behind me. "He's just sleeping."

I hissed at him. I'd believe it when I saw proof. Turning back to Bosh, I yelled, "Wake him up then!"

Bosh blinked sleepily before I'd even finished.

I sagged in relief.

A silly grin crossed his face as he woke up, interrupted by a yawn. He stretched lazily. "Isn't that incredible?"

"So incredible," I agreed in a flat, clipped voice. "I'm going to wait for the new arrivals in the reading room."

Behind me, Bosh's voice rose higher in confusion. "What did I miss?"

Whoever answered spoke too quietly for me to hear since I'd already entered the atrium.

"Rena, wait!" Bosh called, catching up quickly. "I'm sorry, I thought it'd be a fun surprise. I should've warned you."

"I'm fine," I said, though I slowed to a stop in the atrium. I needed to stay close while the Key was unveiled since those insufferable Jinn had technically agreed to be a buffer when the new arrivals came.

He nudged my shoulder. "You were worried about me, hmm?"

"Obviously." I raised a brow at him, smiling slightly to show all was forgiven. "Would you worry about me?"

"I would," he said quickly, growing serious, but cut off when a flash of light turned the atrium into a dizzying rainbow of colors. A new Gift? Was it meant only to dazzle and distract, or was there a more sinister intent beneath the show?

Lips moving, I hurriedly ran my hand over the Key and veiled it once more.

At least one new Jinni had just arrived.

Chapter 18

Arie

RENA SCREAMED FROM THE atrium. The Jinn in the study were too busy fighting someone with a Gift of Speed who thwarted all their attempts to catch him or her. Maybe there was more than one. It was hard to judge from the blur of motion. I lifted my skirts and ran toward Rena's screams with Kadin and Gideon on my heels.

"What's going on?" I yelled as I dashed inside to find Rena fighting against strange dazzling sparks crackling through the room like lightning. "The Jinn—"

I cut off as a cold metal blade came to rest against my throat.

Another blade knocked it away before I had a chance to even take a breath. "Peace!" a strong female voice called, loud enough to reach the corners of the library.

Risking a glance behind me, I found a Jinni with eyes as deep blue as sapphires and wiry bare arms that hefted her sword as if it were a mere toothpick. "To me!" she yelled, lowering her sword. "They're friends." To the Jinni with the other sword, she added, "Gideon is at least."

Slowly, I swung around to find an enormous Jinni, both in height and width, gripping a much larger blade—the one that had been at my neck. Along the curve was a tiny trickle of red. I touched my throat where it had nicked my skin. Apparently, Rena's spells weren't as Jinni-proof as she'd thought.

She stood gasping on the other side of the fountain, clutching her shell necklace, focused on another Jinni who still held a few tiny crackling bolts of light in his palm. "How come there are so many of you?" she demanded between breaths, eyes darting around the room as new Jinn slipped in from all sides, along with the former arrivals, all of whom moved around one another warily.

The blue-eyed Jinni shrugged as she sheathed her sword. "Tracking an object is much quicker in a group. We've banded together like many others in the human world. Makes life easier." Her sharp gaze swung to Gideon as he appeared in the door, and her stony face broke into a small smile. "Then there are those who prefer to remain alone."

In response, Gideon met her gaze, not speaking. I closed my eyes, turning away. He was speaking into her mind; I recognized the Gift in use right away, even if I could no longer hear it.

The adrenaline of the last few moments drained out of me, and I sagged into an empty chair. All eyes turned to me. Maybe I should have stayed still. Whatever Gideon's secret that only Jinn could know was, it seemed to soften the new arrivals somewhat.

Blue Eyes took the chair next to mine, holding out her hand. "I'm Sapphira. I understand you're a royal." She tilted her head and added, "In the human world."

Taking a deep breath, I forced myself to sit taller and shake her hand with a firm grip. "Call me Arie."

* * *

OVER THE NEXT FEW days, alliances formed as Jinn continued to arrive. Not all the Jinn were willing to join us, but since they couldn't leave, they grudgingly watched from the sidelines.

Once, a second tracker found their way to us a few hours after the key was veiled again and caught us by surprise. After that, we stationed a guard rotation to keep watch. Just in case.

Most of the groups were smaller than the first ones, usually just pairs or a trio. Every so often a solo Jinni was close enough to Hodafez to heed the call of the Jinni Key first.

Beds were brought in, with Kadin's help convincing Captain Navabi and the Shahs. He handled communication with them, as well as coordinating meals and took on even more council meetings on my behalf, since I'd been forced to abandon it completely.

At the end of the first week, we had over three dozen Jinn, though almost half of them were undecided about our cause—or decidedly against it.

Jedekiah was currently debating the merits of transforming a portion of the library into a training center. "We can hardly practice if we have to be delicate or contained. I just don't think it's doable, personally."

"You want to keep everyone divided," Rena snapped, not even bothering to hide her feelings toward Jedekiah. She'd taken an immediate dislike to him.

"Peace," I said, holding my hands out between them. "We'll reconfigure the library to have an open floor plan for the duration of the month." It was one of the largest rooms in the castle, second only to the great hall, and if we moved the shelves, it could house at least a hundred Jinn and a small training arena. Not comfortably. But with only a month to spare, comfort wasn't my focus.

"Moving the shelves should take less than a day," I assured them. That was optimistic, but the change would be worth it. The original groups of Jinn each kept to themselves as much as the newest arrivals. If we continued on in our current atmosphere, there was no way we'd unite long enough to even get to Jinn, much less stop the Crowning Ceremony.

A Jinni stepped forward. "I can help with the shelves." He demonstrated by grabbing the nearest shelf and lifting it, with its dozens of heavy books, as if picking up a chair.

Lining up the bookshelves against the walls ended up taking only an hour.

I stepped out into the newly cleared space. "Will this do for training?" I called, knowing the Jinn could hear me, especially now that the exposed wooden floor in the center made my voice carry.

"It will indeed," Jedekiah said behind me, making me whirl around to face him. "We will begin at once."

* * *

"AGAIN," HE CALLED OUT hours later as sweating Jinn faced off in pairs. They fought the human way: "No Gifts, just sticks," as Jedekiah called it—sticks being swords or other long-reach weapons useful for combat. A few of them were pulled from our own armory, as some of the Jinn had never bothered to learn such a skill or even owned a weapon.

I'd wanted their training to focus on their Gifts, but even Gideon had balked at that idea. He'd pulled me to the side, pretending to go over a supposed library repair.

"It won't be effective," he'd said softly, leaning over the renovation sketches as if studying them. "Gifts are held close, hidden whenever possible. If you ask them all to reveal their Gifts at once, before they've gotten to know each other, one of two things will happen: Either they will use only their known Gifts, fighting handicapped and not helping anyone, rendering the time useless and a waste. Or, if it draws on long enough, someone is bound to use an offensive Gift. It will be like a spark that lights all the others into a roaring flame to all use their Gifts at once. Such a defensive reaction could easily end in complete destruction of not only this room, but of the entire host we're trying to build."

"Well, what do you suggest then?" I whispered back, nodding at the drawings as well for the sake of watching eyes behind us.

"We need to build trust. Only once that is established will they be able to use their Gifts wisely and accomplish anything."

"*Or* you could encourage them to use their Gifts when not expected," Jedekiah interrupted, sauntering up to us without even bothering to act like he hadn't been eavesdropping. "Let them practice in secret when no one is looking. Then you don't have to wait."

"That will counteract the trust we need to build," Gideon argued. "We can't have everyone constantly prepared to defend themselves. That will lead to the same problems as the first scenario, where eventually someone goes too far."

"Well, if we go with your plan, they'll never practice." Jedekiah lounged against the table, ignoring the plans to stare directly at us.

"Why do you say that?"

"Because"—he gestured toward me—"you're planning to call in new Jinn each day, correct?"

Frowning, I nodded.

"Then each day you're bringing in someone with new trust issues. If the queen goes with *your* plan"—he gestured to Gideon—"she has to start from scratch every single day."

Pressure built between my eyes. *Who am I to make this decision?* "Thank you," I said before they could squabble any further. "I'll take both of your points into consideration. For now though, if not training with Gifts, then what *do* you suggest?"

* * *

THAT LED TO THE present, where the Jinn focused on learning new combat skills and the library was filled with the clash of metal on metal.

Only two days into the new routine, Kadin tore up the stairs toward me yelling, "All the swords are gone!"

I jumped up from lunch and ran to the balcony railing.

Three dozen Jinn stood tense in the training center on the first floor, just seconds away from breaking the rules and fighting for real.

Without thinking, I tore down the stairs two at a time. Out of breath, I pulled up short between the two sides. They were so much taller up close, looming. "What did I miss?"

Gideon and Jedekiah scowled as fiercely as the rest. Maybe inserting myself had been a mistake.

The Jinni closest to me, Sapphira, answered before anyone else could. "Someone used their Gift to make all our weapons disappear," she hissed in cold fury.

I turned my gaze toward her, finally noticing the way her hand clenched the air strangely as if holding something.

I tried to summon calm for myself, making my tone casual, curious even. "Are the weapons fully gone or are they still in your hands, unseen?"

Sapphira hefted her half-closed fist up and down as if testing the weight of what appeared to be nothing. "It's still there," she admitted grudgingly.

"Do you remember the shape of it?" I asked next, trying to ease the tension while I searched for a solution.

It seemed to be working. The Jinn within my view relaxed their arms slightly, shoulders lowering. Their faces shifted from fury to curiosity at the strange antics of the human queen.

When she nodded, I turned to those nearby and called out, "Does anyone mind if I borrow their sword? Carefully?" I added with an apologetic grin, as if it were my fault that I couldn't see it.

It surprised them enough that a few smiled, and one even laughed. On my left, a hulk of a Jinni cleared his throat. "You can have mine."

"Handle first?" I overenunciated, making more of them laugh.

The big Jinni grinned and twisted his wrist, taking my other hand to guide me. I could only trust he wouldn't stab me through. Since I didn't care much either way, I let him.

I bit my lip when I felt the weight of it. My arm dropped heavily when he let go, and in the quiet, a loud thunk of metal bit into wood. "Oops," I said on a breathy laugh.

The Jinni who'd handed me the weapon stepped back to give me a wide berth, and others followed his example. I turned back to Sapphira, who stood with one dark brow raised.

"Can we try sparring like this?" I asked because I didn't know what else to do. As soon as the words left my mouth, I wanted to take them back. Stupid. Stupid.

But a slow grin spread across her face. "What a fascinating idea." She stepped into a fighting stance, raising her arms and invisible weapon.

I was too nervous to smile back. Growing up, I'd had *very* few lessons with a sword. Just enough to know the basics, like all royal families. I raised my heavy sword in a block, the most basic step. But from there, I wasn't sure what came next.

I'd made a huge mistake.

Sapphira circled me, eyes narrowing, searching for an opening. But she seemed to be almost as uncertain as me. As far as we could tell, we were both wide open.

At that thought, I shrugged. What did I have to lose? I swung a bit wildly.

She jumped back.

It took two more swings, probably horribly aimed, though thankfully no one would ever know, before steel met steel.

The reverberation shuddered through my arms, and I winced.

A few more swings, and we started to get the hang of it. Mostly her.

My arms grew weak, and sweat dripped down the front and back of my dress. "Truce!" I yelled when my arms were shaking. "Or whatever I'm supposed to say. I give up!"

They laughed again. I hadn't even noticed that the Jinn had settled into chairs along the sidelines to watch the fight.

Sapphira lowered her sword arm and held her other hand out toward me. "Well done," she said with another fierce grin as she shook my hand. "Normally I wouldn't let you off so easy, but since I can't see the blade to accurately hold it to your throat, I'll take the win as is."

I laughed, breathing hard. "Thank Jinn because I have no idea what I'm doing." Taking a chance, though I knew it might backfire, I added, "But I'd like to learn. Perhaps we could have the weapons brought back for my sake? That is, if you don't mind my joining in the training?"

In response, just a heartbeat later, the sword in my hand became visible again. The length of it made my mouth drop open. It was thin but longer than I'd expected. And curved. It didn't seem like it should be nearly as heavy as it was. "I could've done some damage," I murmured, mostly to myself, brows drawing together in concern.

"Mmm, no you couldn't have," Sapphira replied, pulling me out of my thoughts as everyone chuckled. She swung an arm over my shoulder and held up her own wicked blade, which gleamed in the light. "This is practically part of my arm. I'm not going to forget how to use it *that* quickly."

I noticed their laughter came easier now. When Jedekiah and Gideon stepped forward to reset everyone's positions, their shoulders were relaxed and stances easy. They gave me a place to stand as part of the group. Nearby Jinn gave me pointers. Everyone seemed more comfortable. More trusting.

Somehow, it had worked.

Chapter 19

Nesrin

AFTER MALAKAI VANISHED, I forced myself to wait until the next day to visit Maadar Bozorgi. While I lay in bed waiting for sunrise, I racked my mind, trying to remember what she'd said.

You are Khaanevaade. I rolled onto my side. Squeezing my eyes shut, I sifted through what had seemed important at the time and tried to remember what I'd ignored. *Descended from dragons.*

That couldn't be right. Could it?

Dawn crept over the roofs in town, giving them a soft magical glow. The sun hadn't yet peeked over the horizon, but I couldn't wait any longer.

I knocked on Maadar Bozorgi's door just loudly enough to wake her but hopefully not her neighbors.

Shuffling sounded inside. I knocked once more for good measure so she'd know she hadn't imagined it. This early, the narrow streets were quiet and empty.

The door creaked open. Maadar Bozorgi tugged her shawl tighter over her nightgown and squinted at me. "What in all of Jinn has come over you this morning? You're up before the dragons." Scrunching her nose, she tsked and shook her head before swinging the door wide for me to enter. "I'm up now. You might as well come in. Tea?"

"Not on an empty stomach," I replied, turning to close the door behind me.

"Ah, I see how it is." The elderly woman puttered around in her kitchen. "You're hoping I'll make breakfast."

"No, I—"

"I suppose I would enjoy the company." She put the tea on and began breaking eggs and dropping them in a pan. "What part of the cliffs are you climbing today?"

"Oh, I'm not climbing," I said, taking a deep breath to try again.

"Not climbing?" She paused to shake her finger at me. "You're going to see that boy from the Heydari family, aren't you? I may be old, but I still keep one ear pinned on the gossip." She winked while my mouth hung open.

I'd completely forgotten about Adel. I pinched the bridge of my nose and moved to sit at the table, wondering if I should talk to him or just assume that friendship was over. For the ten thousandth time, I had to corral my thoughts of a certain secretive Jinni and steer them back to the shocking secret he'd begun to spill before he'd left.

I accepted the hot mug of tea that she'd poured for me anyway, setting it next to the plate of food. "Maadar Bozorgi, what do you know about the Khaanevaade?" When she stared down at my plate, I took a bite of the eggs to pacify her.

She cackled. "What *don't* I know. The Khaanevaade is our birthright. I've been telling you young ones that for a century."

"Yes, I know—" I cut off, forgetting the eggs and leaning forward. "Wait, do you mean a literal century?"

"Of course." She went back to fiddling in the little kitchen, adding salt to the eggs, tasting, adding a bit more.

My questions fought with one another, and in the end they all poured out at once. "How? And why not everyone else? Or is not everyone in town a so-called Khaanevaade? If not, then who *is* Khaanevaade? And what does that even mean? Are we *really* descended from dragons? That's not possible, right?"

She took my babbling in stride, shuffling over to sit, brushing invisible crumbs off the table. "Of course that's not possible." She shook her head with a small smile.

I deflated, somehow disappointed, before she added, "It's the *dragons* who are descended from *us.*"

* * *

MY HEAD SPUN WITH the answers Maadar Bozorgi had given me. Using the excuse of a climbing day, I headed out of town toward the cliffs, but as I neared my usual ravine, my feet led me into the forest instead.

We were "not the same" as dragons, she'd declared. *Obviously.* Irritated, I kicked the branch in my path out of the way with extra force.

Much of our history, our memories of our history, and our "abilities"—which were still unclear to me—had apparently been lost because of this so-called *suppression.*

When I'd brought that up, wanting to know what it meant, Maadar began railing about the Jinn and their wicked, evil Gifts and how they broke their Unbreakable Laws the way she broke eggs: with reckless abandon and as many as possible.

She'd then slammed her dishes on the counter with such force that one of the plates broke. While sweeping up the pieces and picking the rest out of the rug, she carried on about those "spiteful Jinn" so loudly that a neighbor came over to ask her to keep it down, at which point she began yelling at them instead.

I'd chosen that moment to slip out.

I needed to think.

My feet led me unconsciously toward the last place I'd seen Malakai in dragon form, and now I stood in the clearing created by a wounded dragon. Even two weeks later, it still brimmed with the same heavy sweetness I'd smelled in his lair. The smell of a Jinni under a spell, I supposed.

Unbidden, my eyes catalogued all the broken twigs and branches in the trees and foliage. There was where he'd lain bleeding. And there, a few paces ahead in the trampled shrubbery, was where I'd stood between him and Avizun's arrow. Then the smaller space in the chaotic mess of broken undergrowth: where his Jinni body had taken form. Across the clearing was a tear in the bark of one of the fallen trees where an arrow had landed.

In the daylight, without Avizun's men surrounding us, I had my first opportunity to really study the area. The trees in this part of the wood were even older and larger than their surroundings. Some of the tree trunks could easily fit my entire closet inside. They merged together to create a leafy ceiling that darkened the forest floor. Foliage came up to my waist, making progress difficult, but when I stepped into the clearing, those massive dragon footprints had smashed everything into the dirt.

A circle of sunlight warmed my skin as I stood there in the center, hands on my hips.

What did I expect to find here?

I had no idea.

Still, I moved to a fallen log to sit and pulled out my lunch: flatbread, dried meat, and jujube fruit. The cloying smell of the old spell tickled my nose as I chewed.

On the other side of the clearing, an ancient banyan tree had split, creating a gaping dark hole at its enormous base. In normal circumstances, I might've enjoyed exploring. Today though, I wasn't in the mood. My feet swung idly over the greenery beneath me as I took a long drink of water.

I'd hoped this place might cure me of my infatuation, which was what all these feelings were. Malakai was different from the men I'd grown up with, but that didn't mean he was better. I just needed to get that through my thick skull.

If I could figure out the source of why I cared so much, I could remove it.

My eyes kept coming back to the spot where Malakai had transformed from a beast into a Jinni. When Avizun had shot at us, Malakai had saved me. But he'd also saved himself, so it hardly counted. And I'd stood in front of him, defending him first.

Why did I do that?

Because he'd brought me home when he didn't have to. He'd given me a priceless dragon's egg. He'd saved my family from destitution and given us hope.

Just a few small reasons.

I scoffed at myself and hopped off the log, wandering back to the middle of the clearing to stand in the sun.

Closing my eyes, I turned my face up to the warmth, breathed in the syrupy sweetness, and reminded myself that he was also the reason I'd spent a month in Jinn. That I'd nearly died at the claws of a strange beast, then from the ensuing infection, and even risked the magic of the queen.

But... he'd saved me from them too.

What does that make me then? The damsel in distress? I kicked at the weeds in disgust.

None of this helped me feel better, the way I'd hoped.

It seemed I liked him despite my better judgment.

Chapter 20

Kadin

I WAITED FOR ARIE in the vestibule, which had become a small sanctuary of sorts from the Jinn in the last few days. The servants wouldn't go any farther. Today they waited in the hall to deliver the noon meal. I'd chosen those most trustworthy to keep the secret of just how many Jinn were in the library—over three dozen and growing by the day. As far as the rest of Hodafez knew, there were only one or two Jinn here with their queen, forming a truce between the humans and the Jinn. But even one Jinni was one too many. Everyone gave the library a wide berth, even Captain Navabi, who defended Arie whenever a Shah complained of her absence as a brave and noble queen who was facing the Jinn for her people.

This small vestibule entrance was my sanctuary too. Since Arie usually answered the summons of the bell, it was our only real opportunity to be alone.

That was what drew her now as she slipped inside and shut the door softly.

In a rare moment of vulnerability, she stepped into my arms when I held them out. I pressed my lips into her hair and breathed her in.

Too soon, she pulled back. Turning to open the double doors to the hall, she ushered the servants in with the carts of food.

I touched her back lightly, careful not to let the servants see, and whispered, "Can we talk?"

She nodded absently, turning to face me. "Just for a moment. We're working through a difficult exercise. Which reminds me…" She raised her voice for the servants to hear. "Dinner can be brought in an hour later tonight."

I cleared my throat. "It's about the Jinn," I murmured as the servants gathered old dishes. There was no easy way to say this. "I don't think you should spend so much time with them. Or fight with them," I added, glancing at what she was wearing.

Instead of a dress, she wore riding boots, pants, and a loose tunic.

"Why?" She kept her voice low, crossing her arms. "Because you don't trust them?"

The servants finished with the dishes and moved to take the laundry, brows drawing together whenever they glanced at Arie, eyes filled with pity.

She ignored them.

"That's not it." *Yes, it is,* my traitorous mind whispered. *I can't keep you safe from them.* "I just know you're still dealing with… everything." Tiptoeing around the truth wasn't really my style. "I don't want you to get hurt." *Again.*

"I won't," she replied immediately, stepping back. "You don't have to worry."

I took a deep breath and blew it out. Of course I worried. How could I not? I hated feeling like I was losing her. Like I didn't belong in her world anymore. Or, maybe more accurately, like she didn't belong in her own world—and I did.

Running a kingdom was like running an enormous heist. Publicly. With honors instead of fugitive status. I liked it, but I didn't want it without her.

When the servants opened the door to leave, the guards outside spied Arie. Their faces twisted into the same expression the servants wore, as if they'd practiced it.

I frowned at them, and they shifted back into position, saluting their queen.

There were very few Shahs willing to pass the library these days, but two of them were heading toward the great hall. Once again, pitying expressions transformed their faces at the sight of Arie.

She'd already turned her back on them, heading for the doors as the servants pulled the opposite double doors to the entrance shut. They closed with a bang.

It was just the two of us now. She put her hand on the doorknob. "It's only for three more weeks." She lifted her eyes to meet mine for the first time in the whole conversation, not bothering to hide the sheen of tears. "I need this. Please understand."

I didn't know what to say, so I just nodded and moved to follow her through the vestibule door into the main library.

When she stepped into the training area where the study used to be, it was impossible to miss: instead of the fixed expression of pity, the Jinn grinned at her, coming over to draw her into conversation.

I understood then.

This was what was missing—what she needed to heal. This was the only place where she wasn't made to wallow in her own grief. I'd been so blinded by jealousy that I hadn't seen it until it slapped me in the face.

Three more weeks.

I ground my teeth. While they were distracted, I slipped upstairs to the second floor shelves where there were more places to observe without being seen.

This is temporary. It'll be over soon. I can suffer through it for her.

Even if it physically hurt to watch Jedekiah jump off the balcony and reappear in front of her, bowing formally and holding his arm out to ask for a walk around the room, as if they were at a ball instead of battle training. She smiled at him in a way I hadn't seen in a long time.

I took a long, shaky breath.

Even if my heart might break.

Chapter 21

Arie

I ACCEPTED JEDEKIAH'S ARM and offer to walk around the room with a raised brow.

"Have you given any more thought to my methods of training?" he asked, leading us through the atrium toward the quieter side of the library, away from the sweaty Jinn training in the space where the study had been, past the line waiting to use the small librarian's bath, and ignoring the groups of sullen Jinn who'd refused to join our cause, sitting restless on the sidelines.

I waited until we strolled into the gallery near the front of the library, where some of the kingdom's finest art was displayed, to answer, "Telling everyone to pick a fight whenever they're in the mood with no consequences seems less like a training method and more like asking for trouble."

"Perhaps. But it would build strategy." He spread his free hand wide and grinned, ignoring the art and focusing solely on me. This was why everyone followed him. His Gift of Charm was like a magnet that tugged all your uncertainties and concerns away—or so I'd been told.

I shook my head, thankful for Rena's protection spell. It let me see beneath the Gift to his true feelings, which were slightly frustrated with me. Probably for not giving in. "We need trust more than we need strategy if we're going to take on the queen. If the insurrection doesn't go as planned, it may come to fighting, and without trust we'd end up battling one another."

"Aren't battles and strategy essentially the same thing?" he countered.

I pressed my lips together. "I'm not entirely sure," I admitted, dropping my pretense of admiring the paintings he ignored. "But I have another idea." I strode into the reading room instead, gesturing to it as he followed. "We can set aside a second training area. The first, as it is now, can be for weaponry. And the second, here in the reading room, can be for training with Gifts. We will train daily, but everyone can choose where. That way, those who train with Gifts won't feel forced into revealing themselves, and the trust we so desperately need to keep will stay intact."

Jedekiah nodded thoughtfully, giving me an approving glance that for once seemed genuine. "Well done, my queen. You have more wisdom than most in your position."

I took it as an opening. "Wise enough to know that there's more to your banishment than you're letting on."

"Whatever do you mean?" His eyes flew open with false innocence.

"Don't play virtuous with me," I teased. "You said you broke all three of those 'unbreakable rules.' How exactly did you do that?"

He surprised me by growing serious. "You remember Gideon revealing that my banishment happened fifty years ago?"

I nodded. The hint teased my mind, but I didn't know why.

"Crowning Ceremonies traditionally happen every fifty years," he said, pausing to allow me to put the pieces together.

My lips parted, and I whispered, "You tried to steal the throne."

"Tried," he agreed. "Unsuccessfully, as you may have gathered. Banishment is the greatest possible punishment a Jinni can receive. My kinsmen and I will never be allowed to return unless we can somehow prove our loyalty to the queen." He drew a deep breath and blew it out. "As you can imagine, that's quite difficult to do from the human world." His lips pressed together in a firm line then, as if he'd said too much.

"You certainly have a lot of secrets."

Jedekiah only smiled at that, patting my hand.

My suspicion flared at his abnormal silence. "What are you not telling me?"

We strolled around the outskirts of the library as if at some fancy dinner party. "Even you, my queen, cannot expect to know all my secrets."

I resisted the urge to pull my hand away. Despite all my attempts over the last week, I'd barely made any progress in learning more about him or in curbing the strange impulse all the Jinn had of calling me "my queen." It was a formality so ingrained that I'd given up.

"You know what I like about you?" One side of his mouth quirked as he glanced down at me. "You're quite persistent. It's a good quality. Reminds me of someone I once knew. She was like a dog with a bone."

"Oh?" I let him lead me around a table and past the largest window that looked out over the ocean and the cliffs; we paused to stare at the view. Absently, I asked, "What was this other woman like?"

"Beautiful. Surprisingly kind for her station. Intelligent. Unusual." For once he was quick to answer. And genuine, as if the veil of false charm had been lifted. "Like I said. You remind me of her."

At the unexpected rush of information, I turned to ask who she was to him, but his arm slipped from mine and he stepped back. "My apologies, I must return to my duties. We have a fight to prepare for, after all. Thank you for the lovely walk."

He flashed away without waiting for my response, leaving me with even more questions than when I'd begun.

* * *

ONE SUNNY MORNING, A solo Jinni landed in the center of the training space, but instead of whirling to fight, he held his hands out to the side, palms out in peace.

Sapphira brushed past me, rushing forward to hug him. "Benaiah!"

My shoulders relaxed, and I allowed myself the first deep breath of the morning. This whole process went much smoother when Jinn recognized each other. Naturally, I found myself turning to search for Kadin's reaction, only to feel a small twang of disappointment. He wasn't here this morning.

Our newest guest, Benaiah, smiled as he stepped back. "Sapphira. It's been a full century. How are you?" Taking in the rest of us with a raised brow, he added, "What've I stumbled onto?"

"It's a long story," she replied, and I let her take the lead, assuming she'd know the best way to bring him into our confidence. "What brings you to the human world?" she asked instead, changing the subject abruptly. "I thought you were working your way up in the Guard?"

"I was." He hesitated. "Circumstances came up. I may have fled the Guard on poor terms…"

"May have, hmm?" Sapphira smirked.

I leaned forward, intrigued, hoping she'd ask him more.

Again, she took a different tack. "Why would you desire the Key? I doubt you'd want to use it to return…"

He gave her a crooked smile, though his eyes still drifted across the rest of us as if trying to decide how much to share. "I hoped to find more like-minded Jinn. It's better not to be on your own right now."

When he stopped, she urged him on. "There's no secret love for the queen here, if you're referring to her latest proclamations. Speak plainly."

Nodding, he drew a deep breath. "She's preparing to invade the human world. When I spoke against it, I barely escaped with my life."

Brows raised, I glanced over at Gideon, who stepped out from among the shelves to ask, "What do you mean, 'with your life'?"

"High Commander!" Benaiah gasped, bowing low. "I never thought to see you again!"

"I was banished," Gideon said, frowning. "Did you not know? And is that not still the capital punishment?"

Something about the way he stood still as a statue made me tense.

Benaiah shook his head slowly. "We were told you defected… and just a few months ago the queen decreed the new capital punishment is death."

The room fell silent as a grave.

No wonder he'd fled.

Swallowing a bitter taste of dread, I drew a deep breath. "This doesn't change anything." I raised my voice so everyone could hear. "If anything, it only makes our plans all the more urgent."

* * *

THE NEXT MORNING, A trio of Jinn dressed in wedding garb arrived, though they refused to explain why, as mistrusting as every other new arrival. The following day brought five more, and the next day brought two, and so on each day. They almost always arrived in groups. According to Gideon, any Jinn working together could pool their abilities and track the Key much quicker, though occasionally a solo Jinni would find us first if they were already close by.

Some days I struggled to get out of bed. Tears came without warning, and I'd hide in my borrowed librarian's room under the covers, trying to ignore the voices telling me I wasn't good enough. Other days were easier. Distractions helped—especially when I had a job to do, like I did now.

Breakfast was cleared, and everyone stood, tense, waiting for the day's interlopers.

"I don't think we need to keep doing this every day," Rena mumbled to Gideon and me as she scowled at Jedekiah, who stood close enough to hear. "We have more than enough to stand witness already."

"I disagree," I said at the same time as Gideon. He stopped and gestured for me to finish, and I said simply, "We need as much help as we can get."

Around us, the Jinn already here stood along the edges of the room, still as statues. Waiting.

Kadin hadn't shown this morning or the last few mornings. He avoided this room lately. I should've been thankful he willingly took care of the castle in my absence, but I missed him. His distance was my own fault. Worse, I didn't know what to do about it.

A new Jinni flashed into the middle of the room just a few paces away from us. Another followed.

At this point, though they emerged with weapons raised in fighting stances, the sight of over five dozen Jinn surrounding them usually made our new guests pause long enough to hear us out.

This group was no different, though they still attempted to leave, making the boundary pop and crackle. Every time that happened, the smaller group of Jinn who'd refused to join our cause grumbled and sulked.

Gideon spoke into the minds of our newest visitors. He still refused to tell me what he said each time, but with Jedekiah's encouragement, they'd agreed it was the quickest way to defuse the situation.

I couldn't argue.

Each time, whatever he said would make them stop, reevaluate, and calm down enough to listen.

I hated the secrets.

But I couldn't deny it worked.

Jedekiah had agreed to give me afternoon lessons on the side once everyone else was paired off.

I looked forward to this time of day.

Breathing hard, I forced my muscles to keep the small broadsword upright when everything in me wanted to let it fall. Jedekiah wouldn't hesitate to take that opening if I did. He didn't mind leaving a few slices in clothes—or even skin— as a lesson.

"Better," he said. The praise was blunt, free of his usual Gift of Charm. Somehow, it meant more that way.

I allowed a small smile.

Lunging, I did my best to keep it up. At first, it'd shocked me when the Jinn didn't treat me as fragile. But now I craved it. To be around them and be treated as an equal. Not pitied.

When I managed to hit his sword five times in a row before he got past my block, he allowed a break for a drink of water.

"You have to know your opponent as well as you know yourself," he said as I drank a full cup and filled another. He flipped his weapon in the air, showing off.

I laughed once, darkly, letting my own sword hang limply by my side. "What if I don't know myself?"

"Don't be a fool." This time when he threw his weapon up into the air, he held out his hands and used his Gift from when we'd first met to keep it there.

It startled me. Sometimes when the Jinn kept certain Gifts to a minimum and used others recklessly, it had an unsettling effect of making me forget the ones they didn't use.

He sent the weapon higher and higher until the sharp point gently touched the tall ceiling three stories above, then let it drift back down. "Everyone knows themselves," he continued. "Whether they realize it or not."

"Easy for you to say," I mumbled.

He caught his sword and broke out of his stance to face me, shaking his head. "I said everyone, and I meant everyone." He smiled to take the edge off his words. "If something is hidden, it's only because we hide it from ourselves."

"That's *so* helpful," I replied, swinging at him without warning.

He blocked my amateur move easily, clipping the blade with his own.

The vibrations of the two weapons meeting shivered down my arm.

"It is," he agreed, ignoring my sarcasm. He lunged and distracted me, moving us away from the drink table and back to training.

Chapter 22

Nesrin

"YOUR MOTHER TOLD ME I might find you here," a warm male voice said behind me. I whirled from where I'd been spying on a few members of the Dragon Watch testing arrowheads at the nearby booth to find Malakai's face just a breath away from mine. He stepped back, but only slightly, grinning as if we'd been spying on the Watch together.

"Why did you want to find me?" I pretended to see something I wanted, moving farther into the market square. I didn't want the Dragon Watch to catch me lurking. Not that it mattered much. My hopes of joining them were fading faster than a dragon's shadow.

Malakai put his hands in his pockets as he followed, ignoring the stares that he drew as a Jinni in Heechi, an occurrence about as common as a tamed dragon. "I'd hoped you might take me climbing with you. Show me the ropes, as you say."

He'd left me with a thousand questions and only Maadar Bozorgi's strange ramblings for answers. I had to admit, if only to myself, that I wanted to say yes. Wandering through the market with Malakai on my heels, I paused by the fruit stand. *Do we need fresh plums back home? Maybe I can get some.* When I finally answered, I kept my eyes on the plums. "What if you have to leave again?"

"I've paid close attention to the timing of"—he glanced around, lowering his voice—"when *it* is revealed. It's almost always in the early morning hours, and when it's hidden once more, I've never yet felt it return until the following day."

I frowned. What did that have to do with anything? Turning away from the fruit, I headed down the aisle toward the booth with fresh flatbread.

Malakai kept up with me easily. "What I'm trying to say is that I've already attempted to find... *it* this morning. Unsuccessfully. I should have the rest of the day without any unforeseen demands."

"Good." I swung around to face him. "Then you can explain what you meant when you said there was a feud between our people."

"Don't you see how they look at me?" he asked, brows rising, waving at those forced to walk around us. The men glared at Malakai, women eyed him suspiciously, and children ran the other way.

"Yes, but you're a Jinni."

He grinned. "Take me climbing, and I'll tell you why it's so much more than that."

I blew out my breath. "Let's go." Turning, I took the closest path out of the market. "You can tell me on the way."

Without asking, Malakai took the bag of climbing gear I always carried, slinging it over his shoulder. It was nice not to carry it for once, so I let him. I could see he was trying.

When we reached the dusty road that led into the forest, the only sound was the rustling of wind in the trees and quiet birdsong in the distance.

"Tell me everything," I said, keeping to my side of the path. He kept veering from his own to walk closer to me. I tried not to put too much weight on his actions. They didn't mean anything.

"I don't know much."

I laughed and pointed to myself. "As opposed to nothing?"

"Fair point." He held his hands up in a gesture of peace and smiled. "It was before my time, but I promise to tell you what I know."

His voice fell into a soothing storyteller's rhythm, and he stepped around the root of a large banyan tree as he began. "Long ago, there was a group of human-but-not-quite-humans known as the Khaanevaade. They were said to be part human, part animal. Part dragon, in fact, if the stories are true."

"Maadar Bozorgi says dragons are descended from us," I interjected.

He nodded. "That could very well be. Legend says a queen of Jinn met with the leader of the Khaanevaade. She told him, 'Your people have such excellent sense of smell, such incredible eyesight, such impenetrable skin. It's a shame you can't travel long distances or use other Jinni Gifts. You would be unstoppable.'

" 'We would,' the leader replied, wistfully.

" 'Perhaps we could form a covenant?' the queen offered. 'If we were to marry, our people could join forces and become unstoppable.' "

"We would *never* join the Jinn," I interrupted again.

"It's a very common tradition between kingdoms," Malakai said with an exasperated grin. "Let me finish." He returned to the rolling lilt of his narrator's voice and continued. "The agreement was struck. They would form the covenant in one week's time, where they would bring rings and witnesses.

"The queen arrived alone. Her companion was fetching the ring she said, and she asked if they could begin without her.

"So the leader of the Khaanevaade took the ring he'd carefully crafted from white gold. On it, he'd fastened a perfect ruby for his people and a pure diamond for the Jinn.

"When he slipped it onto her finger, the covenant began. The leader of the Khaanevaade poured all the abilities of his people into that one ring, as she would do as well, on behalf of the Jinn. The trust required was symbolic of the trust forming between their people."

Malakai paused, making me glance away from the path at his puzzled expression.

"The details of what comes next are somewhat lost," he admitted. "Some archives say the queen pretended to wait, while others say she then spit in his face, but they all seem to believe she turned the covenant into a curse by refusing to complete it."

"What kind of curse?" I held my breath, though I'd already guessed at the answer.

"On this, all the stories agree: legend says the queen cursed the ring that'd been given to her so that the Khaanevaade could not access what had been given unless the covenant was completed or a thousand years had passed. And on that day, the Khaanevaade were cursed to forget—to let their animal side fall asleep—for a thousand years."

I considered him in a new light, wondering how much truth there was to these stories. "But it's just a legend—you said so yourself."

His gaze lingered on my face before returning to the curve in the path. "I believe it's far more than that, and I have my suspicions who the queen may have been as well."

My brows rose as I took that in.

"It's said that this queen of Jinn knew that by the time a thousand years came around, the Khaanevaade would've forgotten who they were, and they'd never fully wake again."

As Malakai finished, we rounded the last bend in the path, and the cliffs ahead rose high above us. I'd been so mesmerized by the story I'd barely noticed the walk.

I quietly processed the story. It wasn't until we stood next to the sandy rock wall that I finally said, "It doesn't make sense." Frowning, I held the harness out to him, offering to let him climb first. "Because Maadar Bozorgi hasn't forgotten."

"I don't need the harness," he said with a small smile.

Of course. He could fly. How foolish of me. I pretended the straps needed adjusting and hoped he didn't notice my blush.

"It's true," Malakai said as I strapped the harness onto myself. "There do seem to be a few who refuse to forget, whose ancestors wrote down their history and passed along the stories of the Khaanevaade. Probably contributed to the prejudices against the Jinn."

When I swung around to raise a brow at him, he threw up his hands, chuckling. "With good reason, I agree."

At the cliff wall, I began to search for the best place to begin our climb, and he stepped up behind me. "I'm sure you've noticed the legend has become a fable over time. A simple children's bedtime story. Believing it is seen as foolishness. *That's* how the queen won."

That made me turn away from the wall, forgetting the climb altogether. "Have the Jinn always had a queen as their ruler?" I swallowed, trying and failing to find a sensitive way to ask my next question. "Or do you think there's a chance that the queen in this story is your own mother?"

His lips pressed together in a flat line. "I'm not yet certain. The stories don't say, and we've had many queens before, but... I do wonder."

It was a lot to take in. I needed time to think it over when there wasn't a handsome blue-eyed Jinni staring down at me with a soft smile, making me think about kissing instead.

I cleared my throat and made my tone all business. "The first rule of climbing is to always choose the best possible handholds and footholds. That will be the difference between a successful climb and falling off the wall."

"I'm not afraid of falling," he answered cheekily.

Why did he *insist* on trying to make me blush? I scrunched up my face to make it clear what I thought of that, but it didn't deter him at all.

Instead, he reached out and took my hands. "If we could break the curse, you wouldn't be afraid of falling either."

I let him hold on a half second longer than I meant to before I tugged my hands away. "What do you mean? Are you saying that I could *fly*?" I was incredulous. "Why would I want that? I *hate* flying!"

"I know," he said patiently, prompting me to think about it further with raised brows. "And why do you think that is?"

"Are you saying it's… because of the curse?" My voice came out small, uncertain. I hated it.

Taking a step away from him, I returned to studying the cliffs for a proper handhold. Normally, I'd be a good distance up by now. He was making me unhinged.

He wasn't done either. "Just imagine what you all might be able to do if the curse was broken." He laughed out loud. "Nesrin, you might be stronger than me. By a lot."

I couldn't imagine. Icy fear pumped through my veins, something I'd felt so few times in my life that I didn't know how to handle it. I suddenly didn't feel like climbing anymore. Snatching up my bag, I stepped back from the wall and from him. "Why are you telling me this? Is that why you keep so many secrets from me? Because I'm Khaanevaade and not to be trusted?"

"No." He stayed where he was, scratching the back of his head. His gaze dropped from mine. "It's not easy for a Jinni to share secrets. It's not..." Another hesitation, then he sighed, lifting those pale blue eyes to meet mine. "It's not normal where I'm from—especially for me. If you knew my mother better, you'd understand why."

When I didn't say anything, he hesitated, then continued. "I'd like to be honest with you from this day forward, if you'll allow me. As a first step toward forming an alliance between our people."

"An alliance?"

"Yes." The slight hint of blue on his pale cheeks deepened into a darker hue, almost like a blush. He cleared his throat and spoke briskly. "I don't know if your feelings have changed since we last spoke, but a very common form of alliance in Jinn is through marriage. That is, if you might consider marrying me."

Once again, his words knocked the air out of my lungs as surely as if I'd lost my grip while climbing and slammed into the rock wall. "Doost," I choked out, blushing at the slip. "I told you I can't do that."

He winced and had the audacity to look hurt. "I thought an alliance between our people could perhaps return memories and begin mending the ancient feud." His voice grew soft, wounded, but he continued. "After all, hatred is usually learned, which means it can be unlearned."

"No." I paused and sucked in a deep breath to try again. "I mean, I'm not just going to marry you to make other people happy." *That's not what I want from you.*

"I understand," he said, so quietly I barely heard him.

I swallowed, hating the way he made me feel so exposed. It wasn't fair. An *alliance* of all things. As if that was all that mattered when it came to marriage. I didn't know much about it, but I knew I didn't want it for that.

"It's a no," I said back just as softly, wishing even as I did that I could just say yes and hope it would somehow turn into what I wanted.

"I'll leave you to your climb then," he said, vanishing before I could reply.

Chapter 23

Rena

TWO WEEKS OF THIS torture had passed since we'd begun trapping Jinn in a confined space. That space, so large and extravagant at first, now seemed extremely cramped. When I'd volunteered to help, I hadn't expected it to be so tedious. Or to be quite so outnumbered.

I stood in the center of the training space, same as always, deep in the territory of the Jinn. Sighing, I pulled the Jinni Key out yet again. At first I'd worn it on a chain, but that hurt whenever a rogue Jinni snapped it off, so now I wore it on a thin string. It always returned, of course. Better to just let them think they had it for a few moments and keep my neck intact.

"I'll bet you a ruby that this next one picks a fight." The speaker was a Jinni with unusually close-cropped hair and nearly white eyes whose name I couldn't remember and didn't really care to.

"I'm betting Arie will win them over right away," a female Jinni with deep blue eyes declared, coming to stand on the other side of the room. "She's getting really good at her speech these days." She was one of those who'd been here the longest, but her name still escaped me. No sense getting to know them since they weren't staying long.

I sighed loudly. It seemed odd to pick sides like this, as if it was some sort of tournament, when the fate of their race hung in the balance. Shrugging, I figured it was another Jinni anomaly and made a note to ask Gideon about it later.

He was up on the second floor balcony, deep in conversation with a group of Jinn who were on the fence about our invitation. Then there were those who'd outright refused, judging us from the sidelines. Some just leaned on the shelves to watch out of curiosity while others' glares could've burned a hole through me if that'd been their Gift. Their stares tickled my skin like swimming through a thick school of herrings. Those were the Jinn who swore up and down that if anyone mentioned their names when this went sideways, they'd be out for blood.

"I've got a gut feeling about this one." Jedekiah used his Gift to make his voice rise above the rest. He ambled over to the Arie-supporters' side, winking at her. He was a natural leader, one of the reasons he was so easily accepted by the newer Jinn arriving. Currently, this worked in our favor, but his loyalties could shift as easily as the tides, as far as I was concerned.

I didn't need to glance at Kadin, where he stood in the back and out of the way, to know he'd be irritated. He wasn't the type to pick a fight, respecting Arie too much to put his jealousy on display. But I honestly wondered how she could miss it.

One by one they stilled, waiting for me. There were dozens of Jinn along the edges of the room, male and female, all with raven-black hair, all towering over me, with eyes as different in shades of color as the coral in the sea.

I raised a brow and waited until the whispers died down before I unveiled the Key.

I counted sixty seconds twice before veiling the Key once more—even though there was no sign of a Jinni just yet. Jinn who'd been tracking us, trying to pinpoint our location, found us a bit faster every day.

I'd learned the hard way not to wait.

Slash, slash.

The sound of a knife slicing pierced the stillness.

Where's that coming from?

Gideon pulled the thin blade from his cane so fast I missed it.

I frowned at him until a thin red line of blood grew between sliced fabric on both of his shoulders. The cuts weren't deep. Gideon tensed, weapon raised, bracing for a fight like a soldier—no, I reminded myself, like the high commander of the Jinni Guard he'd once been.

The group by the window cheered and clapped. "Called it!" one hooted.

"It's not final yet," Jedekiah called back. *How can they be enjoying this?*

Gideon slashed at the air but only succeeded in antagonizing the invisible Jinni into another slice across his back, splitting open one of his favorite vests.

"I'd recognize that handiwork anywhere," Jedekiah boomed cheerfully. "Ananias, get down here!"

I squinted up at Jedekiah, who loomed over me. "Have you lost your mind? The attacker is obviously on the ground."

He glanced down at me with a grin.

I hated my height more than ever when I was forced to stand by this whale of a Jinni.

"Trust me, darling." He pointed up at the rafters of the vaulted ceiling. "Ananias, show yourself for the little lady."

Sure enough, a heavyset Jinni winked into existence above us, perching on the thick wooden railing of the second floor balcony, which looked like a little stick beneath him.

"I'd appreciate it if you'd show your weapons also," Gideon said in a dry tone.

Two knives materialized in front of Gideon, just a breath away from his face. They could've gouged his eyes out before he even saw them coming.

His already pale skin blanched whiter.

I'd never seen him scared before.

A few of the Jinn by the window who'd bet on the latest arrival reacting this way snickered. One slash from Gideon's blade, and the knives dropped to the floor with a clatter.

"Just you?" Jedekiah called up to the newcomer.

"Just me," Ananias confirmed, flashing down from his perch to stand on the edge of our wide circle. "I work alone." He eyed Gideon warily. "What's this meeting for?" His voice was higher than I'd have expected from such a big man. "And what are you doing with *him*?"

I sighed.

We'd discovered the hard way that Gideon had personally banished a large number of Jinn over the last couple centuries. Part of the high commander role, he'd explained. He'd made quite a few enemies.

"He's standing with us against the queen of Jinn," Arie said and the Jinn stepped back to reveal her presence.

She moved forward. Both male and female Jinn stepped respectfully aside. "I'm the queen of Hodafez, and I'm asking you to join us."

"I'm sure you've heard the rumors surrounding Hodafez," Jedekiah added casually.

I scoffed at his self-importance, to be so certain we'd caused rumors in just a few short weeks. It wasn't like the arriving Jinn could spread it. *Well...* I made a face. *Can't forget the humans.* They'd probably inadvertently shared more than they'd meant to. It was all they talked about.

Gideon stepped forward then, I assumed to speak to the Jinni with his mind. I hated that trick! The newcomer, Ananias, glanced at him sharply.

"The queen... of Hodafez?" Ananias's tone had shifted into one of respect. "I'd heard rumors..." He trailed off.

Whatever Gideon told these newcomers each time they arrived seemed to work because once again the nervous energy in the room subsided. "I suppose I could hear you out."

"Please, have a seat." Arie beckoned to the circle of chairs along the side of the training area. Our enormous group moved to follow, although most of us were forced to stand at this point. We now housed somewhere close to seventy Jinn and counting.

A few Jinn had repurposed spare tables in the library into a sort of balcony seating around the outside of the circle, and others chose seats on the second floor within earshot.

Low conversations picked up around the room now that the immediate danger had passed, although everyone kept an eye on Arie and Ananias.

"We are building a group of witnesses, as large as possible, to stand up to the queen at the Crowning Ceremony and demand that someone else rule," she said simply. After so many days, she'd compacted her speech down to a few simple sentences. "As you know, the queen's power has gone unchecked for too long. There are also some here who would stay with the humans if our mission is unsuccessful and protect us from any potential invasions, though we sincerely hope it never comes to that."

The big man listened to her plea without expression. His almost-normal shade of green eyes blinking was the only sign he hadn't fallen asleep with his eyes open. He didn't ask the usual questions, such as, *Who will you choose to rule instead?* To which we always suggested a vote. Or, *Why should we help humans?* Which was easier to answer: because it helped them too. If someone else ruled Jinn, they could be pardoned and return home. That was usually a huge draw, but this Ananias only took in the room, one Jinni at a time.

"So you have to help us," I burst in, becoming impatient with the lengthy silence.

"He doesn't *have* to do anything," Jedekiah replied, picking at nonexistent dirt under his fingernails. "Although it would be nice, I suppose, if you wanted to join us, my friend. We could use your talents."

And just like that, he once again had Arie convinced he was helping her.

I crossed my arms. My gut told me he was a puffer fish and one of these days we'd see his true form. Eyes narrowed, I could only watch him.

Arie didn't see it, and Kadin had said not to argue with her because at least now she was eating and had some color in her cheeks.

Grouchily, I stomped away from the circle toward the exit. They didn't need me for anything besides being a beacon? Fine. I wouldn't bother them.

In the atrium, I stormed right past Kadin before I spied him seated in a high alcove behind some tall ferns where he had a narrow line of sight into the other room and could watch the proceedings without being seen.

"They're like slippery eels—making promises they might not keep, luring her in—and she's falling for it," I grumbled, dropping into a nearby wicker chair with a huff. "How can you stand this?"

He only shook his head, arms crossed, slouching deeper into his seat. Misery was written across his face. "I can't."

Chapter 24

Nesrin

AFTER THE WAY HE'D left, I didn't expect to see Malakai again. Just two days later, I stepped into the courtyard with my bow, bored and hoping for some target practice. I plucked a few petals from the rose bushes, planning to shoot them as they floated across the surface of the pool and probably make my mother furious, before I glanced up and stopped still.

Malakai stared across the water at me from beneath the tree on the other side. The reflection of the water made his pale eyes flicker like they held an ocean of their own within.

I forced myself to meet his gaze. I'd missed him, although I wasn't prepared to let him know that.

Neither of us said a word.

My sister came out behind me, nearly running me over. "What's going on? I—Malakai! You're back! Are you staying for lunch?"

He glanced at Zareen, then back at me, as if waiting for permission.

I swallowed quickly and then shrugged. "You can if you want to."

A small smile touched his lips as he turned to Zareen and respectfully bowed. "I'd be honored to stay."

I turned away before he could see that I was glad.

* * *

HE CAME BACK THE next day. And the next. He never mentioned his proposals, and I pretended they'd never happened. Sometimes, when he brought me a drink, or admired my terribly out-of-date clothing, or talked to me instead of to my sisters—no matter how hard they tried to get his attention—I would pretend he'd proposed differently. With emotion and desire driving him instead of some ridiculous alliance. And when I imagined it that way, I almost always said yes.

At one meal, he let his hand linger over mine as I passed him a plate of food.

I blushed uncontrollably. It made me furious, which only made my cheeks flush hotter. I jumped up from the table to fetch something from the kitchen before he could see the stupid smile on my face. I couldn't seem to make it go away.

* * *

WHEN HE SHOWED UP with small gifts for my whole family—soaps and dyes for my sisters, a polish for my brother's sword, fine meat and seasonings for my parents' kitchen, and velvet-soft fabric flowers sewn in intricate designs for me—I spoke without thinking. "You don't need to be so charming. They already adore you. All you have to do is turn those pretty eyes of yours on them and they're gone."

"You think I have pretty eyes?" He turned them on me with the full force of their charm, acting as if he were fascinated by me, though it couldn't possibly be true.

"Did I say that?" I sounded a bit breathless.

That impossible blush began in my cheeks. I cursed it, desperate to make it stop, knowing he could see it.

"That," he said, reaching out to cup my hot cheek and giving me a wicked smile. "That's how I know you feel more than you're letting on. Never stop."

My lips parted to answer him as he drew his hand back, but for once, I was at a complete loss for words.

* * *

HIS DAILY VISITS GREW so consistent that I secretly began to look forward to them, though I'd never admit it.

We strolled through town—ignoring the usual stares— took noon picnics in the forest, spent evening dinners with my nosy family, and on the rare occasion even ate breakfasts together.

We'd often discuss the Khaanevaade and our theories about how the curse could be broken. One day, he jumped up, splashing me as he pulled his feet out of the pool where we'd been cooling off in the heat of the day. "Are there any grand libraries near Heechi?" he asked out of nowhere.

"I'm not sure," I said slowly. "Why?"

"Because we could search for answers in books about the Khaanevaade, if we can find any," he said with a huge grin that I couldn't help returning.

I swung my feet out of the water and rose to face him, standing closer than I meant to in my distraction. "Do you really think it's possible?"

"I do," he said, taking my hands. Our fingers slid together naturally as if we'd done so a million times. "I don't know if we'll find answers in a day, a week, or a year, but I believe the answer is out there if we look hard enough."

"What if the answer is in Jinn?" I asked, then wished I could take it back. It was cruel to mention his home when he might never see it again.

His excitement dimmed a bit. "I can't promise anything…" He still hadn't been able to find the end of the trail to the Key he'd told me about. "But I hope so. In the meantime"—he let go of one hand to tuck a bit of loose hair behind my ear—"I have a feeling there are many other places we could start."

For a half second I forgot what we were talking about.

"As long as you can stomach my Gift of Traveling," he added when I didn't say a word.

Clearing my throat, I let go of his other hand and shrugged. "I'd be willing to try it." But I bit my lip to hold back a grin of excitement and there was no way he could miss it.

* * *

LIBRARIES WERE NOT MY natural habitat. While Malakai could skim a few dozen books in one sitting, my average was much less.

I wasn't entirely sure what I was looking for. Malakai continued to remind me that it might take a while. Sometimes I agreed to go along more for the pleasure of sitting quietly beside him in a comfortable chair in the sun, soaking up the simple happiness of small moments. He'd make the funniest faces if he caught me watching him. Blushing didn't embarrass me quite as much as it used to.

Then one day I waited in the courtyard for hours, taking my breakfast, lunch, even my dinner there in the dusk of sunset. But he never showed.

The next day passed without a sign of him either.

He's done this before, I reminded myself, trying not to be hurt. *You should have known better than to get attached.*

But I *was* attached. There was no hiding my feelings from myself anymore. I'd lost interest in the Dragon Watch weeks ago—truthfully, it'd only ever been a distraction. They didn't want me. And there was someone who *did* want me who I'd taken for granted.

Worse, despite my best efforts to convince myself that he'd abandoned me—that he didn't think I was good enough, just like everyone else—my gut told me that wasn't true. He wouldn't just leave for good without saying goodbye... would he?

Chapter 25

Rena

MY NERVES LEAPT AND spun wildly like a school of fish that scattered each time a shark swam through. We had just one week until the so-called Crowning Ceremony. One week until the Jinn—those who'd agreed to join us, anyway—would storm their home and demand the queen give up her crown. I had a strong feeling it wouldn't go well, and if the longer and longer training sessions were any indication, the Jinn felt that way too, even if none of them would say so directly.

"Come on, darling," Jedekiah called to me, projecting his voice across the huge space. "We know you're there. Some of us want to get this day started."

Arie hadn't joined them yet, and today he'd chosen to side with the less optimistic Jinn, wagering that any arriving Jinni would most likely attack. He was so predictable.

"We don't have all day," someone else called.

"Yes you do," Bosh muttered, but only loud enough for the two of us to hear. We stood in the vestibule with the door cracked, but I'd hoped to walk in with Arie and not spend a minute longer here than necessary. There were just over one hundred Jinn here now. It was an intimidating number.

"Could you go in there and ask Arie if she's almost ready?" I whispered to Bosh.

"You've sent me twice already," he reminded me. As if I could forget. He leaned even closer, dropping his voice so low that I could hardly hear it. "She didn't look like she was coming."

"What? Why not?" I forgot the watching eyes for a moment, turning to frown at Bosh. "Where is she?"

"She's by the back window with Kadin. I didn't want to interrupt."

"Why not?"

"She's having another bad day," he said, which meant she was crying. "Kadin's helping her."

With a sigh, I gave up, stepping fully into the room. I'd been stalling for nearly an hour.

Crossing the atrium, I slowed and tried one last time. "I'm sure she'll be here soon."

"We don't need her here," a Jinni called out.

But Jedekiah's Jinni-enhanced voice boomed, louder than I'd ever heard it. "Calling Her Royal Majesty. Your loyal subjects are waiting."

I winced, plugging my ears a moment too late. "A little warning!" I yelled over the pounding in my eardrums. "The walls are spelled to bounce things back, remember?"

Jedekiah didn't like to look like a fool. He strode toward me. "If you don't get this little show together soon, I'm going to—"

Bosh jumped in front of me, blocking his path, but Jedekiah continued approaching until Gideon flashed between us. "Patience," he said, waving Jedekiah away like a fly. "We can wait a few more min—"

Boots sounded on the wooden floors.

I sighed audibly as Arie appeared between the shelves, followed by Kadin.

"Finally," Jedekiah muttered, but his back was turned as he stalked to the other side of the room, and Arie didn't hear. No one else seemed to care, and by the time he'd reached the other side, he was all smiles again, turning to Arie. "Shall we open the Jinni trap once more?"

"Please." Arie waved a hand for me to begin. She chose a small chair at the edge of the group, close to where the shelves began. "You didn't need to wait for me."

That earned me a glare from Jedekiah.

Huffing at both of them, I unveiled the Key, adding a few personal mutters about Jedekiah's attitude as I finished.

I began counting. *One, two, three...* It was a struggle to leave the Key unveiled for a full minute, let alone a second one. I closed my eyes. It was easier to focus that way.

"It can't be!" Gideon yelled. My eyes flew open. What'd happened? Had someone died? I'd never heard that tone in Gideon's voice before.

I whispered the spell to veil the Key in a hurry.

A new Jinni stood in the center of the room, not attacking, not using any tricks. Nothing remotely upsetting enough to deserve Gideon's tone. At least, not that I could tell.

His silver-blue eyes stared at Gideon for the space of a breath before he broke into a laugh.

Gideon strode forward and grabbed him so roughly that at first I thought a fight was breaking out. Instead, they hugged each other, hands clapping each other's backs.

Murmurs broke out across the room. Jinn frowned, studying the newcomer. Some of them clutched their heads as if they hurt. "What's happening?" one near me asked.

Another hissed, "Why do I recognize him? I feel like I know him, but I've never seen him before."

"I think... I think we *have* seen him before," another Jinni said, raising his voice for those nearby to hear. "I recognize this sensation from my time working with enchantments in the Jinni Guard. They taught us to recognize the disillusionment and the way it pops when you're confronted with the truth..." We all turned to stare at the new Jinni still embracing Gideon and clapping him on the back. Both of them grinned from ear to ear.

"I think," the former Guard member continued in a reverent tone, "I think that's Prince Malakai."

"I remember!" Another Jinni gasped, bringing her hand to her mouth, shaking her head in awe. "How is it possible that all of us forgot Jinn had a *prince*?"

Chapter 26

Arie

"YOU'RE ALIVE!" GIDEON'S VOICE was hoarse. Was he crying? The joy on Gideon's face was contagious. I hadn't noticed before this moment just how downcast he'd truly been, but as I witnessed him welcoming the prince he'd been looking for since before I'd known him, it occurred to me how selfish I'd been to think I was the only one in pain.

The Jinn all around the room approached them. Cheers rang out, and others joined in until the room was in an uproar. Jinn embraced their lost prince with shouts and laughter. "Someone tell the servants to bring us a feast!" Gideon shouted over the madness. "We need to celebrate!"

My own tears hovered near the surface, as they had all morning, but for once I didn't mind. I glanced over at Kadin to see his reaction, but he kept his face carefully blank, arms crossed, as he usually did around the Jinn.

Gideon pulled back, clasping the prince's arms, shaking him a little as if to make sure he was real. "I searched everywhere. When I couldn't find you in Jinn or in the human world, I worried you were hidden away in a dungeon somewhere or secretly beheaded."

"You have so much faith in me," the prince said between laughs. Unlike Gideon, who seemed constantly stiff with a soldier's view of the room, this prince's nonchalant demeanor shouted confidence. His grin was as wide as Gideon's. "It's a long story, but I was neither in the dungeons nor beheaded."

"So it seems." Gideon clapped him on the arm again.

"Introductions?" Kadin said.

"Ah, yes." Gideon finally seemed to notice all the curious eyes. "This is Prince Malakai, son of Noah, son of Elijah, and rightful heir to the throne of Jinn. All of Jinn was—and still is—under a spell to forget his existence."

"How did you remember him then?" Rena piped up from the other side, somewhere beyond the tall crown of Jinn, too short to see.

"He left me clues." Gideon laughed.

"You found my Kathenoth!" the prince said, and another round of cheers went up. I didn't understand.

Thankfully, Rena didn't let them move on without an explanation. "What's a Kathenoth?"

"It's difficult to describe," Gideon said, turning to the prince, who took over.

"It's a will—or more often many pieces of a will scattered across different locations. It also serves as proof of existence."

"Do you need to prove your existence often?" Rena said sarcastically.

The Jinn around us laughed as if she'd told a joke.

I couldn't make out what she said next, but her tone was irritable.

"As bond-brothers, I could sense his absence, even if I didn't immediately know what it was," Gideon told the Jinn looking on. "Thanks to my training in enchantments while in the Guard, I followed the clues until I gathered enough memories to piece them together. The rush of their return can be painful—you may be feeling similar effects now."

One of the Jinn near me wavered, bringing a hand to her brow, which was pale, even for a Jinni. "You're telling me," she muttered. "I need to sit down."

"What's a bond-brother?" Rena interrupted Gideon's story again.

"It's the bond of family," the prince answered for him, searching for Rena in the crowd, frowning a bit when he spotted her. He must've finally realized she was a Mere. Glancing at Gideon in question, he added simply, "Even stronger than family because you choose your bond-brothers and bond-sisters and swear an oath."

"What kind of oath?" I spoke up for the first time when Rena didn't ask anything further.

"The covenant of a bond-brother or bond-sister includes a promise to always keep secrets, always protect, and always trust," the prince said, searching for me in the crowd. When his eyes met mine, he stopped, blinking rapidly, then shoved forward through the crowd until he slowed to stand before me. "I'm sorry," he murmured, shaking his head and seeming to come back to himself. "I thought you were someone else. Forgive me."

I cleared my throat and introduced myself.

"Queen Arie of Hodafez," he repeated, squinting at me. "Your face is quite familiar."

Gideon cleared his throat and asked the prince, "Have you eaten?"

As he and the other Jinn offered the prince food and drink, Gideon's abrupt change of subject struck me as an unusual lack of manners. It seemed perfectly acceptable to the rest of them, even the prince, though his eyes drifted my way frequently.

I shifted to the outer circle, out of sight though still within earshot.

"It took me months to discover you were missing." Gideon's strong voice carried. I peered around one Jinni shoulder to peek at them. "I would've searched every inch of Jinn to find you, but when I discovered the spell, Queen Jezebel banished me."

The prince grew solemn, glancing around the circle. I ducked behind the tall Jinni in front of me again. "As I said, it's a long story. It begins with the enchantment spell that erased me from memory in Jinn. But what even Gideon may not know—at least, not for certain—is that my mother was behind it."

The Jinn around me glanced at one another, shifting uneasily. *Why? Because of the power of the spell? Or because it's a mother and her son?* I hadn't known my mother—she'd died when I was very young—but I'd never imagined one could be so cruel.

It was quiet so long that I risked another glance at them. Gideon's mouth had flattened into a thin line. Finally, he sighed and nodded. "I'd long suspected."

"A regular prison would have been impossible under this spell, for obvious reasons," the prince continued. "Eventually a loyal subject would have set me free." He paused, glancing down at his hands, which he flexed and turned over, inspecting them. "Because of this, I was turned into a dragon."

Gideon stiffened. "A shape-shifting Gift? Those are extremely rare. Are you insinuating someone other than your mother was behind this or that she had help?"

"No." The prince's voice was brittle and almost too soft to hear. "It was my mother alone."

A beat of silence.

Beside me, a Jinni hissed, "The queen... is a *shape-shifter*?" Heads shook in dismay. "How did she keep such a thing a secret?"

"Not just any shape-shifter," another Jinni called into the stunned silence. Her voice rose above the rest. "A powerful one. When was the last time you heard of a shape-shifter strong enough to shift another being besides themselves?"

My heartbeat quickened at the fear that touched the faces around me. *What kind of queen is this, that she scares Jinn?*

"Of course she's powerful." Everyone stopped talking when the prince spoke quietly again. "She has the crown."

It all came back to that.

And the Crowning Ceremony.

"There are very few Gifted with Shape-shifting," Gideon murmured finally. "But it was rumored to run in the queen's family bloodline, along with a few other Gifts that we were led to believe had faded out of existence."

Rena slipped between the Jinn to get closer to the prince, curiosity making her forget how the Jinn felt about her. "You're saying your own *mother* turned you into a dragon? That's heartless, even by Mere standards." She shook her head, oblivious to the way the Jinn tensed. "I'm sure she would've changed her mind soon enough if you were still there."

The prince stared.

Rena blushed, stepping back a bit.

The prince answered simply, "No. She wouldn't have."

"Malakai's been missing for over a year," Gideon explained to Rena. Swiveling back to the prince, he frowned as he added, "Were you spelled the entire time? How did you break free?"

"Nearly." Malakai glanced around the circle again, studying them, measuring his words as he said, "A month ago I was shot out of the sky near the Dragon Cliffs. Truth be told, the dragon hunters there nearly killed me. The spell's power over me was broken that day."

His pale blue eyes fixated on Rena and the Key that dangled from her neck, like a cat on the hunt, slow and steady. "I kept sensing the Key over the last few weeks. I could never find it in time."

She only shrugged, glancing around the room, possibly searching for me to explain. I stayed quiet.

"I honestly thought I might be losing my mind," the prince said. "I feared I only sensed the Key because I wished for it so desperately." He took a slow step toward Rena, then another. "Seeing that it's in the hands of the Mere, I would hope we could strike a deal of some kind. There must be something you want enough in exchange from Jinn. If you help me return home and claim the crown, we can form a new alliance between our people."

"No need to bargain," Gideon reassured him from where he stayed seated. "Rena is on our side. As you can see, we've been gathering forces for the last few weeks with her help. We hoped to form a resistance against the queen. First, to make a stand at the Crowning Ceremony, where I'd hoped—" Gideon coughed, glancing around at everyone.

We'd never shared our full plan, but I could see that he wanted to.

After a long pause, he continued. "The truth is, I'd intended to bring about a mass disenchantment right before the Crowning Ceremony, using our numbers to keep the queen from stopping it. I thought that if we couldn't find you before then, we'd at least make everyone remember—then they'd be forced to search for you."

I stepped forward, making myself walk toward them. The Jinn parted around me. "We also hoped that in the interim— as we searched for you—that these brave Jinn might protect the human kingdoms from any attacks." I stopped beside Gideon, and we both stared at the prince, who still stood halfway to Rena, taking it all in. "Rumor says she's gathering support against the humans." With those words, I glanced over at Benaiah, the defector, who nodded.

Gideon waved at the band of supporters we'd labored to put together over the last month, just over one hundred Jinn. "We're not an army, but we're strong. With you, we may actually have a chance."

Malakai's gaze slowly crossed the room, taking in each of our faces, contemplating our words.

"As you know"—Gideon rapped the floor with his cane to punctuate his statement—"the Crowning Ceremony is in just one week."

Malakai nodded gravely.

I tried to find Kadin's face in the crowd, but he was nowhere to be seen. Gideon's eyes met mine instead, and he gave me an encouraging nod. "If you take the throne," I said softly, fighting the dark voice in my head telling me to stay out of it, "that would not only slow down her plans to attack, but could stop her completely."

"I agree," Malakai said, striding toward us. "And I swear to you I will do exactly that. There are seven days until the ceremony. I will return tonight, and we can form a plan. I only need to make a quick trip before we begin."

Silence fell.

Even the whispering around the edges stopped.

I held my breath.

"I don't understand," Gideon said in a terse tone, gripping his cane until his fingers turned white. "Every spare moment is precious. You are the next heir to the enchanted crown, and without you, your mother could very well rule for another fifty years. What could possibly be more important?"

"Nothing," Malakai reassured him. "Truly. I only need to leave for a short while, but I swear to you on all of Jinn that I will return."

"It's not possible."

Malakai scowled. For the first time since he'd arrived, I recognized the princely tone of voice, the voice that said he expected to be given whatever he was asked without argument. "I didn't give you a choice."

Gideon sighed. "Neither did I, unfortunately."

Malakai clenched his fists. He expected a fight.

Gideon stayed seated.

When Malakai flashed out of sight, we all flinched, waiting.

Everyone had tried it at some point during their stay. Moments later, a sharp cry of pain and the hiss of smoke drifted down from the ceiling mixed with the lightest smell of burning flesh.

Malakai reappeared in the chair before us, eyes hard with fury. "I swore never to let anyone entrap me again. Lift this spell at *once*!"

Chapter 27

Kadin

I SAT IN THE back of the library in a forgotten section with ancient texts and a layer of dust. This tiny back room didn't interest the Jinn. Through the curtains at its entrance, I had a clear view of the training space so I could keep an eye on Arie without being obvious about it. As long as I stayed here, everyone left me relatively alone.

A small sanctuary.

Arie didn't know how often I was here. Though I frequently met with Captain Navabi and the Shahs, checking that everything in Hodafez ran smoothly and keeping an ear to the rumor mill—making sure anyone who mentioned the Jinn in the library had misleading information—I still spent quite a bit of time here as well. I couldn't leave her alone.

Yet I hated to join her in the public spaces.

All last week they'd had a Jinni tail me everywhere I went in the room. No matter where I went, a dark-haired Jinni had followed, disappearing and reappearing around me for added discomfort. The week prior to that, they'd given me a literal tail—a donkey's tail, to be specific. Or the illusion of it, at least. I still wasn't entirely sure. Jedekiah had found a loophole in Rena's armor of spells.

A quick conversation with Rena and a trip to the beach had solved that problem. She'd given Bosh, Arie, Gideon, and me tiny conch shells to wear on a string around our neck, hidden beneath our clothing. It was spelled to protect us from any Gifts being used on our person.

Sprouting a tail shouldn't have embarrassed me, but followed by tall ears and cloven hooves, it had left an awful taste in my mouth. A mix of fear and the old bitterness.

I touched the tiny lump beneath my shirt where the hidden shell protected me. Even with that, I couldn't quite shake it. The Jinn were quite creative.

These days, I kept my distance and tried not to tempt them.

Instead, I slipped inside the library quietly each day and prowled the corners, peering through books, reading the odd volume here and there, and keeping myself entertained as I watched Arie among the Jinn, so at ease.

She looked similar to them—same thick black hair, extra height, tall forehead, regal nose, and lighter skin. Considering she'd had a Jinni's Gift, some part of me had always known she had to also have Jinni blood. But knowing something and seeing it before my eyes were two very different things.

Especially now, as she stood next to the newest arrival. The *prince,* Gideon had called him. Two days had passed since he'd arrived, and the mood in this place had lifted drastically. It practically hummed with excitement.

He even had a dimple in one cheek when he smiled, just like she used to. It was all too obvious. She belonged with them, even without her Gift. *I should just let her go.*

They were bringing in another new Jinni now, showing the prince how the process worked.

I turned away.

A familiar crackle and pop sounded nearby.

The boundary.

I smirked and shook my head. Taking a book titled *How to Pick a Lock* from the shelf, I settled into a small corner chair for a long afternoon.

The shuffle of footsteps startled me awake.

My book slipped from my lap and fell on the floor. I hadn't meant to doze off, especially not around the Jinn. Last time I'd done that, they'd locked me in a prison of books and I'd woken to them cackling at another victory. Sapphira, Uziah, and a few others had banded together to put an end to that. *It's the queen's influence*, they'd said. *She's taught them to hate all humans.* In truth, I understood more than they knew. *It's the same way I used to hate all Jinn.*

It occurred to me that I didn't feel that way anymore. There were those who abused power in every realm, but there were also those, like Sapphira and Uziah, who didn't. Unfortunately, they weren't always around, so I still had to keep my guard up. I'd asked them not to mention that last incident to Arie.

The visitor rounded the corner, and it was the prince. His scowl equaled mine in ferocity. When he reached my chair, he loomed over me. "How does one leave this castle?"

I'd picked the wrong day to fall asleep. If this went anything like previous encounters with those who wanted to leave, it wasn't going to end well. I sighed, rubbing my eyes and resisting the urge to touch the shell necklace beneath my shirt, which would only draw unwanted attention. "You interrupted a perfectly good nap."

"Is that so?"

I stood, stretching. Maybe he'd take the hint and back up. He didn't. "I'm waiting."

"I don't know if this... closeness"—I gestured to the couple inches between our faces—"is normal in Jinn, but it's a little... intimate for the human world."

He surprised me by stepping back, crossing his arms. "There has to be a loophole. Every spell has a loophole. Perhaps you know it?"

Ah, yes. The first efforts at an escape where they would pretend to be my friend. It was easier to let them think they had a chance. I began walking casually; if I could get out into a more public space, he'd be less likely to do something violent. "Maybe I do, maybe I don't."

That earned me a sharp look, and he stepped into my path. "Don't be coy. I have someone waiting for me, and she deserves to know what we plan to do. If the confrontation goes poorly and I don't come back—" His mouth snapped shut, and he shook his head.

That surprised me. Jinni hopes and fears weren't all that different from human ones. "You'll make it back," I reassured him. "Just five more days. She'll never even know you were in any danger."

He didn't say anything.

That clearly wasn't what he wanted to hear.

I shrugged. Picking up my book from where it'd fallen facedown on the floor, I smoothed out the pages and returned to my armchair. Acting like I didn't care if I was alone with a Jinni was my last resort.

"There has to be some way out of here," he repeated, and this time I only shook my head. "Please," he added, and I got the sense that it cost him.

I sighed, flipping through the pages to where I'd left off. "It's not up to me. This place is Jinni-proof. Only humans and Mere can leave. You'll have to ask Rena how it all works." Before he could think of more questions, I added, "Won't your girl understand when she finds out this was your one chance to defeat the—" That may not have been the best choice of words. "To stop your mother from attacking the human world?"

The Jinni's silver-blue eyes took in the dim archives around us once more. His fists clenched and unclenched at his sides, and he turned to pace.

I'd found my page and read the first few lines again when he finally spoke.

"The truth is, I'm not sure I can defeat her." He stared directly at me.

My usual poker face failed me, and my brows rose at the admission. I racked my memories for a time I'd seen such a vulnerable and uncertain expression on a Jinni before. I couldn't think of a single one.

He sighed, leaning back against the end of a shelf and sliding down to sit on the wood floor. "You see? I'm going to let them all down. That is, if we even manage to make it to Jinn. If my mother hears even a hint of this coup, she'll close the gates into Jinn tonight."

I opened my mouth, then stopped. What did I have to say to that? I crossed my arms, frowning in thought at the rows of thick dusty tomes before us.

The only thing that came to mind was what I said to Arie nearly every day, what I said to myself even more often, "You could at least try."

* * *

LATER THAT SAME DAY, I met with Captain Navabi and the Shahs again, as usual, but they were growing restless. "How much longer will these Jinn be with us?" the captain asked. "I would like to speak with the queen. Not to offend you, sir, but we've been lacking in royal leadership as of late..."

I couldn't blame him. But when I found Arie in her small room and relayed his request, she made excuses. "We're far too busy. These last few days are too important. I'll meet with him once this is over."

"Arie." I hesitated, wishing she'd look up from polishing the sword Jedekiah had given her. "Your people are important too."

"Of course they are," she snapped, standing abruptly, finally meeting my eyes. "You think I don't know that? Why do you think I'm here? And in case you've forgotten, I can't leave."

"I haven't forgotten," I said softly.

She paced toward the door, then back to where I stood by the bed. "They don't need me. You've been doing a better job than I ever could."

Under any other circumstances, I might've been proud to hear that. I kept my arms crossed, resisting the urge to reach out and hug her since she tended to interpret that as pity. "You think too little of yourself."

She only shrugged, tears filling her eyes.

Now I couldn't help it. I reached out.

For a brief moment, she let me hold her, then pulled back, returning to sit on the little bed and picking up the practice sword.

"You're right. Running the kingdom is not your place," she said stiffly to the sword. "I will meet with the captain going forward. You don't need to concern yourself with any of this. Consider yourself free of me."

Stung, I didn't say a word.

There was a pressure in my chest, almost like a physical blow. Free of her? She wanted to be free of *me.*

I slipped out of her room, shutting the door softly behind me.

I couldn't say that I hadn't seen it coming. She'd made her choice. Though it hurt worse than anything I'd felt in years, I would respect it.

Chapter 28

Rena

WE WERE FOUR SHORT days away from the Crowning Ceremony. Everyone circled one another like King Fish looking for a fight.

It was midmorning—not even time yet for the final strategy sessions during which we'd pore over every last detail of crashing the Crowning Ceremony—but already they were questioning everything.

"I don't want to be on the losing side," one Jinni snapped.

"I don't care which side I'm on, and they can put a dog on the throne for all I care, but I'm not interested in dying over this."

"Enough," Gideon called over the chaos. "If you aren't willing to take a stand against the queen, no one is forcing you. But if you don't plan to go with us, then you have no place in the discussions."

I scrunched up my nose, annoyed at all of them.

"Want to eat lunch early?" Bosh asked, coming to find me with a big tray of food and a grin.

"Yes please!" I followed him to the table in the small research and collections room where we'd taken to spending our time when we weren't officially needed. Not that anyone really needed us at all lately since most arrivals went smoothly the moment Jedekiah showed his face. He seemed to be the unofficial leader of the illicit Jinn, which in my opinion was more of a mark *against* him than *for* him.

"Oh, wait." Bosh frowned at the tray as he set it down. "They forgot to send butter. I'll be right back."

"I'll wait for you." I folded my fingers together to keep them from grabbing a juicy bite. At least, not until he left.

While he was gone, I snuck a piece of cheese.

Then another.

I rearranged the food so he wouldn't notice.

It was taking him forever to come back.

My stomach gurgled, and I let it have another piece of cheese. And another.

Playing with the arrangement, I found it harder to hide the growing hole where food used to be. *Does the kitchen need to make fresh butter from scratch? What's taking him so long?*

I pushed the bench out from the table to stand when Jedekiah flashed into the room to sit across from me.

Though I knew you shouldn't show a shark any sign of fear, I still flinched. "What're you doing here? Get your own meal."

"Oh, come now, darling. I actually came here to offer *you* something."

"Don't call me that," I snapped, though it had yet to stop him.

"Fine." Jedekiah held his hands up in mock surrender, but that smirk contradicted it. His eyes narrowed, and he leaned forward, dropping his voice to add, "I just thought you might want your little friend to live."

Ice stole over me, filling my bloodstream until I was shaking. "What do you mean?"

"The human boy—not the gloomy one, but the puppy that follows you everywhere. Do you care about him?"

"Of course I do," I snapped. Standing, I placed my hands on the table and leaned forward, even though my diminutive stature didn't allow me to tower over him much. My father had taught me never to negotiate with a floater. "Say what you have to say or you'll regret it."

That only made him smirk again. "We found a loophole. In your little spells."

My mind raced, trying to wrap around his words. *What've I missed? What'd he do to Bosh?*

Even as I racked my brain for the answer, two shapes appeared in the door. The heavyset Jinni in the crew who could make knives disappear and attack at will—and who knew what else—held Bosh tight against his belly with a knife to his throat.

Bosh's clothes were ripped, his lip bloody, and his eye swollen and already darkening into an ugly bruise. "Rena, don't listen—"

The Jinni holding him whispered something in his ear and he cut off midsentence. When Bosh swallowed nervously, his throat nicked the edge of the blade, and a trickle of blood rolled down his neck.

"You were so busy making sure the Jinni magic wouldn't touch you," Jedekiah said, triumph in his voice, "that you forgot the simplest protection, didn't you, darling?"

The lump beneath Bosh's shirt where the shell usually hung with the spell of protection was gone. Trying not to panic, I blurted out, "He's well protected. Let him go before you regret it."

"You mean he *was* well protected." Jedekiah lifted his closed fist, opening it and letting something dangle from the string: the tiny conch shell I'd given Bosh. "It turns out, if you

flip the human upside down, those protection spells"—
Jedekiah swung the little shell around mockingly, dropping it
into his other hand for dramatic effect—"just fall right off,
along with the shell."

I took a deep breath, my hand instinctively moving
toward my own shell necklace where I had plenty of spells
ready to be used.

"Don't. Move." Jedekiah stood, and his looming was
terribly effective as he leaned over me. "One wrong spell and
we slice his throat, understood?"

Behind the tall Jinni who held Bosh, three more Jinn
slipped into the room, each with a knife held at the ready.

Without glancing down, I mentally sorted through my
options: The Lightning Whelk could create a forceful current
of air which would throw them all across the room. It might
possibly even break some necks in the cramped space. But I
couldn't use that without harming Bosh as well. The Horn
Shell could call everyone to me, but they wouldn't arrive in
time to save Bosh if the Jinn truly meant to hurt him. Shark's
Eye, Cerith, Auger—all of them were too risky.

I could stop one or two, but not all of them at once. Not
without risking Bosh's life.

I knew it, and Jedekiah knew it too.

When I met his gaze this time, he didn't smile. "It's just
business, darling. As long as you do what we ask, your little
friend will be fine. This whole venture has given me the
perfect opportunity to prove myself to my queen, and I'd be a
fool to pass it up, which means you'd be a fool to stand against
me."

He flicked a finger toward the knife in the big man's
hand, and it cut deeper into Bosh's neck, causing a long, thin
river of blood to form.

My shoulders hunched in defeat, and I whispered, "What
do you want me to do?"

"Remove the boundary spell."

Obediently, I raised my hand toward my shell necklace again.

"Slowly," Jedekiah snapped. "Don't forget what will happen if you try anything."

I nodded my understanding. When my fingers brushed the two necklaces, I paused. "What about the Key?" Lifting that from where it hung on the string around my neck, I held it out to him. "Take this instead of Bosh. Let him go. *Then* I'll remove the spell."

"I don't need the Key anymore, darling," Jedekiah replied, shrugging. "With a group our size, we have enough combined power to travel to Jinn without it. Originally, we meant for the Key to be a gift to the queen—a way to bargain for our return home. Now, however, we have secrets worth far, far more."

The rebellion. "You wouldn't."

"I would," Jedekiah replied flatly. "The boundary spell. Now."

I finally caved, murmuring the spell to remove it as they'd asked. "Now what?"

"Test it," Jedekiah told the Jinni with the fewest Gifts.

Scrunching up his nose in response, the Jinni shook his head. "No way, boss. I don't trust her."

"Tell you what," Jedekiah said, not bothered in the slightest by the refusal. "Take her with you."

The Jinni grudgingly obeyed, flashing to me, but he couldn't move me. "What in the name of the queen is—"

"I'm anchored," I told him through gritted teeth. He smelled like cigar smoke and peaches up close. The strange mix tickled my nose.

"Ah." He looked to Jedekiah.

"Undo it, love."

"No."

Jedekiah sighed, rubbing his forehead as if I were a five-year-old vexing an adult. "Do it, or there'll be consequences."

Bosh grunted as the Jinni holding him tightened his grip and dug the knife deeper into his skin, making the blood stain his collar. He risked their wrath by hissing, "Don't do it!"

That earned him a knock on the head that made me wince with him.

I moved as slowly as possible, hoping someone would think to come looking for us, to wonder where we'd gone. But Bosh and I slipped away often. They wouldn't be suspicious until dinnertime, if even then.

Only a few mumbled words from me, and my anchor slipped away, leaving me vulnerable.

I nodded, just once, that it was done.

At this signal, the Jinni flashed out of the room with me in his arms, out onto the stone walls of the castle. Just a dozen paces down the rampart stood two guards with their backs to us.

Before I could open my mouth, we'd already returned to the tiny little room at the back of the library.

The others stood staring at the ceiling, waiting for the sound of the boundary catching and throwing us back, but of course, it didn't come.

"Told you," I grumbled, startling them.

They swung around to face us.

With a worried glance at Bosh, then at the hand on my arm, I snapped, "Now let us go."

"Good job, darling." Jedekiah had the nerve to pat me on the head. "All right, one last thing. Give me that little shell necklace of yours."

I clutched it, wanting desperately to injure all of them.

Again, I stopped myself.

I couldn't take them all on without risking Bosh, which was exactly what he was counting on.

Still, these shells held every spell I knew how to make, as well as some I didn't that had been gifted to me.

Slipping the long strand from around my neck, I forced myself to hold them out.

Jedekiah ripped them from my hand. "Go."

At the word, the others flashed out of sight.

Bosh stumbled forward, suddenly free.

In the second my attention was on Bosh, making sure he was alive and well, Jedekiah grabbed my wrist. The next thing I knew, everything around me was twisting and changing until I was no longer in the back room of the library but hovering in the wide-open sky over the ocean with nothing in sight except blue waves below blue sky.

"This is your stop, darling," Jedekiah said.

He let go.

I fell backward, screaming up at him as I tumbled through the air, "This won't stop me!"

I could breathe underwater. If he thought this would hurt me, he was a fool. I flipped over in the air, only to find the water rushing at me with a horrible speed. Maybe I was wrong. I'd never hit it hard before, but I had a bad feeling. I couldn't even use my necklace to bring back my tail. The waves came rushing up at me, as solid as stone, and I was completely helpless to stop it.

Chapter 29

Arie

DAWN OF THE THIRD day before the Crowning
Ceremony, Gideon and I were standing outside my bedroom
door in the hall, conferring before the first strategy session
began, when Bosh came stumbling down the hall toward us,
leaning heavily on Uziah's shoulder. I ran to meet them
halfway. "What happened?"

"He took Rena! He betrayed us!"

"Slow down." Gideon stepped forward as Bosh swayed,
glancing around for anyone listening.

Where's Kadin? I'd regretted my words to him the
moment I'd said them, but pride had kept me from following
him. Still, I would've thought he'd be here by now. *Maybe
he's given up on me,* the dark voice in my head whispered. *I
wouldn't blame him.*

Gideon beckoned for us to enter the gallery. Though we were currently alone, it didn't mean someone wouldn't overhear.

Sure enough, Sapphira flashed into the gallery in front of us, followed by a few others. "Who betrayed us?"

"Jedekiah." Bosh held his side, wincing. "They knocked me out and locked me in the back room!"

"I was checking on breakfast," Uziah added when Bosh paused, panting. "That's when I heard him pounding on the door."

Screwing up his face as they helped him hobble toward a small sofa, Bosh added, "We were about to eat lunch. Yesterday."

"I think his ribs are broken," Uziah whispered.

When Gideon pressed a hand on Bosh's side to check, Bosh paled and his knees gave out. They caught him, lowering him onto the small sofa.

"Give me the names of everyone involved and point me in their direction." Gideon spoke to Bosh with the voice of the high commander he'd once been, waving toward a few of the Jinn he'd determined trustworthy over the last month. "Sapphira, Uziah, with me—"

"It's too late," Bosh interrupted. "They're gone."

"Yes, but where? To the back room?" Fury flickered across Gideon's face.

"No, gone." Bosh spit out blood. "As in, not here."

Again, I wondered where Kadin was. Normally, he'd notice if Bosh went missing for almost a full day.

"How can that be?" Gideon was saying as he dropped into a chair in disbelief. "How could they get past the boundary spell?"

"When they grabbed me, Jedekiah said this was his ticket back into Jinn, that it wasn't personal, but he wanted to go back home." Bosh shifted, then clutched his side, hissing in pain. From his view on the sofa, he couldn't see all the Jinn flashing into the space behind us, and he didn't know to lower his voice. "He used me to blackmail Rena into lowering the boundary spell."

Murmurs rose behind us as the Jinn spread the news.

"Of course he did." Gideon shook his head, dropping it into his hands.

"So, we're free then?" an eavesdropping Jinni said, glancing at her friend. "Let's go."

They began to vanish in small groups, followed by others around the room. For those who stayed, I couldn't honestly tell if it was dedication or curiosity, or if either would hold them for long.

"Stop! You can't leave until the ceremony!" Gideon yelled, but it didn't stop the trickle of disappearances.

"Please," I appealed to those who remained. "For the sake of peace between our worlds, I beg you not to go."

The Jinn who'd flashed into the room continued to vanish. It was difficult to say without gathering the remainder together, but at least half of our small "army" had already deserted us.

Gideon stood to pace, cane swinging wildly. "Was Jedekiah alone? He can't reach Jinn by himself. It takes at least three Jinn to travel that distance—"

"There were five of them," Bosh said on a wheeze.

That sunk in.

None of us said anything.

Prince Malakai stood to the side, conferring with a smaller group of Jinn.

Sapphira stepped forward, reaching her hands toward Bosh's ribs. "Let me help."

Bosh crawled backward, wincing. "Don't touch me!"

"Trust me, human." She pressed her hands to his ribs.

Bosh squirmed, clutching the small necklace in his hand and trying to get it back around his neck. "You can't do anything to me," he said. "Rena's spells protect me—" He dropped the necklace midsentence and stilled.

As I stepped forward to pick it up and hand it back to him, he studied Sapphira's hands. "How are you doing that?"

As far as I could tell, nothing was happening, but he didn't take the shell.

Sapphira didn't answer. Bosh began to breathe easier as he lay there, and the rasping stopped. After another beat, she moved to his split lip. It healed under her hand. When she moved to the bruises around his eyes next, he let her continue, grudgingly.

"You should rest to let the healing take full effect," she murmured as she stepped back, tilting her head toward Uziah.

He knelt by the sofa in her place, putting a hand on Bosh's arm. Moments later, Bosh's eyes rolled back in his head, and he collapsed back onto the sofa.

Uziah glanced up at the rest of us as he stood. "He'll wake when he's ready, good as new."

Gideon stopped pacing. He sank onto the chair again, seeming smaller somehow.

Just around three dozen Jinn remained now, observing Gideon fall apart even as Bosh was put back together.

"Jedekiah will go straight to the queen." Gideon's soft voice carried. "He'll use information on us as his redemption. The only thing we had going for us was surprise."

"We could still try." I heard my voice like someone else was speaking. It was what Kadin said nearly every morning.

All eyes landed on my face, pinning me in place.

I searched for the right words. "You can't just give up. If we don't stop her, the queen rules for another fifty years. Every single Jinni in this room knows what a mistake that would be. And she won't be satisfied with controlling the Jinn; she'll come for the humans next."

I already knew the first human kingdom she was coming for. "We have to at least try to stop her from getting the crown again. We still have a chance. He only has a small head start. Right?" I cleared my throat, forcing the confidence I was desperately lacking. "The Crowning Ceremony is in four short days. We need to go to Jinn now, before they close the gates."

A female Jinni whose black hair was pinned tightly back said in a flat tone, "You still expect us to confront the queen." She pushed off the shelf she was leaning against to glance dramatically around the room at the remaining Jinn. "Us against the Jinni Guard? When they know we're coming? The queen will crush this little revolution before we have a chance to say a word. I'm out." She winked out of sight.

"Jedekiah's probably whispering our plans in the queen's ear right now," Uziah said, glancing at me uneasily. "Or, considering how much time has passed, hours ago. There's no telling what the queen might do to retaliate."

"We don't need numbers or surprise," Prince Malakai said from the midst of a small group of Jinn, all of them leaning forward as if they'd been in the middle of an intense conversation. "I am the rightful ruler."

Gideon stood, as if the prince's confidence bolstered his own. "This betrayal escalates the level of urgency, and we must act immediately, but it does not change our ultimate goal."

"I agree," the prince said, almost to himself. "Speed is of utmost importance."

"Please," I said, forcing myself to raise my voice even though it took every bit of energy I had left. "I know the humans and the Jinn don't always get along, but we need your help. Please stay and help us." I cut off before I could add my last thought. *We have no hope without you.* What was a simple human kingdom going to do against a horde of magical abilities?

The Jinn responded to my plea with shifting feet and muttering.

Glancing back at the prince and the small group of Jinn who'd been with him, I found an empty corner instead.

But he wouldn't have left.

He was probably letting the other Jinn know.

Bosh shifted, blinking sleepily, slowly waking up.

A young female Jinni stepped forward from the back of the room. "Jedekiah doesn't speak for me." Her thick black hair had streaks of green and blue to match her eyes. "I'll stay and fight. And I can track the Mere girl too."

"You can find Rena?" Bosh said groggily as my own hopes rose.

"Not if they took her to Jinn." The girl shook her head, crossing her arms. "But... I don't really think Jedekiah would bring her to our homeland. So there's a good chance I can find her, one way or another."

"What do you mean, one way or another?" Bosh cried hoarsely. "They wouldn't hurt her, would they?" His gaze swung wildly from Gideon, to me, to the Jinni tracker.

"She means dead or alive, kid," another Jinni answered in a gentle tone, even though the words were harsh.

"No!" Bosh paled, groaning. "I told her not to listen to them! This is all my fault."

"If Jedekiah left a trail, I just have to find it," the Jinni told Bosh, ignoring the rest of us. She glanced over at me.

I nodded. "Go."

As she flashed out of sight, the doors to the library opened.

Not just one or two, but a dozen Shah strode toward us, visible from the second floor balcony even at this distance. Captain Navabi led them, shouting across the room as soon as his gaze found mine. "My queen, we're under attack!"

Chapter 30

Rena

I WOKE ON THE ocean floor hours later—maybe quite a few, if the pounding in my head was any indication. My whole body hurt from the impact.

The water above was as black as night. Though that didn't mean much. From the pressure of the water around me, I could only assume the surface was miles away. My gills and sight in the dark didn't fail me, but without my tail, I doubted my scrawny human legs could carry me all the way to the surface without giving out.

I glanced around for predators as I searched for the Key, finding it a short distance away from me in the sand. I murmured the spell into the depths. Once unveiled, my body tensed, waiting for the imminent arrival of a Jinni on instinct.

But of course, nothing happened.

This was Mere.

Jinn didn't come here, to the middle of the ocean beneath enormous stretches of water. Even if they stood at the ocean's edge, I doubted they would sense the Key.

This part of the ocean was barren, too deep for coral, surrounded by sand on all sides no matter which way I turned, along with an occasional rock formation. Not a fish in sight. Which usually meant there were sharks nearby.

My heart thudded as I reached up to my necklace, only to touch my bare throat.

My entire life I'd had my shells to protect me. It was like losing a limb. Was this what Arie had felt like when she'd lost her Gift? I probably should've been more understanding...

There was nothing to do except start moving. I leaned forward and kicked, swimming slower than a minnow. Every movement made my body ache and throb from hitting the water so hard.

When I reached a small group of rocks, I peered closely at the spaces and caverns between them, checking for eels. Once I determined they were empty, I poked through them, searching for a loose rock small enough to carry—preferably one with a sharp edge.

I found some that weren't smooth like those shaped by the current but were sharp and full of pockmarks, about the size of my palm. Old volcanic lava. Ripping a piece of fabric from my dress, I wrapped it around the base of a rock before picking it up so as not to cut myself.

Even one drop of blood in a space like this would be a beacon. Just like the Key, but with entirely different recipients. *Or*—I pursed my lips—*maybe very similar recipients since Jinn are the sharks on land.*

I hoisted the rock, feeling better now that I had a weapon of sorts. Now I just needed a plan. I could watch for recognizable currents and try to swim home, where my family could help me. Once there, at the very least, I could get my spells and tail back.

But I have no idea where the Jinni dropped me. Rusalka could be days or even weeks from here.

Even one week would be too late.

Staring up toward the dark surface, where the light was too distant to reach me, I finally admitted to myself that even if Arie sent Gideon or someone else to search for me, it wouldn't help, even if they *could* sense the Key. It didn't matter if a Jinni was Gifted with breathing underwater or had another way to reach me in the depths; they couldn't.

Jinn weren't allowed to enter Mere territory—not even one toe in the water. It was the law and had been for centuries.

Breaking that law amounted to war.

I was completely on my own.

Chapter 31

Nesrin

JUST FOUR DAYS. THAT was how long it'd been since I'd seen Malakai. It felt like decades. I'd finally admitted to myself, if only because I couldn't deny it anymore, that he mattered to me. A lot.

The problem was, I didn't know what to do about it. I didn't even know where he'd gone. He'd described his search for the elusive Key, but I hadn't paid attention. Why should I have cared about the names of towns he'd passed through? I kicked my bedpost, but it only made my foot hurt.

Still, I tried to hope for the best.

He was just detained. Not hurt. Not gone for good.

I'd skipped dinner in favor of pacing my room and was eying the bedpost again—it looked like it could use another good kick—when a thump sounded behind me.

Whirling around, I found Malakai sagging back against the wall, sliding down to sit on the floor.

"What's going on?" I cried out, running around the bed and dropping to the floor beside him. "Are you hurt? Where're you injured?"

"I'm not," he said on a sigh, eyes squeezed shut, arms around his knees. "Just defeated."

I ran my tongue across my teeth, leaning back on my heels to study him. "What happened?"

"It's not important."

"Clearly," I scoffed. When he didn't say anything more, I added, "You were gone for four days!"

"I couldn't get back," he said quietly, staring down at his hands. "I'm sorry. There was a spell."

There was a dejection in the way his shoulders slumped that I hadn't seen since we'd encountered his mother. Placing a hand on his shoulder, I squeezed and stood. "I'll be right back."

Though the kitchen was dark, I made quick work of heating soup over the stove, grabbing a loaf of bread and drinks, and piling up a tray for the two of us.

When I returned, he was still on the floor, so I set the tray on the rug and sat beside him, crossing my legs. I handed him a bowl, and we ate in silence, shoulder to shoulder.

"I failed them," he said softly as he swirled the last few pieces of potato in the bottom.

I frowned. "Failed who?"

"She wants to enslave the human world, you know," Malakai mumbled.

He was talking in circles. "I don't understand."

"Ever since my sister left Jinn, my mother's gotten it into her mind that humans are worthless. Less than worthless."

When I set my bowl onto the tray with a loud clatter, he held up his hands in protest. "Not my words. And the rest of Jinn doesn't want to attack the human world either, but—"

"You say this like it's actually happening."

"If my mother gains the crown for another fifty years, it will." He described the small group of Jinn he'd stumbled upon when he'd finally found his Key, explaining how they'd gathered information on the queen's plans and had formed a counterplan to fight back.

"This 'boundary' you mentioned," I said, forgetting about my soup completely. "That's what kept you from coming back?"

He nodded. "As much as I despised it, I realize now it was incredibly important. Once they broke through the boundary, over half the Jinn abandoned our cause."

"What about the other half? Are they still there now?" I asked, curling my legs beneath me and leaning against the wall to face him.

"I doubt it," he replied. "Why should they be when I abandoned them?" He finally glanced up at me, shaking his head. "I thought it'd be better that way—if I could just get into Jinn on my own and stop my mother—" He broke off, picking the bread up and breaking it into small pieces. "I asked a small number of Jinn to come with me, just enough to travel the distance. But my mother had already barred every gate. No one is allowed in or out of Jinn until after the Crowning Ceremony. By then, it'll be too late."

When I reached out hesitantly to touch his hand, he curled his fingers around mine, and his foot stopped tapping that anxious rhythm. "They might still be waiting for you…"

"It doesn't matter." He dropped his head into his hands. "I can't face them now, not when we've failed so completely."

I had no words. What was there to say? Nothing would solve this.

Chapter 32

Arie

"THIS IS NO COINCIDENCE," I said to Gideon, gripping the stone wall of the battlement. It was strange to be outside after having been trapped in the library for so long.

Gideon stood beside me, along the castle's inner wall. Past that was the outer wall, even thicker and more heavily defended, and beyond that the town of Hodafez sprawled along the mountainside below, surrounded by yet another wall.

With our high vantage point, the army of men could not approach unseen, but they marched steadily toward the town like a swarm of ants spilling out of their hill. They carried dozens of ladders, other tools, and at least one battering ram, which rolled slowly but surely forward on a cart.

It wouldn't be long before they reached the town wall.

In the courtyard below, Captain Navabi rallied his men to fight.

"The timing is too intentional," Gideon said.

We both knew what the other meant.

Jedekiah.

We couldn't prove it—yet—but the timing was too connected. If he'd gone straight to Queen Jezebel, I could only assume this was her attempt at distracting us until the Crowning Ceremony.

It was extremely effective.

Are they being compelled by the Jinn, or is someone else behind this? It was impossible to know for sure.

Though the mountainside created a natural defense, our numbers were small and we had limited resources for a counterattack.

As the sun crossed the sky, they began their assault. Throughout the day, I met with the captain, the Shahs, Gideon and the Jinn, then the captain again, listening to their suggestions to hold the line, accepting some, rejecting others.

"We should give them the town," one of the Shahs said during a late night emergency council meeting. "The people can defend themselves, and we need all the soldiers we have to guard the outer wall."

I didn't even look up from where I rested my forehead against my palm. "Absolutely not."

"We have the high ground," Captain Navabi assured them, taking my side.

"Perhaps we could evacuate the townspeople first," another Shah suggested.

"We can't just give Hodafez up," I snapped, frustrated. "We keep fighting." I ended the council meeting by walking away. Maybe Bosh had seen Kadin. I still hadn't, and it'd been a full day. I was growing concerned.

Clouds covered the moon, turning homes into shapeless mounds except where streetlamps lit small circles of space. Standing on the battlement, my eyes were glued to the dim shapes fighting along the top of the city wall. The battering ram pounded a steady rhythm against the gate, where it had finally arrived just a short while ago and begun its work.

The soldiers didn't wear the colors of any kingdom, but no group of mercenaries would be this organized. I wouldn't have been surprised if some of those unusually large fires that flickered wildly belonged to Jinn.

"Your Majesty," Captain Navabi said from my shoulder. "We have news on young master Kadin."

I spun to face him.

In the torchlight, his expression was solemn. "I'm afraid someone saw him in town, and he hasn't returned to the castle since."

A boom punctuated his words, heavier than those before it, and wild yells broke out as the attacking army burst through the gate. Captain Navabi left in a hurry.

"No," I whispered, whirling back to lean over the wall and stare into the darkness below. Torches lit the gate, now split in two, and soldiers poured through it. "Why would he leave?"

Because I told him to. This was all my fault. *I pushed him away.*

I couldn't see past my tears, and Gideon was just a blur when he approached to stand beside me.

"They fight bravely," Gideon said, but his flat tone and hopeless expression gave the words a different meaning. Chaos below created a cacophony of voices.

I swallowed thick tears, trying to focus. "They should've been able to hold them for weeks. I don't understand. It's almost like something weakened the gate." *Kadin can take care of himself,* I told myself as I blinked to clear my tears. *He's more than capable.* I could only hope I was right.

Pressing my hands into the cold stone before me, I tried to ground myself in this moment, to think like the ruler my people needed. *They're advancing too quickly for men alone.* "They have Jinni help, don't they?"

When Gideon didn't answer right away, I turned to face him.

Arms crossed, lips flattened in a grim line, he didn't meet my eyes, just nodded.

Exhaustion wrapped a fog around my mind, making even the smallest decisions feel impossible. It was difficult to think past the screams and yells sounding below. *What do I do?* I'd grown up learning leadership in times of peace. Everything in me wanted to let someone else take charge.

But I couldn't give up. Not when it would almost guarantee my people being killed or enslaved.

"I wonder if Jedekiah is leading them."

"He wouldn't," Gideon replied quickly. "I don't think."

Kadin had been right all along. I never should've trusted the Jinn. I wished he were here so I could tell him I'd never doubt him again.

Wrapping my arms around myself, I tracked the progress of the army below instead. They slowly made their way into Hodafez, setting homes ablaze and leaving bodies in their wake. My guards came running to stop them, valiantly holding them back while the townspeople fled. Adrenaline rushed through me. I needed to do something. To the guards still remaining with me on the wall, I said, "Go help them."

"Your Majesty?" one of the four asked. "Captain Navabi specifically requested we don't leave your side—"

"I'm requesting that you disobey his orders," I said firmly, straightening my spine and lifting my chin to face him. "Go help your people. They need you now."

Without another word, all four of them bowed and abandoned their posts.

I could fight. My hand brushed the practice sword at my belt, but I'd not actually learned enough to do any real damage, and I knew it.

It'd be an honorable way to go. The murky voice inside me stirred, whispering the words it'd said so often in the beginning of my Severance. *You might as well give up.*

I gritted my teeth, leaning into the stone ledge, pressing my eyes shut and fighting those familiar feelings. If Kadin were here, what would he do? That only led to worrying about him more.

When I finally turned to Gideon, the orange flames flickered in his blue eyes. "If we don't do something soon, they'll take the outer wall just as easily. And then the inner wall, the courtyard, and the castle. It's not a fair fight."

"I agree." He stood so still he could've been a statue.

Sucking in a deep breath, I moved into his line of vision, between him and the stone, putting the fighting and awful screaming at my back. "We need the Jinn on our side to fight with us."

"You can ask, but they won't use their Gifts," Gideon said, as I'd known he would. "They won't risk breaking the Unbreakable Laws and losing their last remaining opportunity to return to Jinn."

The laws that said Jinn couldn't lie, steal, or harm others with their Gifts. A lot of good that code was when Jinn all around us were breaking it. First Jedekiah and his followers the day before, and now, I felt certain, at least one or more Jinn below. The growing casualties and impossibly swift victories made it clear.

"It's past midnight, which means the Crowning Ceremony is happening in just two days," I reminded him. "If we don't have help, the kingdom will be lost before morning. And if you go to stop the queen without us—without *the humans*—we may not be here when you get back."

"If we break the code, we're no better than the queen," Gideon said stubbornly.

"I know."

Shrieks tore through the night.

"I have an idea." I reached out, placing a tentative hand on his arm. "Can you take me to the library?"

For once, Gideon didn't question me. His worried gaze finally left the flames below and met mine as he took my arm.

The dark starry night shifted into a dimly lit library where only half the candles burned, creating a pocket of light in the center. The few remaining Jinn who'd stayed after Jedekiah's betrayal were either asleep or restlessly sparring in the training area. The sounds of the battle were muted here, but clashes of metal against metal still broke through.

Gideon moved around the room waking everyone until our small remainder of barely two dozen Jinn had gathered in the center. Again, I wished Kadin were there. I never should've told him to leave. Wherever he was right now, it was my fault that I was alone. My gut clenched at the thought that he might be hurt. We needed to take the town back immediately.

I strode up to that small circle of light and raised my voice so the whole room could hear me. "I know we've asked a lot of you since you all arrived: to stand up to your queen, to give us your time, to work with humans. But it was all for your prince and your own." Speaking of Malakai, I found it odd that he was still indisposed. He'd retired to one of the back rooms when the battle first started, and even Gideon hadn't seen him since. When I'd asked about it, he'd said we must respect the prince's wishes. I could only hope he might somehow hear me now. "I need to ask you—no, beg you—to help my people."

Uziah was the first to answer. His gaze swung to the walls, as if he could see the chaos in the town beyond, before coming back to mine. "I wish we could… but we can't break the code."

"I could help heal the wounded," Sapphira said, offering her Gift with incredible directness for a Jinni. "But we can't fight."

I held up a hand as more of them voiced their concerns. "There have to be loopholes."

Talking over one another, they didn't hear me.

"I'm not asking you to fight!" I yelled over the noise.

Colorful gazes met mine, unblinking, as they quieted.

I had their attention.

"I know the code says you can't harm another with Gifts, but what if you didn't harm them? As far as I'm concerned, if a soldier suddenly finds himself an entire day's journey from Hodafez, it's unfortunate, to be sure. But he wouldn't be harmed, nothing would be stolen, and there would be no lie. Am I correct in believing this?"

I held my breath as they considered.

"I suppose," someone muttered.

"I just need you to undermine them," I said, before they could come up with another argument. "To be the golem in the night like the stories say. For example, if the one who made our weapons disappear on that first day of training is still here, well, I don't see any *harm* in that happening to enemy soldiers, do you?"

A few of them nodded, and a quiet Jinni who'd kept to himself—perhaps the one who'd made the swords disappear—said, "Since we're here, we might as well."

"Finally. I was getting bored," someone else called.

"I could whip up a few gentle sinkholes," a Jinni close to me muttered.

"Oh, yes," I said to her, trying to smile. "Start with sinking the battering ram, if you could." That in itself would be a huge deterrent.

Attempting to infuse hope that I didn't feel, I raised my voice and said, "Thank you. When this is over, I will do everything in my power to repay you. For now though, if you could hurry?"

With a few nods around the room, they started flashing out of sight.

Gideon was the last to go, placing a hand on my shoulder and squeezing gently. "Well done."

And then he was gone, and it was only me and Bosh left in the library. He couldn't sit still, waiting on word of Rena that hadn't come. If anyone could understand how he felt, it was me. *I should've asked the Jinn to watch for Kadin.* I chewed my bottom lip, struggling with guilt.

"I need to speak with Captain Navabi and let him know we have help now," I told Bosh. "Keep an eye out at the gate for Kadin, will you? I-I'm worried about him."

Bosh bowed. "Yes, Your Majesty."

My brows rose as he scurried off. He'd never called me that before.

No time to consider it.

I pushed through the library doors, hurrying down the hall to return to the castle wall. The first assault was waning as they pulled back after the initial ambush, but the second wave could come anytime. This fight was just beginning.

Chapter 33

Rena

HOURS OF SWIMMING ACROSS the ocean floor, and the landscape hadn't changed a bit. Just dark depths and sand. Sand ahead. Sand behind. It harbored tiny creatures that burrowed underneath—if I grew desperate, I could dig something up to eat. But if I was here that long... I refused to think that way.

Instead, my mind drifted back to Bosh and the knife at his neck. I played it over and over, but I couldn't see any other way than what had gone down. I'd been helpless then and I was helpless now.

I pushed off for the thousandth time, kicking my scrawny human legs, missing my tail more than ever. If only I'd convinced Yuliya to teach me that spell. I could've created a new shell now and covered ten times this distance. Instead, my legs burned and forced me to rest frequently.

While I hoped to run into a passing Mere, it'd be incredibly embarrassing to be seen like this.

* * *

I DROPPED TO THE ocean floor and rolled onto my back on the sand, staring up at the faraway surface. They'd dropped me in one of the deepest portions of the ocean. As I'd dragged my body through the water, the pressure had increased.

It was too deep, even for a Mere. My body struggled to handle the heavy weight of this depth. As little-Mere, we were taught that if we experienced compression as strong as this, we must immediately swim upward or risk losing consciousness.

If something didn't change soon, my eyes could close and never open again. As a young Mere of only sixteen, nearing seventeen, I'd not spent even half a heartbeat considering death. Why would I? The Mere lived to three hundred easily, sometimes much longer. We ruled Rusalka with an iron fist and controlled the entire ocean from there. The Jinn were the only predators worth worrying about, and they couldn't enter Mere.

Yet here I was, struggling to breathe as the depths pressed in on my lungs. Crushing me.

My eyes scrunched up. From my time on land, I knew I was adding to the salt water around me now, though the tears floated invisibly out into the brine.

Staring into the blue abyss, endless sand and sea stared back.

But then...

A speck.

Swimming toward me.

I hauled myself up to get a better view, narrowing my eyes at the blurry shape.

It grew larger.

Not a speck at all.

I clutched the sharp rock and braced myself for a predator. Only predators swam alone.

If it was a shark, at least death would be quick. Grimly, I pressed on, wheezing.

The dark shape grew too large to be a shark. Orca then.

But no, the lazy approach and increasing size finally revealed my foe: a humpback whale.

Not a foe at all, but a friend of the Mere.

This time when the saltwater leaked out of my eyes to join the ocean, I was smiling.

There must've been a migration stream nearby. The whale was clearly foraging for food and had gotten sidetracked.

I swam to meet it, only to discover it was passing me.

Kicking harder, I ignored the burning in my arms and legs, bringing my hands to my mouth as I swam to sound a dolphin distress trill.

At first it didn't notice, but after the third call, its enormous body angled in my direction.

To the whale, my colorful dress probably looked like a small coral reef with the way it flowed and rippled in the underwater currents.

My hand reached up out of habit to wipe away tears of relief, though they'd already merged with the sea. I'd be home soon.

* * *

AS I SLIPPED OFF the whale's back a few hours later, I scratched his throat in thanks. Without my shells, it was the best I could do. When he pulled away to leave, I swam awkwardly toward the coral palace.

Passing Mere stopped to float in the halls and stare. "What are those?" they asked, mostly to each other, ogling the pale legs that flapped almost uselessly behind me. I ignored them, head held high. Or as high as I could when forced to use my whole body to swim instead of a tail.

When my legs threatened to give out, I dragged myself arm over arm along the coral walls. The sharp coral shredded the outer skirt of my dress, leaving the edges in soft green tatters.

"Yuliya? Anyone seen Yuliya?" I panted each time I encountered someone.

Mere only shook their heads, lips parting.

Many of the passageways that led to the throne room were vertical, since it was near the top of the palace. Gripping the rough coral, I suffered the indignity of yet another break to rest only halfway through the hall, which stretched on high above me. As a group of Mere passed by, one of them reached out to touch my legs.

I kicked him off. "How dare you!"

"Is that the Tsaretska?" Someone finally recognized me. "What happened to your tail? Did it get mangled in a shark attack? Or did something else get you? You poor thing."

I scowled. I'd hoped to find my sister and bargain for her help getting my tail back before anyone saw me in this condition. Too late now. "That's none of your concern. Bring me to the throne room immediately."

Between two of them taking my arms and swimming with their powerful tails, we arrived in the throne room just a few minutes later, passing under the graceful arch of coral.

When they let go, I sank toward the floor and began to kick awkwardly, winding my way through the audience.

A hush fell. My face burned hot enough to boil the sea. Or that was how it felt, at least. This was not the return I'd hoped to make someday.

My parents lounged high above everyone on carefully sculpted coral. Their tridents rested on artful pedestals beside them. At the sudden silence, they turned from their conversation to finally notice my arrival. "Rena, how unexpected," my mother said, almost warmly for her.

"What brings you home?" my father asked, coming straight to the point. He waved a hand to dismiss the Mere they'd been speaking to.

"Mother, Father," I called up to them as I bowed my head. "I need to speak with you. Urgently."

"Oh, Sister, how far you've fallen," Yuliya called unexpectedly from a corner near the ceiling, where she lounged on a natural shelf in the reef. "To show your face here with two stubs where your tail should be."

"I've seen you with two stubs too," I shouted back at her, forgetting myself.

Around her upper arms were the golden circlets of the chosen heir, and in her hand was a trident to match my father's and mother's. She'd gotten her desire from the Key.

"My daughters." My father shook his head, and the nearby Mere laughed as if he'd made a joke. To me, he added in a firm tone, "We'll talk in one hour, after we finish plans for the shark hunt."

I swallowed my argument. On the way here, I'd come up with an almost impossible plan, and if there was any hope for me to succeed, I had to catch them in the best possible mood. Even then, it was unlikely.

With a huff, I sank onto a nearby patch of open coral. It bit into my soft human skin and made me miss my tail, which reminded me of Yuliya.

Crossing the room the long way, sticking close to the edges, I tried to go unnoticed. Since my legs drew everyone's gaze, it was a failed effort.

"Sister." I bared my teeth in a smile. Maneuvering through the water onto the ledge beside her, I forced her to make space. "I brought your Key back."

"Oh?" She kept her eyes on the shark hunters while picking lazily at the coral, but her tail stilled, giving her away.

"How about another bargain?" I wanted this done as soon as possible. "I misplaced my shell that changes tails into legs and back again. If you have a spare, I'll give you the Key back early."

"How early?" she asked, glancing over once. "It's only three days until the deal ends, after all."

"I'll give it to you right now. If," I added an amendment, "I get that spell first."

"Need Mommy and Daddy to take you seriously, hmm?" She grinned wickedly, toying with the many shells around her neck but not removing any of them.

"Yes." I didn't bother lying.

"Why should I help?" She'd forgotten to keep up the ruse of watching the discussion below. "What are you going to ask them?"

"I'll tell you," I said with a smile, hoping my secrets would sweeten the deal, "as soon as you give me the shell with the right spell. I'll need to test it to be sure."

She gave me a thoughtful look before finally unwinding a small conch shell and handing it over.

Despite dozens of eyes still on me, I whispered the words that would bring my tail back. The pale human flesh merged into a strong tail. The stabbing pain was familiar now. And worth it. When the spell ended, I touched a hand to my shining red scales and blew out a sigh of relief.

Handing the Jinni Key to Yuliya, I expected a burden to lift, but instead my chest tightened anxiously. This mess was far from resolved.

As I told her my wild plan, I savored the way her mouth dropped open, a reaction I'd never gotten from her before.

* * *

"IT'S SIMPLE." I FLOATED before my mother and father in a small antechamber connected to the throne room. Though I should've stayed still, the urge to move was too strong. I swam from one side of the room to the other. "War is coming. I've seen proof of the queen of Jinn's preparations. The humans need our help now more than ever. If we don't, I have no doubt the Jinn will conquer the humans and the queen will turn them into slaves."

My parents frowned. They remembered how the Jinn ruled. If I'd paid better attention to their stories, I could've used some of them against them now.

"I'm not asking for much," I said. "I believe if the Mere took a small force to guard the human kingdoms, we could stand with them against any invaders." Which were guaranteed to come if the others didn't find a way to stop that Crowning Ceremony. But my parents didn't need to know that. "An agreement between the humans and the Mere could be enough to force the Jinn into keeping the peace."

"We already have peace with them," my father said, frowning as if my plea didn't make any sense. "Why would the humans' plight concern us?"

"Please!" I begged. "What do we have to lose by uniting with the humans? We could benefit from having access to the land."

"I've no interest in the land," my father declared. "And lives are lost in war. I won't risk losing Mere over a human conflict."

"Lives will be lost either way," I argued. "If Jinn overtakes the human world, they'll come for Mere next. They have Gifts you don't even know about and are nowhere near prepared for. It's not a matter of *if* there will be war but *when.* You can't live in fear!"

My father's grip tightened on his trident while my mother hissed her displeasure. That'd been the wrong thing to say.

"It is not *fear* to stay home and save lives." My father gestured with his trident for emphasis. "It's wisdom."

"It's shortsightedness," I muttered, knowing I'd lost. "And it *is* fear because you know, whether you will admit it or not, that the battle will come here one day. You're not saving anything except time. And it will hurt you more in the end. By the time the Jinn get here, the humans will be beaten, and we'll have lost our only allies."

"We don't need those weaklings." My mother brushed the humans aside with a few words. "If it comes to a fight, the ocean will keep us safe. We'll be fine."

My tail stilled, and I slowly sank. "Did you even fight in the Jinni Wars two centuries ago, or was that all a lie?" I swam closer to them. "If you think something as simple as a body of water will stop them, you've forgotten more of your history than I realized."

"Rena," my father snapped, as if I were just a little-Mere again. "Someday you will understand. The safety of our people is our top priority."

"I disagree," I said as calmly as possible, though I was seething. "Our people's *freedom* should be the top priority. Your precious 'safety' will be the downfall of our people. While you keep them *safe*, the queen of Jinn will make them *hers*."

I spun in the water and fled the throne room before I made things worse than they already were. My plan to help the humans had failed.

Chapter 34

Rena

IN MY OLD ROOMS, I ignored my exhaustion, swimming from one hiding place to the next, pulling out shells with existing spells. I could sleep once I caught a ride on a whale. As soon as I strung the shells into a new necklace, I'd leave. With the shell from Yuliya that allowed me to choose between legs and a tail, I could return to Hodafez, where I'd try my best to help. Alone. I feared I'd be as effective as a minnow against a whale, but I didn't know what else to do.

"Maybe you should stay a bit longer," Yuliya said from the door. Her long pale blond hair floated out from her crown, and she absently rubbed the engravings on her trident.

"Why?" I scoffed, tugging out a piece of red coral that hid three shells behind it. It didn't matter if she learned my hiding places; I wouldn't be coming back.

"Because…" She hesitated, rubbing her brow with a sigh before swimming inside to rest on my bed. "Your little speech made more of an impression than you realize. Perhaps Mother and Father aren't listening, but you've caught my ear. As the official heir, I have a say in our future as well."

I crossed my arms. "You're just trying to delay my helping the humans."

"Who even cares about those creatures?" She laughed. "I hadn't given them a second thought."

"I do," I said, more to myself than to her, pulling out some string to tie my small number of shells together. "I care about them." About Bosh especially, though I'd never said so out loud.

"Why?" She sounded surprisingly genuine. "It's not like they have that much value. They have no magic whatsoever. They can barely swim. They're hardly worth saving."

"They're amazing," I argued. "They're kind, loyal, thoughtful, handsome…" I blushed.

"Ah, you're thinking of that human boy you were with," Yuliya guessed.

"Him, and others. The human race isn't as bad as they say. In fact, they have a plan to face the queen of Jinn—" I cut off. I shouldn't have said that.

"What plan?"

Nadia burst past the open door with such speed the current knocked me back a bit. A second later, she reappeared in the coral arch. "There you are," she said to Yuliya, glancing briefly at me. Her small school of orange-and-brown-striped pet fish caught up in two's and three's. "There's a messenger, just arrived, from the human border."

"So?" Yuliya leaned back farther on the bed, putting her head in her hand.

"If rumors can be believed, it'll be the first excitement we've had in months." Nadia grinned. As she took off again, she called back over her shoulder, "He says the human kingdoms are under attack!"

* * *

I REACHED THE THRONE room seconds before Yuliya to find the rest of my family already there, holding court.

A Mere with pale yellow hair and a long face held audience with my parents. He'd already begun delivering his message. "The humans have been fighting since dawn," he was saying.

To a young Mereman near my shoulder, I whispered, "What kingdom was he posted by?"

He shrugged. "I forget. The human kingdoms all sound the same."

"Was it Hodafez?" I pressed.

"Shh," he answered, scowling at me before pointedly returning his attention to the messenger, who was still speaking.

"Both sides have Jinn." The messenger's long face held no expression, and his voice was equally flat. "The attackers seem to have the advantage. I'd estimate they'll fight through tomorrow. Two days at most. Looks likely the invaders will win."

"We should go watch," one of Yuliya's friends said with a laugh.

"This is not some show," I snapped, and my voice carried. Those nearby turned to look. Including my parents. "They're dying. We have to help them."

"We've already had this discussion, Rena," my mother said.

"That's a very good point. We *did* talk about this exact scenario. I told you the Jinn were going to attack the humans, and *you* told me that was highly unlikely. Well, here we are. And what else did you say was highly unlikely when I tried to warn you?"

"Rena," my father cautioned.

I pushed on. "I said that the Jinn will come for the Mere next." That got a few reactions, though many of the Mere around me were more intrigued by my outburst than my words. Still, I had to try. "You can deny it all you want, but why would they stop with the humans?"

"We're not worried," someone called out from the other side of the room, and other Mere cheered.

This was another failure. I narrowed my eyes, debating which approach to take as a last resort. I wasn't above using my people's pride against them. A split-second decision made up my mind, and I raised my voice to make sure everyone heard. "I made an alliance with the humans."

"You didn't!" My mother was aghast.

"I did." I raised my chin, hoping they wouldn't see through the lie.

In the corner of my eye, Yuliya moved. Despite myself, I glanced over. She held the Jinni Key and whispered a name over it. Even from this distance, I could guess whose name it was.

Above my head, a dark cloud with a vision appeared at the call of the Key, revealing my deepest desire. It was Bosh. His cuts and bruises were gone, and his arms spread wide as I ran into them. My incredibly intimate and embarrassing hope was on full display in the crowded room. I threw all my energy into the desire to get back to him and nothing else. *Please, nothing else.*

"She's very familiar with the human," one Mere murmured, and other voices rose. "Her claims may actually be true."

Yuliya let the vision fade, cold blue eyes on me, considering. "It looks like an alliance to me," she said to our parents, loudly enough for the entire room to hear. The support from her, of all Mere, was so unexpected I could only stare back at her, mouth hanging open. "As much as I hate to say it, this might be a good thing. If Rena promised the humans our help, maybe it's the perfect excuse for us to attack Jinn. After all, they need a reminder of our power; they've been getting too comfortable. Consider that Jinni from last month."

My parents shared a look. What'd gone on here while I'd been away?

"We've much to discuss," my father said over the murmurs. "We'll reconvene at the next tide with a decision."

My lips turned up in a smile that I hid by leaving the room. Not having a decision *was* a new decision since they'd made up their minds before. Or, at least, I hoped so. Some good had come out of Yuliya becoming heir apparent after all. While they barely gave my words a second thought, they listened to her.

I waited in an alcove behind waving red coral until Yuliya swam by. Grabbing her arm, I hissed, "Why are you helping me?"

"Am I?" she challenged. "Or am I helping *me*?"

Brows raised, I asked, "How so?"

"I don't want you here," she snapped. "I doubt you have a real alliance with the humans, but why not make one? Then you can stay with them for good."

"What're you not telling me?" I studied her more closely. On the bottom of her black tail, where the fins splayed out, was thin seaweed sewn in neat rows, making a wild pattern. "What happened?"

"A Jinni happened," she said, eyes bright with fury at someone other than me for once. "And I'm not going to let them get away with it."

"Tell me."

"No."

"Tell me, or I'll tell our parents that I never made an alliance."

"You wouldn't," she said with a slow smile.

"You would test me?"

"I don't need to." She leaned out to check that the hall was empty before swimming out of the alcove. "I already know you won't risk it. That human boy is in love with you, and for some reason you like him enough to show up in Rusalka in a panic with *legs*, so I'm guessing you feel the same."

"You think he loves me?" I whispered back, but she'd already swum off.

I couldn't stop smiling.

* * *

"WE'LL HELP THE HUMANS." The four words I'd been so desperate to hear were spoken that evening in front of everyone, followed by, "We'll send a small contingent in the morning."

"That's too late," I argued from the side once more. "The battle could be over by then!"

"Tomorrow," my father repeated. "We need time to gather supplies and plan."

I could go on ahead. In fact, I could slip out tonight—

"Rena will help Yuliya lead the Mere into battle as her second-in-command since this is her scheme."

"But, Father!" Yuliya and I yelled at the same time.

"No arguments. I've made my decision."

Yuliya yanked me by the arm to where the general's table was carved into the corner of the room. "You will do whatever I say," she hissed in my ear before we reached the others. "You're to be a figurehead only." Fine by me. As long as we got there in time.

It'd been a full day now since Jedekiah's betrayal—I just hoped the humans could last another.

Chapter 35

Arie

WHEN HAD I LAST slept? I wiped the hair stuck to my sweaty forehead with the back of my hand. My fingers were covered in ash from fires put out earlier. So was my dress. We were losing. Badly.

This was the second day, or rather, evening, of the attack. There were still two days until the ceremony, though it felt like a month had passed in the span of one single night. These soldiers didn't fly the banner of any kingdom. In the shadows helping them, we'd counted at least a dozen—if not two dozen—Jinn on their side.

We'd lost the outer wall briefly, then gained it back when our own Jinn joined the fight. That was a broad term for what they were doing. Gideon led the others in my harebrained scheme to pick up humans unawares, travel to a distant or neighboring kingdom—anything at least a day's ride away— and drop them off.

Dwindling numbers had made them pull back to recoup. We used that time to come up with other defensive Gifts from our own Jinn, which led to a more cautious approach on both sides.

Still, they continued to wound and kill my men, taking less care to hide their Gifts with each hour that passed. At any moment, they could decide to reveal their hand and forget about those Jinni rules, breaking the only buffer we had left between us.

"You need to rest," Gideon said, appearing at my shoulder as I moved through the wounded soldiers, checking on them, trying to raise morale. In the chaos, he had to repeat himself twice before I heard him.

"I will once this is over," I shouted back, glancing up at him. Gideon's long black hair, usually swept back neatly, hung tangled and dirty in his face, and he was paler than usual. "Any word of Kadin?"

Shaking his head, Gideon waited until we'd moved out of range from the wounded sprawled throughout the great hall. "There are pockets of resistance throughout the town. They aren't speaking with me or my kind right now, for obvious reasons, but he could be with one of them."

Could be. My eyes fluttered shut for a moment, and I took a deep breath. He *had* to be. "Keep an eye out."

"I will," he said, sagging back against the wall.

"Maybe *you* should rest," I added, turning to listen to a general's report, giving him instructions and then continuing on my weary path. "You're the one using your Gifts. That takes far more energy than my walking across a room. Go lie down for a bit."

"I will if you do too," Gideon said with a weak smile.

The lack of argument was enough to make me stare at his retreating back. Sometime in the last few weeks, I'd finally forgiven him for the Severance. It'd never been his choice. I knew that now. *When this is all over*, I promised myself, *we'll speak of everything we've left unsaid for so long.*

* * *

AS THE THIRD DAY of fighting dawned, just one day before the Crowning Ceremony, I was nearly ready to admit defeat.

The town walls were riddled with gaping holes, homes were still burning, and my people were camped between the inner and outer castle walls, in the courtyard, and inside the castle itself. With the windows boarded over, the great hall was dark, both in lighting and mood. Families huddled together. Hushed conversations filled the room. The sheer number of voices reminded me of when I'd first discovered my Gift. The twinge of pain from that reminder was sharp but didn't last as long as it used to—there was too much going on.

My men worked in tandem with the Jinn, who were no longer bothering to hide, mainly because the Jinn who worked for the queen had finally revealed themselves as well. They were beginning to take prisoners wherever they breached our lines—almost as if to say, by the time this was over, the rules would no longer be relevant. It wouldn't matter if a human was harmed, deceived, or stolen from with a Gift after this battle because if they had anything to do with it, we would all belong to the queen.

"Your Majesty," Captain Navabi said, approaching with brow furrowed.

I tensed, prepared for the worst. "What is it now?"

"That redheaded girl? Ah, the one who lived here before? We caught her entering the castle from the ocean side through the shipping dock. She claims—"

"Arie!" Rena's yell cut him off. "Arie!"

I jumped to my feet, staggering down the hall. When I turned the corner, there she was, lurching forward as if she'd forgotten how to walk.

Tears of relief bubbled up and I hugged her. "You're okay!"

"Good enough," she agreed impatiently. "I brought help, but your captain isn't paying any attention to me. You need to listen!"

"I'm listening." I pulled back. "Go ahead."

"The Mere can combine spells to create an enormous boundary over Hodafez that will push all the Jinn out," she said in a rush, gesturing to the empty hall behind her. "But we need to act fast, before it's too late."

"The Mere?" I asked faintly, glancing at the empty space she'd waved toward.

She sighed. "They're still in the water. They don't want to look foolish attempting to walk on two stubs for the first time with an audience. Not to mention your shipping dock is too small. But we don't have to be on land, we just need your permission!"

"You have it—but wait," I added as she turned. "What about the Jinn on our side? I don't want them forced out."

She pursed her lips. "Hmm. Maybe I could... that could work," she muttered to herself.

I glanced back toward where Captain Navabi, the wounded, and all their families lay just around the bend, depending on us.

"Meet me at the library," Rena said. "I'll bring back the old boundary there. Anyone who's inside *should* be protected and able to stay."

I didn't question her. There wasn't time. Nodding, I told the captain to do whatever she asked as she took off down the hall. Calling back to me as she went, she added, "Tell the Jinn to get to the library immediately. As soon as I set the spell, I'll return to the ocean, and we'll push the Jinn out. If they're not within the old boundary by then, they won't be protected."

That would apply to humans with a Jinni's Gift as well, like me. Turning on my heel, I ran to warn everyone I could find.

* * *

"IS EVERYONE HERE?" I yelled as I raced into the library to find many Jinn already inside, along with Gifted townspeople. Some I'd never met, while others—like the elderly healer who shuffled among them—were familiar. "Where's Gideon?"

"He was coming, my queen," Benaiah answered. I barely registered his face.

"He knows the Mere will act any second, doesn't he?" I couldn't hide my panic.

"He knows, my queen," another calm voice replied. Hands guided me to a chair. I dropped into it, back aching and legs trembling with exhaustion.

Will we know when the spell happens? What if it's too late?

A moment later, a crash like thunder rolled over us. The resounding boom made my skin tighten, as if lightning had struck close by. The Jinn around me tensed.

Had the Mere changed the tide of battle? Instinctively, I looked for the one person I trusted to tell me the truth, but Kadin was still nowhere to be found.

Chapter 36

Nesrin

I KEPT MALAKAI HIDDEN in my room. He didn't want to face anyone. After lunch, I brought kabobs and rice upstairs when no one was looking, hoping he might break out of his dark mood soon. This was my third day of hiding him, and my family was growing suspicious of how much time I spent in my room.

He sat by the window, accepting his plate when I handed it to him, taking a bite the way one might take medicine. "Did I tell you," he said absently, "after we were locked out of Jinn, I was desperate enough that I tried all the *daleth* I knew of—even the one we used when I was a dragon."

At my questioning look, he clarified, "The small portals between the human world and Jinn. Remember? My mother closed all the known daleth years ago. That last one in the cliffs was the only one she hadn't found. Of course, she closed it when her spies found us using it."

"Maybe there are others the queen hasn't discovered," I suggested. He'd barely taken two bites.

He shook his head. "Impossible. The only way I even found it was through my sense of smell as a dragon. Their aroma is so sweet and strong."

His words tickled my memory. Why did that sound so familiar?

He finished eating in silence. It wasn't until I was clearing the food to bring the empty plates back to the kitchen that it hit me. I smacked my cup down with such force that a little crack climbed up the side. "Sweet smelling, you say?"

For the first time since he'd arrived, Malakai grew alert, focusing on me. "Yes. Why?"

"I have something to show you."

∗ ∗ ∗

HE WASN'T CONVINCED UNTIL he stood directly in front of the fragrant banyan tree with the gaping hole in its trunk.

When he leaned into the hole and his head disappeared from his shoulders without warning, I choked.

"It really is a daleth," he said in awe when I yanked him back out. Dazed, he stood there blinking, a slow smile spreading across his lips. "We might actually have a chance!"

When he moved back toward the portal, I grabbed his arm. "Are you going *now*?"

"No, no. I just need to see what island it is," he replied, as if this made complete sense. "I'll only be a few moments."

Biting my nails down to the quick, I paced outside the opening until he finally returned with an even broader grin than before.

"It's Urim, only one island over from the capital city of Resh!" he said with a whoop, swinging me around unexpectedly.

I laughed and hit him on the arm. "Put me down!"

My signature blush came back without warning as I slid down the front of him.

He kept his arms around me.

I didn't step back.

"Do you realize what this means?" His voice was a reverent whisper as he tucked a bit of my hair behind my ear. "Thanks to you, we may still be able to stop the queen's plans."

The full weight of his attention made me tremble a little. Pulling away, I turned to study this daleth again as if I hadn't traced every bump and whorl of the honey-colored bark while I'd waited for him. "What will you do?"

"The ceremony is tomorrow. As soon as I tell the others that we have a way in, our plans can resume." He paused as a shadow crossed his face. "If anyone is still there."

"Will you come back?" I loathed the slight quiver in my voice. I cleared my throat and straightened, turning to face him. "I suppose you'll be far too busy."

"Not too busy for you," he said with a knowing smile. "I'd hoped you might consider coming with me."

"To Jinn?" I tensed.

"Yes. With one stop first, to tell the others."

I'd turned him down before and regretted it. But this was *Jinn*. He wanted me to enter the very den of the dragon—while the beast was still inside.

Despite every instinct that screamed to beware of the Jinn, that old familiar thrill of adventure curled up my spine. A slow smile spread across my face as I nodded. "I accept."

* * *

I GATHERED ONLY A day's worth of my usual supplies, unsure what I'd need for a trip like this, and left a note for my family so I wouldn't be forced to waste hours on explanations.

We didn't have that kind of time.

What I didn't expect, though, was for Malakai's Traveling Gift to halt so abruptly, colliding with an invisible wall that felt like it was made of bricks. My vision turned white with little sparks dancing across it, and the air was knocked out of me. Coughing and blinking tears from my eyes, I dragged in a shaky breath.

Malakai was just an arm's length away in the foliage between the trees, suffering the same symptoms.

"That wasn't"—I coughed—"supposed to happen"—a heavy breath in and out—"was it?"

He shook his head, unable to speak.

We'd landed in nondescript woodlands. The trees here were much smaller and scruffier than those back home, with foliage all the way to the forest floor. They crowded our view, filling it with greenery and blue skies, until I swiveled around to find a mountain at my back. At the tip, balanced on the edge of a cliff, was a small stone castle.

"That's Hodafez," Malakai choked out, still struggling to catch his breath. "That's where we should be right now. Something's wrong."

Chapter 37

Arie

A SMALL GROUP OF Jinn huddled around something or someone in the gallery.

A trembling heat flooded through my veins. I grabbed my skirts and ran toward them, pushing through to see.

No.

It was Gideon.

They'd laid him on a thick rug, where a dark pool of blood was forming beneath his chest. His breathing was labored.

"We need a healer," I cried as I dropped to my knees beside him. "What happened? Where are you hurt?" *Is he dying?* His wound seeped blue blood faster than any human wound I'd ever seen. *I never told him I forgive him for the Severance.*

When Gideon tried to move, a young Jinni held him down, pressing clumps of fabric against his side and chest; both turned blue rapidly. "We think he encountered a rogue Jinni," she whispered. "He didn't say. And my skills at healing are limited to small cuts at best. We need Sapphira... but we can't find her."

The Jinni healer. "Can't find her, as in...?" I couldn't say either fear out loud. *Killed in the fighting, or forced out by the spell?*

She only stared back.

"Move aside, move aside," a woman called, growing louder as she pushed through the Jinn without fear.

It was the elderly healer from the village. I blew out a heavy breath. "Help is coming." I took Gideon's hand. "Hold on."

His eyes were closed, but his chest still moved. "Where's... Prince Malakai?" He coughed into his sleeve, and when the coughing spell passed, there was blood left on the fabric. With help from those around her, the old woman lowered herself to the floor beside Gideon, peeling back the bloody cloth to look at his wounds.

"The prince is still indisposed, High Commander," one of the Jinn said. Her eyes shifted nervously, not meeting anyone's gaze. "I'll let him know you're asking for him."

"I need him *now*," Gideon replied, though his voice was weak and far less commanding from the floor. "Tell him it's urgent. He'll understand."

When the Jinni stuttered, searching for another excuse, my lips parted. "He's not here. Is he?"

Her silence confirmed it.

"Did the spell force him out with the rest?" I asked, hoping for Gideon's sake my suspicions were wrong, but again the Jinni was silent. "He left before the spell," I said for her when it became clear she didn't want to be disloyal to her prince. My last words came in a whisper as I remembered how many days it'd been since we'd seen him. "Long before the spell."

All around us, Jinn shook their heads in disbelief. They'd stayed to fight for their prince, but their prince hadn't stayed for them? It was almost as if I could truly feel their emotions, the betrayal and defeat. I understood completely.

A deep Jinni voice spoke over the murmurs. "Jedekiah would've warned the queen by now anyway. It's time we admit defeat. We've lost."

"It's not over yet," I called back automatically, but my voice lacked conviction. It felt over.

"Arie," Gideon whispered.

I lowered my face to his. "I'm here. What is it?"

"It's my time," he said between breaths. I shook my head, but he wasn't done. "There's something you need to know, something I should've told you." He was struggling to get the words out, his breathing ragged. I barely heard him whisper, "About your mother."

My mother?

What secrets had he been keeping?

"Give him space," the healer said, waving a hand at me.

One look at Gideon's closed eyes and labored breathing, and I reluctantly stepped back.

"I'll try to slow the bleeding first, and do what I can," the woman said, placing a hand over his chest. "Make sure I'm not interrupted."

I opened my mouth to ask questions, then shut it. I nodded to the others. "You heard her."

Uziah shifted beside me. Maybe his Sleeping Gift would help Gideon feel less pain. Squeezing Gideon's hand, I whispered, "It's going to be okay, just rest." And to Uziah, I added, "Can you help him sleep?"

He nodded, kneeling, but Gideon's breathing had already slowed, and his groaning stopped.

"It seems he's fallen asleep on his own," Uziah replied with a small frown.

I hoped that wasn't a bad omen.

"Your Majesty," Captain Navabi said as he burst into the gallery. For once, the couple dozen Jinni eyes turned on him didn't seem to faze him. "We've managed to turn the enemy back. When the Jinn disappeared, the men seemed to think they'd been abandoned and turned tail. We're filling the gaps in the wall now." He hesitated, daring to meet the eyes of the Jinn who'd fought beside him and his men over the last two out of three days of battle. "We hoped we might ask for your help."

The Jinn agreed. Those who could travel flashed out of the room immediately. I took over applying pressure to Gideon's wounds so the young Jinni could go as well. The thought of what they would see on the battlefield terrified me. My people's blood stained the streets. What if this was only the beginning?

"Send men to help quench the fires," I instructed Captain Navabi as he turned to go. "And a messenger to the Mere to ask if they'll reconsider meeting." They deserved our thanks—if they could be persuaded to leave the ocean. "Where's Bosh?"

He moved into my line of sight. "Here."

"Can you go with the captain and help him speak with Rena?" I could only hope she'd bridge the divide between our people. It likely wouldn't be the last time we'd need their spells.

"Rena's here?" He ran toward the door. "Why didn't anyone say so?"

"Keep an eye out for Kadin too," I called after him, and my voice broke a bit.

Bosh was already gone, and the captain followed on his heels.

I leaned over Gideon's unconscious form, carefully applying pressure when the healer told me to, ripping new strips of cloth from my dress when the old ones soaked through. His breathing was ragged. Kadin could be in even worse shape, for all I knew. *Kadin is fine,* I promised myself for the thousandth time. *He can take care of himself. He'll probably be back any minute.*

Gideon's hand was cold when I picked it up, but he was still breathing. "I need to tell you something," I whispered, and I could only hope he heard me. "The Severance wasn't your fault. It wasn't your choice. I know that. And I need you to make it through this so I can tell you I forgive you."

His fingers shifted slightly in mine, but his eyes didn't open.

Time moved in jumps and starts.

I rubbed my eyes with one hand, forgetting the soot until I'd already smeared it across my face.

When Rena appeared at my shoulder, I startled. "I've brought help," she said by way of greeting, kneeling in the blue blood beside me.

Behind her, a small-boned man attempted to kneel as she had and nearly fell over.

"Bend your legs," Rena told him, pointing. "There, at the knee. That's it."

He half knelt, half tumbled to the ground on Gideon's other side next to the healer, who frowned at him warily. Pulling a shell from a great strand of shells around his neck, he ignored her and held it over Gideon's wound. "It's not good," he said after a moment.

My heart sank.

Then he shrugged, pulling another shell from his repertoire, murmuring a spell. "At least it's an old-fashioned sword wound and not Jinni magic," he said to Rena, and he had the nerve to chuckle. "*That* would be a lost cause by now."

Gideon's eyes fluttered. He didn't wake.

I couldn't tell if I was imagining it, but his breathing seemed a bit easier. The elderly healer and I exchanged a glance and let the Mere work.

"This will take a while." The Mere finally addressed me directly, though I noticed he didn't use any honorifics.

I didn't take offense. Taking my first deep breath all day, I turned to Rena. "The battle is won, thanks to you."

She wasn't behind me anymore. I swiveled until I found her and Bosh on the other side of the gallery, locked in a fierce hug. If I'd had more energy, I might've smiled at the sweet reunion, but instead it only served to remind me of Kadin.

"I should go find the captain," I said, mostly to myself since the Mereman clearly didn't care.

As I tried to stand, the room spun and my muscles ached in protest, forcing me to drop onto the nearest sofa. "Rest a moment, Your Majesty," the elderly healer said in a firm voice, helping me lie back. "You can't take care of everyone if you don't take care of yourself."

I nodded. "I'll just rest for a short moment." When was the last time I'd slept?

I closed my eyes in relief and slept a dreamless sleep.

"Arie, Arie!" Bosh's voice broke through the muttering. "I found Kadin."

Opening my eyes, I found Kadin leaning over me, his golden gaze on my face.

"Where *were* you?" I spoke through the thick tears in my throat as I sat up. My fingers twitched, wanting to reach for him.

The dirt on his face came into focus. Had he been sleeping on the ground? "It was a bit difficult to get around the fighting over the last few days," he said as he sat beside me, leaving a small space between us. *A bit difficult.* Typical Kadin understatement for saying it'd been absolutely impossible.

With a glance over at Gideon, still asleep on the rug with the Mereman working beside him, I whispered, "I was worried about you." The library windows were dark. How long had I been sleeping? A few Jinn stood or sat within my line of sight, all of them exhausted. They must've finished helping with the wall and returned for the night.

"You don't need to worry," Kadin said softly, eyes on Gideon, brushing my words away. "I don't want to be another obligation."

"You're not," I argued, frowning.

His head turned, eyes on me now.

"I missed you," I finished lamely. That wasn't nearly the whole truth. Sucking in a deep breath, I scooted toward him, closing the space between us. "I thought you'd left… because of what I said."

For a beat, he didn't answer. His hand brushed mine, and he took it lightly. "I did."

"I'm sorry," I whispered. "I didn't mean it."

"I know." He rubbed his thumb along my fingers. "But I would understand if you did."

I didn't know what to say. Staring down at our hands, I wove my fingers through his. "Kadin… you mean more to me than you realize. Which I suppose is my own fault…"

"Come here," he said, gently tugging me into his arms. We lay back on the sofa, and I rested my head on his chest, soaking up his warmth. It was like coming home. Occasional shuffling of feet, the Mereman's muttering to the healer, and the grandfather clock's ticking were the only sounds as we lay there.

At some point, I fell asleep again, waking when the Mereman awkwardly stood and coughed. He was staring down at the blue blood on his hands as if he didn't know how to clean them.

Reluctantly, I pulled out of Kadin's arms to sit up. "How is he?"

"It will depend on the next few hours," the Mereman said simply as the healer brought him a warm bowl of water and a towel to clean his hands. "He's not out of the shark's circle yet."

Gideon muttered something unintelligible.

The dark room was turning gray with the coming dawn. As the sun rose, the remaining Jinn joined us in the gallery, a few at a time. The mood was somber.

"Has anyone found Sapphira?" I asked no one in particular, staring around the group.

Benaiah stepped forward, unshed tears shimmering in his eyes. His voice was hoarse. "She didn't make it, my queen."

I winced, squeezing my eyes shut for a moment to hold back my own tears. "Who else did we lose?"

They listed a few others. Bosh chimed in with numbers Captain Navabi had shared for my people, and Rena tallied a small number of Mere.

I shook my head, unable to process the shocking amount. "You were just supposed to sneak soldiers away in the night, not fight them. It shouldn't have been so dangerous." I waved at Gideon with my free hand, clutching Kadin's with the other. "This is all my fault. I need to be alone." Pulling away from Kadin, I rushed out of the gallery before they could see my tears fall, moving into the privacy of the shelves.

I'd asked them to fight.

I might as well have killed them myself.

A heavy weight settled over me until I couldn't stand anymore. Curling up in a chair in the corner, I wept.

How had it fallen apart so fast? Just a few days ago we'd had the rightful heir, a full force of Jinn willing to stand for him, and a plan to stop the Crowning Ceremony and declare him the true leader.

Now we couldn't stop anything. Couldn't get into Jinn. Couldn't even be certain Gideon wouldn't die in front of us.

Fury rose at my helplessness. I took a book from the table beside me and hurled it at the wall. It didn't help, but it was better than sitting still. I stood and grabbed the book beneath it, throwing it with all my might at the same spot.

Fists clenched, I whirled to the shelves behind me and ripped the books off them so they tumbled onto the floor. Blood pounded in my ears, and I didn't hear Kadin behind me until he grabbed my hands, stopping another pile from hitting the ground.

I wrenched out of his arms. "Leave me alone!"

"Arie, they've gone insane out there!" he yelled. His grip on my arms was almost painful.

Of course they have. They've lost everything. I pulled away, too upset to speak, kicking at the heavy shelf beside me and wishing I was strong enough to make them all come crashing down on top of us.

Belatedly, the uproar reached my ears. Screaming and yelling came from the gallery, along with a heavy crash I wasn't sure I wanted to know about.

Kadin's hands were in his hair, making it a mess before he reached out toward me, palms up. "Arie," he said slowly, approaching like I was a wild animal. His voice was strained. "Gideon is going to be okay."

Hope filled me at his words, and I stilled. "Did the Mereman say he's going to make it?"

The gallery grew quieter.

"No…" Kadin paused. "I just meant he's going to pull through."

"How do you know?"

"I don't. But you have to have faith that he's strong enough to beat this."

Even as he said it, my hope faded and the anger returned.

Chapter 38

Kadin

"ARIE, YOU NEED TO be calm." I'd followed her into the shelves but had kept my distance until a few moments ago. The golden light of the rising sun lit her hair in a soft halo.

"Why?" she snapped, storming down the aisle. "Everything's fallen apart."

Anger and pain bubbled up inside me too, but I fought it. The pandemonium behind us escalated again. Through the arch that led to the gallery, I had a perfect view of the Jinni who threw a heavy chair into a dainty glass sculpture. Shattered glass flew everywhere, spraying out into the shelves and landing at our feet.

I pulled Arie close, shielding her. "You've got to trust me!" I yelled over the racket. "Take deep breaths."

She tried. Inhaling, she blew out a breath, fists clenching.

I took her hands in mine, smoothing them out, rubbing them as she took a deep breath, and another.

No more sculptures shattered.

Was it my imagination or was the volume lowering as well?

"Arie…" I tried to find the words. "I think… don't get mad, but I think you're doing this."

She frowned. "What do you mean?"

I struggled to find a way to say it that wouldn't sound crazy. "Hold on." I held out my hands as I backed away. "Just stay here. I'll be right back."

Crossing her arms, brow wrinkling, she waited as I ran back to the gallery. There—the Jinni with a clean, careful haircut and thick black brows. I remembered him because he'd calmed the others' emotions that first week when a group of Jinn had been bent on harassing me. "Jonah?" I asked. "Could you come meet with the queen?"

He followed me back to where Arie waited. I didn't waste any time. "Have you met Jonah?"

She frowned. "Of course. He kept the training sessions calm. We've worked together frequently since he arrived." Her brows rose as her eyes widened. "Are *you* behind this madness?" she asked, waving toward the gallery.

Shaking his head, he held up both hands. "I swear to you, I'm not. I don't understand what's happening."

"I do," I said. "Or at least, I have a good guess." As Arie listened quietly, the room calmed a bit more. "Arie, this will sound strange, but… I think it's you."

Arie crossed her arms.

Immediately, I felt defensive. But I was growing better at recognizing when it wasn't actually *my* emotion. This wasn't the first time this had happened, either. Not just in the gallery earlier, when I'd felt irrational bouts of despair, but also in the last few weeks, when I'd experienced small moments of illogical moods that hadn't matched my situation. They'd made me question my sanity. *No.* I paused, stunned. It was even deeper than that. The entire Jinni army had mirrored her mood at certain points, growing dim and melancholy or fiercely resolute. Looking back now, it was clear she'd been developing some kind of ability without any of us even knowing it.

To Jonah, I gestured behind us. "Could you help counteract what's going on?"

He was staring at Arie but tore his eyes away when I spoke and said to me softly, as if to keep it a secret from anyone else, "I'll do my best. If it really is her, she's strong."

"Listen," I said to Arie, unsure how to answer Jonah. "What you're feeling is washing over everyone like a wave. When you cried for Gideon, we all cried. When you thought there was a chance, everyone felt hopeful. When you started throwing things back here, well, let's just say Bosh and I got out of sight pretty fast."

I thought she was considering it, but she shook her head, sinking down to sit on the floor. Leaning against the shelves, she covered her face with her hands. Her words came out muffled. "Kadin, if this is some strange attempt to distract me from what's going on—"

"It's not."

Her face was still hidden, and she didn't answer.

I glanced over my shoulder at Jonah, who stood at the other end of the shelves, focused on the Jinn beyond. The yelling had ceased.

When I turned back, Arie had lifted her face from her hands, tears streaming down her cheeks. "I hate that you're making me think about the Severance."

"I'm sorry." I knelt and pulled her into my arms to cradle her, blinking tears from my own eyes. "That's not my intention, I swear."

She sniffed, swiping at the tears. "Kadin, even if I hadn't had a Severance, it doesn't make sense. That was never my Gift."

"I know." I rested my chin on her head, holding on to her like I'd wanted to for months, and now she was finally letting me. "What I'm trying to say is... maybe it is now."

She shook her head, lightly bumping my chin.

I pulled back to meet her eyes. "It's new, and I'll admit I don't fully understand." I blew out an uncertain breath. "I might be wrong, but... what if I'm right?"

A numbness spread over me. It wasn't mine. Was this how she'd felt the past few months? "Arie, don't give up. It's not over yet."

She didn't answer for a few minutes. We just sat quietly. "It doesn't make sense," she finally whispered. "I've never heard of a new Gift after a Severance."

"No one's survived a Severance this long before," I reminded her bluntly. "Gideon said in all the cases he's known of, the suicide attempts always succeeded eventually." We didn't have time to tiptoe around the truth. Even so, I didn't want her thinking that was a forgone conclusion. "*You're* different. Those Jinn and Gifted humans were always cast out of society, left completely alone. That's not going to happen to you because we're not going to let it."

"I still don't understand how I could have a new Gift..." She shook her head as she said it.

"Trauma changes everyone."

She couldn't argue with that.

From the end of the shelves, Jonah gave me a nod to signal he'd gotten everyone's emotions under control before stepping out of sight to give us privacy.

"There are only a few hours left until the Crowning Ceremony tonight," I said, stroking her dark hair. Some of the pain was hers, but a lot of it was also mine, watching her sink into herself and being unable to stop it. "We can't give up yet."

Whether it was her new Gift or not, I didn't know, but her despair was almost a physical wall between us. "It's too late. We've lost our chance."

"Arie, listen. I know you don't feel hope." I needed to find the right words because I couldn't lose her again. "I don't feel it either. But maybe... maybe you can use your Gift—or the strength I *know* you have inside—and you can *choose* it."

Chapter 39

Arie

"I HAVE TO THINK." I pulled out of Kadin's arms and walked away without a specific direction in mind. I needed to be alone.

Wandering away from the gallery, I found myself in the dusty old workroom in the back of the library where the ancient texts were kept under glass cases. It'd been ages since I'd last come here.

As if they had a mind of their own, my feet carried me toward a specific book. I knew the title without even reading it: *The Land of Jinn.*

Lifting the glass case, I set it to the side softly, then began to turn the pages that I'd read months ago—what seemed like a different lifetime ago. I didn't know what I was looking for until my finger touched her words, my mother's handwriting, there on the page. *They fear us.*

The last time I'd seen it, I'd thought I was only human. Then I'd embraced my Jinni heritage only to have it stripped from me. Now I didn't know what I was anymore.

Of all people to think of in this moment, Jedekiah's voice came to mind.

Everyone knows themselves.

"Stop showing off," I muttered as if he could hear me.

I flipped through the pages to the next place I knew I'd find my mother's handwriting, on the genealogies. There was a long list of names followed by one scribbled in at the very bottom of a Jinni family tree: *Hanna.*

Idly, I kept flipping. I was the daughter of a Jinni and a human king. I was the ruler of Hodafez and the former owner of a Gift. There was no one in the human world more suited to stand up to Queen Jezebel and bridge the gap between the humans and the Jinn.

I could almost hear Jedekiah's voice in response. *Well done, darling. You finally figured it out.*

"I didn't figure anything out," I argued out loud. "I can't do it." My voice in the quiet room brought me back to reality. No one else was here.

I focused on the pages turning until I reached the end of the thick volume. There, on the last blank page, was a tiny inscription I'd missed before. In the same swirly handwriting as the other two notes, it said: *For my daughter, that she might know who she is.*

"That might've been who I was before," I murmured. "But you didn't stay here to protect me. I've changed. Everything's changed. I'm not a daughter of Jinn anymore."

No one argued with me.

Except my subconscious.

Qualified or not, I was the only one left. With Gideon out of commission, the prince missing, and the rest of the Jinn scattered to the wind, there wasn't a single other being trying to stop the Crowning Ceremony that would take place this very evening.

Was Kadin right about my new Gift? Could I actually *choose* hope?

In the depths of the dark feelings swirling around me—self-loathing, numbness, hatred, disgust, and hopelessness—I tried to craft a feeling out of nothing.

It was impossible.

Every other emotion fought it. Honestly, I didn't *want* to feel better. Didn't want to heal. Didn't want to save anyone, least of all myself.

Putting the glass case back over the book, I pushed the thoughts away. "I'm going to try," I said out loud. Speaking seemed to help push some of the darkness away. "I want to try," I repeated.

The tiniest ember of hope sparked.

I imagined lifting it up, protecting it, fanning the flame to make it burn brighter.

I had to figure out how to choose hope.

There was still a chance. We had to try.

When I exited the small room and made my way back to the gallery, the spark wavered, but I held on.

Gideon slept while Rena, Bosh, and Kadin watched over him, and another two dozen Jinn kept vigil. It wasn't until I saw my own hope reflected in each of their faces that I finally began to wonder if Kadin was right.

"We need to do just two things," I told them as calmly as I could. "One, we need to find a way into Jinn before the ceremony. Gideon said it takes place at sunset, which means we have until the end of the day. Two, we need to find the prince."

"Yes, my queen."

Why do they still insist on calling me that?

Kneeling next to Gideon and the Mereman Rena had brought to help him, I asked more quietly, "How is he?"

"He will recover."

My eyes filled with tears again. I nodded. "Stay with him." When he looked to Rena instead, I added, "Please."

Only when she nodded did he agree.

The desire to find my bed, lie down, and let everything run its course was beginning to overwhelm me. When I didn't immediately stand, Kadin moved closer to hold out his hand and pull me up. I gripped his hands until my knuckles turned white before facing everyone else. "Let's get started."

Chapter 40

Nesrin

I'D CAUGHT MY BREATH, but Malakai still wheezed as if he'd run the whole distance.

His words from when we'd first unexpectedly landed here echoed in my mind. *Something's wrong.* He'd crawled backward, away from the mountain with the castle, and kept going past a dozen trees before he stopped.

"What's going on?" I'd followed his slow pace, taking in the quiet wood as I did, noting the sound of metal clashing high above us, echoing down the mountain.

"I can't go any farther," Malakai had managed to say. His already pale face had been white as a dragon's tooth, and he'd swayed a bit, staying seated on the ground. "There's a barrier of some kind." To himself, he'd mumbled, "It doesn't make sense. It's not a Jinni spell... I can't even see it..."

"Well, it's obviously not human," I'd said with a smirk. "So who does that leave?"

"It can't be Mere either. They've barely surfaced in centuries," he'd scoffed, then frowned. "Could it?"

I'd shrugged.

"Well, there was that one Mere girl," he'd contradicted himself. "But one girl could hardly create a spell so vast..." He'd stared toward the castle as if the answers would appear.

I'd followed his gaze, but there'd been only puffy white clouds floating over the distant castle.

Now, though we'd followed the edge of this strange barrier to a road, he was still unable to get any closer to the castle itself. As he dropped to rest on the ground once more, I crouched down in front of him. "Listen," I said, waiting until I had his attention. "You obviously can't go any farther. But I can."

"No," he said, already shaking his head. "It's not safe. There's clearly a skirmish of some kind taking place."

"I'll be fine."

"They won't recognize you," he protested.

"I'll make them." I stood, cracking my knuckles, getting ready for a light jog. I tilted my head at the incline in the road ahead. Maybe a sweaty one. "After all," I said to Malakai, "you said it yourself: we don't have time to waste."

* * *

THE CASTLE WAS FARTHER away than it looked. Or maybe it was the incredibly steep terrain slowing me down.

I'd missed this though—the familiar thrill of adventure making my bones hum with excitement.

Malakai had told me exactly what to say to make sure they listened. He'd made me repeat it word for word until satisfied I wouldn't mess it up.

"I'll be back before you know it." I'd given him a mock-serious look. "Just do me a favor and don't go anywhere for once."

He'd given a weak chuckle, dropping back to sit on the ground. "Don't worry. That won't be an issue."

* * *

THE STREETS WERE SHEER madness when I arrived in the small town. Instead of fighting, though, they seemed to be celebrating. Frowning, I focused on the castle, ducking out of sight whenever soldiers passed. It was easier to avoid questions than accidentally answer them wrong.

The people were different here. Darker skin, but lighter eyes. My black eyes and olive skin stuck out like a dishonest hunter peddling a fake dragon's egg.

"I'm here to see Queen Arie of Hodafez," I told the guards at the entrance to the castle courtyard, just like Malakai had told me to.

"Come back in a few weeks," one of them snapped, lifting his weapon as if he'd been using it a lot lately. "The queen can't be bothered with foreigners at the moment. There's been enough of that here for a long while."

"I must speak with her," I insisted, peering around him to the courtyard inside. There were more guards. Too many to dodge. "Tell her it's about Prince Malakai." The castle rose above us. The only access was through this gate—the other sides were guarded even more heavily by the sea and a steep cliff wall.

"We're not telling her anything," the other guard sneered, stepping forward in an attempt to menace me away since words hadn't worked.

I was familiar with his type and didn't move. Or speak. There was no arguing with a bully.

Malakai's words over the last few weeks came back to me. Every time we discussed something new, he'd say, *You're Khaanevaade. You can do things a normal human can't.*

That gave me an idea. I turned on my heel and ran.

"That's right, turn tail," the guards shouted after me, jeering.

I flung up a crude gesture but didn't stop or even look back.

I had a cliff wall to climb.

* * *

WHEN I REACHED THE top, my muscles burned, but I felt wildly alive. I hadn't done a free climb like that since, well, since I'd met Malakai in dragon form.

I didn't have time to ponder it. When my head popped over a balcony, a guard spotted me. He yelled to others, and half a dozen raced along the battlement toward me.

I flung myself across the balcony, through a door into an empty bedchamber, and on into another room, followed by a hall, down some stairs, yelling at the top of my lungs the entire way. As I raced ahead of the guards on my heels, I repeated the phrase Malakai had told me to. "On behalf of Prince Malakai, I need to see the queen!"

When guards appeared at the other end of a hall, I pulled a knife from my boot and leapt across a decorative pool to get away, racing down another long hall, screaming, "I need to see the queen!"

A door opened ahead of me.

I raced toward it, hoping it wasn't a guard. This castle wasn't *that* large. How long would it take to track down this queen? Maybe I'd passed her.

"On behalf of Prince Malakai," I panted, reaching the door just as a young woman peered out. "I need to *see the queen*!"

"I'm here," the young woman said as I ducked around and behind her, nearly bowling her over.

I expected the guards to rip me away, but when she held up a hand, they stopped.

"Your Majesty," the guards called, surrounding her protectively and forcing me back. "Be careful! She's dangerous."

I snorted at their foolishness but was secretly flattered. *Your Majesty.* Their words sunk in. This was the queen I'd been looking for? I blinked, confused. She was so young. Pretty. With lines of sadness around her eyes.

She glanced at me. "It seems if she wished me harm, she would've done so already."

My thoughts exactly. Out of respect for the young queen, I kept my opinion to myself.

The guards bowed with red faces, glaring at me, unconvinced.

"Queen Arie," I murmured, bowing belatedly when she turned to me.

She was beautiful in a fragile sort of way. Her deep ebony black hair reminded me of Malakai. A pained look that twisted her full lips in worry.

"My name is Nesrin, and I'm here on behalf of Prince Malakai of the Jinn," I said in a rush. Now that I was here, I didn't want to lose the opportunity. "We found a portal into Jinn—a daleth, he calls it." I glanced behind me and jerked back, almost bumping into the queen's guards when I found over a dozen Jinni eyes on me. I swallowed, hard. They didn't seem friendly. "There's some kind of spell keeping him from returning. He sent me to summon you so he could take you to the portal."

"Summon us?" a Jinni said.

"Why should we trust you?" another asked.

"Malakai—*Prince* Malakai,"—he'd been very strict that I say his words exactly—"said he told you of his time as a dragon, when he was cursed by his own mother."

That silenced them all right.

This next part felt awkward, but Malakai had said it'd be crucial for the Jinn to believe me. "I'm the one who broke the curse."

Unlike my people, who would have been in an uproar, these Jinn stood like statues, taking in my words.

"Come," I urged them, my own words this time, since Malakai's hadn't left as much of an impression as he'd thought they would. "We don't have much time. Follow me, and I'll bring you to him."

Chapter 41

Rena

BOSH CAME RUNNING THROUGH the tall grass toward the sandy beach. "Rena! Arie needs to talk to you!"

I stood in the shallows, conferring with Yuliya and the other Mere, discussing how long we should keep up the barrier. "I'll be right back."

Bosh splashed into the water before I reached the sand. Stopping just a breath away from me, he said, "Hi."

"Hi." I grinned, even knowing Yuliya and the other Mere looked on. I didn't care. "Hold the barrier until I get back," I called over my shoulder. "I won't be long."

Without waiting for an answer, I lurched into a run with Bosh across the sandy hills that led to the castle. "Is Gideon okay?"

"He's fine," he puffed between words, "but the prince came back—"

"He's here?" I tripped and nearly fell flat on my face. He caught my arm, taking my hand and pulling me along the upward path. Grateful, I let his momentum drag me forward. "Is the plan back on?"

"I'm not sure." Bosh's fingers were warm against mine.

I tripped a second time before the ground thankfully leveled out, and we ran through the side gate into town. "I'm glad you're okay. In case I didn't say so."

With a grin, he half hugged, half pulled me along. "You're telling me. I was getting ready to come find you myself."

"You would've needed fins and gills for that to work," I teased. That was a nice image actually. I'd think on it again later when my lungs weren't burning. This stitch in my side was demanding to be heard right now, and romantic conversations were difficult to have when out of breath.

When we reached the inner wall and paused for the guards to open the door, I caught my breath enough to ask, "What does Arie want?"

"I have no idea," Bosh replied unhelpfully. It was so good to be annoyed by him. I'd missed this.

Outside the castle door, he paused. "I really don't know what I would've done if you hadn't come back..." He trailed off, serious for once.

Placing my hand on his arm, I grew serious too. "I was always coming back. I hope you know that."

He gave me a wide smile. "Of course." A blush spread up his neck to his face. "You had to because you still haven't told me you like me, and it's not like you to leave something unsaid."

I laughed, catching his hands when he held them out. "If I don't say it out loud, does that mean I have to stick around forever?"

Pressing his forehead to mine, his eyes twinkled. "I think it does."

Neither of us said anything for a moment, then he took a deep breath and turned to knock on the door. "Better not keep Arie waiting."

* * *

ARIE'S LADIES-IN-WAITING were struggling to fit shiny armor over her riding clothes. The unscuffed armor, made when she'd begun training with the Jinn, fit her perfectly—though it'd clearly never seen an actual battle.

When she caught my reflection in the mirror, she waved the servants away. "Give us a moment, could you?" She took a step forward, then stopped to clasp her hands together. "Rena, how can I possibly thank you?"

Twisting the fabric of my sleeve, I shrugged. "It was the right thing to do. I know you would have done it for me. Well, if you could swim for more than a few minutes—"

"No," Arie interrupted. "It's not just the right thing. You saved thousands of lives. And it's more than that. It's also the last few months…" Her voice grew soft. "I know it probably didn't seem like I heard you. But I always did. I needed you more than you knew."

I didn't know what to say. My cheeks grew warm. We didn't spend much time on gratitude in Mere. "It was the right—you would have—you're welcome." I cleared my throat. "Let me see this armor. It's buckled so loosely, it'll fall off at the first big wave. Uh… wind."

She let me redo the work. The leather was tougher than woven seaweed, and the armor breastplate reflected light like the ocean's surface.

Arie took my hands in hers, drawing my attention back to her face. "I called you here because I have something to ask you." She cleared her throat, letting go to face the mirror. "As usual, we're short on time, so this is more informal than I'd like."

Frowning, I stared at myself in the mirror. I still wore the same green dress I'd had on days ago. The bottom was shredded into rags. Next to Arie, in her gleaming armor, blue tunic, and fancy leather buckles, I looked ridiculous. What could she possibly need from me?

"I'd like to know if you might be interested in being an ambassador between the sea and the land."

I forgot her fancy boots with their own armor, meeting her smiling brown eyes with a grin. This was exactly what I'd hoped for. "Are there nice clothes in this deal?"

Arie laughed a little. "There can be. Absolutely. And a room here that's yours whenever you need it."

"I think that could work." This was the deal I'd told my parents was already struck, but she didn't need to know that.

"If you're willing, maybe you could start today?" she continued, taking leather sleeves and buckling them to her forearms. "You'd just have to work with Captain Navabi until I get back."

When she struggled with the ties, I stepped forward to help again. Resisting the urge to complain about how Captain Navabi treated me like a child, since an official ambassador probably didn't go around doing things like that, I just said, "Whatever you need."

As I tied the last knot, frowning at it, she added, "I could ask someone else to assume control while I'm gone, if you'd rather come with us?"

"To Jinn?" I asked, then shivered. "Absolutely not. There's no way I'd break the treaty first. My parents would kill me, right after the Jinn did."

Satisfied, Arie tugged at the buckles again; they were all tied tight. "Good. Because someone needs to look after Gideon and make sure he continues to heal. We also need to talk about what you'll do if I don't return—"

"You'll come back."

"But if I don't, Captain Navabi will be instrumental in finding a successor, and he could use your help—"

"You'll come back," I interrupted, grinning at her. "You haven't given up yet, and even if you tried, I'm pretty sure *he* wouldn't let you." I nodded toward the reflection of Kadin in the mirror, where he'd stepped quietly into the room.

Arie spun around to face him. "Is it time?"

He nodded.

As she turned to go, Arie faced me one more time. "Thank you, again. I mean it." She held my gaze until I nodded before spinning toward the door. "Try to keep the kingdom safe while I'm gone!"

I grinned at the new notes of cheer in her voice. "No promises, but I'll see what I can do."

They left, and I stood in the empty room, gathering my courage to go back into the hall and face Bosh. I couldn't decide which job was scarier, taking over a kingdom or telling a boy how I felt, but both of them were exhilarating. And I didn't want to wait any longer.

Chapter 42

Arie

THOUGH WE'D MOVED GIDEON to a comfortable bed and his wounds were wrapped, Kadin still had to pull me away. "I don't want to leave him like this," I whispered. "What if he doesn't make it? What if I never see him again?"

"You will," he reassured me. "Try to relax."

He didn't need to remind me that I was sharing my panic with everyone. I closed my eyes and breathed deeply.

"We'll be back to check on him before you know it," Kadin said, squeezing my hand.

"I don't know if I can do this," I said softly so no one else would hear.

He pulled me close, pressing his lips to my forehead. "That's what I'm here for. We'll do this together." Turning to the Jinn, he stepped in as he had with the kingdom over the last few months and began calling out orders. "Travel together. Watch for any rogue Jinn once outside the boundary. Follow the road toward Keshdi that Nesrin described." Just minutes later, he'd paired each of the humans and the few Jinn unable to travel with a Jinni partner who could. "I assume that outside this library Rena's boundary will force you out, so I suggest aiming for a good distance outside of Hodafez."

We flashed out of the castle.

The first two times we appeared on the road, Nesrin just shook her head and said, "Farther." My stomach twisted uneasily, and I found myself thankful I hadn't eaten any breakfast.

Respect for the Mere rose in my mind as I glanced back over my shoulder and found my home a distant miniature on the mountain.

When we landed the third time, we'd gone too far. Nesrin pulled away from the Jinni, running back toward the castle and rounding the bend.

We followed. Sure enough, there was Prince Malakai pacing in the road. He didn't notice Nesrin until she flung herself onto his back, laughing. I couldn't tell what they said to each other, but he swung her around and then turned to face us.

We drew up quietly as Nesrin filled him in on Gideon's injury and the few Jinn who remained.

Before I could speak, the prince addressed us as formally as if we stood in a great hall instead of in the woods. "I owe you all a sincere apology." He gazed at each face in turn. "I thought I could face my mother alone, but I was a fool. I couldn't even get home." Drawing in a breath, he continued. "No one can succeed on their own. We all need help. *I* need your help," he amended, gazing at the tall girl under his arm. "Nesrin taught me that."

I turned to look at the girl more closely, along with the rest of the convoy. She blushed. Her nearly black eyes never left the prince.

"It's because of her that we still have one last chance to stop my mother from ruling for another fifty years," Prince Malakai said. "But I won't force you to fight for me, like my mother does. Whether or not you choose to go with us, I will respect your choice."

The Jinn glanced between one another, and Uziah stepped forward to speak for them. "We've already made the decision, my prince—my king."

When Malakai's gaze turned to me, I cleared my throat. "The humans are on your side as well." I glanced up at Kadin, the only other human in the entire party besides Nesrin. His shoulder brushed mine as he nodded back in silent agreement.

The prince, who'd echoed Gideon's formal manners until this point, broke into a grin. "Well then, it's settled. If we succeed, all of you will have a place in the new reign." To all the Jinn with the Traveling Gift, he added, "Follow my trail. I'll lead you to the daleth."

They nodded.

Softly, he added, "Let's hope we can get home in time."

"No pressure, hmm?" Nesrin mumbled, wrapping an arm around his side as his arm settled over her shoulder again. Her olive skin and dark eyes contrasted his light skin and pale eyes; they complemented each other.

Sighing, I copied her with Uziah, preparing to be travel-sick again. "We're ready when you are."

I instinctively glanced back for Kadin, but he'd already flashed away. Another breath, and we followed, leaving the warmth of the woods behind in the blink of an eye.

Our feet touched dirt and grass, and I let go, stumbling a bit. Traveling made me dizzy.

"We're here." Nesrin whispered at the head of the group. "Keep your voices down—we don't want to catch a dragon's attention."

We stood in a clearing. All around us were enormous trees, larger than I'd ever seen before.

Malakai didn't even pause. Stepping up to a tree with a gaping hole at its base, he leaned down to squeeze inside.

He disappeared.

There one second, gone the next.

I gasped as the Jinn cheered.

Nesrin shushed them. "Dragons," she hissed, pointing at the nearby cliffs. "Hurry."

They ducked through one at a time, as quickly as possible, as a roar sounded in the distance. Another joined it.

Kadin cleared his throat behind me, and I ducked through the dark hole with him on my heels.

The world rippled as I stepped into the hollow of the tree, and where I should've run into rotted bark, I stepped into a wide-open space filled with soft morning light. We stood in a forest of pink trees with pale white bark, vivid green grass beneath our feet, and a sun that had doubled in size.

I pointed to where it had begun to climb up into the sky. "I hope we're close because we're running out of time."

Chapter 43

Kadin

I KEPT TO THE edges of the small group. Only sixteen of us remained, and the Jinn who hadn't gone rogue grinned and spoke in excited whispers, showing more emotion in the last few moments than they had the entire last month.

This had been our end goal all along. We were finally in Jinn. My skin prickled.

On the surface, Jinn appeared harmless: rolling hills, vibrant green grass, lush forests with strangely colorful trees, pure-white clouds floating through the cheerful blue sky. The only notable difference was the sun as it rose above the horizon, larger than normal. It cast a pale golden light over everyone.

Arie glanced at me frequently as she and the prince spoke.

I smiled back, reassuring. I'd keep my reservations to myself, but I wasn't naïve. This entire quest was a disaster waiting to happen.

Malakai raised his voice for all of us to hear. "It's decided. We'll travel once more and arrive in full force at the palace gates. That will be the most public and therefore the most impossible to ignore." He held out a hand for Arie and Nesrin. All three of them disappeared.

Unconsciously, I took a step forward as if I could follow on my own. Frustration warred with embarrassment.

"Here." Uziah held out a hand.

I took it. My whole body tensed as we flashed into yet another unknown space.

Unlike previous traveling, where we landed effortlessly, this time we slammed face-first into something solid.

I fell back with a ringing in my ears. An explosion of pain crossed the side of my body where I'd hit.

Hit what?

Groaning, I opened my eyes.

We'd landed in a field of giant flowers. The stalks were as tall as corn. Each one had a blue flower on top as large as my head. No matter which way I turned, there were only blue flowers worshipping the sky.

Our landing had created a small crater. Dragging myself up, I stood stiffly.

The huge stalks rippled in the wind, creating the illusion of standing in a strange sea.

Another pair of Jinn fell backward out of thin air above us.

I scrambled out of the way.

They fell next to our crater, making a new one.

Someone moaned. Peering through the thick stalks, I spied Arie, Malakai, and Nesrin and pushed through the stalks toward them, touching Arie's arm lightly to reassure myself as I asked the prince, "What happened?"

Lips set in a grim line, he stood, dusting himself off. "It seems the queen has placed extra protection spells around Resh, our capital." Malakai exhaled heavily. "We can't travel there."

"How close are we?" I pushed past him through the tall stalks, some of which were thick as my arm, hoping to find the edge of the field. Leaves hit me in the face.

Abruptly, I stopped short.

Just one more step, and the land dropped clean away.

Fluffy white clouds drifted far below.

Malakai snatched the back of my shirt, pulling me away before I fell face-first.

I offered him a silent nod of thanks, trying to catch my breath.

"That's the edge of the island," Malakai said, as if it were the most normal thing in the world. "Resh is one island over. That's what I was trying to tell you."

Island. My brows rose. I turned for a closer look at the drop-off before me.

"Is there a way between these islands on foot?" Arie asked.

If it was a true island, I feared the answer.

As the clouds shifted, other islands appeared and disappeared, floating in the distance. Some were close enough to make out whole cities, rivers, and roads. Others were mere specks in the sky that I would've mistaken for a bird if I hadn't known better.

Each one was widest in the middle. Their dangling roots mirrored the shape of the earth above, making them look like rough diamonds.

"There are bridges," Malakai said with a layer of meaning to the Jinn gathering around us. Some of them shook their heads ruefully while others grew still.

Squinting, I could just make out a thin line dipping between one island and the other, and another, much closer. "Bridges?" I said dryly. "Does anyone actually use them?"

"They do," the prince said slowly. "But each bridge has a small contingent of the Jinni Guard stationed at each end."

"Any chance we can somehow walk right past them?" Nesrin asked, crossing her arms.

The prince took in all of us waiting for his answer and finally said, "We've come this far, so I suppose there's a chance."

I grinned. Trying to sneak onto an island in such an obvious way reminded me of my years of robbing castles. As we followed Malakai through the field of flowers, my years of planning heists kicked in. "What's the Jinni Guard trained for?"

"All manner of Gifts, as well as physical combat," another Jinni whose name I couldn't remember replied.

"Mmm," I murmured. "Is *that* all?"

Malakai frowned at me over his shoulder. "Should they know more?"

I waved him off. "Never mind." I considered the Gifts of the Jinn around me—or rather, the Gifts I *knew* of.

"You." I pointed to the shortest Jinni, trying to remember his name. I should've spent more time with them. There were sixteen of us total, yet the only Jinni I knew well besides the prince was Uziah.

"Zacheus," he offered.

"Zacheus," I repeated, committing it to memory. "You can imitate any music. Can you also imitate animal noises?"

"I suppose... though it would be quite degrading—"

"Good," I interrupted. To Malakai, I added, "Are there any predators in Jinn that would cause your kind to worry?"

"A dragon?" a Jinni with knives strapped to her tall boots suggested. "Tamar," she said, offering her name at my blank look.

Malakai held a hand to his lips, slowing to a stop as we neared the edge of the field.

I shook my head and whispered back, "That'd make them hide. I'm looking for something that'd cause them to go on the offensive."

"Maybe a Lacklore?" Uziah suggested as we all carefully peered out through the stalks toward the bridge. Just as Malakai had described, a small guard shack stood in front of it.

I lifted my brows, waiting for an explanation.

"Sort of a bearlike creature with an ox head," Malakai murmured, and Nesrin shivered where she stood beside him, touching three long scars on her arm.

We peered out at the one visible guard, and Malakai's brow wrinkled. "If Zacheus made a Lacklore call, it'd lead them straight to us."

"That's why you two will travel to the other side of this field, make a racket, and come back."

"They'd track us too quickly," Uziah said.

But Malakai slowly grinned. "Not if we traveled a few dozen times first. We could leave a maze of trails that overlap and make it ten times more difficult."

"We could lead them on a wild chase while everyone else crosses," Uziah finished, nodding to himself. "It could work."

I studied our surroundings, thinking. The flowers cut off in a clean line, making a small clearing of short too-bright grass. Without the stalks to impede our view, the steep drop-off was sharper than a knife. The bridge was larger up close, though still thin enough that if two people met in the middle, one or the other would have to turn back. It glowed a soft unearthly silver, and the rope handrails looked about as sturdy as thread.

"This is a smaller bridge," Malakai whispered to us over his shoulder. "But it'll still be equipped with at least four guards."

276

At least three more inside then. Or out and about? Hopefully it wouldn't matter once we began. Once we'd discussed every angle, Malakai clapped a hand on my shoulder. "We're as ready as we can be."

Hesitating, I nodded. We didn't have time for an elaborate heist. Right now, all that mattered was getting the prince to Resh in time to stop the ceremony. We'd just have to hope for the best.

The three of them flashed away.

After a few moments, an awful gurgling howl arose from the flowers on the far side of the field, soft in the distance.

The guard out front flinched. Another Jinni slammed through the door of the shack at the racket. Three more came through the door behind him, so that made five total.

The leader called out commands, and they scattered. Three took off toward the noise, while the other two stayed by the bridge.

I frowned. It wasn't as effective as I'd hoped, but two would be easier to take down than five.

Waving silently for everyone to wait, I whispered, "I wonder if we can draw those last two out as well."

As they discussed other Gifts that might work, Arie crept up to my side. She glanced at the others, then leaned closer to my ear and drew a breath to speak. But words didn't come. Instead, the same hideous screeching of the Lacklore spewed out.

Up close, it nearly made my ears bleed. I winced and jumped back.

Her eyes flew wide. She clapped her hands over her mouth, cutting off the terrible sound. But it was too late. The two remaining Jinni guards turned in our direction.

The surprise factor was gone.

I grabbed Arie's hand, pulling her in the opposite direction from the bridge, and we ran. Although I wanted to blame Zacheus or another Jinni, I knew what I'd seen.

Crashing to one side of us ended suddenly in a thump. Then another ahead, and another behind. Yells and thrashing struggles followed.

In the corner of my eye, flames lit a patch of flowers on fire. Whether they were from the Jinni Guard or our own, it was impossible to know for sure.

I pulled Arie along faster.

She squeezed my hand back, keeping up with me, holding tight.

Our only hope was to lose them.

We zigged and zagged like rabbits, and as the distance grew, the sounds of fighting softened.

"Here," I whispered to Arie as I tugged her down to the flat ground. Surrounded by stalks, it was as good as any place to stop. We knelt, trying to quiet our breathing. Arie didn't ask questions; she understood. The waving stalks would give away our path faster than anything.

A pair of flower-blue eyes appeared in front of me through the stalks, staring directly at our hiding place, as if the Jinni guard had somehow seen us right through the whole field.

I pulled Arie up by the hand, turning on my heel. "Run!"

Too late.

The breath was knocked out of me as if I'd been tackled. My muscles locked up, and I fell to the ground, hard.

Chapter 44

Arie

I DODGED THE JINNI who reached toward me with hands that glowed luminescent white.

She caught Kadin instead.

Under her touch, he dropped as if he'd had a heart attack.

"No! Kadin!" I tried to catch him. Instead, his deadweight knocked me onto the ground, and he fell on top of me. The impact knocked the air out of my lungs.

"Get up," I choked out, pushing him. He was heavy and unresponsive. "We have to run! Wake up!"

When he didn't respond, I panicked. Gasping, I turned to find his eyes wide-open, blinking furiously—he was still alive, paralyzed somehow by her Gift.

The female guard knelt beside us, staring down at me with a bored expression as she let the glow of her hands flicker out, returning to their normal pale color.

I'd effectively captured myself.

With a shrug, she rolled Kadin off me.

When I tried to land a punch, she snatched my fists out of the air and tied me up with ease. Placing one hand on my shoulder and the other on Kadin's, where he lay still and unmoving, she traveled with us to the guard shack and dropped us on the cold stone floor within.

The small shack was one big room with bars and a cell door blocking off the side that we were in. On the opposite side, narrow bunks were built into the wall, along with shelves full of supplies, and a small table with chairs took up space in the center.

A guard sat at that table, making notes in a ledger as the rest of us were brought in, humming to himself as if he recognized some of the Jinn.

With my hands and feet tied, I awkwardly rolled up to a sitting position and leaned against the wall.

Kadin, still paralyzed, was on the stone floor beside me. Rolling him over, I checked his pulse and his breathing, both normal. I placed my bound hands on his shoulder in comfort, wishing I could help him up. While he still couldn't move or speak, his breathing calmed a bit.

A fierce white handprint glowed on his arm where the Jinni had touched him. Glancing around the cell at the handful of our group who'd been captured, I noticed more glowing handprints on the necks, arms, and even faces, while other Jinn were merely tied up.

They must have recognized one of ours from when they'd banished her the first time. She was gagged and had gloves placed over her hands, which were tied behind her back. *How wild are her Gifts if she can scare the Guard?*

Stuck here, thinking of Gifts, my mind turned to what had gotten us in this predicament. Kadin hadn't said it out loud, but I knew: *me.*

I counted. Ten of us captured so far. Malakai was among those still fighting back. Explosions shook the little shack.

This small cell had four narrow slabs of wood built into the wall for sleeping. Clearly, it wasn't designed to hold all sixteen of us. When the guards flashed in with new prisoners, they knocked into each other, shoving tied-up prisoners aside to find an open place on the floor to set them. They carried tall crystal weapons the length of a spear with a sharp point at the end.

The Severed part of me whispered to just give up. What did any of it even matter? Another part, the little seedling of hope that I'd been nurturing over the last month, fought against the idea. *It's not over yet.* I willed myself to believe it. *It's not over yet. Malakai is still out there.*

A guard flashed in holding a thrashing Nesrin, who, despite her hands and feet being tied, managed to land a solid punch in his gut. He winced, though he didn't double over. Throwing her roughly into the room, he let her land on two of the paralyzed Jinn inside.

"Sorry," she said as she rolled off them and glared at the guard.

That just left Malakai.

But the Guard had more training. More preparation. More everything.

And they were thorough.

It'd taken less than a quarter hour for them to track down and capture every single one of us.

"Silence!" the leader snapped when we tried to murmur to one another. I attempted to communicate hope through a glance instead, meeting their gazes one by one.

Until Malakai was captured too.

Paralyzed *and* tied up, they dangled him before us, or at least before those whose heads weren't angled away, unable to see. "I think this is the one the queen told us to watch out for," the tallest Jinni said to the female guard who'd captured Kadin and me. They still hadn't addressed any of us directly. "I wonder what's so dangerous about him."

"We'll find out after the ceremony," a Jinni with bushy eyebrows and silver-gray hair said. I'd never seen a Jinni as old as him before. He was thin, even a little gaunt, though his skin didn't sag like a humans, and his eyes were still sharp as they crossed over mine. I made myself blink and shrink back as if scared. It wasn't hard to do. I *was* scared. Thankfully, it seemed to work; he didn't look at me again.

It's not over yet, I told myself for the thousandth time. My eyes betrayed me, veering away from Kadin to Malakai's still form in the opposite corner. Nesrin had crawled over the others to get to him, but there was nothing she could do while they were watching us so closely.

Leaning my head back against the wall, I resisted the urge to close my eyes and focused on Kadin instead. If his paralysis wore off, he could untie me, and we could break free.

Of course, the guards were a step ahead.

The silver-haired Jinni finished going through the shelves and pounded herbs together, dropping them into what looked like wine. He brought it to the cell door, which another guard opened for him, and knelt next to the nearest prisoner, tipping the full wine glass to her lips. "Drink."

With almost half our group paralyzed by those glowing handprints, it was quick work. He moved around the room, giving each Jinni a small sip. Some tried to fight, but the guard simply shut their mouth with one hand and plugged their nose with the other until they swallowed the concoction.

He passed over us three humans.

Whatever was in that glass, he didn't think we were enough of a threat to need it.

He didn't stop until every single captured Jinni drank.

"What about the humans?" the tall guard asked.

"No need," Silver-hair replied. "There's not a drop of Jinni magic in any of them; we don't bother blocking Gifts that don't exist. Just put them to sleep."

The other guard stepped forward, waving a hand across Nesrin's face. Though she set her jaw stubbornly, as if she would fight him every inch of the way, it only took three seconds for her eyes to roll back in her head and close. She collapsed against the wall, head tilting at a strange angle.

The guard moved to Kadin next. Another three seconds of holding a hand over his eyes, and Kadin's eyelids drooped, body sagging as his tense muscles relaxed. Clearly asleep.

When he got to me, my heartbeat doubled. He put his hand in front of my face.

I felt nothing.

One second. Two. Three.

After the slightest hesitation, I hurried to close my eyes and slumped over, pretending to fall asleep too.

How did it not work on me? Did he notice?

My heart beat so loud and fast in my ears, I was certain he could hear it too.

But his footsteps shuffled off.

First I have one Gift, then another? And now I'm immune. Was my previous immunity from Rena's protection spells, or was that my own doing all along?

A soft conversation that I couldn't make out followed, and then the door slammed open and shut.

I cracked an eye open.

We weren't alone.

The silver-haired Jinni had stayed behind to watch us, though he was busy writing and didn't bother to look up. Why should he when his charges were all neutralized?

I kept my lids lowered, just in case.

Naomi, a female Jinni with thick black hair to her waist who I'd sparred with once or twice back home, sidled up to the bars, pulling herself closer with bound hands. "Abner," she crooned, leaning into them. "Remember me? I could make it worth your while if you let us go. You don't want Queen Jezebel to reign for another fifty years, do you?"

He ignored her.

"Let Prince Malakai challenge her rule. He's the rightful heir," she murmured.

The guard frowned down at the table, almost imperceptibly, growing still at the mention of the prince. Was he remembering? And if he did, would it matter if his loyalty was to the queen?

"You can't just wait it out like the others," Naomi continued. "After all, you likely won't be alive by the time her reign ends."

His mouth twisted in disgust, and he returned to writing and ignoring us. Whatever progress she'd made was lost.

Malakai gurgled something unintelligible, trying to join her in her plea, but his paralysis hadn't fully worn off yet. Around his neck were two glowing handprints, and there was another on his arm. Still, it seemed that the Gift was slowly wearing off. The handprints on some of the others were slowly fading, and as they did, they began to twitch.

Uziah rolled his head from side to side, struggling to move the rest of his body. His Gift put people to sleep too, though he'd never put his hand out like that guard. Maybe it wasn't necessary for him.

Kadin's voice in the library came back to me. *I think you're doing this.* I'd thought I had Jonah's Gift. And then Kadin's eyes flying wide when that noise had come from my mouth—when I'd somehow used Zacheus's Gift. Even if I didn't understand how, there was no denying it had happened.

A memory of injured Gideon falling asleep when I'd told him to fluttered to the surface unbidden. Had I also accidentally used Uziah's Sleeping Gift without even realizing it?

Soft scratches of a pen on paper came from the guard.

Let's see if I really used the Sleeping Gift.

I pinned him with a hard stare.

Nothing happened.

It'd taken months to figure out my old Gift. If I was right that something new was forming—and that was a big *if*—then we didn't have that kind of time.

I bit the inside of my cheek, narrowing my gaze and focusing.

Still nothing.

What'd made it work the last time? *You're insane. You don't have a new Gift. That doesn't happen.* I argued with myself. Another part argued back, *Who really knows what happens?* Gideon had made it clear no one had survived a Severance long enough to find out. Not because someone had killed them, like I'd originally believed all those months ago, but because of the broken pieces it left behind, something I understood all too well now.

I closed my eyes, playing the painful scene in my head. Gideon had lain there gasping, covered in his blue blood. I'd told him to rest, then asked Uziah for help... I'd *told* him.

I tried to swallow, but my mouth was dry. If this didn't work and the guard heard me...

"Sleep," I whispered to him.

It wasn't quick like the other guard's Gift had been. Abner blinked sleepily. Slowly, he sank back against his chair. Though he fought it, his head eventually dropped into his hands, his eyes closed, and he began snoring.

Then, and only then, did I stand.

The Jinni closest to me flinched and yelped, startling the rest of them.

I froze, eyes on the old guard I'd put to sleep.

He didn't wake.

A flurry of whispers followed from the Jinn who were only tied up. "How are you awake?"

"What did you do?"

"Get us out of here!"

I swallowed, holding up my bound hands, and asked my own question. "Why didn't the Sleeping Gift work on me? Are Rena's spells still in effect?"

Rena had said her spells would give us a tingling effect whenever a Gift was used, but I'd never felt that—had I blocked the Gifts of other Jinn in a different way all along? If... if I was truly a mirror of other Jinni's Gifts, then perhaps I reflected their own Gifts back? I couldn't think of another explanation; I tucked the thought away to ask Kadin when he woke.

Malakai's hands were bound behind his back, and the gag was still over his mouth. I made my way across the room to pull it out, attempting to untie him next.

The Jinn around the room hushed one another, eying the sleeping guard warily.

Malakai's paralysis was still wearing off, causing him to fumble as he tried to rub his sore wrists. He lisped slightly as he answered, "You did this?" He gestured toward the guard.

"I'm... not sure," I whispered, hesitating. "But I think so."

He shook his head. "Incredible. I don't understand it..."

My cheeks grew hot. Moving back to sit beside Kadin, I placed my hands on his side to make sure he was still breathing. I wished there was something I could do.

"Who else would it be?" Uziah spoke up from the other side of the cell. His words were slurred too, though the handprint on the back of his neck was almost completely gone. "The other humans are sleeping, and they forced every single one of us to drink Teshuvah. Our Gifts are completely blocked."

I frowned at the unfamiliar word and looked to Malakai.

"The elixir the guard made us drink," he explained. "It buries our Gifts out of reach, like a wall built up between us and our abilities."

A wall. Buried. I took a slow breath and let it out. A thought had come to me, but I was almost too afraid to voice it. "Is that... is there any chance that's how... how a Severance works?"

Malakai's brows rose, and the Jinn around the room murmured in speculation, but no one had an answer. Gideon had always described a Severance like losing a limb, but what if the loss was temporary? What if my Jinni side had never truly been removed, only blocked?

Uziah was the one who finally answered. "Unless one of the guards is secretly helping us, which I highly doubt, you are quite literally the only one capable, my queen, so I suppose it must be so."

I had trouble swallowing and blinked away unexpected tears. Hearing someone else say what I'd been thinking confirmed it. *I'm not without Gifts after all.*

Pretending confidence, I cleared my throat and asked Uziah, "How exactly does your Gift work?" I tilted my head toward the sleeping guard. "Will he wake up if we startle him, or is he fast asleep?"

"What does it matter?" Naomi grumbled from the corner. "We're stuck here."

"He shouldn't wake for quite some time," Uziah answered respectfully, ignoring her. "It would take a stampede to wake him."

"It still doesn't matter," Naomi muttered again.

"I disagree," Malakai replied with a grin. "It matters very much. If what everyone has told me is true, and Queen Arie can imitate all our Gifts, then I believe she could free us."

For once, the Jinn were struck speechless.

I swallowed hard. "Tell me what to do."

"No," someone said. "Too dangerous."

Others disagreed. "How else are we going to get out of here? It's either her letting us out or Queen Jezebel. I vote her!"

As they argued, I moved back to check on Kadin. Still asleep. *What if I could wake him?*

While they continued debating in hushed whispers, I put my bound hands on Kadin's arm and murmured, "Wake."

Nothing happened.

"Stop sleeping."

Still nothing.

To Uziah, I dared to ask, "How does your Gift work when you're reversing sleep?"

His brows drew together sympathetically as he shook his head. "My Gift only works one way. Once they're asleep…"

"Maybe the other guard's Gift would wake him?" I suggested.

That still didn't help me with the actual steps, however. We were quiet for a moment. Malakai cleared his throat. "If you're mirroring Gifts, it's hard to say if you need proximity, recent exposure, or other knowledge that comes from practice and careful training."

"Let's give her some training then," Naomi said with a wicked grin. "Try to remove those ropes."

Holding up my hands, I studied the knots around my wrists. "How?"

"Trust me." Naomi winked. "If you can truly mirror or mimic me, or whatever it is you do, you won't have a problem."

"I don't know what how to do 'what I do'," I muttered, then squinted at the rope and knot anyway.

Nothing.

The Jinn offered suggestions. No result. "I don't even know what you can do!" I snapped after a few minutes. "How can I imitate a Gift or duplicate it or whatever it is that I can do, if I don't know what the Gift even is?"

That led to a lengthy explanation of how her Gift made every impossibility possible.

It didn't help me at all.

Frustrated, I threw up my still-bound hands and said to the closest Jinni, "We don't have time for this. Just take this off for me. I have another idea."

Chapter 45

Arie

THE JINNI UNTIED MY ropes, dropping them to the floor.

I drew a deep breath and blew it out. There was no promise that this would work when the attempt to remove the rope with a Gift had been such a complete failure.

A little voice in my head whispered that I couldn't control this. It would only ever happen by accident.

Another breath. Another exhale.

I refuse to believe that.

Instead, I imagined Gideon, who'd taught me to control my former Gift. It seemed like years had passed since that moment instead of a few short months. He'd shown me just how powerful it was to believe you could do something. To study how you did it, and do it better the second time. Though it'd still taken me a long time to master it, it'd been possible.

So was this.

The most common Gift, which over half of them had and which I'd seen in action more than any other, was the Traveling Gift—crossing enormous distances in a heartbeat. Simple. My traitorous heart skipped a beat.

I tensed my body and willed it to move.

Nothing.

Pressing my lips together, I focused on the small ring of brass keys where they hung on the opposite wall. Where I wanted to be.

Malakai followed my gaze, putting two and two together. "Just picture yourself already there," he whispered.

I closed my eyes and did.

A slightly unsettling feeling passed through me.

When I opened my eyes, I stood in front of the key. "I did it!" I yelled, then clapped a hand over my mouth, darting a glance at the guard.

He still slept soundly.

The Jinn in the cell gave a muted cheer in return, silently clapping for my success.

"Get us out of here!" one hissed.

Another said, "Open the door!"

"Get the key!"

"All right, settle down!" I waved a hand in the air for them to be silent.

Surprisingly, they obeyed.

Snatching the key ring off the wall, the metal clinked together softly in victory.

I darted across the small room and slid the keys into the lock, looking for the right one.

The bolt clicked out of place, and the door opened.

Another subdued cheer rose from our little group as they crowded one another, all trying to leave the cell at once.

"Someone get Kadin and Nesrin," I hissed. Malakai was already untying Nesrin's hands before he lifted her. Another Jinni went back for Kadin, lifting his sleeping form with ease.

At the jostling, Nesrin cracked an eye open. "She's waking up!" Malakai cradled her as she slowly blinked at our surroundings and then focused on his face.

I spun to face Kadin, but he hadn't moved, and his slow breathing didn't change. *Why is she waking up when he's not?* "Don't let anything happen to him," I ordered, trying to keep the worry out of my voice.

"Yes, my queen," the Jinni replied solemnly, bowing his head slightly as he carried Kadin out of the cell. *Again with the title.*

Packing into the small front room, shoulder to shoulder, they kept a careful distance from the sleeping guard and took turns peering out the small window in the door.

Malakai set an unsteady Nesrin on her feet, and she leaned on him as she woke up. "Wait," he called as one of the Jinn put a hand on the doorknob. "If the guards see us, we'll just land right back here. We need a way to overpower or get past them."

A Jinni stepped forward.

"Lyra." He acknowledged her with a nod. She was the one that the guards had bound extra carefully earlier. A party of tattoos played across her skin, and she'd shaved half of her stick-straight black hair, but when I tried to place her and her Gifts, I had almost no memory of her in the library. She'd been one of the Jinn who'd stuck to physical combat and avoided training with Gifts.

Her tattoos changed colors, and she pulled off the gloves that the guard had put on her hands as she said, "I can help with that. I'm a Puppeteer." She wiggled her fingers as if to demonstrate. "My Gift requires touching them, but once I do they cooperate."

Jinn within an arm's reach of her stepped back.

A slow smirk spread across her face.

"That could work." I lifted my chin to project a confidence I didn't feel. "There are only four other... guards."

I stumbled, almost calling them men, though of course the Jinn were not truly men at all. "If we face them one at a time, we could walk them right into that cell and turn the lock."

Malakai nodded. "I agree. Except on one point. It cannot be 'we.' With the drugs from the Teshuvah in our system, none of us can use our Gifts."

My stomach clenched. "How long will that last? You can't expect me to do this on my own!"

"You can, and you must." He held my gaze. "They didn't give us careful doses, so I can only guess at maybe tonight or tomorrow. Of course, they would dose us again long before that, to be safe. If we wait for either of those two instances, it'll be too late." He bent to peer through the small window in the door. "Judging by the sun, the Crowning Ceremony is in just a few short hours."

That explained why I was starving. We'd wasted half the day already. I hid my hands in my skirts so no one would see them shaking. "I can't do it. I couldn't imitate Naomi's Gift, and I won't be able to do Lyra's either because none of you can show me what to do."

"Just try. Try it on me," Lyra offered, blinking rapidly but holding my gaze. "Make me go back into the cell." She took my hand and placed it on her arm.

I sighed.

With a glance at the door, I nodded. "Someone keep watch. This'll take a while."

"That's all right," Malakai reassured me, turning to give commands, sending Jinn to watch the door and to check for more of those crystal spears or other weapons. Five Jinn carefully tied up the sleeping Guard and force-fed him Teshuvah without waking him. To me, Malakai added, "Take your time. Make sure you understand it fully."

Though he appeared calm, I could only imagine the approaching ceremony weighed on him. Throwing back my shoulders, I lifted my chin and faced Lyra. "Explain it to me. In detail. Don't leave anything out."

It took a few dozen attempts. My head ached by the time I figured it out. What surprised me was how easily it came once I stopped trying so hard and let the Gift work on its own.

Lyra took one methodical step after the other until she was inside the cell.

The moment I let go of her arm, she whirled around and raced back out, eyes wide. "That felt terrible. Well done."

High praise from a Jinni.

The others had pretended not to watch, as if that were possible in such a cramped space, and now those nearby clapped me on the back and grinned.

I strode toward the door before I could lose my nerve.

Malakai stepped in front of me as my fingers grasped the handle. "Wait. Next try to puppeteer someone *and* travel."

I hadn't thought of that. I nodded.

Every Jinni within an arm's reach stepped back. "Fine!" Lyra threw up her hands. "I'll do it."

"Seems only fair," someone mumbled. I was too busy stepping forward to take her arm to see who.

First, I took control. It was slippery, but I managed to make her take a step.

"Now, keep your hold on her and travel at the same time," Malakai encouraged, glancing at the door as if he couldn't help himself.

A small part of me was thankful I'd grown up with an audience; still, the pressure of everyone watching was almost unbearable.

"Does Lyra have the ability to travel?" I asked when nothing happened.

"I don't think so," one of the twins said.

"I'll have to copy someone else then," I said to myself, turning all my focus to imitating Malakai.

A second later, we stood in the cell, but Lyra's gaze was no longer vacant, and she pulled away with ease. When I put my hand on her shoulder to travel again, she pulled out of my grip before I could.

"Seems you can only mimic one Jinni's Gift at a time," Lyra called over her shoulder as she hoofed it out of the cell, like she couldn't stand to be in it a second longer. From outside the bars, she stood, breathing hard, and added, "That could be a problem."

"Someone's coming," the Jinni watching the door hissed.

"Everyone back in the cell, now!" Malakai commanded in a voice that wouldn't brook disobedience. "Arie, behind the door. You must catch him by surprise before he sees that the cell door is not truly shut."

I nodded, stepping around the flow of Jinn to the small nook behind the door. On the way, I caught Lyra's arm. "I need you with me." Just in case. I didn't know how close I needed to be to imitate someone else.

She followed, breathing a sigh of relief.

There wasn't time to plan anything further. This had to work. I peeked through the small window, ducking back quickly. They were close. *They.* "There's more than one!" I hissed. To Lyra, I whispered, "Can your Gift handle two at once?"

She nodded that *she* could, but the worried wrinkle between her brows told me she wasn't so sure what *I* could do. Grabbing a small metal pan off the hook on the wall, she said on a breath, "We'll take care of them. One way or another."

The doorknob turned.

Hard shoes hit stone, and the door began to swing shut. The guard closing it opened his mouth, eyes flying open at the sight of us, but my hand was already on his arm. His panic softened into obedience. He was mine.

The other guard was quick to spy the guard we'd tied up in the cell. He turned with a yell, swinging, but the guard under my control was already there, obeying my instincts. I made him take a solid swing at his friend, who ducked. Fortunately, in my direction. The second I got my hand around his wrist, he froze, then straightened into a calm standing position.

Both were under my control.

It took all my focus to walk them into the cell. As soon as Malakai understood, he waved all the Jinn out in a stampede.

"Don't let go," he called as I got the two guards inside the cell. "*Don't let go!*"

Liquid pouring into a cup sounded behind me. "More," Malakai said to someone. "Add this." Footsteps crossed the stone, and Malakai appeared in front of me with the same wine glass and familiar deep red drink. "Make them drink the Teshuvah."

When the guards were fully bound, blocked, and on the floor of the cell, I let go. They immediately began to struggle. Pulling my lower lip into my mouth, I met Uziah's gaze across the room. He nodded. As I imagined taking on his Gifts, Lyra's abilities floated away from me like a cloud, suddenly out of reach. I took a deep breath and whispered over the guards, "Sleep." They sagged back, wide eyes drifting shut, and I let out a breath in relief that at least one Gift came easily.

As they slept, my gaze veered toward Kadin for the thousandth time, where they'd laid him on one of the bunks.

Stepping out of the cell, I moved to his side.

Still asleep.

His pulse beat strong and sure.

I sighed, lowering myself to the ground next to him.

The only sounds in the room were soft breaths and shuffling feet.

Without looking up, I asked, "Now what? Do I go out and lure the last two Jinn into the cell by myself?"

"I have a better idea," one of the twins said. "How about you stay here. Let them come to us."

"Another ambush?" Malakai rubbed his jaw, considering the idea. "I like it."

So did I. I hadn't been entirely sure I'd make it back to the guard shack if I left. But I didn't say that. I only asked, "Do we have time before the ceremony begins?"

Malakai judged the time by the sun and hesitated before he nodded to himself. "I expect they'll return shortly when their comrades don't reappear." When he waved everyone back to their original positions, the Jinn reluctantly returned to the cell, though they left the door open and one of them stayed to keep watch at the door.

Malakai pulled out a chair for Nesrin to sit at the small table, taking one himself and gesturing for me to join him. "While we wait, we must make a new plan for the ceremony. First, we must describe our Gifts to Arie in great detail and discover how her own works. Second, we must devise a way for her to steal the crown."

I started shaking my head as a couple of the Jinn inhaled sharply. "That wasn't the plan. Why would we steal it?"

He steepled his fingers, meeting our gazes. "I think it has become necessary. At this point, we are *all* unable to travel until the Teshuvah wears off, which means we're forced to take the walking paths and may even arrive *after* the ceremony has already begun. We may not get a chance to present our case to the people until it's too late. And if I don't get there in time to challenge the crown, the only other candidate is my mother. No one will even contest it. Arie is the only one who can get there in time."

Chapter 46

Arie

THE LAST TWO GUARDS took us by surprise, coming around the corner from our blind spot. "Get down! They're here!"

Flustered, I searched for Lyra as the Jinn swarmed into position in the cell, trying to switch from Uziah's Gifts to hers, but the door swung open before I'd found her.

There.

Locking eyes on her, I struggled to access her puppeteering ability as the door closed and I came face-to-face with both guards.

I caught the first guard's arm, but the other dodged out of reach. It was the one with the Paralyzing Gift, and her hands glowed as she leapt toward me in a surprise attack.

With one hand still on the other guard, I could only duck behind him.

She overshot me, but just barely, paralyzing the guard under my grip instead.

He fell to the floor.

As she leapt over him with arms stretched out, I panicked, losing my grip on Lyra's Gift completely.

My back hit the wall.

The guard's glowing hands were about to touch my skin when a huge clay pot crashed into her head from behind. It shattered, flooding the room with white flour that had been inside.

She dropped like a stone beside the first guard.

Behind her, as the flour settled, Kadin's determined face appeared, clutching the remaining clay pieces. He swayed a little, groggy.

I jumped over the guard and hugged him. "You're awake!"

"That was close," Malakai said from beside us, where the rest of the Jinn had flooded out of the cell to help, just a few seconds too late. "Now, can you run?"

Kadin leaned heavily on me as we left the guards behind, tied up and drugged in their cell, and ran toward the shining white bridge suspended over the clouds. Kadin lurched forward, stumbling frequently as he wrestled with the drowsiness. Uziah ducked under his other arm to help carry some of his weight.

"Remember," Malakai called out from the front of the group as we reached the bridge and stopped. "Even without the guards to call on the magic of the bridge, it still has defenses of its own. If anyone is on it too long, they'll trip the alarms as well. Once your feet touch the surface, never stop moving."

I tensed.

Taking a deep breath, I nodded with the rest of them. There was no time for uncertainty.

The first Jinni began to cross, then the next, and the next. Uziah pulled Kadin onto his back, and Kadin was too tired to complain as he began to run.

Toes flying across the slats of the bridge, hands not bothering to touch the rails, each of them tore across, ignoring the way the bridge dipped and swayed.

I swallowed hard, the last to go besides Malakai. He held out a hand to help me onto it. "Go! I'll be right behind you."

I ran.

Out of breath, we tumbled onto the bright grass on the other side of the bridge. I dropped to the ground beside Kadin. The Jinni Guard could burst out of the shack on this side at any moment.

"Use my Gift this time," the hulk of a Jinni who'd never deigned to speak to me before said as he knelt beside us with a thud. He cracked his knuckles, eyes on the guard shack.

"It would have to be very simple," I said on a breath, glancing over my shoulder at the door. It was opening. "I don't have time to learn!"

"Just imagine the wind," he said, grinning, "and then shove it toward them!"

Swallowing, I tried not to overthink it. *Wind. Obey me.* A heavy gust rushed over us, knocking me slightly off-balance. *More,* I thought, trusting in the Gift a bit more as the squall grew wild.

I lifted my hands and literally shoved them forward. *Hit.*

A current of air lifted the guards pouring out of the shack up into the air before slamming them into the dirt with force.

"Hold it," the hulking Jinni encouraged me, waving to the others. "Go get them!"

As soon as they were fully disarmed and knocked unconscious, I let go of the Gift.

Glancing up at the sun, which continued a fast descent toward the horizon, Malakai turned a worried gaze to me. "We need to hurry."

"I'll help him from here," Uziah said from Kadin's other side.

"Why would I..." Kadin mumbled, eyelids drooping. He struggled to stand. "Where is she going? Why can't I go?"

"I have to go on alone." I knelt to face him, taking his hands. "I'm going to use Malakai's Gifts to stop the ceremony, but I can't travel with more than one. I have to take him for our plan to work."

It was a terrible explanation, but Kadin squeezed my hand weakly. "Go."

"I'll see you again soon." Tears made him a watery shape in front of me.

"I'll be here. Or"—he glanced toward Uziah as I blinked to clear my vision—"wherever it is we're going."

I nodded but didn't get up. I'd never told him how I felt. *This might be my last chance.* "I think I've loved you since the day you rescued me in that market," I whispered.

"I know." He grinned, golden eyes growing more focused.

I hit him lightly on the arm.

He caught my hand. "And I've loved you longer than I even realized."

"We have to go," Malakai broke in. "No time for heartfelt conversations just now. I swear if I'm crowned king you can talk for a century, but right now..." He motioned rapidly toward the castle looming in the distance in the middle of the large city.

I took his hand and stood. "See you soon," I said to Kadin, swallowing hard as he nodded.

Squaring my shoulders, I recalled Malakai's Traveling Gift, hoping the transition between Gifts would eventually feel smoother and less like stripping off an entire wardrobe for another. "Just tell me where to go."

Holding on to me with one hand, he pointed with the other, describing each landing point as we went. "That place where the forest comes to a point by the small town."

I didn't quite make it that far, struggling with accuracy. Gideon had made this look easy.

"Good," Malakai said. "Now a bit farther next time so you don't tire too quickly. That building at the far edge of town with the steeple, do you see it? Aim for the very tip of the roof. There will be a ledge."

We traveled again and again, crossing this new island in spurts. The castle quickly grew closer. Malakai was careful to choose locations where we wouldn't be spotted.

The others were far behind now. If they managed to run on unhindered, Malakai claimed they could make it to the castle around sunset, though there was a chance they'd miss the beginning of the ceremony.

We flashed up to the main gates, hiding in a small alley. "What now?"

"Now you walk right through the gate."

Chapter 47

Arie

A HUMAN INVADING THE land of Jinn. *Foolishness at its finest.*

The castle loomed in the distance. Its gleaming white stone walls and pointed light blue turrets were surrounded by an ocean of lavender flowers and a vast garden.

"What do you mean *I* walk through the gate?" Terror rose as Malakai turned back to me. "You're coming with me, aren't you?"

"The castle is covered in protection spells." He pressed his lips together, shaking his head. "They've been in place for centuries. I'm afraid the only way is through the gates, and the next Gift I'm going to teach you will only work on you. I can't go past this point."

"No. I can't." I took shallow breaths. "I can't do this."

He held my gaze. "You can."

I shook my head again. "No. I can't. I can't do anything. I can't even lead my people. I shouldn't be here. I shouldn't be their queen at all—"

"Arie, being a leader doesn't mean the fear goes away."

That caught my attention, enough to make the surroundings stop spinning for a minute. I focused on the different shades of pale blue and silver in his eyes. "*You're* not afraid."

"I am. All the time," he said immediately. Hesitating, he added, "But I was arrogant. I thought I could lead on my own, do everything on my own, and didn't need anyone—that this made me fit to rule."

He paused, staring out at those pale stone walls. "Knowing you need people keeps you humble," he added, almost to himself. "It's all right if we're not enough because we're not alone. No one should try to lead alone."

He turned back to me, standing taller. "It occurs to me now that I wanted to lead the way my mother does. Without any input or advice. But that's what makes her unfit to rule. You, Arie, are nothing like her. You will be—and already are—a wise queen."

The voices that followed me everywhere whispered, *He's wrong. You're not good enough to be queen.* I took a deep breath.

His words repelled them. *It's true. I'm not good enough. But I'll try. And that's what matters.*

I glanced over his shoulder at the gleaming light blue turrets, biting my lip. "What is this new Gift?"

"You have to swear you'll keep it a secret," he said instead, fixing me with a serious stare. "There are only three others in the world who know. Four, once I share with you."

I hesitated. "I'm not a quick learner," I reminded him. "I have to understand it, know what it looks like."

"In this case, it'll be what it *doesn't* look like." Malakai smiled a little. "Swear to me you won't tell anyone else?"

I hesitated. I didn't want to keep things from Kadin anymore. *If we both manage to leave here alive and see each other again...* "I promise not to tell anyone *who* I got the Gift from," I compromised.

"That'll have to be enough," he said, glancing at the castle yet again. He drew close enough to whisper in my ear. "Invisibility."

Brows raised, I immediately understood why he wanted to keep it a secret. "No one else knows? Truly?"

He shook his head. "It's what allowed me to attend meetings I shouldn't have overheard, to stay aware of what was going on in my kingdom. If my mother hadn't known, I may've even been able to stop her before she exiled me."

Thinking through all the Gifts that had been described to me earlier, I whispered, "That might be the most valuable Gift of all."

In the quiet alley, my words seemed loud.

Malakai nodded. "When I was young, my mother taught me to hide it. The way she hides many of her own Gifts." He added the last part with a bitter twist to his mouth but continued before I could ask what he meant. "I'm going to teach you to use it. Start by closing your eyes and imagine that the blanket of invisibility is a literal blanket."

I obeyed.

"You let it fall over you," he continued in a rhythmic cadence, "all the way to the ground. Good."

I didn't dare peek to see if it was working.

"Eventually, it will stay in place as if a second skin, but for now, if it helps, imagine clutching the blanket. Raise your hands and actually grip it, mentally." A short pause. "Are your hands raised?"

I'd raised them immediately. It caught me by surprise that he didn't know, so much so that my eyes flew open.

Instead of my raised hands before my face, I stared at the white castle gate before me. Startled, I let go of the Gift. My hands materialized.

"Again," Malakai said.

I envisioned a blanket again, draping it over my head and shoulders, down to my feet.

When I opened my eyes, my hands had vanished once more. Glancing down, I found only the dark tar of the alley.

"You're ready." Malakai smiled at a spot slightly to my left.

Letting go of the so-called "blanket" of invisibility again, I gave him a wavering smile. Some of my old fire simmered. "Ready enough."

"Don't forget the plan." He'd described the castle in incredible detail earlier. "Find my mother. She'll be getting ready in her rooms. The crown will be with her."

"Three floors up," I repeated. "Follow the royal portraits to the largest doors at the end." Another thought occurred to me, and I paused. "What do I do if she's still wearing it?"

"Oh, she'll undoubtedly be wearing it."

"What?" My voice rose a bit too loud. We glanced around, but no one came running.

"The queen never removes her crown. At least, not to anyone's knowledge. It hasn't left her head in a century and a half."

"Why in the name of Jinn *not*?"

"Because of the enchantment." There was that tone again, as if I should have been born with this knowledge. "It enhances all her Gifts. While wearing it, she's invincible. Without it, she's vulnerable."

Chapter 48

Arie

"YOU KNOW WHAT? LET'S just get this over with," I muttered, pulling the invisibility blanket over myself and stepping out into the street.

Malakai chuckled behind me. "You're just like your mother."

I would've questioned the familiarity, but I'd already begun walking.

The guards stood at the gate with long crystal spears, ready to stop anyone who tried to enter without permission. Their gazes roamed the crowd, searching for someone. The prince? Probably.

Clutching the air in front of me with both hands, picturing the invisibility like the thickest blanket I'd ever seen, I walked right past them.

I dodged other Jinn walking the wide path with me, running up the huge castle staircase and into the broad entrance hall. The ceiling rose a stunning four levels above me with a giant shimmering chandelier. I stuck close to the walls as I searched for the staircase that Malakai had described.

This castle was ten times larger than Hodafez and designed to confuse, with hallways splitting constantly in all directions, paintings that looked similar, and no other specific markers.

My stomach clenched every time someone looked my way. Even though they looked right through me, it didn't stop my heart from racing until they looked away.

If Malakai hadn't told me to watch for the floor-to-ceiling paintings of deer frolicking in the woods and pay attention for one with a handle, I'd never have guessed it was a door. *The fastest way to the royal rooms,* he'd explained back in the guard shack after swearing all the other Jinn to secrecy.

When I reached for the handle, I fumbled at first, unable to see my own fingers grasping it. Opening it, I hurried to close it softly behind me before taking in my surroundings. A thin staircase stretched ahead, lit by softly glowing Jinni lights.

I took a deep breath.

In and out.

I could do this.

As I climbed the stairs, there was only the plush red carpet runner where my feet should've been.

By the time I reached the third floor, I was breathing hard. I slipped out of the hidden staircase, letting the tall painting click shut seamlessly behind me and paused to lean against it.

Two guards in ceremonial armor decorated with velvet red draping turned the corner, surprising me. I leapt out of the way just before one of them crashed into me.

At the thump of my hitting the wall, one guard turned, frowning briefly. When the other guard didn't stop, he gave the empty landing a final once-over before hurrying on.

It took a few more minutes to find the right hallway, following the portraits as Malakai had directed, but once I did, the queen's door was impossible to miss. Outside of it, two more guards stood in the same ornamental armor.

Their helmets covered their faces. All that was visible were their pale blue eyes.

Creeping forward, I struggled with my instincts, which screamed at me to run. As I got closer, I moved even more carefully, one painfully slow step at a time.

In my pocket was the letter Malakai had pressed into my hand during a quiet moment at the guard shack.

"Slip this under the door," he'd said. The simple paper was sealed with uncolored wax from one of the guard's candles. "Then be ready. When my mother calls for the guard, they'll open the door in response. You must slip inside *immediately*. Do you understand?"

I'd nodded, but that hadn't been good enough.

"There will be an *extremely* small window. She'll ask who was at the door. The guards will be confused and say no one, and she'll dismiss them. That's all the time you'll have. Do you understand?"

"Yes," I'd repeated.

"This is important, Arie." He'd ignored my sigh. "Every detail matters. As soon as you take the crown from her head, you need to run, as if your life depends on it, to the nearest door or window. Do *not* stop. Do not allow them to see you under any circumstances. And most importantly…" He pulled out more of the same wax that he'd used to seal the letter. This time he'd shaped the wax into small molds. "When you reach the queen's door, you must place these in your ears—tightly—and do not remove them under any circumstances until you're far, far away. Do you understand?"

This third time he repeated the words, they were no longer irritating; instead, they gave me chills. I accepted the wax molds. "Why?"

"Because one of her secret Gifts is something indescribable—somewhere between Charm and Persuasion but stronger than both. And she will have no qualms about using it."

"I don't think I can be influenced by Gifts anymore, remember?" I smiled, genuinely thankful for my Severance for the first time.

But Malakai didn't smile back. "You managed to deflect one guard's Sleeping Gift. That's hardly proof. And as I already said, the crown enhances the queen's Gifts. They're a hundred times more powerful. Even if you have developed an immunity of some kind, it will not hold up under the weight of her Gifts."

I hadn't realized how much I'd come to depend on being untouchable. Safe.

Now that I stood before her door, I was brought back to the girl I'd been less than a year ago, terrified of King Amir and his power over me. The same quaking in my muscles that made them liquid. A shiver lifting goose bumps across my skin.

I stepped closer to the guards until I could've sneezed on them. Malakai hadn't warned me how terrifying it'd be to stand within inches of them, knowing even one overly loud breath might mean my discovery.

I stepped past them into the deep doorway. Kneeling down, I pressed the thin letter to the crack beneath the door and pushed it through softly.

As I stood, I brought the wax molds to my ears and shoved them in. They muffled outside sounds and made my breathing ten times louder. My racing pulse joined in the noise.

The hall had been so quiet.

Could they hear me breathing?

I tried to draw air in through my nose as quietly as possible. With the wax in my ears, it was hard to tell if it helped or not.

My instincts urged me to watch the door. It was a struggle to obey Malakai's instructions and face the guards instead.

His voice came back to me. *Whatever happens, do not let them touch you. When they turn to answer the queen, they'll most likely open just one of the two double doors.*

I'd asked why it mattered. I hadn't been able to picture it. Now I understood. I was boxed in between the doors and the guards. If they opened just one door, I could dodge their reach and stand in front of the other. But if they opened both, it'd be nearly impossible to get out of the way in time.

Plan for them to open the door on the right, and stand before the left. The guard will likely be right-handed. But be prepared to be wrong.

And don't let them touch you, I had said before he could, though I'd wanted to roll my eyes.

Standing there now, I touched the wax again. Would I even hear the queen call? I stared at the guards' stiff backs. I'd chosen a place in front of the left door, muscles tensed and ready.

Behind me, a voice finally called out, muffled by the wax.

After that it was a blur.

One of the guards swiveled around.

Reaching out, his hand came directly toward me.

I ducked under his arm and leapt to the other side just before he would've grazed me.

With the wax impeding my hearing, I could only hope the click of the door handle covered my hurried footsteps.

The door swung inward. This made things more difficult—the guard stood in the opening, blocking most of it. Past him, I caught glimpses of ivory walls, a vase filled with flowers on an elegant table, and bright light filling the room.

The guard's back was so close I could've reached out to touch him. If I tried to squeeze through the opening, though, there was a strong chance I'd bump into him. Or at the very least, my skirts might brush his leg.

Once again, Malakai's instructions came back to me. *She'll ask them who was at the door.* With the ear wax, her voice was muffled, but I assumed he was right. *The guards will say no one, and she'll dismiss them.* And his repeated reminder. *You'll only have a small window. Do not hesitate.*

The guard spoke.

If Malakai was right, she was about to dismiss him. This was my last chance. I slid toward the opening, treading softly.

Again, the queen's muffled voice sounded, and the guard stepped back to close the door.

I leapt through it, dodging his arm, and rolled into the room.

One of the wax molds fell out of my ear.

Without it, every sound became magnified—my frantic breathing, the rustle of my skirts as I shifted, fingers feverishly searching for the wax.

It'd been squished underneath me when I'd rolled. To make it fit my ear, I needed to reshape it.

I risked a quick glance over my shoulder as my shaking fingers lifted it and squeezed.

Queen Jezebel sat at her dressing table in front of a large ornate mirror with an enormous jewelry box covering the entire table, filled with stunning necklaces, rings, bracelets, and even crowns. One white-gold ring with a ruby and a diamond rested in an oddly prominent position at the top. Her velvet-covered chair had a tall back, but as she leaned forward, her face became visible in the mirror. On her head was the crown. Woven white-gold metal encircled her thick dark hair.

For a split second, I forgot to breathe. Her gaze pinned me to the wall. But when I dropped low again, still struggling to press the mold back into shape, her eyes didn't follow. It was the door she was watching with those kohl-lined eyes.

The wax mold was still a bit flat, but it would have to do; I lifted it to my ear in a panic.

"I recognize your handwriting, my son."

I froze.

Her voice was gentle and soothing, like the sweet trickle of a waterfall. It made me want to stay and hear more.

"A bit dramatic though, don't you think?" she continued, laughing.

A gurgle of laughter rose in my throat too; I barely cut it off in time. I wasn't even sure why I did. She was hardly a threat. Malakai had overexaggerated quite a bit.

The queen held the letter up and read it out loud. " 'You betrayed me'?" She tsked, shaking her head.

I shook mine too. He really was dramatic.

"You betrayed yourself"—a harsher tone entered her voice as she stood, one that made me tense—"by being too weak for your people."

The wax mold in my still-raised hand dropped to the floor accidentally. It didn't bother me enough to pick it up; I didn't need it.

Her sharp eyes narrowed on it. "Show yourself, darling. I dislike feeling like I'm talking to myself."

This woman was not a threat, I decided.

I let the invisible blanket fall.

Chapter 49

Arie

QUEEN JEZEBEL DIDN'T CALL her guards.

She didn't say a word.

Crossing over to me, she stopped to stare into my face with a strange intensity. "You're not my son," she said finally, not blinking.

My racing heart calmed under the soothing tones of her voice.

"You are the mirror image of your mother," she said softly, gazing into my eyes.

"How did you know my mother?" I whispered back. I couldn't help myself.

Instead of answering, she turned away. "This is an unexpected turn of events." She ran a long, slim finger across the curves and ridges of a chair, all trimmed in gold. "When Jedekiah described the small rebellion forming, I expected my son to lead the revolutionaries himself."

I'd pulled the second piece of wax out of my other ear to hear her better but frowned when she mentioned Jedekiah. "He shouldn't have told you about us."

"Oh, of course he should have." She turned back to me with a smile. "It was very loyal. And I reward loyalty."

I smiled back. Loyalty was a good virtue, I had to agree. It would've been nice if Jedekiah's loyalty had been to us... but I supposed it didn't matter now.

Queen Jezebel was strikingly beautiful, like a painting you couldn't look away from. Her skin was flawless, the pale color a stark contrast to her deep ebony hair. There was a slight blush of rosy pink dusted on her cheeks, and her lips were a dark red.

She waved me toward a set of gold-covered chairs by the window. "Come, sit with me. We have a bit of time before the ceremony begins. That's why you've come, is it not?"

I sank onto the chair she offered. It wasn't as soft as it looked. The gold pearls decorating the back poked me through my dress. "Yes," I answered, uncomfortable about sharing our plan. Had Jedekiah already told her everything? I supposed he had. A worse thought struck me—I hoped she didn't think that I disliked her. That had been before I knew her. "I'm sorry," I offered when she seemed to be waiting for me to elaborate.

"Don't trouble yourself over it, my dear." She waved a generous hand and graced me with another smile. "It's all in the past. In fact, I have a splendid idea." She stood, and I did too, but she waved me back down. "How about you tell me where your friends are? I'll have the Guard gather them up so they can watch the ceremony from the best possible view."

I bit the inside of my lip. They wouldn't like it. But she was so kind to offer, I could hardly say no.

"And," she added, clasping her hands together, "I have a special role in mind for you in the ceremony itself. It's usually the priest's responsibility, but I think you'd do it wonderfully, if you wouldn't mind?"

Her thoughtfulness touched me. No one cared about me this much, not even Kadin. The thought of him caused me an odd moment of hesitation; he wouldn't like this at all. But Kadin trusted me to make the necessary choices for my kingdom and for myself. I knew he would understand.

"I'd love to," I agreed, returning her smile.

"Wonderful." Her smile grew, and she held out a hand. "Come. You can tell the guards where to find them, and then you and I can begin making plans. We have much to discuss and very little time."

I followed her into the hall, where the guards I'd passed earlier appeared startled at the sight of me. The queen gave them a hard look but didn't reprimand them. Instead, she nudged me forward to share everything they needed to know to find my friends. "Hurry now," the queen told them once I finished. "And once the Guard has been told to capture... their attention and bring them to the ceremony, send a retinue to the princess's old rooms to pick us up. We'll meet you there." She leaned forward to whisper something else to them before they saluted and turned to go.

The princess? A faint memory came back to me of Gideon standing in my rooms. What had he said? *The queen's daughter disappeared years ago.* What had happened to her? I couldn't remember if he'd said.

The queen held her arm out to me, and I took it eagerly. It was only two hallways over before we stopped in front of a dimmer set of doors, almost dusty. They creaked when the queen pulled them open.

Inside, the furniture was covered in sheets, but the sun shone in brightly. It was less than an hour from setting now; the ceremony would begin soon.

The queen took the sheets off the nearby chairs and pulled the gold curtains back from the bed. Dust flew in the air. The ceilings were so tall that the room felt twice as big as it actually was. She stepped away to the tall windows, putting her back to me. "This was my daughter's room."

There was a raw tone to her voice, as if her words were more real than anything else she'd said to me.

I took it in with new eyes. The room had to have sat empty for years. But the furnishing was for a young lady, maybe even my age. Tasteful. Lots of gold, white, and silver blended together. The windows let in so much light we could have been standing outside, but they were locked tight. The queen didn't try to open them, and I assumed from the way they appeared glued shut that she couldn't.

"What happened to her?" I asked hesitantly. I didn't want to upset her, but she'd brought me here for a reason. It almost seemed as if she wanted me to ask.

Queen Jezebel's hand fell from the sheer white curtain. "She disobeyed me." She sighed, still not turning to face me. "I only wanted her to spend a little time away from home, to see just how good she had it here. Then she developed feelings for that fool of a human king."

I frowned at the description. What had this king done? He must have been terrible.

The queen turned to face me, and the tears in her eyes made my own well up. "She wouldn't come home. I'd lost her to the humans. And when she died a few years later, I was heartbroken."

"I'm so sorry," I said in a thick voice, tears clogging my throat. Memories of my father's death sprung up unbidden. It was still so fresh and raw. I understood her pain.

"You look just like her, you know," the queen whispered. "Like my sweet Hanna."

My heart missed a beat.

That's my mother's name.

"*Your* Hanna?" I asked slowly, though the answer stared me in the face.

The queen's skin was much lighter, and her eyes a pure ice-water blue, but the rest of her face was so familiar it was like looking in a mirror.

"Are you my... grandmother?" I asked on the heels of the first question.

Queen Jezebel's eyes tightened at the corners, and her lips pressed together briefly, but then she smiled. "I suppose I am, though I dislike that word. It makes me sound far too old."

I just stared at her, taking in her features. My grandmother was the kindest, most beautiful woman who'd ever lived. "I wish I'd known you sooner."

That made her take my arm and tuck it into hers with a smile, leading me back to the door we'd come in. "Oh, I always kept an eye on you, you know. From afar. In fact, when they brought back images from your coronation, it took my breath away how much you reminded me of her."

"How come you never came to see me?" I hesitated. "I had no idea. My father never told me..."

She just patted my hand. "I doubt he knew. But I was planning a visit quite soon actually. You beat me to it."

Warmth flooded through me. I had family again, and she'd wanted to see me.

We stepped out into the hall where the guards waited for us, and the queen shut the door of her daughter's—my mother's—room carefully.

"If you'd like," she said to me conspiratorially as we began to walk down the hall, "you could stay here with me, in your mother's rooms." She brought my hand back under hers, and I leaned into her. My grandmother. "They're quite comfortable," she continued. "You'll never want to leave. I know your mother didn't."

That contradicted what the queen had said earlier, but she didn't give me a chance to ask about it. "I would like you to be the one to crown me as queen once again during today's ceremony."

My brows rose. "Why me?" I couldn't believe the luck. To suddenly have a grandmother. For her to want me to play such a huge role in her coronation.

"It will mean a great deal to my people to learn that Hanna's daughter is the one placing the crown on my head," the queen explained as we turned on the landing and began down the next set of stairs. "Family means a great deal to the Jinn. And on top of that," she added, almost to herself, "it will silence the human sympathizers."

"Sympathizers," I repeated, trying to understand. The politics in Jinn were so foreign to me.

"Some of my people think I'm not as considerate of the humans as I should be." The queen didn't look at me or at the guards who followed, keeping her gaze focused on the hallway ahead that I knew from Malakai's description led to the throne room. "Isn't that absolutely ridiculous?"

I laughed. "It is."

"After all, here you are, my human granddaughter." She did look at me then, appraisingly, noting the grass stains on my once-regal dress.

I wished I'd found a way to change before meeting her. To represent her in the ceremony like this would be an embarrassment. I opened my mouth to back out for her sake, but she'd turned to the guards. "Bring one of the former princess's gowns." She glanced at the hem of my dress again. "A full ensemble to replace what she's wearing now."

We stepped into a small side room, presumably near the stage, to wait for the crowds to gather. Queen Jezebel—my grandmother, I reminded myself, though it didn't feel any truer now than it had the first time—didn't speak to me. She was probably nervous.

As she paced the length of the room, she stroked the woven metal of her crown absently.

I sat on yet another gold couch to wait.

At one point, a guard knocked. Once the queen spoke to him, she seemed to grow calmer, coming to sit across from me on a separate couch. "We've found your friends," she told me. "Aren't you glad you'll get to see them at the ceremony?"

I nodded, smiling slightly. Yes, I was happy to hear they were okay, but I was also nervous about their reaction now that they'd been found out. Were they furious with me? I'd explain as soon as I could.

"What exactly will I do in the ceremony?" I asked, hoping she wouldn't mind my intrusion now that she was more relaxed.

"For most of it, you will sit to the side," she said, brushing at unseen lint on her dress, admiring herself in the mirror. She'd barely looked at me since we'd arrived. "It is a lengthy ceremony. When it is time for me to remove my crown, I'll signal for you to join me and take it. You'll repeat a few words given to you and place it back on my brow." Finally, she brought her eyes to mine, warmth infused in them, comforting me that she hadn't forgotten me already. "Isn't it simple? It will be over before you know it."

"Are you sure I'm the right person for such an important role?" I asked once more. Something didn't feel right about it.

"My dear," Jezebel said, standing to come sit beside me, taking my hand in hers. "You're a queen in your own right. A queen in the human world and, perhaps," she added, strangely unblinking, "a future queen of Jinn, hmm?"

All those times the Jinn had called me "my queen" came rushing back. They'd *known* I had royal Jinni blood all along? How was that possible?

I snapped my mouth shut when I realized it was gaping open and nodded quickly. I would be whatever she needed me to be.

Something softened in the queen's face, and that same vulnerable tone returned to her voice. "The way you lift your chin like that. So resolved. Just like her. Some days I wonder—" She cut off, shaking her head, and the moment was gone. She stood and returned to her own couch.

"Jedekiah has told me of your Severance, child." Her tone was warm, but her eyes seemed cold, distant. "I know that you are Giftless as any human."

I opened my mouth to contradict her, but she wasn't done.

"The cruelty of the humans never ceases to amaze me. I'm truly sorry to hear it." Her hand drifted up to the crown once more, tracing the lines of it like a habit she was barely aware of anymore, eyes on mine. "Help me finish this Crowning Ceremony, and I will do everything in my power to bring back your old Giftings, even give you a dozen new Gifts besides."

Again, I opened my mouth to explain that she didn't need to worry.

But she held a hand up to stop me. "You'll be the second-most powerful ruler to ever exist, second only to me. No one will ever be able to sever anything from you again. You will never again have to feel the way you do now."

I hadn't paid much attention to how I felt over the last few days. So much had been going on that, for once, I hadn't curled into myself.

The revelation distracted me from telling the queen about my new Gifts, and when I looked up, she was already standing, waving an impatient hand for me to follow. "Come," she said, dropping her hand before I could take it and striding toward the guard who'd appeared at the door with the requested clothes. "Change quickly. It's time."

Chapter 50

Kadin

WE WOKE IN YET another cell. This cell was much larger than the guard shack, with iron shackles, stone benches, and only a tiny shaft of sunlight streaming in through a small vent high above. We were underground. Our little group of sixteen—fifteen with Arie gone—hunched over in small groups throughout the room.

I winced at the bump on my head where I'd landed on the hard ground outside the castle gate. The Jinni Guard had been waiting to ambush us in Malakai's hiding place. We'd never had a chance.

I jumped up, frustrated at how powerless I was in this world to have been knocked unconscious twice in one day. Two guards stood on the other side of the bars. "You're making a huge mistake!" I yelled at their backs. "This is your prince!"

"I've already tried that," Malakai murmured from the ground. He leaned against the stone wall, head bowed, body still. "It's as if they can't even hear me."

"Then we'll make them hear," I said, shaking the bars, yelling louder. "Your queen has you under an enchantment! Turn around and open your eyes—I guarantee you'll recognize him."

"Silence, human," the guard growled. "Before I silence you myself." The disgust in his voice made me step back just seconds before the heavy pommel of his crystal shoved through the door where my chest had been. "Filth," he muttered, turning back around.

I stepped up to the bars again, careful not to press too close. "I know you hate my kind." I paused, blowing out a breath. "Honestly, I used to hate your kind on sight." The Jinn inside the cell glanced up at my words.

Nesrin nodded slightly from where she sat on the bench beside Malakai. "So did I," she murmured.

"I finally understand we're all the same," I said, more to them than to the guards. "Evil runs in every race." I shrugged. "So does good."

I studied the uneven stone beneath my feet. What'd happened to my brother wasn't their fault. It wasn't Malakai's fault, or Gideon's, or any of the Jinn here. Not even the soldiers, who had stopped listening. "I don't want to hate someone I've never met for what someone else did," I murmured to myself. "It's not worth it."

Crouching in front of Malakai, I leaned my elbows on my knees. "You're going to become king," I told him firmly. "I don't know how, and I don't know when, but I know the difference between rulers who lead out of trust versus fear." His eyes lifted to mine. "Fear doesn't last. A true ruler inspires trust. Like you. Queen Jezebel can't keep the crown through fear alone, no matter how powerful it is. It's just a matter of time."

"That's it," one of the guards snapped, whipping his keys out and unlocking the cell door. "I think the two of you need a lesson."

Chapter 51

Arie

THE SETTING SUN CAST a golden light over the entire throne room and everyone present. It danced around the queen, giving her a soft halo.

I played with the black lace sleeves of my new dress, which was a much slimmer fit than I was used to. Jinn fashion seemed dedicated to detail, and the stunning lacework covered my arms, overlaying a sleek bodice and skirt made of black satin.

Lifting my chin, the way Jezebel said my mother used to, I strode out after her down the long carpeted aisle.

The crowd of Jinn stood all around us, filling the main hall and overflowing past the pillars into the outer room on all sides.

When I moved to follow the queen up the shining white steps onto the high stage, guards took my arms and pulled me to the side, a bit more roughly than I liked.

They deposited me at the base of the stage instead. Tall stone seats lined the wall.

Remembering my grandmother's words, that she would call me when she was ready, I settled onto the hard gray stone. They were roomy enough, but they were not designed for comfort.

Jezebel continued up one set of stairs, then the next, the third, and the fourth, until she reached the throne at the top. I had to crane my neck to see her from this angle. She lowered herself onto the velvet cushions and lifted a hand for the ceremony to begin.

As different Jinn took turns speaking at length about the queen's reign from a small platform between me and the queen, I turned my gaze to the audience, searching the pale faces and dark hair for the "special seating" the queen had promised our group.

It was difficult to see much when I was seated and the Jinn were standing. Past the first few rows, I could only glimpse a face here and there. It was tempting to stand, but I didn't want to risk ruining the ceremony, so I stayed still.

About a half hour into the ceremony, a Jinni approached in the corner of my eye. He had a familiar swagger. Bent to speak with the guard, I couldn't see his face, but whatever he said made the guard wave him through.

Jedekiah.

Fury made my entire body flush until my ears burned. *How dare he show his face here?*

He sauntered past me, dropping into the seat beside me, turning his face to the queen, who was in the midst of lighting candles. Each candle had a meaning, all of which I'd already forgotten.

I shifted in my seat, putting my back to the guard as much as possible, pretending to be engrossed in the ceremony, and hissed in Jedekiah's ear, "What are you doing here?"

"Helping you, of course," he murmured back, not taking his eyes off the queen.

"Helping?" I repeated, incredulous. "You *betrayed* us."

"Betrayed is such a strong word." He tilted his head just enough to wink at me. "I prefer to think of it as looking out for my own interests."

It was a struggle to keep my voice low when I wanted to scream at him. "I'm sure you do."

"Furthermore, just because I wanted the queen to clear my name and allow me to return home does not mean I want her to rule," he continued, as if he hadn't heard the venom in my voice. "When my kinsmen noticed you were caught in her thrall, I supposed I should help untangle you from the spider's web."

"Don't you dare speak of my grandmother that way," I snapped.

He hummed to himself, shaking his head. Almost under his breath, he said, "It's worse than I thought." Then louder, to me, "I thought you'd be stronger, darling. You resisted *me*, after all. That's no mean feat."

He waited for validation, which I refused to give.

I glared at him instead. He didn't respect the queen like he should. I could see why she'd banished him. "You knew."

A slight wrinkle appeared between his brows as he leaned toward me. "Knew what, darling?"

"That she's my grandmother. When I said so, you didn't even blink."

"I did," he agreed, readily enough. "Gideon told me the day we met."

My feeble, patched-together heart ripped a brand-new tear. *Gideon knew.*

Thick tears clogged my throat, and I whispered, "How could he?"

"It was a promise to your mother," Jedekiah said. His tone was soft for once, gentle. "I knew her too, though not as well as Gideon. He loved her. Dearly."

Loved. My mother. Gideon.

When I returned home, he and I would be having words.

I caught myself shaking my head and stopped. "He told everyone," I whispered slowly, remembering those few moments each time a new Jinni had arrived in the library, where Gideon had stepped forward and spoken into their mind. "Every. Single. One of you." I tilted my chin higher, staring up at Jezebel where she was lighting the last of the candles, to keep the tears from spilling from my eyes. A tiny crack broke my voice as I added, "Everyone except me."

Jedekiah's mouth flattened into a thin line as if, for once, he didn't have a comeback or satisfying remark. "That was his choice, darling. His, and your mother's."

"It should've been my choice."

Some tension in Jedekiah's shoulders eased as he slouched back to lean on his elbow, looking for all the world like he might fall asleep there. "I agree. As should what happens today. Which brings to me to why I'm here."

The queen lit the last candle, and the attendant intoned the significance of it, which stood for the relationship between the Jinn and their ruler. I tuned him out. "I assume you're here for some favor. If the queen wants to hear you out, she will."

"Not at all, my queen," Jedekiah replied. "I'm here to do *you* a favor. Personally, I think you should rule. Nothing against Malakai, of course. I just like you better. But unfortunately, that'd require you to view your grandmother a bit differently. Have you ever heard the story of the boy who believed two impossible things?"

Taking a deep breath, I let it out in a lengthy sigh and shook my head.

"Well…" He paused, shifting in his seat. "It's too long to tell now. Suffice it to say, he spends his life trying to obey both masters, but they never agree on anything. Instead of choosing, he merges them together in his mind and creates a monster that spins webs full of lies. In the end, he's eaten by the monster." He tapped my arm subtly. "Don't let the monster eat you, darling."

The corner of my mouth lifted in a smile. "I'm sorry if my change of heart doesn't fit your plans, but I trust my own eyes. Truthfully, I should have known better than to believe rumors over a firsthand account. Perhaps it was your intention all along to set us against the queen, when you knew better." This time I was the one who shifted enough to bump his arm with my own for emphasis. "Maybe you hoped all along to lead us astray so that *you* could steal the crown."

He splayed a hand over his chest. "You wound me. And also compliment me at the same time. If only I'd come up with such a brilliant plan. But no." For the first time since he'd sat down, he risked facing me fully, eyes growing more serious than I'd ever seen. "I doubt it's possible in the time we have to force you to face the monster, so instead, I would ask of you just one thing."

"Why should I do anything for you?"

"For your mother's sake," he replied, not breaking my gaze. "For Hanna. It is a very small thing. It won't hurt anyone. I swear to you on my honor."

Frowning, I tried to find the scheme beneath his words, but for once he seemed entirely genuine. "I'll consider it."

"When Queen Jezebel removes the crown and gives it to you so that you may place it on her head, do this one thing: don't place it on her head immediately."

"Why?" I drew out the word. "Are you trying to embarrass her by ruining the ceremony?"

"Not at all," he replied easily, although that could mean anything. "Just hold on to it for as long as it takes to count the number of candles that have been lit. It will build the suspense. Trust me."

"Trust you," I said flatly. "You mean the way I trusted you not to harm anyone or tell the queen of our plans?"

"Exactly like that," he said. "And if you do, I'll tell you about your mother."

I stilled. My father had rarely talked about Hanna. She'd died when I was born. I knew next to nothing about her. "My grandmother can tell me what I need to know."

"Not these stories," Jedekiah said, grinning. He leaned forward, preparing to stand. "Just think it over, darling. What could it hurt? A few precious seconds of dramatic flair for a lifetime of tales? I'll be holding my breath to see what you choose."

He slipped out of his seat without waiting for an answer, pausing once he reached the back of the room to bow low behind the backs of the assembled Jinn and disappear through the door.

I frowned at the space where he'd been until the guard beside me cleared his throat.

Quickly, I turned around to face the ceremony once more.

The queen sat on her throne as a Jinni far below on the floor with us spoke of her valor, her honor, and her goodness. The back of her throne stretched a full story high behind her, tipped with a sun emblem that danced in the fading sunlight as if alive. It was mesmerizing. Time passed slowly as I stared at it and tried to find elusive answers.

When the queen stood and waved to me, I'd grown so complacent that I didn't immediately react. The guards stepped forward as if prepared to drag me up to the throne.

I stood, waving them away.

Taking the wide pale steps one at a time, I made my way up to the first platform, and the second, and by the time I reached the fourth and final level where the queen waited, I was thoroughly out of breath.

She didn't speak, so I didn't either.

Between us, a Jinni had set a short pillar with a red velvet pillow on top.

Gravely, the queen took my hand and held it up, turning to her subjects. "This is my granddaughter, Queen Arie of Hodafez, daughter of Hanna, daughter of Jezebel."

Unlike humans, the Jinn reacted with utter stillness, as if so trained in keeping their emotions to themselves that even this shock didn't break the façade. The queen continued as if she'd expected this. "As a human, she has agreed to stand with me today, strengthening the unity between our kingdoms; and as family and a fellow Jinni, she has agreed to offer me the crown on your behalf."

While she spoke, my eyes drifted across the stoic Jinni faces, searching for Kadin, or Malakai, or Nesrin. They were nowhere to be found. I frowned slightly before remembering where I was and wiping the emotion off my face. Where were they?

The queen took my hands and flipped them over, palms up, before reaching toward the crown still on her brow. She picked it up with a soft intake of breath. There was a long pause as she stood staring at it before she placed it on the velvet pillow.

Confused, I kept my open hands out beside the crown.

"Take it, child," the queen urged me. Her voice was flatter now, a bit more crisp. Irritable even. She seemed smaller somehow.

The crown warmed to my touch, heat soaking into my bones in a way that straightened my spine and lifted my chin, drawing confidence up from a well inside me I hadn't known existed. The sheer power flooded through me.

Jedekiah's words came back to me. *Just hold on to it for as long as it takes to count the number of candles that have been lit.*

There were at least two dozen candles.

One.

When I dragged my gaze away from the crown to count the first candle, my grandmother's lips quirked in a kind smile.

Slowly, as if she'd aged a bit in the moments since she'd removed the crown, she bent down, using the small pillar to balance until she knelt before me.

Two. Three.

"Just place it on my head, dear," she murmured, leaning forward a bit in anticipation, "and then you can go sit back down."

Four. Five. Six.

Her affection for me was still tangible, like one ocean wave after another, washing over me with pulsing regularity.

Seven.

There was something... *wrong* with the waves though.

I blinked to clear the confusion. *Eight. Nine. Ten.*

I lifted the crown slowly. *Eleven. Twelve.* Just a little bit of drama, Jedekiah had said. For stories of my mother. That seemed more than worth it.

Thirteen. Fourteen. Fifteen.

A nagging thought tugged at my mind. Affection felt like the sun on a hot day, hugging your skin tightly. The queen's warmth was like an imitation sun. All light, but no heat. No true feeling.

The crown was at eye level. My gaze dropped below it to hers, involuntarily. *Sixteen.*

"Don't dawdle," she said through her teeth, which were bared in a smile that no longer seemed so genuine.

Seventeen.

What was it Malakai had told me about her Gifts? *Something between charm and persuasion... powerful... the crown will enhance them...*

She wasn't wearing the crown now, however.

I forced myself to smile back at her, turning the crown in my hands as if in awe. *Eighteen. Nineteen.* Almost there. "Where are Malakai and the others?" I whispered to fill the remaining seconds. *Twenty. Twenty-one.* "You said they'd be here."

Jezebel's jaw clenched, but otherwise her loving smile didn't slip. "Don't worry about them now, dear. Remember how important it is for you to finish this task."

The responsibility tugged at me with her words.

Twenty-two. Twenty-three.

It was like living through two experiences at once, happening over top of each other.

As I reached the last candle, instead of lowering the crown onto her head, I clutched it tighter.

I'd never thought I'd be thankful for my experience with King Amir, but it was the memory of him that stayed my hand.

Twenty-four...

There was a lie here.

I just didn't quite know what it was.

"Is your son even here?"

The audience below us couldn't help but notice the drama unfolding now. It hit me as I said the words—her son was also my uncle. *Does he know too? And never told me?* The room spun slightly. The queen's expression blurred. The unraveling of all the secrets threatened to overwhelm me. *How could they not say anything?*

"How dare you question me," the queen hissed back, forcing me back to the present. She still knelt, waiting for me to crown her, unable to do anything without ruining the atmosphere of her precious Crowning Ceremony now that she'd put the power in my hands. "You're just a pathetic human. My choices are none of your concern. Place the crown on my head *now.*"

The lingering effects of the crown had all but vanished. I barely even felt her Gift anymore as my *own* Gift—the one I'd refused to even acknowledge as a Gift before but recognized now—created a safe buffer around me.

My gaze drifted past the crowd of Jinn to the back of the room where I'd last seen Jedekiah, almost expecting to find him standing there, winking at me. Of course, he wasn't. But his request had worked nonetheless.

I finally saw my grandmother for who she truly was: a hateful liar who'd manipulated me into—almost—giving her the throne.

A Gift of Manipulation.

Stronger than Jedekiah's simple charm and far worse than King Amir's persuasion, the queen's manipulation had utterly replaced my desires with her own.

Could her Gift be turned against her? "You don't really want to be queen, do you?" My nerves turned it into a question instead of the statement I'd intended.

Her face twitched in a snarl that she was trying to keep hidden. "How are you defying me?" she snapped, ignoring my question. "You shouldn't have *any* Gifts. You were given a Severance to make sure of it."

"What do you mean to make sure of it?" I took a small step back from her unconsciously. "You were behind that? Behind King Amir? And Enoch?" Another thread began to unravel, this one going all the way back to the choice that had led me to run away from home. "My Severance was because of *you*?"

For the first time since this entire ceremony had begun, a murmur rose from the audience. That last bit hadn't been as hushed as I'd thought.

"You don't want to be queen," I said, soft and hurried in case it didn't work. "You don't want any of this. You want to give it to your son, the rightful heir."

She didn't seem the least bit swayed by my attempts to turn her Gift on her. "You're a fool." With a glance at the hundreds of watching eyes, she turned her glare back on me and ground out, "This is your last chance, girl. Put the crown. On my head."

Her guards could easily climb the stairs and end this the moment she called. If I didn't get a handle on her Gift soon, it'd be too late.

How had she won me over earlier? *With a smile and a bit of truth mixed in with the lies.* I swallowed and stretched my mouth into the best imitation smile I could manage. After years of smiling through boring hearings with the Shahs back home, I hoped it would suffice. "You did love my mother, didn't you?" I asked.

Her face softened, almost imperceptibly. "Of course I did."

I squeezed the crown, feeling the way it pulsed in my hands, and imagined pulling strength from it. Still smiling, I asked another question, hoping those below had quieted enough to listen. "Did you ever mean for my mother to rule?"

"No."

The Jinn below were nearly invisible to the queen now. Her gaze was on mine. Their gasps hardly registered with either of us.

I should've focused on the crown, but there was another question I needed to know the answer to. I hesitated, then smiled at her again, holding her gaze, which seemed to help. "Did you truly want me to stay here?"

"No," she replied. "I was going to lock you in Hanna's old rooms." Almost as an afterthought, as if she regretted it now, in the thralls of her own Gift being used against her, she added, "I wouldn't do that anymore though. I can see now you're much more than a useless human."

I nodded along, trying not to feel the sting. The rejection shouldn't have hurt. I'd only known her for a few hours.

"Let's focus on the crown right now, shall we?" I gripped that same item as tightly as possible, afraid that if I let go I might lose my fragile control over her. If she would admit to his existence, it would change everything. Her people wouldn't let her move forward if they knew he existed. "Do you also love your own son? Prince Malakai?"

"Of course," she said agreeably, shifting a bit as if kneeling was beginning to hurt. "He's my baby boy. He's just a bit misguided, that's all. I'll help him."

I was tempted to ask how *exactly* she thought she would help him, and if it'd be anything like the previous *help* she'd offered. Instead, I simply asked, "Where is he now?"

"He's here," she said, waving to the other side of the stage where we'd entered. "I was going to bring him out for the feast."

"Let's bring him out now," I said cheerfully, gritting my teeth to maintain the smile. To the guards below, I said, "On the queen's orders. Please," I added when they didn't immediately move.

"I'd rather not," she said.

My grip on the crown tightened again. The edges of the smooth white-gold metal were surprisingly sharp. If I squeezed much harder, it might cut me.

"I'd like him beside me when I crown you," I crooned, "so he can see his mother take on the throne for another fifty years. To…" I searched for another half-truth she would like. "To lead her people bravely into the future."

"Yes, the future," she murmured. "I have many plans for it."

"Let's bring him up here. I'm sure he can't see a thing from wherever he is. Don't you want him to see his mother's finest moment?"

"I do," she finally acquiesced, and to the guards, "Bring him to me."

"And the others too," I added, trying to keep my tone light.

"Oh, those humans and the Jinn who helped them? They're already sentenced to beheadings in the morning. After all, I can hardly banish someone a second time. It would take all the meaning out of it."

I tried to control the panic squeezing my lungs. "Th-then they should witness your true power more than anyone," I stuttered, trying to find the right words to convince her. "I'm sure you want me to put this crown on your brow as soon as possible." I laid it on thicker than ever, hoping my hold on her was strong enough that she wouldn't simply seize the crown and finish this ceremony without my contribution. "The fastest way to get your wish is to bring them here."

The queen sighed and finally gave in. "If it will speed up this process, I suppose." She sent a second pair of guards to the dungeons to fetch them.

Chapter 52

Nesrin

THE BITE OF THE guard's weapon had felt more like a bee sting than the wild, burning pain that Kadin and Malakai seemed to feel. I'd tried to help and had earned a nasty shock from those crystals, then a knee in the back when it didn't affect me the same.

I knelt by Malakai and held his hand through the discomfort.

Though he winced as he sat up, his eyes had a hopeful light again. *May Kadin forever escape the dragons and grow rich*! I could kiss him for that speech.

Currently, Malakai fiddled with a set of shackles on the wall that had been damaged. He was pulling one of the loose chain links out.

Unexpectedly, he dropped to his knees before me, holding the little circlet of chain in his palm. "Nesrin, I don't know how the humans do this," he began.

My mouth dropped open, and I started to shake my head. *Not this again!*

Ignoring my reaction, he cleared his throat and took my hand. "Nesrin Ahmadi, I've asked you to marry me before. Twice actually." The Jinn around us chuckled, all eyes on us. "Once out of jealousy, once to offer an alliance, and now, this third—and I hope final—time."

My lips twitched into a small smile at the wry tone in his voice.

He grew serious. "Those were never the real reasons. The truth is, I *love* you. Wholeheartedly. I have since you helped me regain consciousness in my dragon form. I love the way you're fearless except when it comes to ridiculously simple things like talking through how you feel."

My cheeks burned as hot as a flame. Smiling down at him, I just shook my head, overwhelmed.

"I love how you aren't afraid to tell me when I'm wrong."

"I can definitely do that." My voice shook slightly with nerves. This was the proposal I'd daydreamed of but had never believed would truly happen.

"I'd like to help you bridge the gap between our people, if you would let me—"

"Yes," I interrupted.

He bounced up from where he knelt. "Yes you'll bridge the gap or—"

"Yes." I laughed. "And *if* we survive, I'll consider marrying you. So maybe"—I added on a whim—"if you wanted to, you could kiss me now." *How was* that *for sharing how I felt?* I wanted to add, even as my face caught fire. I was likely the same shade as a tomato, especially with an audience, but I didn't care.

He slowly leaned down, taking my face in his hands, and brushed his lips against mine, so softly.

There was nothing else quite like it.

Nothing even came close.

Not even finding a dragon's egg.

I could *definitely* look forward to a future that held more of that.

"Okay," I said, grinning against his lips, eyes still closed. "You've convinced me."

He picked me up in excitement and swung me around until I yelled at him to put me down. Slowly, I became aware of cheering. The Jinn surrounded us, clapping us on the back, congratulating us. Somehow, it felt like the most natural thing in the world.

Kneeling again on the broken stone floor, Malakai held that small chain-link ring out again, gently taking my hand.

I nodded, letting him put the slightly crooked piece of metal on my ring finger.

A pulse of energy threw me to the ground. Convulsing, I barely heard Malakai and the others shouting to the guards to get help.

Between one blink and another, my world shifted. The gray stone ceiling above me came into sharp focus with all its cracks and crevices. A crystal clear drip of water, so small I shouldn't have noticed it, dropped through the air toward me. It was a perfect teardrop shape with a dozen shades of blue.

Kadin and the Jinn jumped back, smelling of fear. *Since when can I smell fear?* Even Malakai drew up, eyes widening as he stared down at me. He smelled of a mix of concern and surprised excitement. Again, I frowned, wondering how I knew what that smelled like.

In the growing silence, I picked up a conversation down the hall between guards coming to get us. They were running. Every word they spoke between pants was clear. "The queen said to get him. So we get him."

"Did you hear that?" I jumped to my feet. Instead of standing, I flew into the air, nearly to the top of the high ceiling. Dropping back down on light toes, I felt the same awe that I smelled throughout the room.

"Hear what?" Malakai asked hesitantly .

"The guards." I gestured toward the door, frustrated. "They're coming to get you. What's going on?"

He swallowed loudly. "I think... I think we finished the covenant."

"What?" I gasped, glancing around at the way the Jinn kept their distance, eyes glued to my face.

"It's your eyes," Kadin said. "They're... like a cat? A snake?"

"A dragon," Malakai whispered reverently. "Nesrin, I think you've become fully Khaanevaade."

I didn't know what to say.

Something had certainly happened, and I wasn't sure I liked it. Tilting my head, taking in the way every detail of the room was clear down to the pulse of the guards on the other side of the door, I decided I didn't hate it either.

The guards I'd heard coming arrived, speaking quietly with the others.

"They want to take you to the ceremony," I whispered to Malakai. "Do you want me to fight? I think I could take them."

He shook his head, still staring at me with wonder. "No. Not yet," he amended. "Let's find out what my mother wants. This is more than I could've expected."

But they'd come for him alone.

"Malakai!" I called, slamming into the cell door as they closed it. A few of the iron bars bent. On the other side, the remaining guards took a few steps back, pointing their weapons in my direction.

I snarled at them.

Wrapping my fingers around the metal bars, I was about to try pulling them apart with my bare hands—might as well test my new strength—when another conversation reached my ears. "She wants all of them now. I don't know why she's listening to the human girl."

"They're coming for us," I growled to the Jinn behind me, then caught myself at the waves of fear rolling off everyone. Straightening up, I added in a more normal tone, "Get ready."

Thanks to my warning, we were lined up at the door when the guards arrived. It was time for me to meet this queen and give her a piece of my mind about how she treated her son.

Chapter 53

Arie

MALAKAI APPEARED SHORTLY AT the base of the stairs with a guard on each side. They hauled him up toward us. His feet skimmed each step, barely touching down, and his forehead was sweaty, eyes bloodshot.

"What's wrong with you?" I whispered as they set him on a step below and held tight.

"They just gave me another dose of Teshuvah," he mumbled, fighting to keep his eyes open as he swayed. "No Gifts."

This wasn't at all what I'd hoped for.

Still.

The alternative was my grandmother.

At the back of the room, Kadin, Nesrin, and the Jinn in our small group shuffled in under guard. It solidified what I knew I had to do.

I lifted the crown again, high and regal. "Bow your head," I told Jezebel.

When she did, clearly thrilled that bringing Malakai onstage had made me finally obey, I turned to the quiet audience of Jinn. Their colorful eyes pinned me in place.

Could I do this?

It'd have to be quick.

There was no telling how long this Gift would keep the queen in place.

"Before you is Prince Malakai," I called out to them. "The son of Queen Jezebel, whom you've somehow forgotten. The rightful heir of Jinn."

I'd taken two steps before the queen opened her mouth to yell for the guards. They faced outward with Malakai between them, one step lower, which suited my purposes perfectly since he was quite tall.

"Hold still," I whispered in his ear.

I sucked in a breath, lifting the crown high, and brought it down to rest on his head.

As I let go, the power that flowed from the crown and tingled through my veins disappeared.

A bloodcurdling scream poured out of Jezebel as she tore at her scalp where the crown would have been. "What have you done?"

The effects on Malakai were just as instantaneous.

His pale skin warmed, eyes growing calmer, steadier, as the Teshuvah seemed to expel itself from his body through the sheer power of the crown. "Unhand me, if you want to live," he said to the guards, tone quiet but not at all soft.

They flung themselves back, bowing, eyes wide and frightened. "My king." They dropped to their knees, then lowered farther until their faces were pressed to the ground. "Long may he live, long may he reign."

Below us, a wave of Jinn lowered themselves as well, bowing first, then kneeling, then faces to the floor. "Long may he live," they intoned as one. "Long may he reign."

"Long may I be a good ruler," he replied, as if that was part of the ceremony. And for all I knew, maybe it was.

He stilled, staring at the floor, pausing long enough for everyone to hold their breath, before lifting his gaze to face the solemn Jinn before him. "Please rise."

As they shuffled to their feet, somehow graceful even then, he began to descend the stairs. One level, two, three, until he stood on the marble floor among them. "Let them go," he said to the guards arriving with Kadin, Nesrin, and the banished Jinn. Immediately, they obeyed.

To the Jinni hovering in the background who projected his and the other speakers' voices, Malakai spoke softly, though I heard him clearly. "Make sure this next part can be heard as far as your range will allow."

The Jinni swallowed nervously, nodding her head and squaring her shoulders.

"There's a spell I was researching before I disappeared," Malakai began, moving among his people, making an effort to look each Jinni in the eye as he passed. "Before my own mother *made* me disappear," he added, waving toward where she stood gaping behind me, shaking her head at him.

Malakai ignored her.

Though many Jinn still tried to hide their emotions, the difficulty was written all across their wide eyes and parting lips.

"Some of you may recognize it by its name," he continued as the Jinni projecting his voice and the guards who'd stepped forward to protect him hurried to follow him through the crowd.

Malakai paused, in both words and movement, for dramatic effect. "The *B'har*."

The stiffening shoulders and necks in an attempt to *not* glance around at one another said more than any whispers could. *This spell scares them.*

When the prince spoke again, he was too quiet to hear from where I was, still high above on the stage. He had to turn to the wide-eyed Jinni girl and remind her to use her Gift. "I understand my mother forbade looking into the B'har," he repeated softly. "But I believe that needs to change."

He drew a breath, and even that was projected. The Jinni girl was focusing so intently that it sounded as if he stood beside me. "If you were born within the last century, you may not have even heard of this enchantment. But it was something the ancients crafted to allow the crown *itself* to choose who ruled the next fifty years. To choose someone worthy of the people. Someone the people *wanted.*"

The room was so quiet that a soft cough echoed.

Malakai was moving through the crowd again. "It took me years to dig up the full spell from where it'd been buried, likely by rulers before my mother, though I assume that when she learned of my findings that may have been part of why she sought to get rid of me."

He was riveting.

All eyes followed him to the back of the room, where the least important stood.

He joined them.

Took the crown from his head.

Soft inhales joined mine.

"My mother didn't want you to have the freedom to choose," he said softly, yet still as clear as if we were a hand's breadth apart. "But I do."

The Jinni girl who'd followed him with the guards tentatively spoke, projecting her own voice in a tinny, fearful way. "Even if it means we don't choose you?"

Malakai nodded slowly, raising the crown above his head as I had just minutes prior. But he whispered words in a language I didn't recognize, rehearsed, growing stronger and making the crown glow as he did.

With a shout, he finished the spell, and a crackle of energy filled the air, rushing through like a wind out the door with a heavy whoosh, then returning moments later in a violent gale that nearly knocked me off my feet. The gust circled the room, lifting the crown from Malakai's hands and bringing it into the swirling chaos.

One Jinni got cocky and leapt into the whirlwind, snatching the crown out of the air. He attempted to pull it down, but it didn't budge. Dangling in the air, all eyes on him, he swore and dropped to the ground, disappearing in the crowd and leaving the crown behind.

Malakai spoke once more, staring up at the crown with the rest of us. "From now on, every fifty years, the *crown* will decide who rules. It will choose what the people want."

A cheer rose from the stoic Jinn, breaking them out of their masks of indifference into a wild joy made all the more beautiful by the contrast.

"I choose Malakai!" someone yelled over the crowd.

"As do I!" Other shouts rose up until the refrain blurred into hundreds of voices shouting the prince's name.

At first, the crown didn't respond. It merely dangled in midair where it had seemingly landed, as if daring anyone else to try to take it.

Malakai only waited.

There were thousands of Jinn in this land. Who knew how many islands. How long would a spell like this take?

Their patience was rewarded, and the cheers grew louder as the crown began to slowly sink from the high vaulted ceiling toward the floor. Toward nothing at first. An empty space. But as it lowered, it began to drift to the side.

Toward Malakai.

Until finally, once again, it rested on his head.

I didn't know how much time had passed, only that my legs trembled and my lungs burned from how little I'd been breathing.

The sun had set by now, but Jinni magic lit the lamps more brightly than anything could back home, making the wild joy on their faces impossible to miss.

When Malakai turned, meeting my gaze across the room, his eyes were clear. "Thank you," he called simply, voice breaking slightly.

Before I could answer, his eyes moved behind me to where the queen still knelt. "Where is my mother?"

I whirled. The white marble floor behind me was empty. There was nowhere to go, yet she was gone. Glancing down to the main floor, Kadin and the others were making their way through the crowd toward the stage. Nesrin wasn't with them anymore.

"Find her!" Malakai yelled, running up the steps as every guard within earshot sprang into motion. "She cannot be allowed to escape!"

Panicking, I searched the entire stage: behind the throne, beneath the tablecloths, and every nook and cranny, coming up empty as he reached the top of the stairs. "What if she traveled outside the castle?"

"She can't," he replied, even as he gestured for the guards to block the exits to the throne room. "The Traveling Gift is blocked by a spell within these walls—it's impossible. The only way to leave is through a door or a window."

There were dozens of both.

Nesrin landed softly between us—she'd dropped down from the ceiling! I gasped at her eyes, instinctively stepping back at the eerie shape. Almost like a dragon...

"Don't move," she whispered to Malakai, eyes on his back, approaching in a crouch. "She's still here. I can smell her."

"Where?" Malakai hissed back.

Her nose twitched violently, and her hand darted to the back of his neck.

Standing next to Malakai, I heard his soft intake of breath as she lifted a tiny venomous Phidar as black as her eyes by one of its dozen legs. It'd been poised to strike.

"Here she is," Nesrin whispered.

My mouth fell open. *That's the queen?*

The insect bared sharp fangs and tried to sink them into Nesrin's hand.

She only stared down at the green venom as it dripped harmlessly down her fingers. Her skin remained unbroken.

I blinked, trying to clear my eyes. *I must be seeing things.*

"Khaanevaade," Malakai whispered to her in a reverent tone.

What's that? Is that a Gift? Now was not the time to ask, in front of hundreds of Jinni eyes, but Nesrin wasn't the same girl we'd arrived with. She seemed more *right* somehow, like the girl I'd known before had been wearing a mask and this was her true face.

Reaching out to the table with the ceremonial wine, Nesrin dumped the red drink on the floor and flicked the tiny Phidar inside where it scrambled dizzily against the sides. She cupped her hand over the top quickly, suffocating the queen. Drawing it up to her ear, she listened, though for what I couldn't say. Only once satisfied did she remove her hand. "Better get some more of that drink you all use before she comes to, or you'll have a problem on your hands."

"Bring the Teshuvah!" Malakai shouted, and someone delivered it within moments. "Figure out how to make her drink it. She can swim in it if necessary." His voice, though still powerful, had grown flat. She was, after all, still his own mother. "And bring her to the dungeons immediately. The strongest cells. Make sure she has a fresh dose of Teshuvah every hour until I can determine what to do with her." As they obeyed, Malakai's gaze grew less hard and more lost.

A reverent whisper from someone in the crowd seemed loud in the silence. "Prince Malakai took down the queen!"

Someone began to clap. Every eye turned toward the sound.

It was Jedekiah.

He clapped slowly as he ambled toward us. The crowd parted to let him through, though the guards in front of Malakai and me did not.

Stopping in front of them, acting as if they were a part of any normal conversation, Jedekiah grinned. "I wasn't sure you could do it."

Malakai's gaze was cold, but there was an awe in his voice as he raised it for all to hear and turned to me. "I couldn't have done it on my own. We took her down together."

The Jinn cheered. It was a far cry from the stoic reactions they'd had when I first met them. If anything, they grew louder.

Before Malakai could say anything further, I placed a hand on his arm in question. His gaze softened. Did he see his sister when he looked at me? He nodded permission to lead, and I turned to Jedekiah.

"We needed everyone's help to change the course of this day," I told him, knowing the Jinni girl was still projecting our voices, wanting oddly enough to save this obnoxious Jinni who'd somehow saved me. "Even yours."

epilogue

Arie

THREE WEEKS HAD PASSED since the Crowning Ceremony. Kadin found me in my mother's old rooms, curled up on the big four-poster bed with its gold curtains. This time when he crawled onto it to lie beside me, I rolled over to face him with a smile.

His dark brown hair had grown past his brows again, and it contrasted with the soft white satin pillows.

I reached out to brush it back, letting my hand linger.

The sunlight danced in his eyes, highlighting one of my favorite features: the golden flecks in the brown-and-honey colors. He put his hand over mine and turned his head to kiss my palm.

We lay there in happy silence. Another thing I loved about him—most days—was his quiet patience. And I did love him.

I knew that now.

I didn't want to break this spell. Didn't want our time here to end. We'd gone back and forth between Jinn and Hodafez a few times since the Crowning Ceremony, but this time would be more permanent. I needed to face my kingdom, face the state I'd left it in, and—hopefully with Kadin's help—build it into something even better than it'd been before. I pulled my bottom lip into my mouth. I hadn't actually asked him that yet.

He raised a brow at my worried expression.

I wanted to ask him to come back to Hodafez with me. Well, more specifically, to *stay* in Hodafez with me once we returned. Instead, I asked simply, "Are they ready for our departure?"

There was going to be a big send-off. Malakai had declared lots of fanfare was fitting for a member of the royal family.

In private, the prince, now king—and my uncle, though he looked hardly a decade older than me—had told me he meant to end the hatred between the Jinn and the humans. Publicly, his first act toward that goal was to pardon the banished Jinn who'd fought on our side to bring Malakai home, declaring them loyalists to the true king and friends to the humans all in the same honorable mention, linking the two together. "Honoring someone is more binding than dishonoring them," he'd said casually, but the words had stuck with me, as much of his leadership did. Binding people together was the antidote to hatred. Love built up more common ground than anger ever could. I hoped to someday be even half the ruler he was already.

"They're ready and waiting," Kadin replied with a smile in his voice. He lifted his head as if to get up.

"Wait." I tugged on his hand so he'd curl back up beside me. "A few more minutes couldn't hurt."

He relaxed back onto the pillow. "What's on your mind?"

This was the perfect opening for my question. I opened my mouth but closed it again, rolling onto my back. "I'm going to miss Rena," I hedged.

He reached out to squeeze my hand in comfort. "She'll only be gone a month. The time will go by before you know it." When he didn't let go, I wound my fingers between his, savoring the feeling.

"If anything," he continued as he held my hand, rubbing my thumb absently, "you might want to plan ahead for where she'll stay when she comes back to Hodafez. I have a feeling she'll be anxious to be near Bosh."

"About that, I was thinking…"

He turned to stare into my eyes until my cheeks grew warm and I looked away, feeling ridiculous.

"Maybe with Rena as ambassador from the sea, and Gideon as ambassador from Jinn, once he's fully recovered, we could cultivate Bosh to be an ambassador for the humans?" My blush grew hotter. I'd said it accidentally. *We.* Had he noticed?

Kadin's lips twisted in a smile, but I couldn't tell if it was from my phrasing or the idea. "He'd have his hands full between the two." He laughed.

I tried not to be disappointed that he hadn't caught my slip. After all, I *still* hadn't actually asked him anything.

"I think it'd be a wise move though," he continued. "If there's anyone open to their cultures, it'd be him."

"It'd be a lot to take on," I agreed, grinning. For one thing, Gideon would be frustrated. To ask an ancient to speak to a sixteen-year-old about the fate of their countries would heavily stretch his boundaries of what was acceptable.

I'd help him understand. He'd grown more flexible since I'd first met him, and in spite of his occasionally condescending manner, I could tell he'd grown to like Bosh.

It seemed even the ancients could change.

If he could, then so could I.

Maybe when we got back I'd ask him to help me train with my new Gifts. Once I was certain he was fully recovered, of course. He shouldn't push himself. He still had a lot of explaining to do about my mother, but one thing I could tell simply from the way he talked about her was she'd meant the world to him.

I wonder... A thought struck me, and not for the first time. *Could others survive a Severance too? Is there a chance it'd transform someone else as much as it did me?*

I explored the tendrils of the most recent Gift I'd borrowed, the one that let me see the colors that hung over a person. Kadin's colors were the same amber gold as his eyes, all warmth and happiness. There was a tendril of yellow. Uneasiness? I wasn't familiar enough with the new Gift to know for sure; it was possible that I was projecting my own feelings onto him.

It was time to ask.

No more beating around the bush.

He spoke before I could, still holding my hand and playing with my thumb as he stared up at the gold canopy. "The men tell me there's a new job in the south near Jinyue." He cleared his throat.

I couldn't breathe. *He's going to leave?*

"But I'd like to—"

"Stay!" I cut him off.

"—stay," he finished, slowly turning to meet my eyes.

I swallowed. A warm white color that could only be labeled as joy filled the air above him. I assumed I had the same colors because I was nearly floating. I splayed my free hand against the soft bed covers just to double-check, but floating had been yesterday's Gift. This was pure feeling.

I leaned forward until his lips were just inches from mine.

He closed the distance.

"Do you think," I whispered against his lips a few moments later, unwilling to move away even for a second. "If it wasn't too much of an imposition… that you might someday want to be a king?"

He grinned. "Only for one kingdom. Or maybe I should say, one queen."

"Oh, good." I laughed, feeling the string tying his heart to mine wrap tighter where I'd worried it would be cut. How silly I'd been to think it was fragile thread when it was clearly something stronger. Like I'd turned out to be. "That's the queen I had in mind."

THE END.

If you loved this book, support the author by leaving a review—it helps more than you know!

Gideon

a short story

BETHANY ATAZADEH

GIDEON

One Year Ago

"GIDEON, A MOMENT," THE queen of Jinn's voice
rang out like the largest bell in the castle tower. Everyone in
the halls pretended not to hear, even as they sidled closer to
eavesdrop.

I turned sharply on my heel and bowed in one smooth
motion. "Yes, my queen."

Queen Jezebel stopped before me. She waved a hand at
my insistence on formality. "Up, up." But her perfect red lips
curved in a smile, as always. The power radiating from the
crown she wore made her every feature brighter, younger.
Though she was at least two centuries my senior, her long hair
was still raven black and shining, her skin free of wrinkles,
and her blue eyes sharp.

Her mind was guarded against mine. When my Gift
brushed up against it, it was like running into a steel wall. Most
Jinn kept a vigilant guard over their thoughts, whether they
knew they were in the presence of a mind reader or not.

I stood stiff, staring at the pale crown on her brow instead
of her eyes as she made me wait, studying my face. Thank the

stars she didn't have my Gift. With the crown to enhance her abilities, she'd know all my secrets. And like everyone in Jinn, I had plenty.

"Have you any word of my daughter?" she asked, after two members of the Jinni court reached the end of the long, white hall and were out of hearing.

The princess had disappeared two decades prior and no one had heard from her since. Not even I. Still, the queen asked for news occasionally; twenty years was hardly long enough to be declared dead for a Jinni.

The small wince of pain that I allowed to reach my face was real. "Sadly no, my queen. My latest journey to the human lands revealed no new information on that front. However, I wrote in my report of the enormous increase of the Gifted humans abusing their abilities, along with many of our own kind. They're breaking the laws of Jinn with alarming regularity—"

"Yes, I read the report," she murmured. "It's unfortunate, but the human troubles seem insignificant in comparison to my daughter's absence. I miss her so. Gideon, do you not miss anyone?"

It was a layered question.

Dangerous.

Did I miss anyone? Yes. Did I miss her daughter? Deeply, which I knew she suspected, though for now, it worked to her advantage, so she allowed it. Did I miss anyone else? That was possibly the true question, buried beneath the others.

I'd spent the last few weeks questioning a missing piece—a place in the mind where a memory should've been. In the Jinni Guard we were trained to recognize spells and enchantments, and I knew enough to recognize that one haunted me now. Without meaning to, the queen had led me to wonder if the missing piece was actually a missing person.

"My queen," I began, running through my options in one breath. "I must admit that my work has kept me too busy to miss anyone."

Her eyes flickered, and I thought I read satisfaction in the small twist of her lips, but also suspicion in her narrowed gaze. It was difficult to say if she believed me, but she nodded and turned to walk, leaving me to follow. "That's probably for the best."

"Yes, my queen," I agreed easily. I would hide what I'd learned until I could make sense of it. Especially from her.

* * *

Want to read the rest of Gideon's story?

Sign up for Bethany Atazadeh's author newsletter to get a free download of this short story, as well as be the first to learn about new releases and receive exclusive content for both readers and writers!

WWW.BETHANYATAZADEH.COM/CONTACT

ACKNOWLEDGMENTS

It's finally hitting me that our time in this world I've created is ending—at least for now. *She says like it's a hint, even though she has no idea what's coming next.*

I'm so thankful God led me to this writing career because creating for a living is an absolute blast! Let me take a minute to rave about all the amazing people who helped me take this book to the next level:

First of all, my amazing critique partners Brittany Wang and Jessi Elliott are the literal best. It takes a true friend to spend hours reading a messy draft (which for a long time didn't even include an ending—how rude!) and somehow they still gave me such incredible feedback.

My beta readers who've read through this whole series are the dream team. As usual, they inspired me to add *way* more to the story than I originally had. Like, roughly 20,000 more words! Huge shout out to: Athena Marie, Amelia Nichele, Emma Woodham, Katherine Schober, Lia Anderson.

I also want to give a huge shout out to my amazing editor, Natalia Leigh, who is the queen of detailed edits. She polished a lot of rough edges in my writing. (How do I *still* not get the difference between further and farther after all this time? Ha!)

I'm very spoiled when it comes to cover design because I get to work with my good friend Mandi Lynn on all my covers, and she does a fantastic job at bringing my vision to life.

My lovely mama is the best proofreader in the world—hi mom! Thanks for always supporting and encouraging me. You know, you were the first one to suggest that I should try writing more seriously (sorry I brushed the idea off at the time, mothers really do know best).

Huge thank you to my sweet hubby who still hasn't read the books (and probably never will) because he's "waiting for the movie." Your writing advice cracks me up (and I will never use it, but it always makes me laugh so thank you for trying)!

And have I told you about my amazing patrons over on Patreon? Each one of these people is the absolute best! To each of you who support me, I appreciate you more than you know—it's because of your support that I've been able to write and publish these books as quickly as I have.

Last but not least, to *you* as you read this, I don't know if you realize it, but the fact that you know about this magical world I made up still blows my mind. Thank you for sharing The Stolen Kingdom Series and making it spread so much further (or is it farther? I give up!) then I ever could on my own. <3

NOTE TO MY READERS:

When I first started writing this story, I intended to touch on a really difficult topic which affects a lot of people, including myself: depression.

Over the almost three years that it's taken to finish Arie's story, it has transformed into something unexpected. Something similar and related to depression, but not quite the same: grief.

While depression is built into grief like a foundation is part of a building, grief also encompasses other symptoms that are unique to loss.

Losing a loved one is not the same as losing an ability, but there is still an innate grieving process to losing anything that holds significance in your life.

Loss can derail plans, hopes, dreams, even purpose. It is a defining moment, no matter how much we might wish it wasn't. Grief is dark. The deepest night.

But when we write about darkness, I think it's also extremely important to write about the light.

In this case, that light is hope.

Sometimes, hope in the midst of pain.

It's the hope of knowing that this is not all there is, that the pain won't last forever, that the gaping wounds will heal, even if they do leave scars.

"Surely he took up our pain and bore our suffering… and by his wounds, we are healed." (Isaiah 53:5)

Most people don't understand suffering or loss until they've gone through it—I know I didn't. But through such excruciating pain you can have someone who understands what you're going through better than anyone, a comforter, a healer, a light in the darkness: Jesus.

For those of you who read this and feel like I'm talking directly to you—you are the ones I'm praying for as I write this. I'm sending you a hug and a reminder that you'll get through this, and that you have access to the God of the universe who loves you. You are not alone.

GLOSSARY

Abner (AB-nur) – Jinni

Adel Heydari (Ah-dell Hey-dar-ee) – Dragon Watch initiate

Arie (ARE-ee) – the queen of Hodafez

Ananias (Ann-nun-NIGH-us) – Jinni

Amir (Ah-meer) – the former king of the human kingdom of Sagh

Auger (Ah-gur) – a Mere spell

Avizun (Ah-VEE-sun) – the lead Dragon hunter

Baba (BAH-buh) – means father

Benaiah (Ben-NIGH-ah) – Jinni

B'har (Bah-har) – a Jinni spell

Bond-brother / bond-sister – a Jinni relationship that's considered the same as a blood brother/sister, though not related by blood

Bosh (BAH-sh) – member of Kadin's crew

Captain Navabi (Nah-VAH-bee) – captain of the guard in Hodafez

Cerith – a Mere spell

Crowning Ceremony – an event that takes place in Jinn every fifty years

Daichi (DIE-chee) – member of Kadin's crew

Daleth – Jinni portal into human world (Hebrew word for door)

Dokhtari (Dock-TAR-ee) – a title of affection (persian word for daughter)

Doost (Dew-st) – the name Nesrin gave to Malakai's dragon form (persian word for friend)

Enoch (Ee-knock) – the violet-eyed Jinni who helps King Amir

Gideon (GID-ee-un) – Jinni

Hanna (HAH-nah) – Arie's mother

Hashem (Hah-SHEM) – boy Nesrin dances with

Heechi (Hee-chee) – town where Nesrin lives (persian word for nothing)

Hodafez (Ho-DAH-fes) – Arie's kingdom (loosely translated persian word for goodbye)

Hoishi (HOY-she) – Daichi and Ryo's home

Horn Shell – a Mere spell

Illium (ILL-ee-um) – former member of Kadin's crew

Jedekiah (Jed-uh-KI-ah) - Jinni

Jezebel (JEZ-zuh-bell) – queen of the Jinn

Jinn/Jinni (Gin/GIN-nee) – Jinn is the name of the country and the race of Jinn as a whole (i.e. *the Jinn, the land of Jinn*); Jinni is the singular, used to refer to an individual Jinni and also as a possessive (i.e. *a Jinni, a Jinni's Gift*)

Jinyue - a human kingdom

Jonah (JOE-nah) - Jinni

Kadin (KAY-din) – leader of the crew of thieves

Kathenoth – scattered pieces of a Jinni's will and proof of existence (Hebrew word for protection)

Khaanevaade (Hah-nah-vah-DAY) –a fable even older than the Jinn, the supposed ancestors of dragons (persian word for family)

Lacklore – a beast in Jinn with an ox head and bear body

Lightning Whelk – a Mere spell

Lyra (LEER-rah) – Jinni

Maadar (Moh-DAR) – persian word for mother

Maadar Bozorgi (Moh-DAR Boh-ZOORG-ee) – an old woman in Heechi (persian word for grandmother)

Malakai (MAL-uh-kye) – prince of Jinn

Mere (Meer) – meremaids and mereman, also known as mere-folk

Nadia (NAH-dee-ah) – Rena's third older sister

Naomi (Nay-OH-me) – Jinni

Naveed (Nah-VEED) – member of Kadin's crew

Nesrin (NEZ-rin) - girl from Heechi who broke Malakai's curse

Phidar (FI-der) – a venomous insect

Rena (REE-nah) – youngest daughter of the Sea King and Queen

Resh – capital city in Jinn (Hebrew word for head)

Rusalka (Roo-SULK-ah) – the underwater kingdom of the Mere

Roohstam (Roost-tom) – Nesrin's older brother

Ryo (RYE-oh) – member of Kadin's crew

Samson (SAM-sin) – Jinni

Sapphira (Sah-FIRE-rah) – Jinni

Sea King and Queen – Rena's parents

Severance – when a Jinni's Gift is severed from its owner

Shadi (Shah-dee) – Nesrin's older sister

Shah – interchangeable title for a governor of provinces within a
    kingdom or for a monarch (persian word for king)

Shahs Council – council of local Shahs from across the kingdoms that
    meet to decide common laws and rules

Shark's Eye – a Mere spell

Tamar (TAY-mar) – Jinni

Teshuvah – an elixir that blocks a Jinni's Gifts for a period of time

Urim (Yer-um) – an island in Jinn

Uziah (oo-ZI-uh) – Jinni in Jedekiah's crew

Yuliya (YOU-lee-yuh) – Rena's eldest sister

Zacheus (Zack-KEE-us) – Jinni

Zareen – Nesrin's youngest sister

Three Unbreakable Laws of Jinn:

1)   Never use a Gift to deceive

2)   Never use a Gift to steal

3)   Never use a Gift to harm another

Bethany Atazadeh is best known for her young adult fantasy novels, The Stolen Kingdom Series, which won the Best YA Author 2020 Minnesota Author Project award. She is obsessed with stories, chocolate, and her corgi puppy, Penny.

Using her degree in English with a creative writing emphasis, Bethany enjoys helping other writers through her YouTube a.k.a. "AuthorTube" writing channel and Patreon page.

If you want to know more about when Bethany's next book will come out, visit her website below where you can sign up to receive monthly emails with exciting news, updates, and book releases.

CONNECT WITH BETHANY ON:
Website: www.bethanyatazadeh.com
Instagram: @authorbethanyatazadeh
YouTube: www.youtube.com/bethanyatazadeh
Patreon: www.patreon.com/bethanyatazadeh